Praise for *Born at Midnight*

"*Born at Midnight* is addicting. Kylie's journey of self-discovery and friendship is so full of honesty, it's impossible not to fall in love with her and Shadow Falls . . . and with two sexy males vying for her attention, the romance is scorching. *Born at Midnight* has me begging for more, and I love, love, love it!"
—*Verb Vixen*

"There are so many books in the young adult paranormal genre these days that it's hard to choose a good one. I was so very glad to discover *Born at Midnight*. If you like P. C. and Kristin Cast or Alyson Noël, I am sure you will enjoy *Born at Midnight*!"
—*Night Owl Reviews*

"I laughed and cried so much while reading this. . . . I *loved* this book. I read it every chance I could get because I didn't want to put it down. The characters were well developed and I felt like I knew them from the beginning. The story line and mystery that went along with it kept me glued to my couch not wanting to do anything else but find out what the heck was going on."
—*Urban Fantasy Investigations*

"This has everything a YA reader would want. . . . I read it over a week ago and I am still thinking about it. I can't get it out of my head. I can't wait to read more. This series is going to be a hit!"
—*AwesomeSauce Book Club*

"The newest in the super-popular teen paranormal genre, this book is one of the best. Kylie is funny and vulnerable, struggling to deal with her real-world life and her life in a fantastical world she's not sure she wants to be a part of. Peppered throughout with humor and teen angst, *Born at Midnight* is a laugh-out-loud page-turner. This one is going on the keeper shelf next to my Armstrong and Meyer collections!"
—*Fresh Fiction*

"Seriously loved this book! This is definitely a series you will want to watch out for. C. C. Hunter has created a world of hot paranormals that I didn't want to leave."
—*Looksie Lovitz: Books and Wits*

Born at Midnight

c. c. hunter

ST. MARTIN'S GRIFFIN ✖ NEW YORK

BORN AT MIDNIGHT. Copyright © 2011 by C. C. Hunter. All rights reserved. Printed in the United States of America. For information, address St. Martin's Press, 175 Fifth Avenue, New York, N.Y. 10010.

www.stmartins.com

Book design by Kelly S. Too

Library of Congress Cataloging-in-Publication Data

Hunter, C. C.
    Born at midnight / C. C. Hunter.—1st ed.
        p. cm.
    Summary: Sixteen-year-old Kylie Galen thinks her misbehavior in the wake of her grandmother's death and her parents' separation are the reasons she has been sent to Shadow Falls Camp, but learns it is a training ground for vampires, werewolves, and other "freaky freaks," of which she may be one.
    ISBN 978-0-312-62467-5
    [1. Supernatural—Fiction. 2. Camps—Fiction. 3. Interpersonal relations—Fiction. 4. Ability—Fiction. 5. Family problems—Fiction.] I. Title.
    PZ7.H916565Bor 2011
    [Fic]—dc22   2010043573

10 9

To Lilly Dale Makepeace.
Just looking at your smile reminds that magic
is alive and thriving in this big old world.

Acknowledgments

They say it takes a village to raise a child; well, it also takes one to get a spark of an idea and turn it into a book. First I want to acknowledge my editor, Rose Hilliard. Your faith in me means more than you'll ever know. And here's to my other village people: My husband for being supportive to the point of perfection. I'll love you forever, baby! My agent, Kim Lionetti, who takes my dreams and helps them become a reality. What's next, Kim? My village angels who are my critique partners and writing family: Faye Hughes, Jody Payne, Suzan Harden, and Teri Thackston. Girls, thank you for the support, but mostly, thank you for the friendship.

Born at Midnight

Chapter One

"This isn't funny!" her father yelled.

No, it wasn't, Kylie Galen thought as she leaned into the re-frigerator to find something to drink. In fact, it was so not funny she wished she could crawl in beside the mustard and moldy hot dogs, shut the door, and not hear the angry voices spewing from the living room.

Her parents were at it again.

Not that it would go on much longer, she thought as the mist of the fridge seeped out the door.

Today was the day.

Kylie's throat tightened. She swallowed a lump of raw emotion and refused to cry.

Today had to be the suckiest day of her life. And she'd had some pretty sucky days lately, too. Acquiring a stalker, Trey break-ing up with her, and her parents announcing their divorce—yup, sucky pretty much covered it. It was no wonder her night terrors had returned full force.

"What have you done with my underwear?" Her father's

growl spilled into the kitchen, snuck under the refrigerator door, and bounced around the hot dogs.

His underwear? Kylie pressed a cold diet soda can to her forehead.

"Why would I do anything with your underwear?" her mother asked in her oh-so-nonchalant voice. That was her mom all right, nonchalant. Cold as ice.

Kylie's gaze shot out the kitchen window to the patio where she'd seen her mom earlier. There, a pair of her dad's tighty-whities dangled half out of the smoldering grill.

Just great. Her mother had barbecued her father's shorts. That's it. Kylie was never eating anything cooked on that grill again.

Fighting tears, she shoved the diet soda back on the rack, shut the fridge, and moved into the doorway. Maybe if they saw her, they'd stop acting like juveniles and let her be the kid again.

Her dad stood in the middle of the room, a pair of underwear clutched in his fist. Her mom sat on the sofa, calmly sipping hot tea.

"You need psychological help," her father yelled at her mom.

Two points for her dad, Kylie thought. Her mom did need help. So why was Kylie the one who had to sit on a shrink's sofa two days a week?

Why was her dad—the man everyone swore Kylie had wrapped around her little finger—going to move out today and leave her behind?

She didn't blame her dad for wanting to leave her mom, aka

the Ice Queen. But why wasn't he taking Kylie with him? Another lump rose in her throat.

Dad swung around and saw her, then shot back into the bedroom, obviously to pack the rest of his things—minus his underwear, which at this moment sent up smoke signals from the backyard grill.

Kylie stood there, staring at her mom, who sat reading over work files as if it were any other day.

The framed photographs of Kylie and her father that hung over the sofa caught her attention and tears stung her eyes. The pictures had been taken on their annual father and daughter trips.

"You've got to do something," Kylie pleaded.

"Do what?" her mom asked.

"Change his mind. Tell him you're sorry you grilled his shorts." *That you're sorry you've got ice water running through your veins.* "I don't give a flip what you do, just don't let him go."

"You don't understand." And just like that, her mom, void of any emotion, shifted her attention back to her papers.

Right then, her dad, suitcase in his hand, shot through the living room. Kylie went after him and followed him out the door into Houston's stifling afternoon heat.

"Take me with you," she begged, not caring if he saw her tears. Maybe the tears would help. There'd been a time when crying got her whatever she wanted from him. "I don't eat much," she sniffled, giving humor a shot.

He shook his head but, unlike her mom, at least he had emotion in his eyes. "You don't understand."

You don't understand. "Why do y'all always say that? I'm sixteen years old. If I don't understand, then explain it to me. Tell me the big secret and get it over with."

He stared down at his feet as if this were a test and he'd penned the answers on the toes of his shoes. Sighing, he looked up. "Your mom . . . she needs you."

"Needs me? Are you kidding? She doesn't even want me." *And neither do you.* The realization caused Kylie's breath to catch in her lungs. He really didn't want her.

She wiped a tear from her cheek and that's when she saw him again. Not her dad, but Soldier Dude, aka her very own stalker. Standing across the street, he wore the same army duds as before. He looked as if he'd just walked out of one of those Gulf War movies her mom loved. Only instead of shooting at things or being blown up, he stood frozen in one spot and stared right at Kylie with sad, yet very scary eyes.

She'd noticed him stalking her a few weeks ago. He'd never spoken to her and she hadn't spoken to him. But the day she pointed him out to her mom, and Mom hadn't seen him . . . well, that's when Kylie's world slid off its axis. Her mom thought she was making it up to get attention, or worse. With the worse being that Kylie was losing her grip on reality. Sure, the night terrors that had tormented her when she was a kid had returned, worse than ever. Her mom said the shrink could help her work through them, but how could she do that when Kylie didn't even remember them? She only knew they were bad. Bad enough to have her wake up screaming.

Kylie wanted to scream now. Wanted to scream for her dad to turn around and look—to prove that she hadn't lost her mind.

At the very least, maybe if her dad actually saw her stalker, her parents would let her off from seeing the shrink. It wasn't fair.

But life wasn't fair, as her mom had reminded her more than once.

Nevertheless, when Kylie looked back, he was gone. Not Soldier Dude, but her dad. She turned toward the driveway and saw him shoving his suitcase in the backseat of his red convertible Mustang. Mom had never liked that car, but Dad loved it.

Kylie ran to the car. "I'll make Grandma talk to Mom. She'll fix . . ." No sooner had the words escaped Kylie's lips than she remembered the other major sucky event she'd had plopped into her life.

She couldn't run to Grandma to fix her problems anymore. Because Grandma was dead. Gone. The vision of Nana lying cold in the casket filled Kylie's head and another lump crawled up her throat.

Her dad's expression morphed into parental concern, the same look that had landed Kylie at the shrink's office three weeks ago.

"I'm fine. I just forgot." Because remembering hurt too much. She felt a lone tear roll down her cheek.

Dad moved in and hugged her. The embrace lasted even longer than his usual hugs, but it ended too soon. How could she let him go? How could he leave her?

His arm dropped from around her and he physically set her back. "I'm just a phone call away, Pumpkin."

Swiping at her tears, hating her watery weakness, she watched her dad's red convertible get smaller as it buzzed down the street. Wanting to be alone in her room, she started to run inside. Then she remembered and looked back across the street to see if Soldier Dude had pulled his usual disappearing act.

Nope. He was still there, staring, stalking. Scaring the bejeebies out of her and making her angry at the same time. He was the reason she had to see a shrink.

Then Mrs. Baker, her elderly neighbor, toddled out to get her mail. She smiled at Kylie but not once did the old librarian glance at Soldier Dude taking up residence on her front lawn, even when he stood less than two feet from her.

Weird.

So weird it sent an unnatural chill tiptoeing down Kylie's spine, the same kind of chill Kylie had gotten at Nana's funeral.

What the hell was going on?

Chapter Two

An hour later, Kylie walked down the stairs with her backpack and purse over her shoulder.

Her mom met her in the entryway. "Are you okay?"

How could I be okay? "I'll live," Kylie answered. More than she could say about Grandma. Right then, Kylie had a vision of the bright purple lipstick the funeral home had put on her grandmother. *Why didn't you take that off of me?* Kylie could almost hear Nana asking.

Weirded out by the thought, Kylie looked back at her mother.

Her mom stared at Kylie's backpack and her worry wrinkle appeared between her eyes. "Where are you going?" she asked.

"You said I could spend the night with Sara. Or were you too busy grilling Dad's shorts to remember?"

Her mom ignored the grilled-shorts comment. "What are you two going to do tonight?"

"Mark Jameson is having an end-of-school party." Not that

Kylie felt like celebrating the event. Thanks to Trey dumping her and her parents divorcing, Kylie's whole summer was headed for the toilet. And the way things were going, someone was going to walk by and flush it.

"Are his parents going to be there?" Mom raised one dark eyebrow.

Kylie flinched emotionally, but physically didn't blink. "Aren't they always?"

Okay, so she lied. Normally she didn't go to Mark Jameson's parties for that very reason, but blast it, look where being good had gotten her. She deserved to have some fun, didn't she?

Besides, hadn't her mom lied when her dad asked about his underwear?

"What if you have another dream?" Her mom touched Kylie's arm.

A quick touch. That's all Kylie ever got from her mom these days. No long hugs like her dad gave. No mother/daughter trips. Just aloofness and quick touches. Even when Nana, her mom's mom, died, Kylie's mom hadn't hugged her and Kylie had really needed a hug then. But it had been her dad who'd pulled her into his arms and let her smear mascara on his suit coat. And now Dad and all his suit coats were gone.

Drawing in a gulp of oxygen, Kylie clutched her purse. "I warned Sara I might wake up screaming bloody murder. She said she'd stake me in the heart with a wooden cross and make me go back to bed."

"Maybe you should hide the stakes before you go to sleep." Her mother attempted to smile.

"I will." For one brief second, Kylie worried about leaving her mom alone on the day her dad had left. But who was she kidding? Her mom would be fine. Nothing ever bothered the Ice Queen.

Before walking out, Kylie peered out the window to make sure she wouldn't be assaulted by a guy wearing army duds.

Deeming the yard to be free of stalkers, Kylie ran out the door, hoping that tonight's party would help her forget just how badly her life sucked.

"Here. You don't have to drink it, just hold it." Sara Jetton pushed a beer into Kylie's hands and ran off.

Sharing elbow room with at least thirty kids, all packed into Mark Jameson's living room and talking at once, Kylie clutched the ice-cold bottle. Glancing around at the crowd, she recognized most of them from school. The doorbell rang again. Obviously, this was the place to be tonight. And according to every other kid at her high school, it was. Jameson, a senior whose parents never seemed to care what he did, held some of the wildest parties in town.

Ten minutes later, Sara still MIA, the party shifted into full swing. Too bad Kylie didn't feel like swinging along with them. She frowned at the bottle in her hand.

Someone bumped into her shoulder, causing the beer to splash on her chest and run down in the V of her white blouse. "Crap."

"Oh, I'm so sorry," the responsible bumper said.

Kylie looked up into John's soft brown eyes and tried to smile. Hey, being nice to a cute guy, who'd been asking about her at school made trying to smile easy. But the fact that John had been friends with Trey kept the thrill down to a minimum.

"It's okay," she said.

"I'll get you another." As if nervous, he shot off.

"It's really okay," Kylie called after him, but between the music and the hum of voices, he didn't hear her.

The doorbell rang again. A few kids shifted around and gave Kylie a view of the door. More specifically, the shift gave her a view of Trey walking inside. Beside him—or she should say plastered against him—sashayed his new slutty girlfriend.

"Great." She swung around, wishing she could teleport herself to Tahiti, or back home would be even better—especially if her dad would be there.

Through a back window, she spotted Sara on the patio and Kylie darted outside to join her.

Sara looked up. She must have read the panic on Kylie's face, because she came running over to her. "What happened?"

"Trey and his screw toy are here."

Sara frowned. "So, you look hot. Go flirt with some guys and make him sorry."

Kylie rolled her eyes. "I don't want to stay here and watch Trey and what's her name making out."

"Were they already making out?" Sara asked.

"Not yet, but get one beer in Trey and all he'll think about is getting into a girl's panties. I know because I used to be the girl in the panties."

"Chill." Sara pointed back at the table. "Gary brought margaritas. Have one and you'll feel fine."

Kylie bit her lip to keep from screaming that she wouldn't feel fine. Her life had toilet-bound stamped all over it.

"Hey." Sara nudged her. "We both know all you'd have to do to get Trey back is to grab him and take him upstairs. He's still crazy about you. He found me before I left school today and asked about you."

"Did you know he was going to be here?" Betrayal started unraveling the little sanity she had left.

"Not for sure. But chill."

Chill? Kylie stared at her best friend and realized how different they'd become these last six months. It wasn't just Sara's need to party or the fact that she'd given up virginhood. Okay, so maybe it was those two things, but it seemed like more.

More as in Kylie had a sneaking suspicion that Sara longed to rush Kylie to join the partying-non-virgin ranks. Could Kylie help it if beer tasted like dog piss to her? Or if the idea of having sex didn't appeal?

Okay, that was a lie, sex appealed to her. When she and Trey had made out, Kylie had been tempted, really tempted, but then Kylie remembered her and Sara talking about how the first time should be special.

Then she recalled how Sara had given in to Brad's "needs"— Brad who was the love of Sara's life—yet, within two weeks of giving in, the love of Sara's life had dumped her. What was so special about that?

Since then, Sara had dated four other guys, and she'd slept

with two of them. Now, Sara had stopped talking about sex being special.

"Look, I know you're worried about your parents," Sara said. "But that's why you need to just let loose and have some fun." Sara tucked her long, brown hair behind her ear. "I'm getting you a margarita and you're going to love it."

Sara darted off to the table by the group of people. Kylie started to follow but her gaze slapped against Soldier Dude, looking as scary and weird as ever, standing by the group of margarita drinkers.

Kylie shot around, prepared to bolt, but she smacked right into a guy's chest, and darn it if more beer didn't jump out of the bottle and fall right between her boobs. "Great. My boobs are going to smell like a brewery."

"Every guy's dream," the husky male voice said. "But I'm sorry."

She recognized Trey's voice before she did his broad shoulders or his unique masculine scent. Preparing herself for the pain that seeing him would cause, she raised her gaze. "It's okay, John's already done it once."

She tried not to stare at the way Trey's sandy brown hair fell against his brow, or the way his green eyes seemed to lure her closer, or the way his mouth tempted her to lean in and press her lips to his.

"So it's true." He frowned.

"What's true?" she asked.

"That you and John have hooked up."

Kylie considered lying. The thought that it would hurt him appealed to her. It appealed to her so much that it reminded her of the stupid games her parents played lately. Oh, no, she would not stoop to their "grown-up" level.

"I haven't hooked up with anyone." She turned to leave.

He caught her. His touch, the feel of his warm hand on her elbow, sent waves of pain right to her heart. And standing this close, his clean, masculine scent filled her airways. Oh God, she loved his smell.

"I heard about your grandma," he said. "And Sara told me about your parents getting a divorce. I'm so sorry, Kylie."

Tears threatened to crawl up her throat. Kylie was seconds away from falling against his warm chest and begging him to hold her. Nothing ever felt better than Trey's arms around her, but then she saw the girl, Trey's screw toy, walk outside, carrying two beers. In less than five minutes, Trey would be trying to get in her panties. And from the too-low-cut blouse and too-short skirt the girl wore, it appeared he wouldn't have to try too hard.

"Thanks," Kylie muttered, and went to join Sara. Luckily, Soldier Dude had decided margaritas weren't his thing after all and left.

"Here." Sara took the beer from Kylie's hand and replaced it with a margarita.

The frosty glass felt unnaturally cold. Kylie leaned in and whispered, "Did you see a strange guy here a minute ago? Dressed in some funky army outfit?"

Sara's eyebrows did their wild, wiggly thing. "How much of that beer did you drink?" Her laughter filled the night air.

Kylie wrapped her hands tighter around the cold glass, worried she seriously might be losing her mind. Adding alcohol to the situation didn't seem like a good idea.

An hour later, when three Houston cops walked into the backyard and had everyone line up at the back gate, Kylie still had the same untouched margarita clutched in her hands.

"Come on, kids," one of the cops said. "The sooner we move you to the precinct, the sooner we can get your parents to come get you." That was when Kylie knew for certain that her life really had been toilet-bound—and someone had just flushed.

"Where's Dad?" Kylie asked her mom when she stepped into the room at the police station. "I called Dad."

I'm a phone call away, Pumpkin. Hadn't he told her that? So why wasn't he here to get Pumpkin?

Her mom's green eyes tightened. "He called me."

"I wanted Dad," Kylie insisted. No, she needed her dad, she thought, and her vision clouded with tears. She needed a hug, needed someone who would understand.

"You don't get what you want, especially when . . . my God, Kylie, how could you do this?"

Kylie swiped the tears from her face. "I didn't do anything. Didn't they tell you? I walked a straight line. Touched my nose and even said my ABCs backwards. I didn't do anything."

"They found drugs there," her mother snapped.

"I wasn't doing drugs."

"But do you know what they didn't find there, young lady?" Her mother pointed a finger at her. "Any parents. You lied to me."

"Maybe I'm just too much like you," Kylie said, still reeling at the thought that her dad hadn't shown up. He'd known how upset she'd been. Why hadn't he come?

"What does that mean, Kylie?"

"You told dad you didn't know what happened to his underwear. But you'd just flame-broiled his shorts on the grill."

Guilt filled her mother's eyes and she shook her head. "Dr. Day is right."

"What does my shrink have to do with tonight?" Kylie asked. "Don't tell me you called her. God, Mom, if you dare bring her down here where all my friends—"

"No, she's not here. But it's not just about tonight." She inhaled. "I can't do this alone."

"Do what alone?" Kylie asked, and she got this bad feeling in her stomach.

"I'm signing you up for a summer camp."

"What summer camp?" Kylie clutched her purse to her chest. "No, I don't want to go to any camp."

"It's not about what you want." Her mom motioned for Kylie to walk out the door. "It's about what you need. It's a camp for kids with problems."

"Problems? Are you freaking nuts? I don't have any problems," Kylie insisted. Well, not any a camp could fix. Somehow she suspected going to camp wouldn't bring Dad home, it wouldn't make Soldier Dude disappear, and it wouldn't win Trey back.

"No problems? Really, then why am I at the police station at almost midnight picking up my sixteen-year-old daughter? You're going to the camp. I'm signing you up tomorrow. This isn't up for debate."

I'm not going. She kept telling herself that as they walked out of the police station.

Her mother might be bat-shit crazy, but not her dad. He simply wouldn't let her mom send her off to a camp filled with a bunch of juvenile delinquents. He wouldn't.

Would he?

Chapter Three

Three days later, Kylie, suitcase in hand, stood in the YMCA parking lot where several of the camp buses picked up the juvenile delinquents. She freaking couldn't believe she was here.

Her mom was really doing it.

And her dad was really letting her mom do it.

Kylie, who'd never drunk more than two sips of beer, who'd never really smoked one cigarette, let alone any pot, was about to be shipped off to some camp for troubled kids.

Her mom reached out and touched Kylie's arm. "I think they're calling you."

Could her mom get rid of her any faster? Kylie pulled away from her touch, so angry, so hurt she didn't know how to act anymore. She'd begged, she'd pleaded, and she'd cried, but nothing worked. She was about to head off to camp. She hated it but there was nothing she could do.

Not offering her mom one word, and swearing not to cry in front of the dozens of other kids, Kylie stiffened her back and

took off to the bus behind the woman holding the sign that read
SHADOW FALLS CAMP.

Jeez. What kind of hell hole was she being sent to?

When Kylie stepped on the bus, the eight or nine kids already there raised their heads and stared at her. She felt an odd
kind of stirring in her chest and she got those weird chills again.
Never, not in all sixteen years of her life, had she wanted to turn
and run away as much as she did now.

She forced herself not to bolt, then she met the gazes of . . .
oh, Lordie, can you say freaks?

One girl had her hair dyed three different colors—pink,
lime green, and jet black. Another girl wore nothing but black—
black lipstick, black eye shadow, black pants, and a black long-
sleeve shirt. Hadn't the goth look gone out of style? Where was
this girl getting her fashion tips? Hadn't she read that colors
were in? That blue was the new black?

And then there was the boy sitting almost at the front of the
bus. He had both his eyebrows pierced. Kylie leaned down to
peer out the window to see if she could still see her mother.
Surely, if her mom took a look at these guys, she'd know Kylie
didn't belong here.

"Take your seat," someone said, and stepped behind her.

Kylie turned around and saw the bus driver. While Kylie
hadn't noticed it earlier, she realized even the bus driver looked a
little freakish. Her purple-tinted gray hair sat high on her head
like a football helmet. Not that Kylie could blame her for teasing
her hair up a few inches. The woman was short. Elf short. Kylie
glanced down at her feet, half expecting to see a pair of pointed
green boots. No green shoes.

Then her gaze shot to the front to the bus. How was the woman going to drive the bus?

"Come on," the woman said. "I have to have you kids there by lunch, so move it along."

Since everyone but Kylie had taken their seats, she supposed the woman meant her. She took a step farther into the bus, feeling as if her life would never, ever be the same.

"You can sit by me," someone said. The boy had curly blond hair, even blonder than Kylie's, but his eyes peering at her were so dark they looked black. He patted the empty seat beside him. Kylie tried not to stare, but something about the dark/light combination felt off. Then he wiggled his eyebrows, as if . . . as if her sitting beside him meant they might make out or something.

"That's okay." Kylie took a few steps, pulling her suitcase behind her. Her luggage caught on the row of seats where the blond boy sat and Kylie looked back to free it.

Her gaze met his and her breath caught. Blond boy now had . . . green eyes. Bright, very bright green eyes. How was that even possible?

She swallowed and looked at his hands, thinking that maybe he had a contact case out and had changed his lenses. No case.

He wiggled his brows again, and when she realized she was staring at him, she yanked her suitcase free.

Shaking off the chill, she moved on to the row of seats she'd chosen as her own. Before she turned to sit down, she noticed another boy in the back. Sitting by himself, he had light brown hair, parted to the side and hanging just above his dark brows and green eyes. Normal green eyes, but the dusty blue T-shirt he wore made them more noticeable.

He nodded at her. Nothing too weird, thank God. At least there was one normal person on the bus besides her.

Sitting down, she gave blond guy another glance. But he wasn't looking at her, so she couldn't see if his eye color had gone weird again. But that's when she noticed the girl with three different hair colors had something in her hands.

Kylie's breath caught again. The girl had a toad. Not a frog—a frog she could have probably handled—but a toad. A huge honking toad. What kind of a girl dyed her hair three different colors and carried a toad with her to camp? God, maybe it was one of those drug toads, the ones people licked to get high. She'd heard about them on some stupid crime show on TV but had always thought they'd made it up. She didn't know which was worse: licking a toad to get high or carrying a toad around just to be weird.

Pulling her suitcase up on the seat next to her just so no one would feel the need to join her, Kylie let out a deep sigh and looked out the window. The bus was moving, although Kylie still didn't see how the bus driver managed to reach the gas pedals.

"Do you know what they call us?" The voice came from the seat where toad girl sat.

Kylie didn't think she was talking to her, but she turned her head that way, anyway. Because the girl looked directly at her, Kylie figured she might be wrong.

"Who calls us?" Kylie asked, trying not to sound too friendly or too bitchy. The last thing she wanted was to piss these freaks off.

"The kids who go to the other camps. There's like six camps in the three-mile radius in Fallen." Using both hands she pulled her multicolored hair back and held it there for a few seconds.

That's when Kylie noticed the girl had lost her toad. And Kylie didn't see a cage or anything where she could have tucked it away.

Great. She would probably have some freak's humongous drug toad hopping into her lap before she knew it. Not that toads totally scared her or anything. She just didn't want it jumping on her.

"They call us boneheads," the girl said.

"Why?" Kylie pulled her feet up in the seat just in case a toad hopped by.

"The camp used to be called Bone Creek Camp," the girl answered. "Because of the dinosaur bones found there."

"Ha," said the blond boy. "They also call us boners."

A few laughs echoed from the other seats. "Why is that funny?" the girl wearing all black asked in a tone so deadly serious that Kylie shivered.

"You don't know what a boner is?" Blond Boy asked. "If you'll come sit beside me, I'll show you." When he turned around, Kylie got another look at his eyes. Holy mother of pearls. They were gold. A striking feline gold. Contacts, Kylie realized. He had to be wearing some kind of weird contacts that were doing that.

Goth Girl stood up as if to join the blond guy.

"Don't do it," Toad Girl, without her toad, said and stood up. Moving out into the aisle, she whispered something in Goth Girl's ear.

"Gross." Goth Girl slammed back in her seat. Then she looked over at the blond boy and pointed a black-painted fingernail at him. "You don't want to piss me off. I eat things bigger than you in the dead of night."

"Did someone say something about the dead of night?" a voice came from the back of the bus.

Kylie turned to see who'd spoken.

Another girl, one Kylie hadn't known was there, popped up from the seat. She had jet black hair and wore sunglasses almost the same color as her hair. What made her look so abnormal was her complexion. Pasty. As in pasty white.

"Do you know why they renamed the camp Shadow Falls?" Toad Girl asked.

"No," someone answered from the front of the bus.

"Because of the Native American legend that says at dusk, if you stand beneath the falls on the property, you can see the shadows of death angels dancing."

Dancing death angels? What was wrong with these people?

Kylie swung around in her seat. Was this some nightmare? Maybe part of her night terrors? She pushed deeper in her cushioned seat and tried to focus on waking herself up from the dreams the way Dr. Day had shown her.

Focus. Focus. She took in deep breaths, in through the nose, out the mouth—all the while silently chanting, *It's just a dream, it isn't real, it isn't real.*

Either she wasn't asleep or her focus had gotten on the wrong bus, and darn if she didn't wish she'd followed it onto a different bus. Still not wanting to believe her eyes, she gazed around at the others. Blond Boy looked at her, and his eyes were black again.

Creepy. Was none of this coming across completely off the normal chart to anyone else in the bus?

Turning in her seat again, she looked back at the boy she'd dubbed the most normal. His soft green eyes, eyes that reminded her of Trey's, met hers, and he shrugged. She didn't exactly know what the shrug meant, but he didn't appear all that weirded out by everything. Which in some small way made him as weird as the others.

Kylie swung back around and grabbed her phone from her purse and started texting Sara. *Help! Stuck on a bus with freaks. Total, complete freaks.*

Kylie got a text message back from Sara almost immediately. *No, you help me. I think I'm pregnant.*

Chapter Four

"Oh, shit." Kylie stared at the text message thinking it would disappear, or that she'd see a "just joking" magically appear at the bottom. Nope. Nothing disappeared or appeared. This was no joke.

But please. Sara couldn't be pregnant. That didn't happen to girls like them. Smart girls . . . girls that . . . Oh, hell. What was she thinking? It happened to everyone and anyone having unprotected sex. Or sex with a faulty condom.

How could she forget that little film at school, the one Mom had to sign for her to see? Or the pamphlets Mom had brought home and unceremoniously left on Kylie's pillow like a bedtime snack?

Talk about a mood killer. She'd arrived home from one of the hottest dates she'd had with Trey, wanting to enjoy the high from his hot kisses and bold caresses, only to find the statistics of unwanted pregnancies and equally unwanted sexually transmitted diseases waiting for her. And her mother knew Kylie always had to read herself to sleep. No sweet dreams that night.

"Bad news?" someone asked.

Kylie looked up to see Toad Girl sitting in the aisle seat across from her, her legs pulled up to her chest and her chin propped onto her knees.

"Uhh. Yeah . . . no. I mean . . ." What she meant was it was none of her damn business, but being that blunt or rude never came easy for Kylie—well, not unless the person really pushed the wrong buttons—buttons that her mom seemed to know so well. Sara called Kylie's unwillingness to state her mind the "too nice" disease. Her mom would have called it manners, but because her mom excelled at hitting Kylie's buttons, her mom considered Kylie lacking in the manners department.

Kylie pulled her phone closed just in case Toad Girl might have super twenty-twenty eyesight. Then again, she guessed the person she should worry about having super eyesight was the blond guy, with his . . . She cut her gaze to where he sat and found him staring at her with . . . blue eyes. O . . . kay, at least one thing was clear, it couldn't get any weirder.

"It's nothing really," she said, forcing herself to look back at the Toad Girl and not stare at her multicolored hair. The bus came to a quick stop and Kylie's suitcase dropped to the floor. Aware that the blond guy still stared, and afraid he might take the empty seat as an invitation to come sit beside her, she moved over.

"My name's Miranda," the girl said, and smiled, and Kylie realized that other than her hair and her pet toad, the girl looked pretty normal.

Kylie introduced herself, giving the floor a quick check to confirm the toad hadn't decided to visit.

"Is this your first time at Shadow Falls?" Miranda asked.

Kylie nodded. "Yours?" she asked out of politeness, then she looked down at her phone, still clutched to her stomach. She needed to text Sara back and say . . . oh heck, what was she going to say to Sara? What did you say to your best friend who just told you that she might be . . .

"My second time." Miranda pulled her hair up and bunched it on top of her head. "Though I don't know why they want me to come back, it's not like it helped me the first time."

Kylie stopped trying to mentally write the text and met the girl's hazel eyes—eyes that hadn't changed colors once—and curiosity had Kylie almost stuttering. "What . . . what's it like? The camp, I mean. Tell me it's not too bad."

"It's not terrible." She released her hair and it fell into waves of black, lime green, and pink around her head. Then she glanced to the back of the bus where the pale chick now sat up and leaned forward as if listening. "If you don't mind the sight of blood," she whispered.

Kylie chuckled, hoping beyond hope that Miranda would, too. But nope. Miranda didn't even smile.

"You're joking, right?" Kylie's heart did a cartwheel in her chest.

"No," she said in a completely unjoking manner. "But I'm probably exaggerating."

A loud clearing of a throat echoed in the bus. Kylie looked up to the front to where the bus driver stared into the big mirror. Oddly, Kylie felt as if she stared right at Miranda and her.

"Stop that," Miranda hissed in a low voice, and clapped her hands over her ears. "I didn't invite you in."

"Stop what?" Kylie asked, but the girl's odd behavior had Kylie shifting farther away. "Invite me where?"

Miranda didn't answer; she frowned up at the front of the bus and then bounced back into her seat.

That's when Kylie realized she'd been wrong. Wrong about the fact that it couldn't get any weirder.

It could, and it did.

Not terrible. If you don't mind the sight of blood. Miranda's words played like scary music in Kylie's head. Okay, the girl admitted to exaggerating things, but come on, losing even a little blood was too much. *What kind of hellhole had her mother sent her to?* she asked herself for what was probably the hundredth time since she'd gotten on the bus.

Right then Kylie's phone buzzed with an incoming text. Sara again. *Please don't tell me . . . u told me so.*

Kylie pushed her own problems aside to think about her best friend. They may have had a rough few months, but they had been best friends since fifth grade. Sara needed her.

Kylie started texting. *OMG, wouldn't say that. Don't no what 2 say. R U OK?? Do ur parents no? Do you no who the father is?* Kylie deleted the last question. Of course Sara knew who the father was. It had to be one of three guys, right? Unless Sara hadn't been honest about what she'd done on the dates with her two last guys.

Oh, God, Kylie's heart went out to her best friend. Even considering Kylie's terrible circumstances of her parents' divorce, Nana's death, and being sent to "bloody" Shadow Falls Camp with some very strange people, Sara had it worse.

In two months, no matter how bad things were, Kylie would

go home. By then, she'd hopefully have gotten over the shock of losing her dad, and Nana. And maybe over the summer, Soldier Dude would lose interest in her and disappear permanently. But in two months, Sara would have a belly the size of a basketball.

Right then, Kylie wondered if Sara would even go back to school. God, Sara would be so embarrassed. To Sara, fitting in was . . . everything. If blue eye shadow was the rave, you can bet Sara would have blue eye shadow before the week was out. Heck, she'd missed nearly a week of school when she got a big pimple on the end of her nose. Not that Kylie liked going to school with a big zit, but duh, everyone got a pimple every now and then.

But not everyone got pregnant.

Kylie could only imagine what Sara was going through.

Kylie reread her text, added a little heart, and hit send. As she waited for Sara to text back, Kylie realized she'd never been happier than right now that she hadn't given in to Trey.

"Ten minutes for bathroom breaks," the bus driver said.

Kylie looked up from the phone to the convenience store. She didn't have to go, but considering she wasn't exactly sure how much longer the ride would be, she dropped her phone in her purse and stood up in the aisle to follow the others off the bus.

She'd taken two steps when someone wrapped a hand around her arm. A very cold hand. Kylie jumped and swung around.

The pale girl stared at her. Or at least she assumed she stared at her. With her almost-black sunglasses, Kylie couldn't be sure.

"You're warm," she said as if surprised.

Kylie pulled her arm away. "And you're cold."

"Nine minutes," said the bus driver firmly, and motioned Kylie forward.

She turned around and walked out of the bus, but she felt Pale Girl's stare bore into the back of her. Freaks. She was stuck with freaks all summer. Cold freaks. She touched her arm where the girl had held her and could swear she still felt the chill.

Five minutes later, bladder empty, she started back to the bus and saw a couple of the other kids paying for drinks. Goth Girl looked over at her from the front of the line. Then the boy with all the piercing who'd sat at the front of the bus walked past Kylie without saying a word. Deciding to grab some gum, she found her favorite grape flavor and went to stand in line. When she felt someone step behind her, she looked back to see if it was Pale Girl again. Nope, it was the boy from the back of the bus, the one with soft green eyes and brown hair. The one who reminded her of Trey.

Their gazes met.

And held.

She wasn't sure why he reminded her of Trey. Sure, their eyes were similar but it was more than that. Maybe it was the way his shirt fit across his shoulders, and the certain air of . . . distance. Trey hadn't been the easiest person to get to know. If they hadn't been assigned as lab partners in science class, she didn't know if they'd ever have gone out.

Yup, something about this guy seemed hard to get to know, too. Especially when he didn't even speak. She started to swing back around when he raised his eyebrows in some kind of weak greeting. Taking his lead, she raised her own brows at him and *then* turned around.

When she faced forward, she saw Miranda and Pale Girl talking by the door and they were both looking right at her.

So, they were now ganging up on her, were they?

"Great," she muttered.

"They're just curious," the deep voice whispered so close to her ear that she felt the warmth of his words against her neck.

She looked over her shoulder at him. This close, she could really see his eyes, and she realized she'd been wrong. These weren't Trey's eyes. This guy had flecks of gold around his pupils.

"About what?" she asked, trying not to stare.

"You, they're curious about you. Maybe if you opened up a little . . ."

"Open up?" Okay, that annoyed her. She'd been giving him the benefit of the doubt about being the normal one, but not if he was going to start acting as if she was being the unfriendly one. "The only ones who spoke to me were the blond guy and Miranda, and the other one, and I talked to all of them."

He quirked the other eyebrow at her. And for some reason that pushed her button. "Do you have a nervous twitch or something?" she asked, and then bit her tongue. Maybe she was overcoming the too-nice disease. Sara would be proud. Her mom . . . well, not so much.

Her mom.

Just like that, the image of her mom standing there in that parking lot filled Kylie's mind.

"You don't know . . . do you?" the boy asked, and his eyes widened, his gold flecks seemed to sparkle.

"Know what?" she asked, but her mind seemed stuck on her mom. On the fact that she hadn't even hugged her good-bye.

Why had Mom done this to her? Why had her parents decided to split? Why did any of this have to happen? The familiar knot, the need-to-cry knot, formed in her throat.

He looked over at the door and when Kylie followed his gaze, Miranda and Pale Girl were still there. Had all three of them gone to the camp before and they were like buddies and she was the new kid on the block? The new kid they'd decided to pick on?

The lady behind the counter spoke up. "Hey, you wanna pay for that gum?"

Kylie looked back at the cashier. She dropped a couple of bucks on the counter and left without getting her change. She brushed past Miranda and the other girl with her chin held high and without blinking. She dared not blink for fear the flutter of her eyelashes would bring on tears.

Not that their snotty attitudes made her want to cry. It was her mom, her dad, Nana, Trey, Soldier Dude, and now even her concern for Sara. Kylie couldn't care less if these weirdoes liked her or not.

Chapter Five

An hour later, the bus pulled into a parking lot. Kylie had seen the Shadow Falls Camp sign posted in front. A wiggle of fear stirred in her stomach. She shifted her gaze around, almost surprised the place didn't have a high fence and a locked gate. They were, after all, considered to be "troubled" teens.

Kylie heard the bus engine rumble to a stop. The bus driver jumped down from the seat and stretched her little chubby arms up over her head. Kylie *still* didn't know how she reached the gas pedals.

"We're the last bus to arrive, guys," she said. "Everyone is waiting in the mess hall. Leave your things in the bus and someone will bring them to your cabins later."

Kylie looked at her suitcase. She hadn't put a tag on it. How would they know it was her suitcase? Easy—they wouldn't. Great, she could take the luggage with her and risk getting in trouble for not following the rules, or leave it and risk losing all her clothes.

She was not going to lose her clothes. She reached for her suitcase. "They'll bring it to you," Miranda said.

"It doesn't have my name on it," Kylie replied, trying to keep the sharpness from her tone.

"They'll figure it out. I promise," she said as if trying to be nice.

But was Kylie going to believe her? *No.*

Suddenly, the green-eyed Trey lookalike moved into the aisle. "Believe her," he said.

Kylie looked at him. While she didn't trust Miranda, there was something about this guy she believed. While standing there, he reached in his pocket and pulled out some money and dropped it in her hands.

"Excuse me," Goth Girl, said, and pushed past Miranda.

Kylie stared at the dollar and few coins.

"It's your change from the store." He motioned for her to step into the aisle.

She dropped the money into her purse and started out. His footsteps dogged hers. She felt him behind her. Felt him lean in a little closer, his shoulder brushing against her back.

"My name's Derek, by the way."

Caught up in listening to his deep voice and feeling Derek behind her, she didn't see Blond Boy jump out into the aisle. In mid-step motion, Kylie had one of two choices. Plow into Blondie or fall back into Derek. An easy decision. Derek's hands caught her by the upper forearms. His fingers pressed against her bare skin where her sleeves ended.

She looked up over her shoulder and their gazes met.

He smiled. "You okay?"

Amazing smile. Like Trey's. Her heart did a little jump. God, she missed Trey.

"Yeah." She pulled away, but not before noting Derek's warm touch. Why that seemed important she didn't know, but the pale girl's coldness had left an equally odd impression.

They moved out of the bus and made their way into a large cabin-like structure. Right before Kylie entered the door, she heard a strange kind of roar. Like a lion. She paused to see if she heard it again, and Derek bumped into her. "We'd better move inside," he whispered.

Kylie's stomach fluttered with fear. As she took that first step over the threshold, she somehow sensed her life would forever be changed.

About fifty or sixty people filled the huge dining hall that had large picnic tables running parallel to each other, and the air smelled like pork-n-beans and grilled hamburgers. Some of the kids were sitting, others were standing.

Something felt off, odd. It took her a minute to realize what it was. Silence. No one spoke. If this was the school's lunch room, she probably wouldn't be able to hear herself think. And that's what everyone appeared to be doing right now. Thinking.

A quick sweep of the crowd had Kylie once again feeling as if she didn't belong here. There was a large amount of what Kylie's mom would call "rebellion evidence." Sure, Kylie rebelled. But she guessed she did her thing in less noticeable ways, not so much with her clothes and such, but in her surroundings. Like the time she and Sara had painted her room purple without permission. Her mom had freaked.

These kids, they didn't just paint their rooms, they wore their rebellion boldly. Like Miranda's hair or that other kid on the bus who had nose rings and piercings. As Kylie's gaze shifted around, she noticed a couple of kids had tattoos or shaved heads. And there were tons more goth-dressed kids. Black obviously had not gone out of style with troubled kids.

Uneasiness started crawling on Kylie's skin. Maybe she had hung out with Sara too long, but it seemed evident that she didn't fit in. But unlike Sara, Kylie wasn't so eager to become one with this crowd.

Two months. Two months. She repeated the words like a litany in her head. In two months, she'd be out of here.

Kylie followed Blond Boy to an empty table in the back. And when she got there, she realized all her bus companions had hung together. Not that she felt as if she belonged with them, she hadn't even had eye contact with some of them, but face it, a known freak was better than an unknown one.

Suddenly, Kylie started feeling people turn and look at her. Or were they looking at all of them? The new kids were on display. The crowd's gazes became a collage of cold stares with different-colored eyes, but similar expressions and a lot of eyebrow twitching.

Weirded out to the max, she looked at Derek, then Miranda and even Pale Girl and Blond Boy, and damn it if they were doing it, too. The eyebrow thing. It wasn't cartoonish, and not as noticeable as Sara's whole roll your eyes and pucker your brows kind of thing, but just a little twitch.

Like Derek had done back at the convenience store.

What was it with the eyebrows?

Looking back into the crowd, fighting the urge to look

down at her shoes, she forced herself to hold their gazes. Face it, she didn't want to be the chicken of the bunch. The one everyone picked on. And if that made her like Sara, so be it.

"Looks as if we are all here," a female voice said from the front.

Kylie tried to find the face behind the voice, but her gaze clashed with another stare—a cold, bright blue-eyed stare that somehow stood out from the rest. Pulling her attention away from just the eyes, Kylie noticed the boy's jet-black hair. And just like that, she remembered.

She remembered him.

She remembered . . . her cat.

"It can't be," she muttered under her breath.

"What can't be?" Derek asked.

"Nothing." Kylie forced her gaze to the front where the woman spoke in a singsong type of voice.

"Welcome to Shadow Falls Camp. We are . . ."

The woman, probably mid-twenties, had long red hair that hung almost to her waist. She wore jeans and a bright yellow T-shirt. Standing beside her was another woman about the same age, but good God, she wore goth. All black, even her eyes appeared black. Somebody really needed to subscribe to a fashion magazine or two.

Kylie looked over at Goth Girl who'd been on her bus. The girl stared at the woman with a sense of admiration.

"My name is Holiday Brandon and this is Sky Peacemaker."

Right then the cabin door opened and a couple of men walked in. They looked like lawyers, or some other serious type of profession that demanded they wear matching black suits.

Kylie watched the two women up front shift their gazes to the visitors and frown. She got the feeling the two men weren't expected. That they were even unwelcome.

Sky, the goth leader, walked over and led the men outside and Holiday continued. "Okay," the singsong voice said. "First we're breaking down into newbies and returnees. Everyone who has been here before will move outside. You'll find some helpers out there with your schedules and cabin assignments. As always, the rules of this place are posted in your cabins. We expect you to read them. And let me make something clear right now, we're not going to rearrange cabin assignments. You are here to get along, and get along you will. If a serious problem arises, bring it to the attention of either myself or Sky and we'll discuss it, but not until after twenty-four hours. Any questions?"

Someone in the front raised a hand. "Yeah," the female voice echoed in the room. "I have a question."

Kylie leaned to the right to see the girl. The girl, another goth-dressed individual, turned around. "It doesn't have anything to do with the rules, but . . . I want to know, who the hell is she?"

The girl pointed—pointed right at the table where Kylie stood. Or was she pointing right at Kylie? No, she couldn't be.

Oh, damn. She was. She was pointing *at* Kylie. "Crap," she muttered when about sixty pair of eyes all turned and focused directly on her.

Chapter Six

"Relax," Derek said in a voice so low she was certain no one else heard it. And she could barely hear him thanks to the thumping of her own heart.

"Introductions will happen over lunch," a female voice said. Kylie thought it was Holiday again, but she couldn't be sure. They all continued to stare. Stare at her. Her mind raced and her heart pounded. Gushing sounds echoed in her ears.

Tearing her gaze away, she eyed the door and fought the urge to run. Run fast and run hard. But face it, she'd never been a good runner, and too many freaks stood between her and the door. Then, oddly, she remembered something she'd learned about wild animals. If you run, they think you're dinner and will chase you.

Oh, double crap. Okay, deep breath. Then another one. Her lungs expanded. These weren't wild animals, just weird-ass teenagers.

Right then, Kylie's phone beeped with another incoming text. Probably Sara. Kylie ignored it. And for the first time, Kylie decided she possibly could have been wrong about Sara's situation being more difficult than her own. She wasn't a hundred percent certain of that, but something deep in her gut said this wasn't just about her going to Mark Jameson's party.

But what else could it be about?

And why? Why of all the freaks in the room had she been singled out? Was it because she didn't twitch her eyebrows? Oh, she could twitch her brows as good as the next person. And darn if she wouldn't be practicing that as soon as she got alone. Problem was, she just didn't understand the whole twitching thing. Was it the Shadow Falls Camp version of a secret handshake?

"Come on. Let's get things moving," the singsong voice said again. "Returnees, outside. Newbies, hang right here."

Kylie experienced the tiniest bit of relief when the crowd stopped staring and started shuffling around, reaching for purses and backpacks. Or at least most of them stopped staring. Kylie looked over to the right and saw the black-haired boy with bright blue eyes standing there, his gaze locked on her. *Lucas Parker.* She recalled his name, even though it had been a long time since she'd seen him.

I'm glad they left, she recalled her dad saying. *Take my word on it, that kid is going to grow up to be a serial killer.* Kylie felt a fist wrap around her heart and squeeze. Was she really at a camp with a possible serial killer?

Could it really be him? Of course, she could be wrong. It had been, gosh, over ten years. Chills tiptoed up her spine, and then he turned and moved into the flow of other returnees out the door.

Kylie saw Miranda take a few steps. She stopped in front

of Kylie and said, "Good luck." Kylie couldn't tell if the girl was being a smartass or serious, so she just nodded.

The blond boy stepped behind Miranda and grinned at Kylie. "Wouldn't want to be you," he said as if joking, then he followed Miranda out.

Knees locked so she wouldn't crumble, Kylie came to her senses long enough to realize that at least half the crowd had gone. And of her bus buddies, the only ones remaining were Pale Girl, Goth Girl, Derek, and the guy with all the piercings.

"Okay," Holiday said. "Now, what I want is for all of you who know why you're here, to move to the far left. All of you who don't, move to the far right."

Kylie remembered her feeling that this was about more than her trip to the police station and started to move to the right, but she noticed everyone shifting to the left. Not wanting to be singled out any more than she already had been, she went to stand beside Derek.

He shot her a look of disbelief. Deciding to practice the whole eyebrow thing, she crinkled her forehead.

When she looked over, only four people stood on the right side of the room. One of them was the pierced boy from her bus.

Holiday looked at both groups and Sky walked in and stood beside the redheaded leader. "Okay, righties, come with me. Sky is going to talk to everyone else." Holiday started out, then stopped and glanced back over her shoulder. Her gaze slapped right into Kylie. "Come with us, Kylie."

Shocked the women knew her name, she shook her head. "I know why I'm here," she lied.

"Really?" asked Holiday.

Deciding to take a stab at it, she said, "I got caught at a party where drugs were found."

A few snickers filled Kylie's ears.

Holiday frowned at the snickerers and motioned Kylie forward.

"Is it because my parents are getting a divorce?" she asked, feeling desperate.

Holiday didn't say anything, but then she didn't have to. The look she shot Kylie reminded her of her mom's don't-go-there stare. And the one time Kylie had gone there, she'd been grounded for a month. So Kylie followed Holiday and the four others out of the dining hall.

When they walked past the crowd standing outside, Kylie felt all the eyes turn toward her. Miranda nodded and mouthed the words "good luck." For some reason, Kylie suspected the girl's intentions were genuine.

Then Kylie spotted Lucas Parker standing beside the goth girl who'd raised her hand and asked about Kylie in the big meeting. They had their heads together, whispering, and they both stared at Kylie as if she didn't belong there. And damn if Kylie didn't agree with them. That's when Kylie realized that Lucas was dressed goth, too. Or at least he wore a black T-shirt. Of course, he looked really good in that shirt. It fit his upper torso—his very lean yet muscular upper torso—like a glove. So unfair, how guys didn't have to follow any fashion guidelines to look good.

Realizing she was staring at the guy's abs, and that the goth chick was smirking at her, Kylie turned away and pretended she hadn't noticed the girl's rude expression. Now if she could just pretend none of this was happening. Right then the pierced guy fell into step beside Kylie. She glanced at him and tried to smile. They might be strangers, but at least they'd ridden the same bus and he seemed just as clueless as she was.

He leaned in. "You wouldn't have brought any drugs with you, would you?"

Kylie's jaw dropped open in shock and mortification. *Just shoot me now.* Friggin' great. Thanks to her little slip in the dining room, everyone now considered her a druggie.

Holiday, her red hair flowing down her back, led them into a smaller cabin with a tin roof, located right behind the dining hall. From the wooden-plank porch hung a sign that read CAMP OFFICE. Kylie and the other four followed her to a back room that looked like a classroom.

"Have a seat, guys." Holiday leaned against the desk in the front as she waited for everyone to settle in.

Kylie felt the woman's gaze on her every few seconds as if she thought Kylie might try to bolt. Much to Holiday's credit, the idea had crossed Kylie's mind more than once. Hence the reason she chose the desk closest to the door.

Yet something kept Kylie from running, something besides the fact that she had never excelled at the fifty-yard dash. Something more than fear of being caught trying to escape.

Curiosity.

For an unknown reason, Kylie sensed that whatever Holiday had to say, it was going to explain things. And Kylie desperately wanted an explanation.

"Okay," Holiday said, and offered everyone what appeared to be a relax-everything-is-cool kind of a smile. Nevertheless, it was going take more than a smile to convince Kylie.

"What I have to say is going to be a relief to most of you, because deep down you've known that something was . . . different. Some of you have known it all your life, some of you have only recently come upon your destiny, but either way, this is probably going to be a shock." Holiday's gaze shifted to Kylie. "You guys are here because you are special. Gifted."

Holiday paused and Kylie waited for someone to ask the question, and when no one did, she blurted it out. "Define special."

"We've all read about the supernaturals, thing of legends, and from childhood, we're taught that they don't exist. The truth is that they do exist. Not everyone in the world is alike. And some of us are a lot more different than others. Some of us were born like this, some of us were changed. But no matter how this happened to you, if you are here it is because this is your destiny. It was chosen for you."

"Wait a minute," Kylie said before she could stop herself. "What are . . . I mean, are you saying that . . . that things like . . . like—"

"Vampires exist?" Pierced Guy asked. "Oh, shit. I knew I wasn't crazy. That's why I got really sick."

Kylie had to swallow to keep from laughing. She'd been about to say things like angels, but this was . . . it was stupid. The boy had obviously done too many drugs. Everyone knew that . . . that vampires and crap like that didn't exist.

She waited for Holiday to correct the guy. And then waited

some more. During that second delay, Kylie remembered how cold Pale Girl's touch had been. She remembered Blond Boy's ever changing eye color, she remembered Miranda's disappearing toad. No. She refused to let herself start to . . .

"That's right, Jonathon," Holiday said. "They exist. And yes, you were turned last week."

"I knew they weren't just dreams," said the other girl. "The wolf I dreamed of. It was real."

Holiday nodded.

"No." Kylie held up her hand and shook her head so hard that blond hair brushed back and forth across her face. "I'm not going to believe this."

Holiday met Kylie's gaze. "I'm not surprised that it's you, Kylie, who finds this the hardest to believe."

"What am I?" blurted out the other sandy-haired girl.

What am I? The girl's question vibrated in Kylie's head. Not that she had the least bit of desire to ask it herself. She didn't believe in this crap. *I do not believe.*

Holiday smiled at the girl and gave her a soft accepting look. "Your birth mother was fairy. You have healing gifts. And I know you have suspected this."

The girl's eyes widened with what appeared to be relief. "I healed my little sister, didn't I? My parents thought I was crazy," she said. "But I knew I'd done it. I felt it when it happened."

Holiday gazed at her with sympathy. "That is sometimes the hardest part of this. Knowing what we know and not being able to share it with others. But very few ordinary humans can accept us for who we are. This is part of the reason you are here—to learn how to deal with your gifts and how to live in a normal world."

Kylie's mind raced. She recalled the strange things that had been happening—the return of her night terrors and . . . Soldier Dude, the stalker that only Kylie seemed able to see. Panic started to unravel her logic. She closed her eyes and desperately tried to wake herself up. It had to be a dream.

"Kylie?" Holiday's voice had her opening her eyes. "I know this is hard for you to accept."

"It isn't just hard. It's impossible. I don't believe—"

"But you are scared to ask, aren't you? Scared to ask the reasons you are here, because deep down, you know you belong here."

I know that neither my mom or dad want me. That's why I'm here. "I shouldn't be here," Kylie snapped. "I haven't been having dreams of wolves. I have night terrors. I'm hardly able to remember my dreams. I haven't been bitten by a bat, and I haven't healed anyone."

"Vampires and werewolves are not the only supernaturals that exist." Holiday paused and then pressed her palms together in front of her. "What do you want, Kylie? Proof?"

Chapter Seven

"Yeah, proof would be good," Kylie said, unable to keep the sarcasm from her voice. "But now you are going to tell me that you can't give me that, right? You're going to tell me some little speech about how I have to believe in it anyway, right?"

"No, actually, I planned on giving you the proof." Holiday's voice held an odd kind of calm that made Kylie take a deep breath. It also scared the bejeebies out of her. What if Holiday was telling the truth? What if . . . Kylie recalled how cold the pale girl was on the bus. No way. She was not going to believe in this. Vampires and werewolves existed in fiction, not in real life.

The woman pulled a cell phone from her jeans and made a call. "Can you send Perry into the office classroom? Thanks."

She placed the cell back in her pocket. "Now, all of you are welcome to stay and see this. Or if you'd like to go on out, each of you have a mentor waiting out front. They are here to answer your questions."

Kylie watched them look among themselves and they all

agreed to stay. It made her feel better knowing she wasn't the only one having doubts about any of this.

After a few minutes, long minutes during which silence penetrated the room like a fog, she heard the sound of footsteps in the front of the cabin. The door opened, and the blond boy from her bus, the one with weird eyes, walked into the room.

"Hi, Perry. It's good to see you again," Holiday said with sincerity.

"It's good to be back." His gaze met Kylie's and her breath caught when she found herself staring at eyes so dark that they didn't appear human. Right then, his creepiness level moved up in leaps and bounds.

"It would make me very happy if you'd do the honor of showing us your special gift."

Those non-human eyes didn't shift from Kylie. Perry grinned. "So you have some non-believers, do you?" Turning his head, he focused on Holiday. "What would you like to see?"

"Why don't we let Kylie decide?" Holiday looked at her. "Kylie, this is Perry Gomez, he's a very gifted shape-shifter, one of the most powerful ones there are. He can probably become anything you can imagine. So why don't you tell him what you'd like to see him become?"

Kylie kept moving her gaze between Holiday and Perry. Realizing they waited for her to say something, she forced herself speak. "A . . . unicorn."

"Unicorns don't exist," Perry said, his expression seeming to say he felt insulted by her choice.

"They used to," Holiday added, as if coming to Kylie's defense.

"No shit?" Perry asked. "They really existed?"

"No shit," Holiday repeated. "But we should work on our language." She smiled. "Just think of a horse with a horn. I know you can do it."

He nodded, then he pressed his palms together and Kylie saw his black eyes roll back into his head. The air in the room suddenly felt weak, as if something had sucked the oxygen out of it. Kylie stared at Perry even when everything inside her said not to. Right then her curiosity, her need to know evaporated into the not-so-breathable air. She'd never understood that saying, "Ignorance is bliss," until this moment. She wanted to remain ignorant. She didn't want to see, didn't want to believe.

But she did see.

She saw sparkles forming around his body—sparkles as if a bucket of floating glitter had been spilled around him, as if a thousand lights came on and reflected each miniscule piece of glitter. The hundreds of diamond-shaped twinkles swirled around him. Slowly the sparkles fell to the floor and left standing where Perry had once stood was a huge honking white unicorn with a pink horn in the middle of its forehead.

Chapter Eight

The unicorn, aka Perry, swatted its tail back and forth, as if strutting its stuff, then swung around in Kylie's direction. The beast took two steps toward her, close enough she could have touched it if she'd been so inclined. But no inclination existed.

It reared its head, made a neighing noise, then one of its deep dark black eyes winked at her.

"Shit!"

"Damn!"

"Oh my God!"

"Holy cow!"

"Mo fo!"

Kylie wasn't sure who said what, one may have even leaked out of her mouth, for all five responses had shot through her addled brain. Taking in another gasp of air, she looked at Holiday, who stared at her with soft green eyes.

"It's okay," Holiday said. "Perry, change back now."

Kylie dropped her forehead against the flat, cool surface of her desk top and concentrated on breathing and *not* thinking. If she let herself think, she'd cry and the last thing she wanted to do in front of these people was show any sign of weakness. Hell, these freaks probably fed on weak people.

"You guys should leave now," Holiday's voice, now with an authoritarian tone, seemed to echo in the room, bouncing inside Kylie's head.

She counted to ten and then somehow managed to sit up. The desks around her stood empty. Perry, back to his human form, and the others shuffled out of the room. Perry gave her a quick glance over his shoulder. His brown eyes, normal-looking eyes this time, almost appeared apologetic.

Remembering Holiday's order about leaving, Kylie forced herself to stand. If she could just get out of here, she might be able to find a secluded place where she could freak out in private. Where she could cry, and attempt to come to terms with . . . No. Don't think yet. Not yet. She swallowed the few tears crawling up her throat and her sinuses stung.

"Where are you going?" Holiday asked.

Kylie looked back her. It hurt to talk around the knot of emotion lodged between her tonsils. "You said we should leave."

"They should leave. *You* need to stay."

"Why?" A watery film coated her vision and hopelessly, Kylie realized she couldn't stop it. The tears had arrived. *Why?* The one-word question plowed through her confused mind and morphed into dozens of questions. Why was any of this happening? Why was she being singled out again? Why did her mother not love her? Why did her dad turn his back on her? Why couldn't Trey give her a little more time? Why did all these freakish kids act as if she were the weirdo here?

She blinked back a few tears and dropped back into the seat. "Why?" she asked again. "Why am I here?"

Holiday sat in the desk beside her. "You're gifted, Kylie."

She shook her head. "I don't want to be special. I just want to be me—normal me. And . . . and to be completely honest with you, I think there's been some huge mistake made here. You see, I'm not . . . gifted. I . . . I certainly can't turn myself into anything. I don't suck at anything, except maybe algebra. But I've never been great at things, either. Sports are so not my thing, and I'm not super talented or even the extra smart type. And believe it or not, I'm okay with that. I don't mind being just average . . . or normal."

Holiday laughed. "There is no mistake, Kylie. However, I know exactly how you feel. I felt just like that when I was your age and especially when I realized the truth."

Kylie swiped at her face to hide the evidence of her tears and then forced herself to ask the question she'd been trying not to think about since the whole thing started. "What am I?"

Chapter Nine

"Can you handle the truth?" Holiday asked softly, her eyes filled with empathy.

Handle it? I just saw a boy turn himself into a unicorn. Can it get any worse?

Seconds after Kylie asked herself that, she got a chill. What if it could get worse? She recalled Holiday saying there were other types of supernaturals besides vampires and werewolves, which in Kylie's mind had to be the worst kind of supernatural, not that she had expertise in the field or anything, but what if Holiday had only said that to calm her down? Would she have lied?

"Yes, I can handle it," Kylie said, sounding braver than she felt.

But when Holiday opened her mouth to speak, Kylie blurted out, "No." She dropped her face into her hands, then removed them and stared again at the redheaded camp leader. "I don't know if I can handle it."

How could she when it was just too much?

Kylie bit down on her bottom lip so hard it hurt. "I mean, if you are about to tell me something like I'm dead, that I need to start acquiring a taste for blood and I can't even eat sushi, I won't be able to handle it. Or if you're going to tell me that I'm going to start howling at the moon, eating people's cats, and will spend the rest of my life having to get waxed if I want to wear a bathing suit, then I don't think I can handle it, either. I like cats and I tried waxing once, and that hurt like a son of a gun." She dropped her hand between her legs, remembering.

Holiday laughed, but Kylie had been as serious as a heart attack. Waxing had really hurt and she hadn't let Sara talk her into anything like that since.

"Do you think I can handle it?" Kylie asked, afraid of the answer.

"Honestly, I don't know you very well yet, but I trust Dr. Day's assessment of you."

Kylie blinked. "What does my shrink have to do with this?"

"Your shrink—as you call her—is the one who recommended you to us. She recognized your gifts, she's half fairy, you know."

Kylie tried to process that information. "I'm here because of her? That woman is . . ." Kylie leaned closer, almost as if whispering might make it less of an insult. "She's a few fries short of a Happy Meal." Kylie dropped her hands on the desk. "I wouldn't lie to you. She's a flake."

Holiday frowned. "Unfortunately, all supernaturals come off a bit flaky when viewed from the normal prospective. She spoke very highly of you."

Kylie felt a little guilty then, which she suspected had been the camp leader's intent.

Holiday dropped her palms on top of Kylie's hands. "I won't

lie to you, either, Kylie. The truth . . . the truth is, we don't know what you are."

Kylie sat up a little straighter, chewing on that bit of information, and Holiday sat quietly as if allowing Kylie the time to adjust. Not that Kylie was adjusting. Oh, hell no. She was working on finding a positive slant to all of this. "Don't you see? That's because I'm not anything. I'm just me. Normal me."

The woman shook her head. "You have gifts, Kylie. Those gifts could have come from various supernatural forms and almost always they are hereditary."

"Hereditary? Neither of my parents are . . . supernaturals."

Holiday didn't look convinced. "In rare cases, it could skip a generation. It could be fairy, it could be you are a descendent of one of the gods. It could be—"

"Gods? Gifts? What gifts?"

Holiday cleared her throat, and her eyes met Kylie's with empathy. "You can talk to the dead—sometimes in your sleep. Other times when you're awake."

Warmth spread into the top of Kylie's hands, but cold spread into her heart. "The dead?" Her mind started filtering though images, all of them Soldier Dude, since she couldn't recall anything from her night terrors.

"No, you're wrong. I never talked to them. Never, ever. Not one word. Mom taught me to never talk to strangers, and I've lived by that."

"But you've seen them, right?"

Tears welled up in Kylie's eyes again. "Just one. And I'm not sure he's a ghost. Sure, my mom didn't seen him, but my mom . . . she's always in her own little world." But then there was her neighbor, the way she had walked right past Soldier Dude and never even glanced at him. *Oh damn. Damn.*

"It's scary, I know," Holiday said. "I remember when I first started experiencing it."

Kylie pulled her hands out from under Holiday's grasp. "You . . . you have the same . . . talent?"

Holiday nodded and looked over to the left.

Kylie gave the room a visual sweep. "But none are here now, right?"

Instantly, Kylie felt it. That cold . . . the eerie in-the-bones kind of cold that she'd experienced so often lately.

"They are always here, Kylie. You're just turning your mind off."

"Can I do that?" Kylie asked. "Can I just turn my mind off permanently?"

Holiday hesitated. "Some people can, but this is a gift, Kylie. To not use this gift is a waste."

"A waste? Oh no, I didn't ask for this gift." Her own words echoed inside her head and she realized she'd practically admitted that this was real. She didn't want it to be real. Didn't want to accept it or believe it. "I'm not sure I have this gift. I mean, I hear about normal people seeing ghosts all the time."

Holiday nodded. "It's true. Some ghosts accumulate enough energy that even a normal has been able to see them."

"Then that's what's happening to me. I'm just dealing with a super-charged ghost. That's it. Because I'm just normal."

"The evidence says different."

Her breath caught. "What evidence?"

Holiday stood up and motioned for Kylie to follow. Her

knees felt weak when she stood, but she followed. Holiday spoke as she walked. "First, there's the fact that you are unreadable."

"Unreadable?" Kylie asked as they walked into a small office.

"All supernaturals have the ability to get a sneak peek into other minds. When reading a human, we see a similar pattern with everyone. When reading other supernaturals, we can generally sense what they are. Unless they are purposely blocking us out. Which most don't do as a sort of courtesy to others."

"Is that the eyebrow-twitching thing?" Kylie asked.

"You don't miss much, do you?" Holiday smiled. "And the thing is that people with the gift of ghost whispering are often slow at reading others and are very difficult to read. We're not being rude, but our minds function on a different plane than everyone else's does. With practice, however, we can train ourselves to open up enough so that we aren't coming off as holier than thou. Your pattern, and the fact that you are unreadable tells me that you are more than human. And then there's this evidence." The camp leader pulled out a file drawer. She drew a piece of paper out of a file with Kylie's name on it and placed that paper in Kylie's hands.

Kylie looked at the copy of her birth certificate. Nowhere on the document did it say anything about her being supernatural or about her seeing ghosts. She glanced up at Holiday with questions running through her mind.

Holiday must have either read her thoughts, or her expression, because she answered, "You were born at midnight, Kylie."

"So? Why is that supposed to mean something?"

Holiday ran her finger over all the files. "Everyone here was born at midnight."

Kylie's heart thumped a little harder. She watched Holiday's red-painted fingernail move over the file tabs where the names appeared in bold type. None of the names meant anything to Kylie until her gaze found one that did.

Lucas Parker.

Not that he mattered. His name only leapt out at her because it was one of the few familiar things here. Another sweep of icy emotion tiptoed up her spine.

Kylie swung around and her breath caught when she saw him. Not Lucas, but Soldier Dude. And he just stood there, closer than ever before, and stared at her with his cold, dead eyes.

Less than ten minutes later, Kylie sat at a lunch table.

Alone.

Only her, Holiday, the other camp leader, and the two men, occupied the dining hall.

Every few minutes, Kylie's mind would try to wrap around everything that had happened—everything from the unicorn to her not being human. But her mind wasn't in a wrapping mood.

Deny it. Deny it. The words played like a song in her head.

The sound of the voices in the front of the dining hall brought Kylie's gaze up. Holiday had received a call from Sky, and because it was almost lunch time anyway, Holiday had told Kylie to just come with her and she'd show her to her cabin after lunch.

Holiday's gaze shifted to Kylie. Kylie stared at her phone, pretending she didn't feel uncomfortable, while Holiday and the other camp leader, Sky, stood at the front with the two black suits who had dropped in earlier.

Kylie couldn't hear the conversation, but whatever it was, she could tell it wasn't good. She peered up between her lashes again. Holiday and Sky were frowning. Holiday seemed the most anxious of the two, tapping her foot and twirling her hair in a tight rope.

Then one of the men raised his hands in the air and spit out, "I'm not pointing fingers, but I'm telling you like it is. Get to the bottom of this and make it stop or I swear, higher-ups are going to shut the camp down."

Shut the camp down? Kylie lowered her gaze and pretended not to hear, but she couldn't stop the hope from building in her chest. Ever since Holiday had left her alone at the table, Kylie had been tempted to call her parents and beg them to come get her.

Ah, but what would she tell them? *Hey, Mom, Dad, guess what? You sent me to camp with real freaks, a bunch of bloodsuckers and cat killers. And oh, I'm a freak, too, but they don't know what kind yet.*

Kylie's stomach clenched at the thought of how that conversation would turn out. Chances were her mom would yank her out of the camp and commit her to a psycho ward. Not that it would be worse than what she was in now.

Staring at her hands, Kylie remembered what Holiday had said about her gift being hereditary. Did her mom or dad see ghosts? Not her mom, otherwise she wouldn't have brought in the mental doctor the first time Kylie brought up Soldier Dude.

And her dad would have told her if he had any special abilities, wouldn't he?

Not that Kylie had accepted that she had any gifts. It was still highly probable that Holiday was wrong about her being one of them. Maybe Soldier Dude was just a high-powered ghost, like Holiday said could happen. And surely there were normal people who were born at midnight, right?

Nevertheless, the idea of trying to tell her parents any of this seemed absurd. Seemed absurd? Who was she kidding? It was over-the-top completely one hundred percent crazy, and if she hadn't seen Perry change himself into a unicorn, she wouldn't have believed it, either.

The conversation up front got a little louder, but not as loud as before, not loud enough for Kylie to distinguish words. So she stared at her phone and pretended to read Sara's last text, but in truth, she'd already read it.

Her friend hadn't told her parents about her missed period, and as soon as Sara's mom left for her lunch appointment, Sara was going to the store to buy a pregnancy test. Some time this afternoon, Sara would know if she was pregnant.

Kylie hadn't asked Sara about the father, she hadn't even asked Sara if she would consider an abortion. For some reason, Kylie didn't see Sara doing that. But six months ago, Kylie would have sworn that Sara would never find herself pregnant, either.

Kylie let herself worry about Sara for a minute before she shifted back to her own issues. Like how she was going to survive the next two months. And by survive, she didn't mean just mentally. Vampires and werewolves killed people.

Only the bad ones, Holiday had explained on the walk over

here when Kylie had almost jumped out of her skin anytime someone came close. Was Holiday certain that no bad ones were at the camp? Some of them had looked pretty grim to Kylie. Not that she considered herself an expert at distinguishing bad supernaturals from good ones. But in a way it sort of compared to how Kylie felt about snakes and spiders—there were good ones, and there were bad ones. But for safety's sake, she avoided all of them.

God, Kylie hoped she didn't get stuck rooming with any of them. Surely Holiday wouldn't expect her to sleep in a cabin with someone who . . . who might be tempted to kill her while she slept. Then again . . . Great, that meant she'd probably be sleeping with one eye open the entire two months.

The conversation between the two black-suited guys and the camp leaders came to an end and the two men started to leave. But one of them, the taller of the two, turned around and looked right at Kylie. And then he did it. He twitched his brows at her.

Kylie looked away, but she sensed him standing there in that same spot, still staring and twitching. She felt her cheeks heat up.

The door to the dining hall shut, but then she heard it open again. Kylie looked up and saw the other teens start to filter into the room. As each one entered, Kylie found herself guessing— fairy, witch, werewolf, vampire, or shape-shifter. Were there other kinds of supernaturals? She'd have to ask Holiday about the different types, like what "descended from the gods" meant.

Kylie started trying to put the types she did know into one of two groups: supernaturals who wouldn't consider a human a part of the food chain, and those who did.

Derek walked through that door and Kylie found herself

curious about what type of supernatural he was. He stopped a few feet in the room and looked around. The moment his eyes lit on her, she knew he'd found what he'd been looking for. He'd been looking for her. Even not knowing what he was, or exactly what group he belonged to, the thought that he liked her enough to look for her made her feel less lonely.

As he moved toward her, a very small smile appeared in his eyes, and she thought again about how he reminded her of Trey. Was that why she liked him, or at least liked him better than everyone else? Because he did look like Trey a little?

She'd have to be careful, she told herself, not to confuse familiarity for something more.

"Hey," he said as he sat down beside her. When she looked up at him, she realized her shoulder barely came to his mid-forearm. Which meant he was taller than Trey—probably by a couple of inches.

Kylie nodded and dropped her phone in her purse.

"So . . . ?" he asked.

Kylie met his green eyes with flecks of gold. She knew exactly what that one-word question asked. He wanted to know what she was. She started to answer him, to tell him she didn't know what she was, just her gift, but she suddenly found she wasn't ready to say it aloud. To say it aloud meant she believed it. And she didn't, not yet.

"It's been a crazy morning," she said instead.

"I can imagine," he answered, and she sensed a bit of disappointment in him. He'd wanted her to trust him.

Good luck with that, Kylie thought. Between people dying on her—meaning Nana—people divorcing on her—meaning her parents—and people breaking up with her because she wouldn't put out—meaning Trey—her ability to trust anyone had taken a dive off some very high cliff. And it had landed on the bottom of some gully, a mangled mess, right beside her heart.

Miranda dropped down in the seat on the other side of Derek. "Hey . . ." She leaned over and looked at Kylie. "We're rooming together. Isn't that cool?"

"Yeah." Kylie quickly tried to figure out exactly what Miranda was. She remembered the toad and for some reason guessed her to be a witch.

"I'm in with you guys, too," someone else said, and sat down on the other side of Kylie.

Kylie turned and found herself staring at her own reflection in Pale Girl's dark shades.

Chills ran up Kylie's spine. Kylie didn't know if she was a werewolf or a vampire, but something told her she was one of the two. Which basically meant, she fell into the humans-are-on-the-food-chain group.

The girl lowered her glasses, and Kylie got a look at her eyes for the first time. They were black and slightly slanted, exotic, as if she was part Asian. "My name's Della . . . Della Tsang."

"Uh . . . Kylie Galen," she managed to say, hoping her hesitation didn't come off as fear. But it was fear and Kylie couldn't deny that.

"So Kylie," Della said, pulling her glasses down another inch, "do tell. Exactly *what* are you?"

Was it her imagination that at least a dozen other teens turned and looked toward their table? Did they have super hearing? Kylie's phone buzzed. "Uh, I should . . . take this."

She grabbed her phone from her purse, stood up, and went to stand in the corner, away from everyone.

Glancing at the screen to see who to throw handfuls of praise to for calling at the right moment, Kylie's heart did a tug. She'd expected it to be Sara, maybe her mom or dad. She hadn't expected it to be Trey.

Chapter Ten

"Hello?" she answered hesitantly, and her chest immediately filled with a familiar kind of missing-Trey achiness that until she saw him at the party had almost disappeared. Almost.

"Kylie?" The deep sound of his voice did another pull on her emotions.

She swallowed a knot down her throat and visualized him in her mind—his green eyes staring at her like he did when they made out. "Yes?"

"It's Trey."

"I know," she answered, and closed her eyes. "Why are you calling me?"

"Do I need a reason?"

Since you're sleeping with some other girl, you do. "We're not together anymore, Trey."

"And maybe that's a mistake," he said. "I can't stop thinking about you since I saw you at the party."

She'd bet he stopped thinking about her when he got his new bang toy alone that night. Lucky for them, they'd left about fifteen minutes before the cops had arrived. So while Kylie had been sitting at the police station, Trey had probably been expanding on his luck by getting lucky with his new girlfriend.

"Sara told me that you were at some camp in Fallen," he said when she didn't say anything. "She said your mom sent you there because of the party."

"Yeah," she answered, even though she realized it wasn't the whole truth. But she couldn't tell Trey the truth. Not even part of the truth. That's when it hit her, how many lies she'd have to tell everyone she knew. That's when she realized something else. Her mom hadn't been lying when she'd said Dr. Day had convinced her that Kylie needed to come here. Maybe her mom hadn't wanted to get rid of Kylie as badly as she thought. That should have made her feel better, but the achiness in her chest grew.

She missed her mom. She missed her dad. She wanted to go home. The gonna-cry knot formed in her throat and she swallowed it.

"Are you allowed to get phone calls?" Trey asked, his voice bringing her back to the moment and away from her thoughts.

Allowed? Kylie hadn't considered that. "I think so. No one's told me I couldn't." But she hadn't read the rules that were supposed to be posted in her cabin, either. Not that it was her fault; she hadn't been allowed to go to her cabin yet.

She looked up to see if anyone else was on a phone. She spotted two people talking and two more texting. One of the texting kids was Jonathon, aka Piercing Guy, who stood with two other guys. Beside them stood Goth Girl, who hung with a crowd of other goths.

Kylie also spotted Lucas Parker. Not on the phone but talking to a group of girls that looked like his personal fan club. He was smiling at something someone said. And she could see the girls holding on to his every word, practically swooning all over him. Let them laugh and swoon, Kylie thought. He hadn't killed their cat.

"I'm going to a soccer camp in Fallen next week," Trey said, bringing her back to the conversation. "I thought maybe we could . . . maybe we could find a way to get together. To talk. I miss you, Kylie."

"I thought you were with that girl, Shannon."

"We weren't ever really going out. But we're not seeing each other anymore. I could never talk to her."

But I'll bet you did other things. It hurt to remember how the girl had hung all over him at the party.

"Say you'll at least meet me," he said. "Please. I really miss you."

Her chest grew heavier. "I don't know if I can . . . I mean, I don't know how things are run here yet."

"I think our camps are just a mile or so apart. It wouldn't be hard for us to meet."

She closed her eyes and thought how good it would be to see Trey. To see anyone she knew wasn't a freak, but especially Trey. He had always been her go-to person when things bothered her. Which was why his breaking up with her had broken her heart.

"I can't make any promises, not until I figure things out here." Kylie looked up.

Holiday and Sky were moving to the front of the room.

"Lunch is ready," Sky said. "Let's let the new people start first. And then we'll jump into introductions."

Introductions? The thought of having to talk to the group had butterflies nosediving in her stomach.

Kylie saw Derek turn and look at her as if wondering if she wanted to get in line together. She kind of liked the idea of standing beside him, instead of standing alone.

"I have to go, Trey," she said.

"But Kylie—"

She hung up. She hadn't done it to be mean, but the idea that he might feel a bit rejected didn't bother her too much. Payback could be hell.

Derek stood up and waved her over. Yup, Derek was taller than Trey. Moving Derek's way, Kylie tried not to flinch when Della joined them, and the three of them walked to the line together.

Della ended up behind Goth Girl from their bus and they started talking.

Derek turned and focused on Kylie.

"Boyfriend?" he asked.

"Huh?"

"The phone call?"

"Oh." She shook her head. "Ex." Instantly she remembered how several of the other kids had looked at her when Della had asked what she was. She leaned closer to Derek. "Could you hear me on the phone?" She lowered her voice. "Could everyone hear me?"

"I couldn't. It was just . . . your body language." He seemed to note how she looked out in the crowd. "But yes, some of the others have super hearing."

"But not you?" She hoped he would tell her what she wanted to know. That he'd tell her what he was.

"Not me," he said, and they moved a few steps forward. His arm brushed up against hers and for a second, she didn't know if she wanted to back away or lean closer. The fact that he wasn't cold seemed to make closer an option. When her arm met his again, something so comforting spread through her.

"So what are you?" she asked, and then bit her tongue. It wasn't fair for her to be asking questions that she herself didn't want to answer. "That's okay, you don't have to answer that."

She looked away, embarrassed, and listened to the chatter of the crowd. Unlike earlier, when silence had reigned, now if she tried really hard, she might convince herself that she was in a room filled with regular teens.

And that's when Kylie knew that she'd stopped trying to deny it.

Laughter along with a few of the more feminine squeals filled her ears. She should have found the "regular" thought comforting, but she couldn't push away the truth. The truth was none of these people were regular or normal.

Not even her.

That thought shot a wave of panic into her stomach and she wondered how in the hell she would manage to eat anything now.

"I'm half Fae." Derek's voice came close to her ear. The tickle of his breath sent flutters to her stomach. Not the kind that stemmed from fear, but something different. Pushing that aside, she tried to concentrate on what he said.

Fae? The synonym search in her brain started spinning through files until she recalled reading once that Fae was French for *fairy*.

Her mind started spitting out data. Holiday was fairy. Holiday had said Kylie might be fairy.

She turned and met his green eyes. In a voice so low it barely came out a whisper she asked, "Do you . . . do you see ghosts?"

"Ghosts?" His eyes widened as if the question were unbelievable. But duh, how could that seem crazy when . . . when . . .

Her train of thought came to an abrupt halt when Kylie felt someone behind her. Her heart raced to a fast song and she feared it would be Soldier Dude. But the cold, the one she'd suddenly realized always came when he was near, didn't seem to be present. She watched Derek's gaze rise over her shoulder. He nodded.

She turned her head and her breath caught when she found herself staring into the light blue eyes of Lucas Parker.

"I think you lost this." His voice reminded her of a radio announcer—deep with a rumbling quality that made it unique—memorable. A quality that made him sound older than he appeared.

Aware that she stared, she jerked her gaze to his hands where he held out her Coach billfold that her grandmother had splurged to get her last Christmas.

Immediately, Kylie looked back at the table where she'd left her purse. It sat on top just as she'd left it. How had he gotten her billfold?

She took her wallet from his hands and fought the temptation to make sure her mom's credit card was still tucked safely inside. Her mom would be so pissed if she lost it.

Torn between doing the socially acceptable thing of saying thank you or questioning him on how he'd gotten his feline-murdering hands on her possession, her mind spun. Then because she mostly always did the socially acceptable thing, the two simple words, "thank you," formed on her tongue, but she couldn't spit them out.

She couldn't help wondering if he remembered her. She couldn't help noticing how his blue eyes seemed to look inside her, just as they had all those years ago. They hadn't been friends, but neighbors for a very short time. He hadn't even been in her grade. But they had to walk the same three blocks home from school every day, and she could remember that walk being the best part of her day. From the first time she'd seen him riding his bike on her street, he had fascinated her in a mysterious kind of way.

And just like that, she remembered with clarity the last time she'd seen him. The sense of fascination shattered, leaving in its place a cold wind of fear.

She'd been sitting on a swing with her new kitten in her hands—the kitten her parents had given her because Socks had come up missing. Lucas's head had popped over the fence, and his blue eyes met hers. The kitten had hissed and scratched her, trying to run for cover. The boy stared and then said, *Be sure to take the kitten in the house at night. Or what happened to your other cat will happen to it.*

She'd run to her mother crying. That night her dad and mom had gone to talk to Lucas's parents.

Her parents hadn't told her what happened, but she recalled her daddy looking angry when they'd returned from the visit.

Not that it mattered, because the next day Lucas Parker and his parents were gone.

"You're welcome," Lucas said, his deep rumble now slightly laced with sarcasm. Then he turned and walked away.

Oh, great. All she needed was to start making enemies of one of the humans-are-on-the food-chain gang—especially one she knew was capable of doing despicable things. But face it, being nice to Lucas Parker was going to be hard. After all, he had killed her cat and threatened to do the same to her kitten.

Chapter Eleven

During lunch, the introductions proved to be as embarrassing as Kylie thought they would be. Everyone had said their name and "what" they were, but when her time came, she'd only offered her name. The silence in the room had felt suffocating in the seconds afterward. Holiday had jumped in and explained that the origin of Kylie's powers was still being deciphered and that her "close-mindedness" was not intentional, but a product of her gifts.

If anyone in the room doubted that she was the freak of all the freaks, they had now been informed of the fact by the camp leader. Oh, Kylie suspected Holiday had been trying to help, but Kylie could have really done without it. Luckily, she had already managed to force down half a turkey sandwich because after that, there was no way she could swallow another bite.

Right after her embarrassing moment in the spotlight, Kylie's phone rang. She saw her mom's number on the call screen and turned the phone off. The last thing she wanted was for her conversation with her mom overheard by the super-hearing individuals.

As soon as the official lunch meeting ended, Kylie found Holiday to get her cabin directions. Dinner was set at six and until then, the afternoon was free. During downtime, mingling and getting to know your camp companions and cabin roomies was encouraged.

Instead, Kylie spent the four hours mingling with her emotional turmoil and hidden away in her closet of a bedroom. Hey, she understood the difference between "encouraged" and "required."

Sitting up on the bed, she noticed again the size of her room. Not that she was complaining. The fact that she had her own room made the size a non-issue. Considering the night terrors that plagued her three or four nights a week, the privacy was much appreciated. She just hoped the walls were thick enough to contain what her mother called "bloodcurdling screams." The walls at home sure as heck weren't.

Biting down on her lip, Kylie wondered again how her mom could do this to her. Send her here when only a week ago, her mom had suggested she not spend the night off anywhere because it would be embarrassing for her to let others see her in a sleep-dazed terror.

Shaking off thoughts of her mom, Kylie looked around the room again. Her afternoon hadn't been a total waste. She'd unpacked her things, called her mom—aka, the Ice Queen—back, tried to get in touch with a MIA Sara—who still hadn't called or texted—read the camp rules, and indulged in a good ol' fashioned meltdown with lots of tears.

A much-deserved meltdown.

For sixteen years she'd tried to figure out who she was. And while she'd always known she'd had a ways to go, she'd felt pretty confident in her discoveries. But today she realized not only was she wrong about who she was, but she didn't even know *what* she was.

Talk about an identity crisis.

Her phone buzzed again. She looked at the caller ID and saw her dad's name.

Her dad who'd left her.

Her dad who hadn't picked her up at the police station.

Her dad who hadn't visited her before she'd been forcibly shipped off to camp.

Her dad who obviously didn't love her near as much as she'd thought he did.

Her dad who in spite of everything, Kylie missed with all her heart.

If that made her a daddy's girl, so be it. Besides it was probably just a temporary condition. Sooner or later she'd give up loving him so much like he'd given up on her. Right?

Her throat locked up. The temptation to answer and beg him to come get her was so strong that she tossed the phone onto the foot of the bed. She listened to the buzz and knew if she answered that call she'd tell him about supernaturals and about her being one of them—about running into Lucas Parker the potential serial killer.

Keeping secrets from her mom had always felt easy, because it seemed her mom kept her own secrets; but keeping things from her dad was algebra—damn hard.

So instead of taking the call, she plopped her head on the pillow and gave in to another bout of tears. When someone knocked on her bedroom door, Kylie still wore the watery evidence of tears on her cheeks.

Before Kylie could decide what to do, the door opened and a nose peeked through the crack. "Are you awake?"

Since Kylie sat up on the bed and saw Miranda's eyes right above the nose, Kylie didn't lie. "Yes."

Miranda stepped in—uninvited.

"Hey, I just . . ." Miranda's hazel gaze lit on Kylie's face and the girl's mouth dropped open.

Kylie knew exactly what had the little witch gaping. Kylie envied the girls who could cry and barely smear their mascara, but she lacked that particular skill. When Kylie cried, her fair skin broke out in big red dots and her eyes swelled so much that she didn't look human.

Wait. According to Holiday, Kylie wasn't human. Who knew?

"Are you okay?" Miranda asked.

"Fine." Kylie forced cheeriness into her voice. "Allergies."

"Should you go see a nurse? Seriously, you look terrible."

Thanks. "No. I'm fine. It'll go away in a bit."

"It's not contagious, is it?" Miranda stopped a few feet into the room.

"I sure as heck hope not," said a voice at the door. A voice that belonged to Della, who still wore her dark shades, and who Kylie had learned during the introductions was a vampire. Yup. A real vampire.

"I'm not contagious," Kylie said, and realized she should have said yes so they'd leave her alone.

Miranda moved in and sat on the foot of the twin bed, and

Della followed her but didn't sit down. Instead, the girl removed her sunglasses and eyeballed Kylie up and down. Her dark expression reminded Kylie of a how a person on a diet stared at a Girl Scout cookie right before it became mouth mush.

Kylie's skin crawled at the thought of becoming mush in anyone's mouth.

"You are coming to dinner and the campfire, aren't you?" Miranda asked.

"Is . . . is it mandatory?" Kylie asked, hoping her reaction to Della didn't show.

"Are you scared of me?" Della blurted out, axing all of Kylie's hopes of hiding the fact that Della scared the pee out of her.

"Why . . . why would I be scared of you?"

"Because I have sharp teeth?" She opened her mouth and exposed her pearly whites that did indeed showcase two sharp canines. "Because I might suck your blood out?"

It took effort not to cringe at Della's words, especially when the girl ran her tongue over her lips.

"Quit teasing her." Miranda laughed and rolled her eyes.

"That's just it." Della waved at Kylie. "Her heart is racing and her pulse is running off the chart. Look at the vein in her neck, it's throbbing. I don't think she knows I'm teasing."

The fact that Della mentioned Kylie's veins had her blood pumping harder. "Of course I do," Kylie lied. "Holiday said everyone here was good . . . people."

"And you believed her?" Della's black eyes accused Kylie of being dishonest.

Kylie decided right then that Della's ability to read her vital signs surpassed her ability to lie. "I want to believe her. But I'll admit it, I'm still trying to wrap my mind around the fact that . . . that supernaturals exist."

"But you're a supernatural," Miranda said. "How could you not know—"

"Holiday *thinks* I'm a supernatural." Yeah, somewhere in the last few minutes Kylie had gone back to hoping Holiday's analysis was meritless.

"You are a supernatural," both Miranda and Della said at the same time, both their eyebrows twitching ever so slightly.

"Or at least, you aren't all human," Della said. "We can tell that by looking at your brain pattern."

"And you guys are never wrong?" Kylie clutched her knees tighter to her chest.

"Everyone's wrong once in a while," Miranda said.

"But not very often," Della added.

Nevertheless, their answer spurred Kylie's hope. "But it does happen. Right?" The heaviness in her chest lightened.

"Yeah, there are the people with brain tumors," Della added.

Kylie dropped her forehead on her knees. She was either a supernatural or dying of a brain tumor; she didn't know which was worse.

"And a few whose brains are just loopy," Miranda added.

Kylie raised her head. "Loopy?"

"Yeah, like a frog's hair from being loco."

"Then maybe I'm just loopy. I've been accused of that before."

"No, wait," Miranda said. "Didn't Holiday mention you had gifts?" Miranda and Della both raised inquisitive eyebrows.

Kylie shrugged. "Yeah, but that could just be because I'm dealing with a super-charged ghost."

"Ghost?" Miranda and Della said in unison.

Kylie could be wrong, but both girls looked appalled and scared. Their shock reminded her of Derek's reaction earlier when she'd asked if he could see ghosts.

"You can see the dead?" Della stepped back from the bed. "Oh, hell. I do not want to room with someone who has ghosts hanging around. That's too freaky."

Even Miranda popped up off the foot of the bed. Kylie stared at them, completely befuddled. "You're joking right? You two are scared of me? You're a witch." She pointed at Miranda. "And you're a vampire." She wagged her finger at Della. "And ya'll are calling me"—she poked herself in the chest—"freaky?"

Miranda and Della exchanged a look, but neither girl denied what Kylie had just said.

"Fine, forget it then," Kylie said, hurt by their attitude. "But just for the record, I don't talk to them." Then she realized that both girls were looking at her the same way she'd been looking at them all day. The bitterness of tasting her own medicine had Kylie turning things over in her mind.

"So they just hang around you?" Della started eyeballing the room. "Please tell me there's not any here right now."

"There's not," Kylie snapped, but her anger wasn't directed at her, just the situation. Because dad-blast it, if she'd heard someone could see ghosts, she'd probably be afraid of them, too.

"Good." Miranda reclaimed her spot at the foot of the bed.

Della continued to glance around. "Nope. Too weird. I don't want to room with you."

"I'm not any weirder than you are." Kylie stared at the vampire and for some reason wanted Della to accept her.

"She has a point," Miranda said to Della. "We're probably pretty scary to her, too. I say, let's try to make this work. You know, be buds."

Della let out a deep breath. "Okay, but you'll tell us when you see a ghost hanging around?"

Kylie nodded, but quickly realized how hard that request was going to be to keep, because the familiar icy feeling of a ghostly presence hit right then. The saving grace was that she didn't "see" the ghost. Not that she looked hard, but who could blame her not wanting to clash gazes with a dead person?

Kylie hadn't thought she could eat, but when the warm, spicy scent of pizza hit her nose, she realized how little she'd eaten all day. She'd managed to down one slice of thin pepperoni and cheese and eat half her salad before she started feeling self-conscious from the occasional twitching stares. Some of the campers were still trying to figure her out. Well, good luck with that. She took another bite of salad and hoped that if they managed to do it, they'd let her in on the secret.

As Kylie moved her gaze around the room, she found Derek sitting at another table. There was a red-haired girl sitting next to him, and from her body language she found Derek more interesting than her pizza. The girl leaned so close to Derek that her left breast brushed against his arm and from the way Derek leaned into the girl, Kylie figured he enjoyed the girl's attention.

The tiniest bit of jealousy echoed in her chest, but Kylie pushed it back. It was just because he looked like Trey. Biting down on her lip and her emotions, she knew she'd have to be careful where Derek was concerned. It would be easy to confuse her feelings for him.

Right then the half-fairy looked over his shoulder at her. Their gazes met and held. The flutter, the good one, started happening again in the pit of her stomach.

"I think he likes you," Miranda whispered.

Realizing she and Derek had drawn attention, she glanced away. "He's probably just curious about me like everyone else," she whispered back.

"Nope. He's hot for you," Della said, reminding Kylie of the supernatural hearing of some of the campers. "When he was sitting by you at lunch, he oozed so much testosterone that it was hard to breathe. He wants your body," Della teased.

"Well, he's not getting it," Kylie said.

"So you don't like him?" Miranda asked, sounding thrilled.

"Not like that, I don't." It felt like a lie, but she ignored it, because she knew any feeling she might have stemmed from his looking like Trey. She had enough stuff going on in her life right now. She sure as heck didn't need to start falling face-first into another relationship, especially one based on a lie. Derek wasn't Trey.

And Trey wanted her back. Or at least he'd insinuated that on the phone earlier. With all the other stuff she'd been zapped with today, she hadn't had time to consider how his confession made her feel. Happy? Sad? Angry? Maybe a little of all three?

Trying to prevent emotional overload, Kylie reached for her glass of diet soda and watched Della pull the pepperoni off the pizza and pop it in her mouth. The very tips of her sharp canines caught Kylie's attention and her thoughts skipped past Trey issues and landed on living-with-a-vampire issues.

As another piece of pepperoni disappeared down Della's throat, Kylie realized that the girl was eating. From the fictional books she'd read, she'd assumed vampires didn't eat. They only drank . . . Kylie's gaze slammed against Della's glass filled with some red, thick liquid.

"Oh crap." Kylie's stomach heaved, and she placed a hand over her mouth.

"What?" Della asked.

"Is that . . . blood?" she muttered, and looked around the dining hall, noticing the glasses filled with the red substance that were occupying the tables in the room.

Miranda leaned in. "It's gross, isn't it?"

"Hanging out with toads is gross." Della's voice came edged with anger.

"I don't hang out with toads," Miranda snapped, her hazel eyes grew bright with what appeared to be embarrassment. "I put a spell on this guy. He deserved it, of course, but now I can't seem to reverse it so whenever he misbehaves, he automatically turns into a toad and pops in to see me."

Desperation echoed in Miranda's voice, but Kylie barely paid it any heed. For some reason the fact that Miranda could turn people into toads didn't bother Kylie near as much as the fact that Della was drinking blood. But holy hell. What kind of blood was it?

Della looked at Kylie and read her disgust. "Seeing dead people is gross, too. This"—she picked up her glass and took a big gulp—"is not gross."

When Della pulled the glass away, a couple of red drops beaded right below her bottom lip. Della's pink tongue shot out and caught the droplets.

Kylie's stomach knotted and the pizza, now a lump in the bottom of her gut, wanted to find its way up.

"Of course"—Della's smile came off wicked—"you guys will find that out when you have to try it."

"I tried it last summer and it was gross," Miranda said. "It tastes like a dirty penny smells."

"What?" Kylie swallowed hard. "I have to drink blood? I'm not doing it. Nope. Not me." She put her hand over her mouth and concentrated on not barfing.

"Not drink it, just taste it," Miranda said. "We all have to learn about each other's cultures toward the end of the summer. We, the witches, put on a ceremony and show some of our magic; the werewolves, last time we actually saw Lucas Parker transform himself. It was scary. Whatever you do, don't piss off a werewolf."

Kylie's mind stopped fixating on drinking blood and fixed on Lucas Parker transforming into a wolf. Then she remembered their little meet-up during lunch. The one where she'd probably pissed him off.

Of course, she didn't need to hear Miranda's warning. She knew firsthand what he was capable of doing. Then for some crazy reason, she found herself trying to find him in the crowd. He either wasn't there, or had his back to her.

"Werewolves aren't as badass as vampires," Della said, defending her species with enthusiasm. "Werewolves only have full power once a month. Vampires—we're a hundred percent twenty-four/seven. It's *my* kind that you don't want to piss off."

Kylie sat there trying to digest the conversation while her shaky stomach worked on digesting the pizza.

"And then the shape-shifters—that was weird, but not scary," Miranda continued.

"What did the Fae do?" The question came from a deep, obviously male voice.

Kylie recognized Derek's voice before her eyes found him. And when she did find him, she realized he'd found her, too. He stared right at her.

Her already knotted stomach knotted some more. Only these knots, like the flutters, weren't all unpleasant. Yup, she was going to have to be extra careful with Derek where her emotions were concerned.

"Well," Miranda said, her tone a little higher pitched than normal. "Because fairies have different gifts, each one did a short presentation." Miranda gave her hair a twirl and smiled extra wide.

"What's your gift?" Della asked Derek as she pulled another piece of pepperoni off the pizza and slipped it between her lips. Lips that had just drunk blood.

A long pause followed the question. Derek's posture stiffened. "Who said I even have gifts?" His tone implied he didn't like to be questioned. Or could he be like her, and wasn't too thrilled to have his gift?

"One of the fairies last year could read people's thoughts," Miranda continued, obviously not picking up on Derek's mood. "Can you read my mind now?" She bit down on her lip and sent him a sultry look.

Kylie's gaze shot back to Derek. Could he read minds? No, she didn't think he could, because he'd asked earlier what she was. Or was he just making conversation?

She recalled thinking some private thoughts about his body, comparing it to Trey. Oh, great. How embarrassing would that be if he knew she'd imagined him without his shirt? Then she realized she was doing it again. Kylie felt her face flush and Derek, still staring, didn't miss a thing.

"Another fairy could move objects with his mind," Miranda said louder as if trying to get Derek's attention on her. "Of course, witches can do that, too."

"Really?" Della sounded honestly amazed. "Do it now. Move my plate." She leaned back as if to give Miranda room.

Miranda's gaze shot to Della and she frowned. "I can't. It's against the rules."

"Rules? Screw the rules," Della said. "Do it. No one is going to know but us."

"I can't." Miranda's cheeks turned pink, almost as pink as the streaks in her hair. It was good to know Kylie wasn't the only one who suffered from blushing.

"Why not?" Della argued. "Just because of some stupid rule?"

Miranda glared at Della. "Why don't you just go drown

yourself in blood?" Miranda glanced at Derek, who she'd obviously wanted to impress, and turned pinker.

"Oh, stake me!" Della snapped.

"Be careful, or I might," Miranda shot back, her expression passing embarrassment and going straight to anger.

Kylie's gaze shifted from Miranda to Della as they took turns slamming each other with insults.

Great. Now her two roommates were going to be trying to kill each other.

"You two should chill," Derek said, as if he'd read her mind.

"I'm already as chilled as I can get," Della said, and focused on Miranda. "Somebody's got a chip on her shoulder. And you'd best be careful, because I'd be more than happy to knock it off for you." She jumped up and before Kylie could focus on her, she was gone.

"Cool," a new voice in the crowd said.

Perry, aka Weird-Eyed Boy who'd turned himself into the unicorn, stood beside Derek. Kylie stared at his black eyes, and her heart raced to the tune of panic.

"Hey," Perry said to Miranda. "I'd love to watch you two go at it and rip each other's clothes off."

"In your dreams," Miranda said.

"Yeah." Perry chuckled. "Especially the clothes off part."

"Grow up." Miranda grabbed both hers and Kylie's trays and shot off to drop them off.

"Thanks," Kylie said to her, but looked from Derek to Perry, not sure which one made her more nervous—Derek who made her feel things she didn't want to feel, or Perry who just plain freaked her out. Her phone buzzed. She pulled her cell from her purse, hoping it was Sara with not-pregnant news and not her dad. A sigh escaped her lips when she saw Sara's number.

"Later," Kylie said to the guys. Then, eager to escape, she took off outside where she could have a private conversation. Though who the heck knew how far she'd have to go so the super-hearing supernaturals couldn't listen in?

Chapter Twelve

"Just don't panic," Kylie told Sara thirty minutes into their conversation. "It'll probably be fine." Kylie couldn't say that with a huge amount of enthusiasm, but she gave it a shot. That's what friends did. Yet deep down, Kylie knew if Sara was pregnant, and there seemed to be a good chance she was, it wouldn't be fine.

"Thanks, Kylie," Sara said. "What am I going to do without you all summer?"

"Survive," Kylie said. "That's all I'm planning to do, too."

Kylie had spent the entire conversation hiding behind the office, sitting on the ground, leaning against a tree and trying to calm Sara down.

Sara's mom had canceled her lunch and insisted her daughter spend the day with her, going to the art museum and then shopping. The Museum of Fine Arts in Houston was great and Sara actually liked art. As for the shopping, who wouldn't love that? But not with your mom while you're afraid you were pregnant.

"I totally can't believe this is happening," Sara continued. She hadn't even picked up a pregnancy test yet. She was too freaked.

Not that Kylie wasn't up to her eyebrows in her own issues, but talking to Sara about her problems helped Kylie not to focus on her own. Plus, focusing on Sara was pretty much the norm for them. Face it, when Sara was upset, and sometimes even when she wasn't, Sara tended to be a tad self-absorbed. Kylie never minded. She'd always preferred listening to other people's problems than blabbering about her own.

Good thing, Kylie supposed, since right now she couldn't talk about what was going on. Well, not to any normal person, anyway.

"Well, I should go," Sara said.

One of the last sprays of the day's sun shot a golden glow around the green scenery. With dusk closing in, the heat index no longer felt so suffocating.

"Call me when you get the test," Kylie said.

"I will. And thanks."

Kylie closed the phone and her eyes. Leaning her head against the tree, she recalled her newfound hope that maybe Holiday was wrong about Kylie being a supernatural. She also remembered the two black-suited guys saying the camp could be closed down if "it" didn't stop—not that Kylie had any idea what "it" was. But if both of those hopes came true, Kylie could almost see her life being tolerable.

Or at least somewhat tolerable. The issues of her parents, Nana, and Trey almost felt manageable now. Amazing how one's perspective altered after learning you might not be human.

Holiday's voice played through Kylie's mind: *The truth . . . the truth is we don't know what you are. It could be fairy, it could be you are a descendent of one of the gods. It could be—*

Kylie recalled interrupting the camp leader, and now she wished she'd hadn't. Even though she hadn't given up on being normal, she couldn't help but wonder what else she might be.

Trying to stop the emotional jitters from making her stomach twitch, she concentrated on not thinking and just listening. A late-afternoon breeze stirred the leaves of the tree, crickets warmed up for their night song, a baby bird called to its mama. Kylie remembered the hiking trips she'd taken with her dad. Should she call her dad back now?

Later, she told herself. Maybe then she would know what to say to him about why he hadn't come to get her at the police station when she called him. For now, she was just going to sit there and absorb nature and almost relax. She closed her eyes and slowly the tension faded.

Kylie wasn't sure how long it had been, ten minutes or an hour, but something jarred her awake. Her eyes sprang open to darkness. She sat very still, listening. Not even the crickets breathed. Fighting the fear of the unknown, she remembered real monsters existed.

A deep, sinister roaring, like a lion, filled the dark silence, and then came the howling of dogs . . . or were they wolves? She glanced up at the black sky. The moon, not a full moon, looked blurry from the smear of clouds crawling past it. The sudden need to go somewhere where she felt safer shot through her. Before she moved, she heard a twig snap.

She wasn't alone.

Her heart raced and she considered her options—scream or run. Maybe both. Before she could do either someone spoke up.

"Still afraid of me, huh?"

She recognized Della's voice and her heart stopped most of the racing. Most of it. "Not as much as before." Kylie looked up. The vampire loomed over her.

Della laughed. "I like the way you mostly tell the truth."

"You can really tell when people are lying?" Kylie asked.

"Not everyone. Depends on how good of a liar they are. The good ones can control their pulse enough so I don't hear it. Then there's the people for who lying is so second nature it doesn't affect them."

Kylie stood and dusted the grass and twigs off the butt of her jeans. She'd have to be careful and not lie to Della. Or either get better at it.

"Holiday sent me to sniff you out."

"Sniff me out?" In the dark, Kylie could barely make out Della's expression, but she could tell the girl was smiling. Her white teeth seemed to almost glow in the night.

"You can smell me?" Kylie brought her arm up to her nose.

As if Kylie was a communal sniffing project, Della leaned in and sniffed. An appreciative moan left the girl's lips.

The tips of Della's sharp canines appeared at the corners of her mouth and Kylie jerked her arm back. Della's smile faded. Kylie got the odd impression that the vampire honestly didn't want Kylie to be afraid of her. So vampires had feelings, too. Somehow, realizing that made the girl more human and less scary.

"Everyone is at the campfire." Della started walking.

Kylie moved in step with her, not an easy task since Della's pace wasn't for wimps. "Do I really smell good to you?"

Della didn't look at her. "Do you want me to lie so you'll feel better? Or do you want the truth?"

"The truth . . . I think."

Della stopped and her tone came out huffy. "There's blood in your veins, I really like blood, so yes, you smell yummy. But it doesn't mean . . . Let me put it like this. Imagine you're hungry and you go into a hamburger joint. Every table is filled with people and their plates of big juicy hamburgers and greasy fries. The smell is ambrosia. So . . . what do you do?"

"Hurry and order," Kylie answered, not getting the point.

"You mean you wouldn't go steal any food off anyone's plate?"

"No," Kylie said.

"Okay, so if stealing someone's lunch is bad, you can imagine stealing a few pints of blood might create a tad more of an issue than swiping a Big Mac. I'd have to be really starving. Or really angry before I'd do that."

The girl came off pretty dang angry. Kylie asked, "Do you get *really* angry a lot? Have you ever got that mad?"

Della let out another exasperated huff. "I've never killed anyone that I can remember. Is that what you want to hear me say?"

"Yeah." Kylie smiled. "So vampires really aren't a threat to humans?"

"I didn't say that," Della said.

"Meaning?" Kylie asked.

"Meaning just like there's good and bad humans, there are good and bad vampires. And really bad vampires who belong to gangs and purposely try to cause havoc everywhere they go."

"What kind of havoc?" Kylie asked.

"Let's just say they'd steal your Big Mac. Or worse."

"Okay," Kylie said, pretty sure she knew what "worse" meant, and she didn't like it one bit.

"Then there are the betweeners," Della continued.

"Betweeners?"

"Like humans who have been known to get into some trouble, but aren't totally bad. Vampires can be like that, too."

Kylie nodded. They started walking again and her curiosity grew. "What are your gifts? If . . . you don't mind me asking?"

"Heightened senses. Heightened strength. And—oh, shit! I just remembered your gifts." She came to an abrupt halt. "There aren't any ghosts around here, are they?"

Kylie did a quick check for coldness. "Nope. But seriously, I don't think I'm really gifted."

"You don't want to be gifted, do you?" Della asked.

"No," Kylie answered, coming close to lying. Then she remembered Della was a human—make that a "nonhuman"—lie detector.

Kylie realized they were heading into the woods; a spray of clouds passed over the moon and darkness cloaked the area. That's when Kylie heard it again, the deep roar of what sounded like a jungle cat.

"Did you hear that?" she asked.

"You mean the white tiger?"

"The what?" Kylie reached out and grasped Della by the elbow. The coldness of her skin had Kylie letting her go even quicker than she grabbed her. The roaring stopped but the temperature of Della's skin sent a chill up her arm. Were vampires really dead? She didn't think she could ask that question.

Della looked back at her as if she knew the coldness repulsed her. Kylie looked down and tried to pull free a twig that had clung to her jeans, hoping to keep Della from seeing too much.

When Della started moving again, Kylie remembered what they'd been talking about. "This is Texas. We don't have white tigers."

"You do at wildlife parks. There's one a few miles from here. It's both a refuge and a park. Like a zoo. Visitors can drive through and even feed the tamer animals."

"I went to one once," Kylie said. "I just didn't know there was one here."

"Yup." Della raised her nose in the air and sniffed. "And most of the animals need their litter boxes cleaned. Stuff stinks. Especially the elephants' crap."

Kylie inhaled, fearing the stench, but only the scent of the woods, of moist earth and green vegetation filled her nose. She supposed having a heightened sense of smell wasn't always a good thing.

Each step took them deeper into the woods. Thorn bushes caught on her jeans. She had to speed walk to keep up.

"Where is the bonfire?" Kylie asked, feeling winded.

"About a fourth of mile. A little farther than our cabin."

"Why didn't we take the trail?"

"It's quicker this way."

Maybe for a vampire. They continued on for another three or four minutes without talking. Kylie thought of all the questions she'd like to ask Della, but didn't know if she would be offended.

Concentrating on the ground to avoid the largest thorn bushes and stumps, Kylie plowed right into the back of Della.

"Sorry—"

Della swung around so fast, Kylie only saw a blur, but there was no mistaking the girl's cold hand pressing over Kylie's mouth. "Shh." Della's fierce expression added a menacing touch to her warning. Then she swung back around, her head tilted as if listening.

Kylie tuned her own ears to hear. But like earlier, when Kylie had just awakened, only silence filled the woods—no insects, no birds. Even the trees held their breath.

Why?

A blast of cold air shot past as if something had flown by. But nothing was there. Then Della made a low guttural growl.

Kylie looked up. The girl's eyes were glowing, and a lime green color beamed from her face, making her look anything but human. Fear took up residence in Kylie's chest, crowding out her heart and lungs.

The whisk of wind passed again. Kylie looked back over her shoulder, and when she looked back around, she saw him. He stood far too close—taking up half of her personal space. Blinking, she took in his jet-black hair and Asian eyes. Eyes similar to Della's, but his eyes glowed gold not green.

His surreal stare focused on Della. "Hey, Cuz."

He cut his cold, gold gaze back to Kylie and leaned in. His nostrils flared. "I see you brought us a snack."

Chapter Thirteen

Before Kylie could think to react, Della jumped in front of her. "What are you doing?" Della demanded. "You can't . . . you can't be here."

"Don't worry, Cuz," he said. "They can't hear or smell me this far away. I know their limitations."

"Forget their limitations. *You* aren't supposed to be here," Della snarled.

"So I can't come see my favorite cousin?"

"Not here." She waved her hand. "Now leave before you get my ass in all kinds of trouble."

"You're not going to introduce me to this yummy-smelling individual." In a flash, he moved to stand in front of Kylie again. This time even closer. She could see an ugly scar running alongside his chin. The smell of his breath wafted up her nose. It smelled like the grocery store when you got too close to the meat department. Raw meat.

One word echoed in her panicked brain. *Run!*

Fear kept her from obeying.

Della growled and less than a second later, her vampire roomie had sandwiched herself between Kylie and the scar-faced cousin. "Leave her alone, Chan. You're scaring her."

He took a step back. "I'm just joking. I had my dinner." He ran his hand down his shirt—a light colored shirt that Kylie noted had stains down the front. Stains that could very well be . . .

Fear froze her lungs as the coppery scent of blood filled her nose. A noise escaped her lips. She took a step backward and almost tripped on her own feet.

Della shot her a quick glance, then refocused on Chan. "Go home. I'll see you when camp's over."

"So you're going to join us when you get out of this joint?" he asked.

"I don't know what I'm doing when this is over. That's why I'm here, to figure that out."

"Your parents will never accept you. You can't live in that world anymore," Chan said.

"You don't know that," Della said, pain sounding in her tone.

"I do know. I tried it. Save yourself and them the heartache and just come and live with us. We're your new family."

"I told you I'll make my decision when I leave here."

"This place is going to feed you a pack of lies. They want to change us . . . all of us. It's a ploy by the government."

"They aren't feeding me anything. They made it clear, it's my choice. Now go away before you get me thrown out of here."

"Trouble is my middle name, Cuz."

"Chan." Della made that low snarling sound again.

"You are no fun," he said, and then took off, moving so fast he left only a cold wake of fear behind.

Kylie found a tree to lean against. Della stood there, head tilted as if listening and staring off in the direction Chan had disappeared, no doubt making sure he'd left.

Slowly, she turned to Kylie. Her eyes had faded back to her own shade of black. The moon found its way from the clouds, allowing Kylie to read the emotions in Della's face.

"I'm sorry," Della said, and her expression matched her words.

Kylie couldn't answer; she hadn't even gotten her breathing under control. Back still against the tree, she wrapped her arms around herself to fight off the chill that had nothing to do with the temperature.

"He wouldn't have hurt you," Della said.

"He called me a snack," Kylie insisted, managing to eke the words out from her shaking lungs.

"He enjoys scaring people. He wouldn't have done anything."

Kylie arched a brow in disbelief. "Is he . . . does he belong to one of those gangs that harm humans?"

"No, he just likes to act out sometimes."

"Is that why you kept getting between us?"

"I did that because I could smell how afraid you were."

While Kylie couldn't totally buy into Della's words, she sensed Della believed it. Or at least she wanted to believe it.

The normal noises of the woods returned. A few insects chirped in the distance. Della stood there almost fidgeting. "Can I ask you a big favor?"

"What?" Kylie asked.

"Don't mention this to anyone? Other supernaturals aren't supposed to visit." The pleading in Della's voice seemed to cost her.

"What if he comes back?" Kylie could almost smell the scent of raw meat that had lingered on his breath.

"He won't. I'll make sure of it." Pausing, Della studied Kylie's face. "Please. If they find out, I could be sent home and I really need to be here right now."

Kylie remembered how Della had protected her and for reasons Kylie didn't quite understand, she trusted the vampire to protect her again. But did she trust her enough to put her life in her hands? Probably not, but her gut instinct made the decision for her.

"Just make sure he doesn't come back. I don't want to become another blood spatter on his shirt." Saying the words sent another chill down Kylie's back.

When the chill hung on longer than it should, she wondered if the cold stemmed from her panic or was it from something else? Was someone else here? Someone other than . . . .

"Thanks." Della smiled. "I knew I liked you. Come on— let's get to the bonfire before they send someone after us."

They started walking again, but every other step had Kylie looking over her shoulder. What frightened her more—finding a ghost or Della's cousin—she wasn't sure.

The smell of wood smoke grew stronger as they made their way through the woods. The half moon shifted in and out behind clouds, shrouding them either in moon shadows or complete darkness. The strange animal sounds kept playing in the distance—lions, elephants, and even wolves. But thankfully, the cold faded into the darkness.

Della never seemed to lose her way so Kylie stayed close, ignoring the feel of thorns and bushes catching on her jeans. Finally, a reddish glow appeared between the trees.

Able to think clearly at last, Kylie took advantage of their last few minutes alone to ask Della a few questions. "Is . . . your cousin the one who did this to you?"

Della looked over her shoulder. "Did what to me?"

"Turned you into a vampire."

"Oh. No. I was born with the virus. But yes, it was probably the contact with him that activated it."

"I thought you became a vampire by getting bit? Or is that just a myth? I mean, I realize there's a lot of myths about supernaturals. I saw you could eat pizza. And you were in the sun."

Della smiled. "The sun and I don't get along, but sunscreen mostly takes care of that. I can eat—not like I used to. I mostly need blood. And yes, some humans can be turned by being . . . bit. There are parts of the myths that are true. However, most of us are born with the virus. But it takes being exposed to another vampire before the virus is activated."

Kylie tried to understand. "So you knew you were a vampire all your life?"

Della chuckled. "Hardly. The virus runs in my family but we never knew anything about it because it only affects one in fifty family members, and even then it may not be the active virus. Everybody thought Chan died in a car accident when he was in France. Then one night I saw him, at this party. Freaked me out."

"I can imagine." A lot of this was freaking her out.

"Anyway, he of course could sense that I had the gene and having come in contact with him, he knew I'd turn and get sicker than hell. He showed up to help me. He told me that I was a vampire. It was a big friggin' shock to my system. Sort of like what you're going through right now."

"Yeah, but I haven't been sick. We're not sure if I'm anything."

"Yeah, denial is a big part of it," Della said. "I remember. I swore I just had a bad case of the swine flu."

Kylie bit back another denial and let Della continue. "I went through it all. Of course with vampires it's worse. The change is damn painful." She moved a few branches out the way and held them back for Kylie to pass.

"So your parents don't know?" Kylie asked.

"You kidding?" Della asked. "They would freak."

They kept walking and Della continued. "I got really sick at first. The doctors didn't understand it, either. Chan explained everything to me. He hid in my bedroom and took care of me for almost two weeks. I owe him big for that."

"Enough to leave your family for him?" Kylie asked, remembering what Della and her cousin had argued about. Then Kylie recalled her own family drama and sympathized with Della's plight. Losing someone you loved hurt like hell. An image of her father flashed in Kylie's mind and her chest tightened.

Emotion made Della's eyes bright. "There's a community of vampires who live in Pennsylvania. Chan thinks it's best if I go there and live. It's hard to live with family and keep this from them. I just . . . I don't know what's right. We . . . my family and

I, used to be so close. Well, Dad's always been a hard ass, but I know he loves me. Mom was my best friend and I have a little sister and I can't imagine leaving her."

"Would your mom let you go if you asked her?" Kylie asked.

"No. I'd have to run away and I know that would break their hearts. Which is why most young vampires fake their deaths, so the family moves on. I don't want to do that, but . . . I'm pretty much breaking their hearts now anyway. It's like a war zone at home."

Della's voice shook and Kylie didn't look but she figured there were tears in her roommate's eyes. Then again, Kylie wasn't sure if vampires could cry. But tears or no tears, she could hear the pain in Della's voice.

"It's hard," Della continued. "I had to go out at night to get blood. It's not as if I can keep a supply in the fridge. I'm basically nocturnal now, so staying awake at school during a boring class was almost impossible. The school convinced my mom I was either doing drugs or depressed. My parents, even my mom, were riding me and accusing me of all sorts of shit. All we did was fight, and I couldn't make it stop. So Chan may be right."

Kylie struggled for something to say. Staring straight ahead she spotted the red and orange flickers from the bonfire. The voices of the campers who were standing around a fire filled the night. She glanced at Della and offered her the only thing she could. "If it makes you feel any better, my home life sucks right now, too."

They walked out from the last line of trees into the clearing and they almost collided with a dark figure that leapt out of the trees, landing with almost a silent thud. Della growled. A startled yelp filled Kylie's throat, but then she recognized the dark figure with very blue eyes.

Lucas Parker.

"That's a good way to get hurt," Della snarled.

His gaze stayed fixed on them, harsh, accusing.

Kylie froze under his intense stare, but Della, unaffected by his ominous presence, gave Kylie a cold nudge to continue walking.

Lucas fell in step beside her and his deep voice came out as little more than a whisper. "If he comes here again, I won't sit by and do nothing." With that, Lucas took off.

"Shit," Della muttered.

Ditto.

Kylie watched Lucas move into a circle of other campers, and all of them greeted him as if he was some kind of leader. Before Kylie could look away, the girl who always seemed attached to Lucas's hip glanced back and her eyes turned greenish gold as she stared daggers at Kylie.

"Someone's jealous," Della snapped.

While the idea was laughable, Kylie could swear she did see jealousy in that girl's eyes.

A short time later, Kylie found herself alone, staring at the fire and listening to the strange animal sounds in the distance. Her gaze followed the trail of smoke that seemed to snake up to where the half moon hung in the sky. Breathing in the scent of burning wood and charred marshmallows from the sticks of several campers, Kylie fought emotional overload. Then, gazing at the flickering fire, she found herself missing Sara like she'd never missed her before.

At first, Kylie didn't understand the upheaval of feelings for her best friend, but when she glanced around the crowd the reasons became clear. Blindingly clear.

Welcome to the world of cliques.

School had always been about the cliques. Among the many, there'd been the cheerleader/popular clique, the school band clique, and then the smart/college-focused clique—completely different from the geek clique—and the art club clique. Then there was the one Kylie and Sara belonged to, the cliqueless clique.

Not that it was the worst one to belong to. In truth, it wasn't even a clique at all; they just belonged to the group that was considered floaters. They hung—not really belonged to, but just hung—with one group for a while, then they'd move to another. Thankfully, people didn't dislike them or poke fun at them like they did some of the unpopular groups. How could they poke fun at them when people hardly knew they existed? Or at least that's how Kylie had always felt at school. Not really disliked, or mistreated, just invisible.

And the reason for missing Sara right now, well, that was a no-brainer. Kylie might have been a floater, but she'd never had to float alone. Since fifth grade, she and Sara had been a team. And Sara had definitely been the head floater—the role naturally taken on since she was the one who worried the most about fitting in.

Inhaling another gulp of smoke, Kylie moved to escape the

path of the wind. As her gaze moved from one group to another, one of Nana's old sayings filled her head, birds of a feather flock together.

The flocks, or cliques, were different at camp than in high school. She spotted Della and the pierced boy, Jonathon, crowding around a group of kids, all vampires, no doubt.

Standing close to the fire, roasting marshmallows, was Perry, the shape-shifter, and with him were two other guys and a girl. Kylie wondered if they could all turn into unicorns.

Derek stood to the side of another crowd, as if he wasn't so sure he wanted to belong. She assumed these must be the fairies, or Fae as he called them. Not that she blamed him for using the different version. No straight guy would want to be called a fairy. Not that anyone could mistake Derek for gay. Something about the way he walked and carried himself was overtly female-loving male—like Trey.

Staring under her lashes, she let herself admire Derek's overtly male body. The wide shoulders, the square jaw, the way he filled out his jeans. That's when she realized she was doing it again—comparing Derek to Trey. She really, really didn't want to get caught up in that emotional storm, so she looked away.

Luck would have it that her gaze shot straight to another hard male body among a different flock of campers. Lucas. His warning about Della's cousin echoed in her head as she let her gaze move over his tall frame. Not that she planned to allow herself to appreciate the view for long. The fact that she appreciated it at all annoyed her. She owed her cat more loyalty than that. Right?

Before she could force her gaze away from his solid torso

wrapped in the black T-shirt, she noticed his goth-dressed girl-friend standing next to him. Her body was pressed so close, that nobody would dare come between them.

Lucas turned around as if he'd sensed her staring. Kylie attempted to look away, but his gaze locked on hers. She felt caught. Then the strangest thing happened. A forgotten memory surfaced. She'd been walking home from school, and a few of the older boys had started picking on her. One of the bullies had picked up a rock and slung it at her, but Lucas appeared out of nowhere and caught the rock. Like some kind of pro baseball player, he slung it back at the kid and hit the bully right between his legs.

The boy fell in the street moaning. Lucas had walked beside her the rest of the way home—as if to protect her. Those bullies never bothered her again.

Realizing she continued to stare at Lucas during her memory recall, she swung around. She noticed Miranda chatting with an artsy-looking crowd—obviously the witches of the group. Still feeling the tingle of Lucas's gaze, and needing something to get her mind off both him and her ex-boyfriend's lookalike, she started moving toward Miranda.

Hopefully, Kylie had learned enough floater skills from Sara to get her through the next few months. Because face it, why should camp be any different than high school? Belonging to a group and fitting in just wasn't in her cards.

Kylie's pillow didn't smell right—didn't feel right, either. Nothing felt right. She'd been the first to leave the campfire. When

Holiday stopped her on her way out to ask how she was doing, Kylie had been tempted to hit the leader with a deluge of questions. *Couldn't I just be a bit loony instead of gifted? And if I'm truly gifted, how do I find out what I am? And . . . What's the real chance that camp could be closed down by those black-suited dudes? Oh, and can I do anything to make sure that happens?* Okay, she wouldn't have asked the last two questions, but not from a lack of wanting.

More than anything in the world, Kylie wanted to go home—back to her own miserable life, back to her own miserable world.

Nevertheless, standing in front of Holiday, Kylie recalled the supersonic hearing of some of her campmates and put her questions on hold. According to her schedule, which had been handed out at the campfire, she'd have an hour counseling session with Holiday before lunch tomorrow.

Before that, right after breakfast, Kylie was to show up for the daily activity of Meet Your Campmates Hour. Supposedly each camper was to be paired up with someone for an hour to get to know a little about each other, their gifts, and the culture of their species.

Now, wouldn't that be fun? Not.

Sure she was curious, yet it would be kind of be nice to figure out what she was, or hopefully what she "wasn't" before investing in what everyone else was. And if she could prove she wasn't anything but human maybe she could go home.

She rolled over for about the hundredth time, knowing part of the reason she couldn't sleep was the fear that she'd have another night terror. Good God, she didn't want to have to explain that to her cabin mates.

The sound of her stomach grumbling filled the lonely darkness. Was there anything to eat in the fridge? Slipping out of bed, wearing a pair of navy boxers with hearts and a pink tank top, she moved to the door.

The door creaked when she stepped out of her room. The eeriness seemed to bounce against the log walls. Kylie gazed at the two closed doors leading into the other bedrooms. She'd heard Della and Miranda come in and listened to see if the two of them were still planning to kill each other. Hey, if she was going to have to wake up to a bloody mess, she wanted to be prepared.

Fortunately, the two of them had exchanged a non-combative conversation. It seemed all Miranda wanted to talk about were the boys. Derek included. Not that Kylie minded, of course.

A couple more steps and Kylie looked again at the bedroom doors. Hopefully, they were now both dead asleep. Okay, maybe *dead* wasn't the best word. Especially considering she didn't know if vampires were dead or not. Did they even sleep? And for that matter, were they immortal like the books said they were?

Kylie's bare feet pressing against the plank boards brought on a moan-like sound from the old wood. She recalled the visit from Della's cousin. Then she remembered the vampire gangs. Clutching handfuls of her tank top in both fists, she debated skipping a snack, for fear of becoming one.

And then the boards creaked again.

Chapter Fourteen

Kylie took one backwards step closer to her bedroom door. Then another noise made her stop short. She listened, recalling the wild animal sounds from earlier that night. This sound wasn't so wild, though. Breath held, she tuned her ears to pick up the noise. She heard it again, a very faint mewing. A soft, gentle sound.

A movement at the window caught her eye. Kylie swung around. Fear entered her chest first, but melted as soon as she saw the orange kitten perched on the outside window ledge. Startled by her sudden movement, the kitten fell from the ledge. "Don't go," Kylie muttered, at first not understanding her sudden concern for the kitten. Then understanding hit. What if Lucas or one of the werewolves happened by?

Kylie hurried to the door and opened it. She knelt down at the threshold and made the squeaky little noise that she knew cats loved.

"Come here, baby. I'll take care of you," she cooed. Her words were met by a rustling in the bushes. "Trust me." A few seconds later, the little yellow fur ball came swaying over.

"What a cutie," she whispered, and with a gentle finger stroked its white chin. The kitten turned on its purring machine, moved in, and started rubbing itself against her bare calves. She scooped up the creature and stared into the gold eyes, snuggling the purring little animal against her breasts, and then carried it inside.

The cat meowed and tried to escape from her arms, as if it didn't want to be shut inside, but Kylie held it tight. "No, no," she cooed. "There are monsters out there. You're safe here."

The animal seemed to relax as she passed her fingers softly over the back of its ear. "You hungry?" She butted her nose against the top of the kitten's head and cradled it closer against her chest.

She walked to the fridge, opened it to see what she could munch on, as well as offer the poor kitten.

A door creaked open behind her, and Kylie turned and watched Miranda, wearing a large yellow T-shirt and a pair of long pajama bottoms with smiley faces printed on them walk out of her room. Her tri-colored hair was a tad mussed and Kylie noticed she looked younger without her normal makeup.

"Hey," Kylie said.

"I thought I heard . . ." Miranda stopped and her eyes grew round. "What's that?"

"A kitten. Isn't she . . . or he adorable?" She held the animal up to check its sex. The kitten started twisting, even hissed, but Kylie held it tight. "It's a boy. *He* was peering in our window." She cradled him against her chest again and glanced back at the fridge. "I think he's hungry."

"Oh, no." The annoyance level in Miranda's tone had Kylie turning back around.

"What?" Kylie asked, genuinely confused. "Are you allergic to cats?"

"Same old trick, huh?" Miranda said, but Kylie didn't think her roommate was talking to her.

Instead, Miranda pointed a finger at the kitten and started wiggling her pinky finger back and forth. "Roses are red, violets are blue, show your true self or I'll put a hex on you."

"Stop. I'm changing back." The words spewed from the kitten.

Kylie stood frozen. *Words.* Oh, what the hell! Was she dreaming? Cats couldn't . . . talk. She looked at Miranda, not completely ready to toss the kitten across the room, but close. "Did I imagine . . . ?"

Miranda looked at Kylie and her lips twitched almost in a smile, but she held it back, and directed her gaze back to the kitten. "Do it now, Perry!"

Perry.

Kylie looked down at the kitten cozied up against her breasts. Sparkles, diamond-shaped sparkles floated around the red tabby. Then *poof.* Perry appeared, standing in front of Kylie, his head plastered against her breasts.

Kylie screamed.

Della shot into the kitchen. "What's . . . ?" She blinked. "Do you guys want to be alone?" She snickered and motioned to Kylie and Perry.

Snapping out of her stupor, Kylie grabbed the little twerp by the ear and yanked him off her chest. "He's leaving now."

"Ouch. Ouch," Perry muttered as Kylie dragged him past the kitchen table. "Let go of my ear!" he ordered in a roar that sounded like some kind of angry beast.

But Kylie wasn't feeling up to taking orders and she was too mad to be scared of him. Holding on to his ear like a tick to a dog, she dragged Perry past the small coffee table, yanked open the door with her free hand, and then shoved the pervert out the door with such force that he landed on his ass.

But she wasn't finished with him yet.

She pointed a finger at him. "You come anywhere near my breasts again and it won't be your ear I drag you out by next time. And in case you don't know what body part I'm referring to, let's just say the next time you turn yourself into a kitten, you'll find you've been *neutered*." She slammed the door with a loud *whack*.

"Creep." Kylie swung around, clenching and unclenching her fists.

Both Della and Miranda stood there, eyes wide and mouths hanging open in a kind of warped shock.

Miranda giggled first. "Sorry," she muttered. "But that was so freaking funny."

"Was not," Kylie snapped, still fuming, her throat tightening with anger.

"Oh, yes it was." Della started laughing so hard that she fell against the table. "You have spunk hidden behind your innocent face. I *like* it."

"Either that or she's stupid," Miranda said, and then snorted. "Do you realize what Perry is? He's like the most powerful shape-shifter in the world right now. Everyone knows you don't piss off a shape-shifter. They have terrible tempers."

"I . . . he . . . he tricked me into letting him snuggle up against my breasts." She recalled hearing the twerp's voice morph into a very threatening roar.

Okay, so maybe her actions had been a tad stupid, but nothing, nothing made her blood boil more than someone making a fool out of her, and that's what he'd done.

Fighting the tears, because she always cried when she was mad, she spotted the fridge still open and marched over to shut it. The cold blast from the white box hit her face the same time as she remembered . . . "Gross, I checked out his privates."

Behind her, both Della and Miranda spewed more laughter. Then for some off-the-wall reason, what hadn't seemed funny suddenly did. Kylie leaned into the closed fridge and started laughing. For the next five minutes, they sat at the kitchen table, giggling until they had tears in their eyes. It reminded Kylie of what she and Sara would so often do.

Or had until everything had changed.

"You should have seen his expression when you were pulling him by the ear," Della said. "I wish I'd had a camera."

"I almost felt sorry for him," Miranda said.

"Sorry for him?" Kylie asked.

"Yeah, he's kind of cute in that boyish kind of way. Don't you think?"

"Cute? Oh, heck. He's a freak," Kylie insisted.

"Aren't we all?" asked Della, her humor fading just a notch.

Not sure I am, Kylie thought, and almost said as much, but something plopped down on the table. Kylie screamed when she saw the toad.

Miranda rolled her eyes and snatched up the creature.

"Being bad again, Mr. Pepper?" she seethed at the amphibian, holding the beast a foot from her face, his toad legs dangling almost to the table.

"What did he do for you to put a spell on him?" Della asked, studying the toad in disgust.

"Like our friend Perry, he's a member of the pervert club." Miranda gave the toad a little shake. "He's my piano teacher and he tried to start playing something besides the piano, if you know what I mean."

Della snarled at the toad. "Why don't we just make him a midnight snack and be done with it? Do toad legs taste as good as frogs?"

"Hmm. Don't know." Miranda glanced at Della. "But I'm willing to find out," she said, and eyed the toad.

Kylie could be mistaken, but she could swear the toad's eyes grew large with fear.

Miranda laughed. "If only I was that type of witch."

"What kind of witch are you?" Kylie asked, somewhat relieved.

"A screwed-up witch." Miranda frowned and then scowled at the toad. "You know the drill, Mr. Pepper, stop thinking bad thoughts and you'll go back to normal."

The toad wiggled his legs and then vanished into thin air.

"What kind of curse did you put on him?" Della asked.

Miranda moaned in frustration. "If I knew that, I could stop it."

"You mean, you don't remember?" Della asked.

Miranda lowered her gaze. "I remember what I thought I said, but I'm . . . I'm dyslexic and I get my spells wrong sometimes, and I have to know exactly what I said to make it stop. So until then, every time that pervert thinks about an underage girl, he's transformed into a toad and pops in for a visit."

Kylie leaned in. "While it sucks for you, it sounds like he deserves it."

"Yeah, *he* does. But he's like a constant reminder that I'm a screw-up."

"True," Della said. "But on the positive side, you're keeping him from doing anything wrong. I hate perverts. I had an old neighbor who would stand at his window, empty lotion in his hand, and whack off in front of me or other girls."

"That's disgusting," Miranda said.

"Yeah, but what I hated was that a girl down the street had already told me he did it to her, too. She told her parents, the parents called the police. The police came back and said that he's a deacon of the church and it was basically my neighbor's word against his and they believed him."

"That's why I did the whole curse thing," Miranda said.

"But I handled it." Della grinned.

"What did you do?" Kylie was almost too scared to ask.

"I broke into his house and replaced his lotion with some really bad-ass superglue that my dad uses at his lab at work. You should have seen the look on his face when he couldn't get his hand off his dick. Then I made an anonymous call to the police and reported him. I mean, how could he deny doing it? His hand was stuck to the crime scene."

They all burst out laughing. Wiping the tears of laughter from her eyes, Kylie looked at Della and Miranda and she could have sworn they were just normal teenage girls.

Well, she could have sworn until the blast of cold snuck up on her from behind. Kylie glanced over her shoulder hoping beyond hope nothing was there.

But hopes were often futile.

Soldier Dude stood only a few feet from her. Too close. Closer than he'd ever been. The chill from his presence sent an icy fear climbing her spine.

"Kylie?"

She heard Miranda call her name—or was that Della? Kylie couldn't tell because it sounded as if it came from another world. A world in which ghosts didn't exist. A world Kylie wanted to get back to, but couldn't.

The dead guy kept his eyes on Kylie while he slowly reached up and removed his helmet. Blood, bright red blood, gushed down his forehead. Kylie's breath caught as she watched the blood trickle down his face. Then everything went into slow motion. Kylie stood up, wanting to escape.

Drip. Drip. Drip.

Blood droplets splattered onto the floor and left tiny speckles of red on the top of her bare feet. The drops kept coming. The specks of blood kept landing on her feet and then they started forming letters and then a word. *Help* . . .

Kylie tried to inhale, but her lungs refused to take in the frigid air. Letting go of the oxygen trapped in her mouth, she saw a cloud of cold air float up from her own lips.

"What's wrong?" Miranda's voice seemed to float in Kylie's mind.

Good question, Kylie thought.

Too bad she didn't have a freaking clue.

"Do you guys smell that?" Della's voice registered in Kylie's awareness but in a distant kind of way, like background music in a movie. "Something smells yummy."

"I don't smell anything." Miranda's words followed. Their conversation continued but suddenly it rang like a distant echo. "Oh shit . . . shit . . . shit. Kylie's aura is turning black. Black . . . black . . . black. I think there's a ghost. Ghost . . . ghost . . . ghost."

"Damn," Della said. "I hate this shit." Footsteps sounded, her friends were running away. A door slammed. Kylie wanted to run, too, but she couldn't. She couldn't move. The blood continued to spatter on her feet, but she refused to look to read the words.

"Wait." Della's tight voice sounded through walls. "She stopped breathing. Kylie's stopped breathing. We have to do something."

Kylie heard the door swing open. Heard her name being called. But that's when everything went black and her body slumped to the floor.

Chapter Fifteen

Coolness whisked across Kylie's brow and stirred her into a semi-alert state. One that brought on all the "w" questions: Who, What, When, Why, and Where. The musty smell of the pillow answered the Where question.

Camp. Still at camp.

The emotional overload from the last few days filled her chest. She forced her eyes open. Holiday sat on the edge of the bed. Her red hair hung free over her shoulders and concern appeared on her face and shined from her bright green eyes.

"Is she awake?" The hauntingly familiar masculine voice filled her ears and Kylie could hear echoes bouncing around her head. She shifted her gaze to the left.

Holy crap.

Holiday moved the damp cloth across Kylie's brow again. "Hey, you with us now?"

Kylie wasn't listening, or looking at the camp leader. She gazed at . . . Lucas Parker—cat killer extraordinaire.

And protector from bullies, Kylie's subconscious pointed out.

Though why her subconscious wanted to defend him was beyond Kylie.

What was going on?

Lucas leaned down as if to touch her. Kylie shot up, pushed the cloth from her face. "What happened?" And then, just like that, it all came back at once.

The ghost.

The blood. So much blood.

Then she was hit by another mind-boggling piece of information. She must have passed out. How geeky was that?

"You fainted," Lucas said, his big voice filling the small room and making it feel even smaller.

Did he have to point out the obvious? And why was he here anyway? Wasn't there some of kind of "no boys in the bedroom" rule? If not, Kylie needed to see about getting it added.

She glanced over at Holiday.

"It happens sometimes," Holiday said. "When the ghosts start getting closer."

"I'm fine now." She lunged out of bed and doggone if the room didn't start spinning on its axis. Round and round. Lucas caught her elbow.

His touch was tight, but not enough to hurt.

His touch was warm and somehow warm tingles danced up her arm and made her even more light-headed. But at least things quit spinning.

Her first impulse was to jerk away, but afraid that would be too telling, she forced herself to appear calm. Of course, if he could read her heart rate like Della, she was pretty much screwed.

And speaking of Della, where were . . . Kylie shifted her focus to the doorway. Della and Miranda stood there, shoulder against shoulder, peering in as if Kylie was the nightly entertainment. Oh damn, how embarrassing. She could just imagine them running from their hiding spot—because she had the vague memory of hearing running footsteps—and them finding her on the floor. But how had she gotten in the bed?

Kylie glanced away from her roommates to Lucas. Had he picked her up? Held her in his arms? Her heart rate started climbing again. That's when she realized that he was still touching her.

"I'm fine." She gave her arm a quick jerk.

He released her, one finger at a time, as if afraid she might fall on her face again. Right before his last finger let go, she noticed his gaze sweep downward. While her pajamas weren't indecent, she became instantly aware of how thin her top was—and even more aware of how the scoop neck of the tank scooped lower than most of her tops. Or as Sara would say, her girls were trying to peer out and say howdy a little more than usual.

Kylie took a step back and crossed her arms over her chest.

"Why don't you let me talk to Kylie alone," Holiday said to Lucas, who still hadn't stopped staring, though his gaze had shifted from her chest to her face with a cold indifference.

He nodded, but she saw his dark brows twitch ever so lightly. So he was still trying to read her, was he? Right now, she was relieved knowing that he wouldn't get anything.

And just like that, another memory from the past surfaced and she remembered Lucas Parker doing the eyebrow thing when she was young. Had he tried to read her then? That thought brought up the question that had been bouncing around her head since she'd first spotted him. Did Lucas remember her?

"We can finish our discussion tomorrow," Holiday said to Lucas as if dismissing him.

"Okay," he said, offering Holiday a smile. Then he walked out.

Della and Miranda moved away from the doorway to let him pass. Kylie didn't miss the unfriendly way Della and Lucas exchanged glances. Was Della worried that Lucas had told Holiday about her cousin Chan's surprise appearance at camp? Probably.

"Shut the door," Holiday added as Lucas was almost out.

Kylie looked back at the camp leader, feeling as if she was about to be chastised for . . . for what? Fainting? Or had Lucas told her about Chan and now Kylie was in trouble for not speaking up?

"You don't have to be afraid of Lucas," Holiday said.

Kylie studied her. "Can you hear my heartbeat, too?"

Holiday grinned. "I read emotions, not heartbeats, but I also read your fear from the way you turned white as a sheet when you saw him."

Kylie almost blurted out what she knew about Lucas, but she didn't. It felt too much like tattling. Instead, she asked a question. "Why was he here?"

"He was in the office when Miranda came to get me."

Kylie looked at the clock; it was almost one in the morning. She couldn't help but wonder exactly what Lucas and Holiday were doing at that hour. Sure, the camp leader was older, but not by many years.

"Are you and he . . . close?"

"Depends on what you mean by close." Holiday arched a brow. "This is his third time here. He's assisting us with some things and even training to work with us next year. But that's all." Then she asked, "What happened tonight?"

Kylie swallowed, stalling. How much should she tell?

"The ghost appeared again, didn't he?" Holiday asked in the beat of the indecisive silence.

Kylie nodded, yet more than anything, she wanted to deny it. "Yes, but Miranda and Della said that people who are a little loony sometimes give off the same mental image of not being human. So maybe I'm not gifted and maybe the ghost is just a powerful one, like you said sometimes happens. Or I could even have a brain tumor."

Holiday sighed. "The chances of either one of those are very slim, Kylie. Don't you think?"

"Maybe, but the chance exists," Kylie insisted. "I mean, you said most of the time ghost whispering stems from . . . a condition that's hereditary. That one of my parents had to have been gifted, too."

"Neither of your parents ever . . . showed any signs of being different?"

"No. Never." Yet even as she answered, she reconsidered her mother's cold nature. Could that qualify as "different"?

"I also told you that in rare situations it can skip a generation."

"But I knew my grandparents on both sides. Don't most people know if . . . if they're not human?"

"Most people do, but . . ." Holiday stared at her as if disappointed, and then she folded her hands in her lap. "I suppose that's what you should work on while you're here."

"Work on?"

Holiday stood up. "Everyone here has a quest. Something they're seeking answers for. I suppose your quest is to discover if you are, or are not, completely human. And if, as I suspect, you are one of us, then you must also decide if you'll embrace your gifts to help others, or turn your back on them."

Kylie tried to wrap her mind around the possibility that one of her parents wasn't human, that they might understand what Kylie was going through. Wouldn't they have said something to her?

Holiday placed a hand on Kylie's shoulder. "You should try to get some sleep. We have a busy day tomorrow."

She nodded and watched Holiday almost make it out the door before the question popped out. "How . . . how do I find the answers? I can't go to my parents and ask them if they see ghosts. They'd think I was crazy."

Holiday turned around. "Or maybe one of them would confess the truth to you."

Kylie shook her head. "But if all this is a mistake, then all of that would be for nothing. They already have me seeing a shrink. If I start talking about ghosts, they might have me committed."

"It's your quest, Kylie. Only you can decide how you want to do this."

The next morning Kylie and Miranda walked to breakfast together. Della had already taken off by the time Kylie got up. When Kylie asked about Della, Miranda informed her that vampires often held before dawn meetings where they performed rituals.

"What kind of rituals?" Kylie asked.

"Don't know exactly, but my guess is it has to do with feeding on blood."

Kylie pressed a hand to her stomach, sorry that she'd asked. Of course, her sickly feeling could partly be due to the fact that she'd hardly slept. Then on second thought, nope, it was for sure the blood. The idea repulsed her in a big way. Seeing the red stuff in those glasses during dinner last night had been too much. If nothing else, at least Kylie might lose a few pounds over the summer.

They walked the next few minutes in silence. "How did you sleep last night?" Miranda finally asked, although Kylie knew what her roommate really meant. Namely, was Kylie okay and what the hell had happened to make her faint?

Kylie decided to ignore the subtext and answered the question as asked.

"Fine." Kylie lied, aware the white lies might work with Miranda, just not Della.

In truth, Kylie had stared holes in the ceiling considering what Holiday had said about Kylie's quest. No matter how Kylie looked at the problem, she couldn't think of a way to ask her parents if they were not all human.

But she could think of a lot of questions she'd like to ask someone about herself. Questions like: if I am a supernatural what other kind of species could I be? And if I'm not one of you, do I have some kind of a brain tumor? Kylie didn't know which was worse.

Then the revelation hit. Maybe getting answers to those

questions would help her rule out the possibility of being anything but human. It wasn't the best plan, but it was a start. And she had to start somewhere.

"You didn't look fine last night," Miranda said.

She hadn't been. When Kylie finally went to sleep, she'd dreamed. Crazy, weird dreams that involved Lucas Parker and her. They were swimming. He hadn't been wearing a shirt and neither had she. She'd woken up, feeling out of breath, and tingly. Tingly the way Trey had made her feel when they'd kissed for a long time. How could her body betray her and actually find Lucas Parker desirable? Not that she would let her body win this one. If there was anything she knew about herself, it was that she could control her desire. She'd gotten really good at stopping Trey, even when stopping had been the last thing she'd wanted.

So that gave her a new goal. Not only would she try and find out if she was human, she was also going to make darn sure she didn't get close to Lucas.

"I did okay," Kylie lied again.

"I don't believe you, but let's let that slide for now." Miranda looked away. "Cute vampire dude on the left," she whispered, totally changing the conversation.

"What?"

"The blond wearing a football jersey," Miranda whispered again. "What I wouldn't give to hook up with him."

"I thought you didn't like vampires."

"I never said that. And if I did, it wouldn't apply to the male vampires, anyway."

Kylie couldn't have cared less about a cute vampire, and the last place she wanted her mind to go right now was to thoughts about hooking up with any guy, but her gaze moved to the left on its own accord. No one was there. "Where?"

"Over there." Miranda nodded in the opposite direction.

"You mean right," Kylie corrected. "Not left."

"Right, left. I always get them messed up. I'm dyslexic, remember? But he's a cutie. Maybe I'll get his name in the Meet Your Campmates session today."

The blond guy stood chatting with a group of other boys. Kylie remembered seeing him, but couldn't remember his name. His stature and overall appearance reminded her of Perry, who was not Kylie's type. Especially after what happened last night.

"Are you really okay?" Miranda asked after they passed the group of boys. "You looked out of it last night. Your aura went all freaky."

"I'm fine." And then because she didn't want to talk about last night, she asked, "Are you really dyslexic?"

Miranda didn't answer right away. "Yeah. And according to my family, you'd think it's something I asked for." Her tone had lost the giddiness that seemed constant in her voice.

"So is your family all witches?"

"Yeah, but my mom can be a bitch, as well."

"Aren't all moms?" Kylie asked.

"Maybe." Miranda sighed. "Not that I really blame her. I've sort of let the family down, big time."

"How's that?" Kylie asked.

"I was destined to be the High Priestess next in line. But before I can be given the title, I have to pass some tests. And tests and I just don't get along. So my family could lose their place in the coven if I can't come through."

"Why does it have to be you? Why can't one of them step up to the plate?"

Miranda sighed. "It doesn't work that way. It's me or the honor goes to Britney Jones."

"Wow, talk about keeping up with the Joneses." Kylie gave the joke a stab, hoping to make Miranda feel better.

"Yeah." Miranda's tone implied the joke fell short.

"Sorry," Kylie said. "So what would it take for you to pass the tests?"

"Only to overcome dyslexia. Which is basically impossible," Miranda said. "Ohh, ohh, look to your left—I mean your right. Your purring breast-loving kitten is here. And he's blushing. You know, it has to be terrible on his ego to have been tossed out on his ass by you."

"I hope so." Kylie spotted Perry, and he did appear rather red-faced.

Good.

"You didn't tell Holiday about him, did you?" Miranda sounded concerned. The girl obviously had a soft spot for the twerp.

"No." Kylie frowned. "But I might if he does it again." She didn't know if Perry had super hearing, but she hoped so.

They were almost to the dining hall, just past the camp office, when the two black suits from yesterday came barreling out of the door.

Kylie slowed down and studied their body language. They weren't happy. Watching them hotfoot it to the parking lot,

Kylie couldn't help but hope that their little visit today had to do with the closing of the camp.

Right then, the bigger of the guys stopped and swung around. He stood frozen in one spot, staring and twitching his brows at her.

He leaned down and whispered something to the other man and then they started forward. Right toward Kylie.

Crappers.

Chapter Sixteen

Kylie felt like a trapped animal in the Black Suit's snare.

Dad-blast it. Why was everyone picking on her?

Better question, what in Hades could they want with her? She wasn't even a card-carrying supernatural person yet. And she hoped she got tossed out of the club before she got rubber-stamped.

Lucky for her, at about twenty feet away, the big guy's phone rang. He paused and answered it. Then he turned to his partner and said something and they both shot off.

She let out a held breath. "Thank God."

"What?" Miranda asked, and studied her in confusion.

Remembering that Miranda wasn't a first-timer, she asked, "Who are they?" She nodded to the retreating black-suited men who were now getting into a black sedan.

"Who?" Miranda asked, staring at another group of boys.

"The Black Suits?" Kylie asked.

"Gross, they are way too old for you." Miranda pulled a hair band from her pocket and put her multicolored hair up in a ponytail.

Kylie shot her roommate a glance. *Honestly, were boys the only things Miranda ever thought about?*

"I'm not interested in hooking up," Kylie said, and started walking again. "I'm just curious."

"Oh. They're from the FRU." Miranda fell into step beside her.

"And who are they?" Kylie asked.

"It stands for the Fallen Research Unit. You know, like Fallen, Texas? The city we passed through to get here? The FRU is basically a part of the FBI. The part that deals with supernaturals."

"What?" Kylie stopped and grabbed Miranda by the arm. "You mean, the government knows about vampires and such?"

Miranda made a face. "Of course they do. Who do you think funds the camp?"

"I thought our parents did." Kylie started moving again when she noticed a couple of people staring at them.

"Well, they pay some, but it takes a lot more to keep this place up."

"But why is the government behind this?"

"Well, that depends on who you ask. The camp has caused a lot of controversy in the supernatural community. Mostly just a lot of bigots mouthing off, if you ask me."

"What do you mean?"

"Some of the elders in each species, mostly old farts who don't believe in interracial relationships, claim the camp encourages it and they want the camp closed down. To their way of thinking, each species should stick to their own kind. To me, it's the same thing as race. They say we should maintain the purity of the species, but that's a bunch of bull. The species have been crossing since the beginning of time."

Kylie tried to digest it. "So the government has the camp because they want the species to get married?"

Miranda laughed. "I don't think the government cares who we hook up with. They're doing it to try to promote peace between the species so we don't go bat-shit crazy one day and try to wipe each other off the face of the planet. Humans included."

"Are there problems between the species?"

Miranda looked surprised. "You really are ignorant to all this, aren't you?"

"Yes," Kylie admitted, and didn't even feel bad about it. She hadn't even known other species existed when she'd climbed on board the bus. How could she be informed?

"Okay, here's a quick history slash political lesson," Miranda said. "Vampires and werewolves have been waging war against each other for, like, forever. What do you think the Civil War was really about?" She hesitated. "My own ancestors aren't much better. The Black Plague was set off because they wanted to annihilate fairies."

"You're kidding me, right?" Kylie asked. And to think she'd listened to her history teacher when he'd said it had been spread by infected rodents.

"Serious as a heart attack. However, in defense of my own kind, witches are the species who are succeeding best at conforming into the human world. There're less covens that actually live in groups. But of course, that's also because our lifestyles are easier to blend with the human lifestyle. We also aren't involved in near as many gangs, causing problems for the humans."

"Gangs? You mean like the vampire gang?"

"So you've heard of the Blood Brothers?" Miranda asked.

Not wanting to mention Della's cousin, Kylie shrugged. "Della just mentioned that gangs exist."

"Exist? Oh, yeah. Of all the gangs, the Blood Brothers are probably the worst. They're into everything, all kinds of crimes. A good mix of everything. Murder, robbery."

Stealing Big Macs. The concept rolled around Kylie's brain. "But how come we don't hear about these gangs or crimes on the nightly news?"

"You do. You just don't know they're not human. The crimes are always explained by serial killers, just murders, then there's the missing people. Haven't you heard how many people go missing every year?"

"I guess so." Kylie felt a chill straight through to her bones. She wrapped her arms around her chest and shivered.

"To rogue vampires or werewolves, the rest of us are food," Miranda said.

Kylie thought about Della's cousin calling her a snack and wondered if he was rogue. Then she thought about Della's blending issues and concerns about leaving her family. "This is so screwed up."

"Not any less screwed up than the human race," Miranda said.

"I guess not," Kylie admitted, remembering she had her own human issues happening at home.

Right then she remembered another and more immediate

problem she had to contend with. "What's the Meet Your Camp-mates Hour really about?"

"Oh, it's kind of cool." Miranda grew animated again. "Half of us write our names on a piece of paper and the other half draws. We are paired together and spend an hour getting to know each other. Of course, it's always better if you get a hot guy."

Great, with Kylie's luck, she'd get stuck with Perry. She felt her face grow red when she remembered she'd checked his genitals.

After breakfast, Kylie stepped out of the dining hall to talk to Sara who'd gone to the drugstore to buy a pregnancy test earlier that morning. Unfortunately, she'd bumped into her mom's best friend at the checkout counter. Sara had been able to ditch the test before the woman noticed it, but the whole encounter had brought her right back to where she started—with no idea if she was pregnant or not.

"How's it going at the camp?" Sara asked.

"Just peachy," Kylie answered. She would have loved to have talked to her best friend about everything that had happened but she knew better. No way would Sara understand when Kylie herself didn't.

"That bad, huh?" Sara replied. "Aren't there any cute guys?"

"A few," Kylie answered, and then she changed the subject back to Sara, and they talked for another ten minutes about Sara's dilemma.

Kylie still had her phone in her hand when her mom called a second after she'd ended her conversation with Sara.

"How was your first night?" her mom asked.

"Okay," Kylie lied, still undecided how to deal with her mom and her questions.

"No night terrors?" her mom asked.

"No," Kylie answered. *No, as in I didn't wake up screaming bloody murder. I just passed out when a bloody ghost showed up for a visit. After a visit from a shape-shifting kitten and a perverted toad.*

"That's good," her mom said. "So what all are you doing today?" Her mom's voice had that fake cheeriness that Kylie always hated because she knew it wasn't real.

"I have meetings with one of the camp leaders, a meet-and-greet hour where you meet one-on-one with another camper, and then I think there's some kind of art program and a hike this afternoon."

"Sounds like a full day," her mom answered.

"Sounds boring," Kylie retorted.

Her mom ignored her remark. "Have you spoken with your dad?"

Kylie hesitated. "He called and left a message, but I haven't had a chance to call him back." Another lie. She'd had a chance, she just didn't know if she could lie as well to him as she did to her mom.

"Well, when you do, check and see if he plans to come up Sunday for parents day. If so, I'll wait until next week."

"You two can't even be in the same room together now?" Kylie asked, not trying to hide her feelings. Her throat tightened with emotion. "Couldn't you two have at least stayed together until I left for college?"

"It's difficult, Kylie," her mom said.

"Yeah, on everyone." The emotion grew in her throat, but when she looked up she saw Della walking toward her and she fought back the need to cry. "I've gotta go."

"Okay," her mom said. "Have a good day and call me tonight, okay?"

"Yeah." Kylie closed the phone just as Della stepped up beside her.

"Hey," Kylie said. "I looked for you during breakfast."

"I ate earlier." She rubbed her stomach and Kylie tried not to think about what Miranda said about the vampire rituals. But the thought was already there, making the half of the Danish she'd consumed feel heavy in the pit of her stomach.

"You'll get used to it." Della grinned as if she knew what had caused Kylie's frown.

"Maybe," Kylie said. Then, remembering to be honest with Della, she added, "But I doubt it."

Della chuckled, then her smile faded. "Sorry about your parents. How long have they been separated?"

"Do you make it a habit of eavesdropping?" Kylie slid her phone in her pocket.

"I wasn't trying to listen in." Resentment rang in Della's voice. "It just, you know, happened."

Kylie bit down on her lower lip and let go of her frustration when she remembered that Della had confided in her about her own family issues. "I'm sorry. It's just hard. It happened last week."

"I can imagine." Sincerity creased Della's forehead. Then her expression changed. "Oh, I almost forgot what I came to tell you. Remember I told you Derek had a little thing for you? I was wrong. It's not little. It's a big thing."

"Why do you say that?"

"Because Brian, the blond vampire, just drew your name for the Meet Your Campmates Hour and Derek asked him to swap."

Kylie compared spending an hour with a strange vampire to spending an hour with Derek, who made her miss Trey, and she didn't know which was worse. "What did Brian say?" she asked, unable to stop herself.

"He said no . . . unless Derek was willing to pay for it."

"No way. Tell me he didn't give him cash to get my name."

"Okay. He didn't give cash to get your name." Della laughed and leaned in as if she had some juicy secret to tell. "He's paying in blood, Kylie. A pint, to be exact."

"Blood?" Kylie stood there shocked. The shock quickly turned into disgust. "He can't do that," she said.

"He can and he did. They made a deal. And believe me, you never go back on a blood deal with a vampire."

Kylie shot off to the dining hall to find Derek.

She could not, would not, let him do this.

Chapter Seventeen

Derek came through the door just as Kylie rushed in to find him. "Hey, I was coming to look for you." He held up a tiny strip of paper. "I got your name." He smiled.

His smile came off so warm, that if Kylie wasn't so furious, and disgusted, she could have gotten lost in it.

"Yeah, I know. I heard." She squinted at him in disapproval.

He studied her and then cautiously added, "I thought we'd take a walk. I found a great spot when I went hiking yesterday."

"Look, I'm flattered but you can't do this, Derek," she snapped.

"Do what?" A frown replaced his smile.

"I know what you did to get my name. And I can't let you do that."

"It's nothing." He started walking away from the door, and then looked back at her when she didn't follow. "You coming?"

"It's blood," she seethed, and closed the two steps separating them and grabbed him by the forearm. "Come on, I'm gonna make this right." She gave him a tug, but he didn't budge. That's when she noticed how solid his arm felt under her hand.

He leaned in. "It's done, Kylie. Let's just go spend our hour together, okay?" His scent—a combination of spicy men's soap and Derek—wafted over her.

"You've already . . . done it?" Her gaze shot to his neck.

"No, but the deal's done."

"I'll undo it," she said, trying to ignore his scent and how much she liked it . . . and how much she liked him. Realizing she still held his arms, she let go. Touching him caused her to recall how she used to touch Trey. How much she liked Trey, missed Trey.

Derek's frown tightened. "You can't undo it. So just come on. Please."

She stood there staring at him. "At least let me try."

He closed his eyes for a second, and then he lowered his head closer and whispered, "Please trust me on this, Kylie. There is nothing you can do to change it."

Something about his voice seemed to reach deep inside her and scramble her thoughts. Or perhaps it was how his breath whispered against her jaw line, the soft, sweet tickle right below her ear that made it impossible to think.

Impossible to tell him no.

"Okay." But even as she cratered to his wishes, she told herself she had to be careful. Derek, for whatever reasons, had some kind of power over her and that could be dangerous.

His green eyes focused right on her baby blue ones and he smiled again. "Let's go."

He held out his hand. She almost took it, but managed to refrain at the last second.

"I'll follow." She stuck her hands in her pockets.

Disappointment weakened his smile, but he nodded and started walking. And she did what she told him she'd do. She followed.

They didn't talk for the first five minutes as they started up a trail. Then he turned off the trail and led her up through a thick patch of trees and bushes. Between yesterday with Della and now this, it would be a miracle if she didn't come down with poison oak. Or worse, chiggers.

Just when she was about to say something, she heard the soft sound of running water, as if they were about to come across a small stream.

"It's right here." He glanced back at her, his eyes carrying a smile even when his lips didn't.

She followed him for a few more feet and then stopped and stared at the stream and the humongous boulder, about the size of a twin-size bed, perched on the edge overlooking the trickling water. The morning sun streamed through the trees, making everything seem so green, so lush. So alive.

Kylie inhaled the air, which smelled just like everything looked—fresh, verdant, and wet. In the distance she could hear what she thought was a waterfall—Shadow Falls. It had to be. The sound of cascading water filled the silence and somehow seemed to call out to her.

"Is there a waterfall around here?" she asked.

"Yeah, but it's prettier here." Derek hopped up on the rock. "Come on." Once settled, he held out his hand to help her up.

She moved in but before she took his hand, the question popped out. "Why did you do it?"

He looked down at her. "Do what?"

"You know what," she accused.

"Are we still stuck on that?" He shook his head. "It's not a big deal, Kylie. Now come up and sit down. This place is even more amazing when you look at it from this angle."

She took his hand and with hardly any effort he pulled her up. Letting go as soon as she had her footing, she found her spot, careful not to sit too close.

Not that it helped all that much.

Feeling his gaze on her, she looked out at the stream and tried to refocus. "Wow," she muttered. "You're right. It's prettier from up here." And it was. The extra height offered a better view of the flowing water. The streams of light sneaking from the trees hit the water and made it twinkle. From this angle, the whole place seemed to be bathed in a mixture of shadows and light, and it reminded her of something she might have seen in fairy-tale book. Almost . . . magical.

"Why?" she asked again without looking at him.

"I was curious about you. I've been curious ever since I saw you standing by your mom before you got on the bus. You were so sad and . . ."

She remembered Miranda saying that some fairies could read your thoughts and before he could continue, she spoke up. "Can you read my mind?" Turning to him, she felt her face heat at some of the more embarrassing thoughts she'd had about him.

"No." He smiled and in this light, his green eyes with golden flecks literally sparkled. "Why are you blushing? What have you been thinking about me?" He leaned a tad closer until his fore-head rested against hers. Her heart did a flip and her next breath tasted sweeter. Realizing she was staring, she remembered what he'd asked.

She didn't answer his question, just asked another one. "Then how did you know I was so sad?"

He hesitated and his smile faded. "I can't read thoughts, but I can read some basic emotions."

She looked at him and sensed he was telling her the truth.

"For some reason I cause a mixture of emotions in you. Some positive, some not so positive, but I'm not sure why."

He was being honest, and Kylie felt she owed him the same in return. "You . . . you remind me of someone I know."

He picked a twig off of a tree and studied it. "A good someone, or a bad someone?"

"Both. He's my ex-boyfriend."

"I see." He waited for a minute and then asked, "What happened between you two?"

"He broke up with me."

"Why?" he asked.

She'd offered him some of the truth, but not about this. "You'd have to ask him." It was a lame answer and she knew it the moment the words spilled.

"But he's not here and you are." He took the twig and brushed the leaves across her cheek. Then he followed the path with his finger. He was coming on to her and she didn't exactly know how to stop it.

In truth, she didn't know if she wanted to stop it. Unlike what had been going on lately, these feeling were not so foreign to her. Not that she needed to get caught up in something else right now.

She looked away and tried to clear her head. "What's it like being fairy . . . Fae?"

"Half," he said.

She glanced back at him and remembered thinking that, just like her, he didn't sound too thrilled by the idea of being a supernatural. She also realized this might be her opportunity to learn something about the whole fairy species. After all, according to Holiday, Kylie could be part fairy.

"So what's it like being half fairy?"

"It could be worse, I guess." He stared at the twig.

"Who did you inherit it from?"

He cut his eyes to her again. "For someone who doesn't like to answer any questions, you ask a lot."

He had a point.

"Okay, I'll tell you about me, but then you tell me about you? Deal?"

He arched an eyebrow and actually seemed to consider it. "Okay." He leaned back on his arms and studied her.

The position made his chest seem extra wide. She found herself comparing him again to Trey. And sorry, Trey, she thought, but Derek won the best body award. Then again, it wasn't just his body. She studied his face. His features were . . . more masculine. More chiseled.

Chasing that thought out of her head before she started emitting emotion he might read, she started talking. "I don't know what I am. I think I'm just human but—"

"You're not human," he said, and looked at her in that odd way everyone did here.

She rolled her eyes. "Yeah, I know I don't have a normal brain reading, or whatever it is that you guys read. But I found out that normal humans can give off this same reading if they're a little off, like halfway crazy. And sometimes I'm pretty sure I'm crazy. Or," she admitted with less enthusiasm, "the other option is that I could have a brain tumor. And I've had lots of headaches lately, too."

His expression said he was horrified by the idea. "Have you been checked?"

"No." And until she saw the concern in his eyes, she hadn't allowed herself to honestly be worried about it. But God, what if she really did have a brain tumor? What if . . .

His brow pinched as if confused. "But . . . what about seeing ghosts?"

"How did you know . . . ?" She recalled asking him if he saw ghosts. "Some humans can see ghosts. Even Holiday said so."

He tilted his head in a very disbelieving way. "So you really believe you're just human?"

His question brought a swell of emotion to her chest. "Yeah." She paused and then added, "Okay, the truth is, I don't know what I believe."

And without warning, tears filled her eyes.

"Oh, damn. Don't do that." He reached over and brushed a tear from her lashes. His touch was so warm, so comforting, she almost reached for his hand and held it to her face.

Instead, she moved his hand back and wiped her own eyes. "I'm just so confused. I mean, these last few months have been hell. My boyfriend breaks up with me, my grandmother dies, my parents are getting a divorce, and then I start seeing this dead soldier guy. Now I'm being told that I'm not human and . . ."

He pulled her against him and she didn't fight it. She rested her head on the nice spot between his shoulder and chest and just breathed in his scent. Amazingly comfortable, she closed her eyes. Somehow just being like this made the knot of emotion crowding out her heart go away.

"I'm sorry." She pulled away. "I know guys hate it when girls do this."

"Do they?"

"Trey did," she answered.

"I'm not Trey." Then Derek added, "Actually, it wasn't so bad." He smiled and touched her check. "Besides, your nose is kind of cute when it turns red like that."

She swatted his hand and grinned. She wasn't sure, but it felt like the first real smile she'd had in weeks. "Okay, now it's your turn. Tell me about you."

The playfulness vanished from his eyes. Leaning back a little, he pressed his palms against the rock to hold himself up. And sitting there, his muscles in his arms flexed, his eyes all serious, he looked good. Really good.

"But you are so much more interesting," he said, his voice low as if he could read her emotions and knew the reaction she was having to his presence.

"You promised. Besides, I told you everything."

His tilted his head forward and looked up at her through his dark lashes. "You haven't told me everything." His voice held the slightest hint of an accusing tone. "As a matter of fact, there's the thing I'm the most curious about."

"What thing? What else is there?" she asked, and tried not to get caught up in enjoying the view again.

"What's up between you and—"

"I'm not talking about Trey and me. That's . . . too personal."

"Okay, but I wasn't going to say Trey. I meant what's going on between you and the werewolf?"

Chapter Eighteen

Kylie pushed her hair behind her ear. *Deny it. Deny that anything is up.*

"What . . . werewolf?" she asked, but darn if her voice didn't lack conviction.

Derek's eyes stared right at her. His gaze reminded her of Della's when she knew Kylie had lied.

"Don't deny it," he said. "Your emotions were all over the place every time you glanced at him. Kind of like when you look at me, only . . . more. You either really like him, or . . . he scares you."

"I thought you could read emotions?"

He sat up and crossed his arms over his chest. "Passion and fear read almost the same."

"Well, trust me, it's definitely the latter," she answered, but after last night's dream she knew the truth could have been summed up better with one word. *Both.* But she hadn't admitted that to herself yet. She sure as heck didn't plan on admitting it to Derek.

"So where do you know him from?" he asked.

"Who says—"

Derek held up his hand to stop her. "It's not normal to be that scared of people we don't know."

She glanced down at her clutched hands. "He lived beside me when I was young. Let's just say I knew something was off with him then. I just didn't know what it was . . . the whole werewolf thing."

"Did he—"

"No more." It was her turn to offer him the determined stare. "I've given you all I'm going to. It's your turn."

He looked at the stream and she sensed he disliked talking about himself as much as she did. "What do you want to know?" he asked.

"Only everything," she said with a certain amount of teasing in her voice, hoping to put him at ease.

"My father was Fae. My mother's human."

"Was?" she asked. "You said your father *was* Fae. Did he pass away?"

He picked another twig from the bush and twirled it around with his fingers. "Don't know. Don't care. He left when I was eight. A real deadbeat dad, if you know what I mean."

"I'm sorry." Kylie sensed he cared a lot more than he wanted her to believe.

"Did you know he was Fae?" She brushed an ant from her arm.

"Yeah, I don't remember ever not knowing. But after he left, we didn't really talk about it or him a lot. Mom was crushed that he walked out."

His mom hadn't been the only one crushed. Kylie saw sadness in his eyes that he tried to hide. Her own chest felt heavy—heavy for him, and perhaps a little for herself. Her own father issues hadn't disappeared. They waited in line with everything else she had to fret over and sort out. Then she remembered that this was Derek's time. He'd listened to her and she owed him the same.

"Sorry," she said.

"Why? I'm not. If he didn't want me, I sure as hell didn't want him."

He couldn't lie any better than she could, Kylie thought. "Did you know you were gifted all your life?"

He stared at the piece of stem with a few leaves still attached to it that he had in his hand. "No. I mean, I knew I could read people better than most, but I wasn't even sure it was . . . because of being Fae. It wasn't until about a year ago that tapping into people's emotions got stronger. And then . . . I finally realized I was different."

"How are you different?" She felt her eyes moving to his chest, remembering how good it had felt to rest against him. The craziest thought hit. What would it feel like to kiss him?

He tilted his head to the right and studied her. "How much do I look like your old boyfriend?"

Were her emotions so readable, she wondered, feeling her face flush. "Not that much, but . . . enough that . . ."

"That you're attracted to me?"

Feeling her face heat to a nice shade of red, she looked back at the stream. "I wouldn't go that far."

"Why not?" His breath was on her cheek again. Warm.

Soft. Tempting. When had he gotten this close? Uncomfortable with how near his mouth was to hers, and how tempted she was to let it get even closer, she jumped down from the rock.

"Stop!" he said.

"What?" She turned around to look at him. "I think we—"

"Don't move," he said in low, very serious voice.

"Why? I—"

Something rustled in the bushes beside her. Kylie looked down and saw a huge snake slinking out from the thick underbrush. A huge grayish black snake with a pointed nose, the kind of nose her father made her aware of so she would know the difference between a nonpoisonous and a poisonous snake when she went on their camping trips.

Panic built as she recognized the species. A water moccasin, which just so happened to be the most aggressive snake found in Texas.

And one of the most poisonous, too.

The snake moved in tight S-like patterns—patterns that brought it closer to Kylie. Fear swelled inside her. A scream crawled up her throat. Logic said that she couldn't move away from the snake fast enough to avoid getting bitten. Logic said she needed to stay very still, but . . . the hell with logic—she wanted that thing away from her.

Derek's hand tightened on her shoulder. "It's okay." His voice was so low, so soft. "It's just passing by. Stay very still. Let it go. I'm here. Nothing is going to happen."

His hand grew warmer, unnaturally warm, and just like that, her fear vanished. Her heart stopped racing and the clutching in her stomach eased. She watched the snake's fat, chubby body slither across the tip of her Reeboks as if it were a butterfly passing by. Something in her brain told her that the calm she now felt, the absence of fear, wasn't normal; that somehow Derek had done this to her. She wasn't even afraid of that right now. It was as if Derek's touch had removed her ability to experience fear, leaving only curiosity in its place.

Curiosity about the snake.

About how it moved like that.

Curiosity about Derek. How had he changed her emotions? What would it feel like to lose herself in his kisses? Would he make her feel the way Trey had? Maybe even better?

"You're doing good. It's almost gone," he whispered.

And then it was gone. Its round body slipped into the stream, causing only the slightest of ripples as it sank down and moved with the water's current.

Derek kept his hand on her shoulder as she watched the creature disappear among the rocks. Then, slowly, he lifted his palm away. The storm of emotion hit her so hard that she screamed. When screaming alone wasn't enough, she swung around, and started climbing the rock. Her heart pumped in her chest, as if it might burst, and her stomach felt as if it knotted all the way around her backbone.

Derek caught her as she ascended, but she didn't stop moving, thinking only about getting away from the slithering snake.

"It's all right," he said, laughing, and fell back on the huge rock, carrying her with him. She landed half on top of him. His arms came around her, but not too tightly. His hands gently rested on her back.

Blinking, she felt her panic evaporate, and she met his green eyes. This close, the flecks of gold seemed brighter. Her gaze lowered to his mouth, to his lips that appeared so soft, so inviting.

The warmth of his body melted against hers. His natural scent worked its way into her senses. She caught her breath.

"You okay now?" he asked, his voice deeper.

"Yeah." When he stole her panic, had he taken her willpower, too, because she really wanted Derek to kiss her. Or she could just kiss him. It sounded like a damn good idea to her. She inched a bit nearer until his lips were so close to hers she could feel their heat.

"Let her go!" a dark male voice boomed from behind them.

Chapter Nineteen

"Let her go, now!"

The deeply serious voice rang a few familiar bells, but quicker than she could wrap her brain around it, Derek shot up with a force that sent Kylie rolling right to the edge of the rock.

Right before Kylie fell, Derek caught her. As soon as she felt secure, she raised her head. Lucas leered at them from the edge of the stream. The flickering of sun and shadows surrounded him, adding to his intimidating presence. His light blue eyes pierced into them with the harshest of stares.

"She's fine," Derek said, his tone matching his stern expression.

Feeling suddenly foolish, she felt the need to explain. "I saw a snake."

Lucas inhaled. He looked around on the ground. "A water moccasin."

"I know," she said. "That's why I screamed."

"It's gone," Derek said, and his words implied that Lucas should be gone as well.

"I heard her scream," Lucas said, as if he, too, felt the need to explain his behavior.

The two guys stared at each other, neither saying a word. Kylie got the distinct feeling they didn't get along. She wondered if fairies and werewolves also had bad blood between them. Heck, for all she knew, World War II could . . .

"She's not screaming anymore," Derek said.

"I'm fine." She jumped down from the rock—after giving the ground a quick check for snakes first.

When she looked up, Lucas had turned his disapproving gaze on her. "If you're that scared of snakes, maybe you should stay out of the woods."

"I'm not that scared, it just—"

"I took care of her," Derek said. His tone was dark, almost angry.

"Yeah, I saw how you were doing that."

Derek sat up higher on the rock as if he was ready to leap down. "Look, if you have a problem—"

Lucas apparently didn't care to hear what Derek had to say because he swung around and in less than a second, he was gone.

Kylie blushed, realizing how the situation must have appeared to Lucas. Then seeing the unhappy expression on Derek's face, she said, "I'm sorry. I shouldn't have screamed, it was just—"

"You didn't do anything wrong." Derek offered her his hand to pull her back up. "He was being a jerk and overreacting. He didn't have to come here. I wouldn't have let anything happen to you."

She stared at Derek's hand and remembered how her fear had subsided with his intense touch.

"What happened just now?" she asked.

"He just overreacted—"

"No. Not with Lucas. With your touch . . ."

"What do you mean? My touch?"

Other questions started buzzing around like bees gone wild. "How did you know the snake was here?"

The look, the one that said he didn't like talking about himself, returned but she wasn't about to let him off this hook. Not this time.

"Wait. Did you make that snake come here?" she asked.

He frowned. "Do you think I'd put you in danger just for kicks?"

Did she believe that? "No. I don't. But you knew it was here. You knew it was here before it showed itself."

"I only knew a second before. If I had known earlier, I'd have stopped you from getting down."

The sun sprayed a new bright stream of light through the trees and it hit her eyes, making it hard to see. "How? How did you know?"

He jumped from the rock, landing solid on his feet beside her. "It's part of my gift," he said, but he didn't sound happy about it.

"You can predict the future?" she asked.

"I wish."

"Then what?"

"I can read the emotions of animals and creatures." He tucked the tips of his fingers into his pockets.

"Wow." She attempted to wrap her mind around it. "That's . . ."

"Weird, I know," he growled. "Like I'm Tarzan or something. Holiday says I can shut it off, and that's why I'm here. To learn how. But Holiday's not thrilled about my quest. She thinks I'm going to be letting down some Fae god if I turn my back on my gift. But the Fae god can just go to hell. I didn't ask for this. The only Fae in my life left me and Mom. Why the hell would I want to be like him?"

Kylie heard the pain in his voice and related in a big way. "You wouldn't. I'm sorry."

She meant it, too. Not just because she understood all about parental resentment right now, but because like him, if she turned out to be supernatural, she'd be shipping the gift back to sender. While Derek's plight contained a lot of emotional baggage, Kylie's contained a heck of a lot of questions. And the unknown brought on its own emotional issues. While she knew the truth could prove to be painful, she needed answers.

And standing in the middle of the woods, with the mixture of sun and shadows, feeling submersed in the supernatural world, she became determined to find those answers.

She met Derek's gaze again. "Communicating with animals can't be nearly as bad as . . . some other things."

He kicked a rock into the stream. It splashed and seemed to blend in with the other woodsy noises. "Like seeing ghosts?" he asked, understanding more than she wanted him to.

"Among other things," she said honestly. "I can't imagine waking up and realizing I have to drink . . . blood." Just the mention of the word reminded her of what Derek had done to get her name for this hour chat.

And she couldn't let him do it. She didn't know how to stop it, but she had to try.

She looked at her watch. "We should probably be heading back."

Reaching over, he took her hand in his and turned her wrist over so he could see the time. The feel of his hand sent a sweet electrical current up her arm and it reminded her how close she had come to letting Derek kiss her. Or had she almost kissed him?

"We have a half hour," he said, holding her hand.

She pulled away, recalling how his touch had controlled her emotions when she'd seen the snake. He'd probably saved her life, but that wasn't the point. She didn't like the thought of anyone trying to control her. Or manipulate her, either. "Yeah," she said, "but we still need to see about how we're going to get you out of giving blood."

His expression darkened. "The deal's already made, there's no going back. And besides, it's not an issue."

"What if he turns you into a vampire?"

His eyes widened. "Oh, hell, you think I'm going to let him bite me? No way. It's too risky and way too gay."

She blushed, feeling ignorant. "Then how do you plan to do it?"

"The same way you give blood at a blood drive. With a sterile needle and an IV bag."

She stood there staring at him, questions coming quicker than she could line them up to ask. "You're going to a doctor's office to get it done? How will—"

"No." He laughed. "Most vampires carry their own supplies. They're better than most nurses at finding veins. It's one of the first things a vampire is taught. How to get blood without killing the donor."

Had Della brought her own blood-draining equipment? "How do you know how vampires . . . ?"

"Feed? I've done it a couple of times." His smile made her feel even more ignorant.

"You've given blood to a vampire before?"

He nodded. "Like I've been saying, it's not a big deal."

"Who? And how did you even know vampires existed?"

"Her name's Ellie. We go to school together. And you're forgetting that all supernaturals recognize each other."

Yes, she had forgotten the whole eyebrow wiggling thing. And for a darn good reason, too. She didn't "read" supernaturals, which gave her a little more hope that she wasn't one of them. Then she wondered if she had any supernaturals in her school back home. Besides Lucas for that short time.

"How many are there?" she asked, even though she was afraid to hear the answer. "How many supernaturals are there compared to humans?"

"I think the consensus puts us a little less than one percent, but growing. Why?"

"Just wondering if I went to school with any."

"You could have," he said. "But not likely. Most supernaturals go to private schools or are home-schooled. For obvious reasons."

"What reasons?" she asked.

"Species issues mostly. Most believe that they need to learn a different history. And most of them can afford it since they use their gifts to become financially well off."

They? Kylie noticed that Derek didn't completely view himself as one of them, either. "So you went to a private school?"

He shook his head. "Dad bailed, remember?"

"Yeah." She sifted through her other questions. "What about the girl you know? Ellie, right? She went to your school?"

"She's a recently turned vampire," he said. "She hasn't gone to live with her kind yet."

Kylie thought about Della. "Do they all have to go live with their kind?"

"Not from what Ellie said. But I know it isn't easy for her to blend in with the normals."

Kylie heard the sense of caring in his voice and her curiosities took a U-turn away from Della's problems, away from the whole supernatural business to a more personal business.

"Are you and Ellie close?" Embarrassed at how she almost sounded jealous, Kylie shook her head, but she couldn't stop from continuing. "Duh, you gave her your blood. Of course you're close."

He arched his brows and another one of those almost smiles tickled his lips and made his eyes brighter. "Is this your way of asking if we're still together?" The green twinkle in his eye said he liked her interest.

"No." At least she didn't think it was, but oh heck, she wasn't completely sure.

"We broke up about six months ago."

"Why?" she asked, and then just as quickly wished she could take it back.

"She met a werewolf." Resentment laced his voice.

"Not Lucas?" Kylie asked.

"No, not him."

Kylie remembered. "I didn't think vampires and werewolves got along."

"Neither did the Hatfields and the McCoys."

A soft wind blew and a strand of her hair whipped across her face and caught between her lips.

He brushed it back. The tips of his fingers whispered over her cheek, causing all sorts of tingles to run down her neck. She caught his hand, felt the tingles intensify, and then released it just as fast.

"What happened earlier?" she asked before she lost her nerve. "When you touched me."

He stuck both his hands into his jeans pockets, as if he were trying to fight his temptation to touch her again.

"I don't know what you mean," he said, but she could tell he was lying.

She shook her head. "Don't lie to me, Derek. When you touched me, you changed how I felt and we both know it."

He looked shocked that she'd figured that out. "I just stopped you from being afraid so you wouldn't do something stupid and get bit."

"So when you touch someone, you can control their emotions?"

"Yeah," he said as if wasn't a big deal.

But it was a big deal, to her anyway. How much of the whole attraction she felt for him was even real? How much of it was because he made her feel it?

Something cold and hard wrapped itself around her heart. "Did you do it before?"

"Do what before?" He looked truly confused now, or was he just faking it?

"Mess with my emotions."

He studied her. "Why are you getting angry?"

"Did you do this, Derek? Did you make me feel the way I feel about you?"

He looked insulted. "No," he said with conviction, but she wasn't convinced.

She poked him in his chest. "So help me, Derek, if—"

He caught her hand and she flinched.

"What? Now you're afraid of me?" He shook his head. "First you justified what you feel for me because I look like your old boyfriend. And now you think I'm messing with your emotions. Why is it so hard to think that you could just like me?"

"Because you have the power to do it, don't you? You have the power to make me like you." She took a deep breath and continued. "Have you ever used this to convince a girl to do things she normally wouldn't?"

His eyes tightened. "Wow," he said in an accusing tone. "You are just looking for a reason to dislike me, aren't you? That boyfriend of yours really did a number on you."

Maybe. But that was beside the point. She was almost certain that her feelings now had more to do with Derek than Trey. The simple truth was that liking Derek was going to complicate the next few months. She had enough crap on her plate, and she didn't need this, too.

"You didn't answer my question," she said, standing a little straighter. "Have you ever used this power on a girl to get what you wanted from her?"

His frown grew almost angry, but she could swear she spotted a bit of guilt in his eyes, too. He looked away.

"If you don't answer me, I'll assume the worst," she said.

"Fine." He faced her. "I've used it to get a girl's attention, but I've never used it to get her to sleep with me. That would be rape. And I don't care how much you want to dislike me, Kylie, I won't pretend I'm something bad just to make you feel better." He waved back to the path through which they'd come. "I think we should probably get back."

She heard the hurt in his voice. Instant embarrassment shot through her and she realized what a cold bitch she was being. God, maybe she was just like her mom after all.

He started walking. She followed. They walked in silence. "Hey," she finally said, unable to hold it back any longer.

"What?" He didn't look at her and kept on moving down the trail.

"I didn't mean to imply that you were some kind of rapist."

"Then what were you trying to imply?" He still didn't look at her.

She tried to think how to put what she needed to say. She hated reaching for the old cliché but it was all she could come up with on short notice. "I like you, Derek, I do. But I'm thinking we should just be friends."

He laughed but the sound had no humor. "So you're going to deny that you feel anything." His pace picked up. "You're going to deny that you almost kissed me back there. That you wanted to kiss me."

Increasing the pace of her own footsteps, she wanted to deny it, and almost did, but caught herself before she lied. "No, I'm not denying it, but I can't trust how I feel right now."

He swung around. "Because you think I'm messing with your emotions?"

"No. Yes. Okay, maybe that's a part of it, but it's also because you remind me so much of Trey. Look, I have all this other stuff happening to me right now." Emotion tightened her voice. "Things at home are crazy. I'm seeing ghosts. I have people telling me I'm not all human, and I'm halfway hoping I find out that I'm just crazy or that I have a brain tumor." She blinked and refused to cry again. "I don't need *this*, too." She waved a hand between them. "But I really need a friend."

He sent her a look of resignation. "Okay. If friendship is all you're offering, then I'll take it. Don't like it, but I'll take it."

"Thank you," she said, meaning it.

He nodded and studied her as if reading her emotions again. Heck, maybe he could read them and then tell her what it all meant, because right now she felt like a scrambled mess.

"It's going to be okay," he said.

"Is it?" She paused. "I just don't know where to start to find the answers."

Derek drew a deep breath and then looked around as though he was afraid they might be overheard although there wasn't anyone else in sight. He leaned in closer.

"I don't have all the answers," he said, dropping his voice to just above a whisper. "And I don't even think this is an issue, but . . . there's one thing you might try."

Chapter Twenty

"Tell me," Kylie said, eager for any help she could get. "I'm willing to try anything at this point."

Well, almost anything.

"There's a girl here," Derek said. "She's Fae, too. Her name's Helen."

"I met her," Kylie said. "She was in the group with me when Holiday explained why we were here."

"Yeah. Her gift is healing. But when she was telling us about herself she said that even before her sister's tumor was found, she could see it. Personally, I don't think you have a tumor, but if you're concerned about it, maybe Helen can check you out. At least you'd stop worrying about it."

"That's an excellent idea." Kylie almost hugged him, but decided at the last moment it wasn't wise. She really didn't want to encourage Derek that they could be more than friends. At least not now, a little voice inside her whispered—the little voice that really liked how it felt to be close to him, the same little voice that had wanted her to kiss him earlier. "Thank you," she said.

"You're welcome." He brushed the back of his hand down her cheek and you can bet her little voice liked that, too. "By the way . . ."

"By the way what?" she asked.

He smiled and the gold in his eyes seemed to glow hotter. "Back there. You weren't the only one who . . . I mean, I wanted you to kiss me, too."

"But we're just friends," she said, wishing she could say it with more conviction.

"Yeah." And he didn't say it with a heck of a lot of conviction either.

When they got back to the camp, it was almost time to meet Holiday. Kylie wanted to call Sara, so she decided to go behind the office to the little hiding spot she'd discovered yesterday.

She made it around the building when she realized she wasn't the only one who'd discovered the hiding spot. Kylie shifted herself in reverse, but not quickly enough. Lucas and his attached to-the-hip girlfriend swung around. Lucas grimaced and Goth Girl smiled. Then she reached up and made a show of buttoning her blouse.

"Sorry," Kylie muttered, and shot off. But she felt a pair of light blue eyes burning into her back as she went.

She made it around the front, only to find Miranda and Della standing near the office yelling at each other.

Kylie's first thought was to leave them be, but when she spotted Sky, the other camp leader stepping out of the dining hall, Kylie marched over to break the two up before they got in trouble.

"I swear, if you wave that little pinky finger at me one more time, I'm gonna break it." Della leaned in. "And you know I can do it."

"Stop it," Kylie said, stepping between them. Miranda shuffled back in front of Kylie and bumped noses with Della.

"You lay one bloodsucking finger on me and I'll hex you with the worse case of pimples you've ever seen."

"You can't hex me," Della spouted out. "Your hexes are retarded."

"Stop it." Kylie spotted Sky looking over at them. "We've got company."

"Giving pimples is one hex I got down." Miranda stepped back, but Della moved in.

She obviously didn't like pimples. "Look, if I get one zit, I'll drain your blood while you're asleep and sell it on eBay."

"Would you guys put a sock in it," Kylie snapped, but it was too late. Sky was on the move.

"Is everything okay?" the tall, goth-dressed camp leader asked.

Sky was also a werewolf, or so Kylie had heard. She still couldn't identify the supernaturals just by looking at them.

Miranda pasted a smile on her face. Della attempted to do the same, although Della's smile looked more like a snarl.

"It's fine," they said in unison. "We're just—"

"Arguing?" Sky's eyebrows tightened in accusation.

"Having a little disagreement," Miranda said.

"Over?" Sky asked.

Della spoke up. "She purposely spilled my blood that was in the fridge."

"I didn't purposely spill it. It fell out when I opened the door."

"There's blood in our fridge?" Kylie frowned.

Sky rolled her eyes. "You have to learn to get along." Sky's dark eyes shot to Miranda. "You are a returnee, Miranda, we expect better from you."

"Yeah, well, get in line with the be-disappointed-by-Miranda crowd." Miranda shot off in a huff.

Sky watched her leave and then looked back at Kylie and Della. "Solve your own problems at your cabins, not in public, or Holiday and I will have to get involved. And trust me, you don't want us involved." She turned and left.

Kylie glanced back at a smiling Della who appeared unaffected by Sky's warning.

"So what happened with you and fairy guy?" Della asked.

"Forget that. You and Miranda gotta stop this."

"Stop what?" Della shrugged.

"Stop threatening to do bodily harm to each other." Right then, Kylie spotted Lucas's girlfriend walking toward them. The girl's eyes narrowed in fury and her lips tightened as she zeroed in on Kylie. If looks could kill, Kylie would be a hair away from decomposing. Then the pissed-off werewolf stormed on past.

With the thought of death hanging on, Kylie noticed a slight headache, a consistent throbbing in her left temple. The idea that she actually might have a brain tumor had her catching her breath.

"Threatening isn't doing," Della said. "So spill it. What did you and Derek do? Did you at least get to first base?"

"We didn't do anything." Kylie pressed a hand against her temple. "Look, I like you and Miranda, so both of you need to pull your big girl panties up and stop fighting before they separate us and I get stuck with a different roommate." Someone like Lucas's girlfriend.

"That wasn't a fight. We were just having a tiff."

"You threatened to sell her blood on eBay," Kylie said. "Where I come from, that qualifies as a fight."

"Yeah, but you're not in your world anymore."

Della's statement hit hard like only the truth could. Nothing was the same anymore. A boy had just given a pint of his blood to get to spend an hour with her. She'd seen toads who were really perverts hopping on her kitchen table, and she'd checked a kitten's privates only to have him end up not being a kitten. And don't forget, she was being haunted by Soldier Dude. Her head throbbed harder.

"Besides, I'd never sell her blood. I'd savor every drop of it. Witches' blood is sweet."

Sweet. Kylie held up her hand. "Stop right there. I can't handle this." She looked at her watch. Crap. No time to call Sara. "I have to go meet Holiday," she said. *And figure out my life, because like Dorothy, I'm simply not in Kansas anymore.* Kylie turned to leave.

Della caught her by the arm. "Oh, I meant to tell you—"

"Wait." Kylie held up her hand. "Does it have anything to do with blood?" She couldn't deal with blood talk, period.

Della's eyes tightened. "No," she said, sarcasm in her tone.

"Then you can tell me."

"Or not." Della crossed her arms. "Maybe I should let you be waylaid for being a smarty pants." Della walked off.

Waylaid? That didn't sound good. "Della, wait," Kylie said.

Della turned back around. "If I tell you, will you put a stop to all the 'blood is gross' remarks?"

It was gross. "I'll try."

"Trying is for sissies," Della shot off. Kylie glanced at her watch again. She needed to meet Holiday, but Della's warning about being waylaid . . .

"Della." Kylie caught up with her. "Okay, no more remarks. Now tell me. How am I going to be waylaid?"

Della let go with a huff. "You know those men in the black suits? I'm told they are FBI."

"What about them?"

Della cocked her head. "They're planning on interrogating you."

"Me?" Kylie asked. "Why?"

"Don't know."

The only thing Kylie could think this could be about was . . . "Wait. Is this about your cousin? Are you sure he doesn't belong to one of those gangs?"

"No." Della frowned. "They'd be talking to me if it was. Besides, they didn't say anything about visitors. They said they thought you could be hiding something because you don't let anyone read you."

Kylie tried to wrap her hurting head around the facts, but she just couldn't do it. "Are you sure they said me?"

"Yup. Holiday wasn't happy about it. Yet supposedly they are like the head honchos around here. What they say goes. But I can tell you that Holiday stood up for you. She told them that you were innocent, but they just said they'd find out for themselves."

And exactly how did they plan to do that? Was it the CIA or FBI who were accused of torturing? Oh damn, she already had a headache—she didn't want to add "get tortured" to today's to-do list.

Della's gaze shifted up over Kylie's shoulder. "Uh, don't look now, but I think Holiday's looking for you. And . . . I think she's found you."

A second later, Kylie felt someone beside her. Only it wasn't Holiday. The cold slammed against her side and Kylie knew "he" was back.

She drew in a deep breath, determined not to pass out, but barely managed to get the cold air down her throat. Forcing herself to move, she shifted her eyes ever so slowly, praying she wouldn't see him this time.

Someone wasn't listening to prayers today. But at the least there was no blood this time. Soldier Dude just stood there staring at her with his big blue eyes. Eyes that seemed to want to tell her something. But what? What could he want? She recalled the word *help* splattered in blood the last time she'd seen him. Just what kind of help could he need from her?

The idea of asking him crossed her mind, but somehow she sensed that if she spoke to him, it would bring him closer. She closed her eyes and mentally pleaded for him to go away.

"And here she is." Della's voice registered ever so slightly in Kylie's awareness. Opening her eyes, she saw Holiday move in between her and Soldier Dude.

"You ready?" the camp leader asked.

The cold faded and the goose bumps on Kylie's arms melted back into normal skin. Even the frigid air in her lungs warmed. A wave of relief washed over her.

"Oh," Holiday said, and took a step back. "Did I interrupt something?"

Kylie knew the camp leader didn't mean her and Della. Blinking, Kylie gazed at Holiday and tried to focus. "Can't you tell him to leave me alone?"

"Doesn't work like that," Holiday said.

"What doesn't work like that?" Della asked.

"Ready?" Holiday said again to Kylie.

"For what?" Kylie asked. Why did the FRU want to talk to her?

"Our meeting," Holiday said.

"Can I come?" Della asked.

Kylie looked at her roommate and saw in her gaze that she was trying to help. An effort that Kylie appreciated more than her roomie could know.

"Can she?" Kylie asked.

"Afraid not." Holiday eyed Della. "I think the vampires are holding a group session. You should be there." The camp leader's gaze shifted back to Kylie. "Come on." Holiday put her hand on Kylie's back and led her away.

But just what the hell Holiday was leading Kylie to was yet to be seen.

Chapter Twenty-one

"There're a couple of people who want to meet you." Holiday moved Kylie toward the main office.

"Who?" she asked, hoping that Della was wrong.

"They're from the FRU."

She'd heard the acronym several times since arriving at Shadow Falls Camp. This time, however, when the three letters formed in Kylie mind, a new thought hit. *Freaks-R-Us.*

"They're the people who support the camp," Holiday added as she guided Kylie up the steps.

"Why?" she asked, and stopped at the door. "Why do they want to meet me?" She wasn't even sure she was a freak.

Holiday's gaze softened. "Mostly curiosity. They've never met anyone they couldn't read."

"I thought you said this was common with people who could see ghosts?"

Holiday appeared to be debating what to say. "It's not just because they can't read you, Kylie. It's because what they can see of your brain pattern isn't common."

Kylie's headache resumed its pounding. And the fear that she really could have a tumor stirred in her chest. She envisioned herself with her head shaved and big ugly scars running across her skull. It was horrible.

But so was admitting that she was as much of a freak as the rest of them.

"You're special, and they sense this. So come on. It'll only take a minute and then we can have our meeting."

Holiday's hand on Kylie's back grew warm. Immediately, Kylie knew the camp leader had emotion-controlling abilities similar to Derek's. All Kylie's reservations about having a brain tumor and about meeting the Freaks-R-Us squad dissolved as the warmth of Holiday's hand flowed inside her.

"Why are you doing that?" Kylie stepped away.

"Doing what?" Holiday asked.

"Trying to take away my fear?" She shifted out of Holiday's reach.

Holiday's eyes grew round. "Wow. You can sense this? That's amazing." She touched Kylie again. "That means—"

"Stop doing it." Kylie backed away again. She didn't care about amazing, or what it meant, at least not now. She cared about what waited for her on the other side of the door and about possibly having a brain tumor. "It makes me think maybe I should be afraid."

Holiday shook her head. "You don't have anything to be afraid of." She reached out again and Kylie looked at her hand.

Holiday held up her palms. "Trust me."

"Sorry," Kylie said. "But I have a hard time trusting people who can manipulate my emotions." And yes, in a small way she meant Derek, too.

Holiday sighed. "Believe it or not, Kylie, I respect that. But right now, I need you to meet these two men. Nothing bad is going to happen. I give you my word."

While Kylie still wasn't convinced, with another look into Holiday's expression, most of Kylie's concerns faded. Only this time it seemed to be from her own intuition rather than Holiday's influence. For some reason, Kylie's gut told her she could trust Holiday. Then again, it could just be because she didn't have a choice. In more ways than not, Kylie was a prisoner at this camp.

The introductions were as awkward as Kylie expected. The two men did their share of eyebrow twitching, which only made Kylie feel more uncomfortable. She wanted to tell them they were wasting their time trying to twitch info from her. She didn't, of course. The too-nice disease again. So instead, she sat at a table and tried not to fidget under their intense stares.

The bigger man with darker hair was named Burnett James and the other was Austin Pearson. Up close, Kylie couldn't help but notice how *GQ* perfect the two men were. Not that she was into old guys—or she should say "older" because they looked about ten years older than her—but she could still appreciate perfection.

Kylie also noticed how Burnett kept stealing glances at Holiday when she wasn't looking. He obviously had the hots for her.

Not that Holiday seemed aware of his interest. If anything, Kylie got the feeling the camp leader found both men annoying. Especially Burnett.

"So . . ." Burnett turned a chair around, straddled it, and sat down.

Holiday watched the man and frowned as if disapproving of his sitting position.

"This is your first time to Shadow Falls Camp, huh?" Burnett asked.

Kylie nodded. Then recalling her mother's belief that answering without words showed disrespect, she followed up with, "Yes . . . sir." The "sir" part of the sentence slipped out as an afterthought and she wished she hadn't done it, because it came out sounding sarcastic. Not that she meant it like that, but her interrogators might not realize that.

Burnett placed his elbows on the back of the chair, laced his fingers together, and studied her. After very slow passing seconds, he tilted his head slightly as if listening—listening for something that no one else in the room could hear. Like the sound of Kylie's heartbeat. Just what kind of supernaturals were these two? Were they, like Della, human lie detectors? Somehow Kylie suspected that Burnett had that ability. Which meant Kylie would have to be careful not to get caught in a white lie.

"What brought you to Shadow Falls, Miss Galen?"

Holiday stepped closer. "She was sent here by—"

Burnett held a hand up at Holiday and frowned. "I'd like Miss Galen to answer." While his words could be construed as non-hostile, Kylie noticed his edgy tone.

Holiday must have noticed it, too. She shot the man a glare

that no doubt contained language she probably couldn't use in the presence of the campers. Kylie got the feeling that this wasn't the first time these two had bumped heads. Heck, for all Kylie knew, they might have bumped more than just heads. They could be old lovers.

Austin cleared his throat as if hoping to clear the tension in the room.

"Go ahead, Kylie," Holiday said, then everyone looked back at Kylie.

She sat up a little straighter and tried not to wince. "I was told . . . by Holiday, that my shrink is the one who got me signed up. I think she convinced my mom that this was a camp for troubled teens."

"And are you?" Burnett tossed out the question.

"Am I what?" Kylie asked.

"A troubled teen?" His tone rang with accusations.

"Of course she's not," Holiday insisted.

Burnett shot a frown back at the camp leader. "As a courtesy, I allowed you to be present, but if you keep interrupting—"

"Bite my ass, Mr. James," Holiday snapped, obviously mad enough not to care about Kylie hearing the PG-13 language.

"Don't tempt me," Burnett retorted.

"Tempting you hasn't crossed my mind," Holiday shot back. "You've been a class-A jerk since you came to see me."

Kylie bit her cheek to keep from smiling. The tension between these two could be cut and served up with hot fudge. It was the kind of tension one saw in a romantic flick.

"Maybe it's the icy reception you've given me for no damn

good reason. If I didn't know better I'd think you have a preju-
dice against vampires."

So he was a vampire. Kylie actually felt proud of herself for
figuring it out.

"Don't fool yourself." Holiday squared her shoulders. "It's
not vampires I have a problem with. It's men who think something as inconsequential as a badge gives them the right to in-
timidate others. From the moment you walked into my camp
you've acted as if we should bow down to you. And if that's not
bad enough, you're now accusing my kids of—"

Austin cleared his throat again, louder than before. "I think
we should get back to Miss Galen here."

Or not. Kylie would like to know what it was the FRU was
accusing the campers of doing, exactly. However, her curiosity
faded rather quickly when everyone's gaze shot back to her and
she recalled Burnett's question.

"No, I do not consider myself a troubled teen."

Burnett's right brow arched. "Have you ever belonged to a
gang?"

"No," she answered, and wondered if he was referring to the
Blood Brothers. "I've never really gotten into any trouble."

"Really. Weren't you just hauled down to the police station
during a drug raid?"

Kylie suddenly understood Holiday's dislike for Mr. Tall
Dark and Handsome. He did have a way of making people feel
small.

Maybe it was Holiday's nerve of standing up to the vampire
that gave Kylie courage. Or perhaps it was just that with all the

other crap slung at her today, Kylie's ability to play nice had played out. Then again, maybe she had a brain tumor provoking her to do things she normally wouldn't do.

Tilting her chin up, she let the words roll off her tongue without remorse. "You'd think if you were able to get your hands on that report, that you'd have at least read it. Because I'm sure it stated that I was not doing drugs or drinking."

Burnett's eyes tightened in the corners. But Kylie preferred to focus on Holiday's pleased smile.

"Are you finished now?" the camp leader asked.

"Just a few more questions." Burnett's piercing gaze never shifted from Kylie. "How do you feel about our camp, Miss Galen?"

"It's great." Kylie's heart sputtered when she remembered she couldn't lie. "At least everyone else I've met here seems to like it."

"And you don't?"

Don't lie. "I'd rather be at home."

"And why is that?" Burnett's eyes darkened to black.

"Everything is so . . . new to me."

"What's new?"

"The fact that people like you even exist." It was the truth. However, she didn't mean it to sound so . . . derogatory.

"Like me? As in vampires?" he asked, clearly offended.

"Supernaturals," Kylie corrected.

"And what do you think you are?" he asked smugly.

"I'm not sure," she answered truthfully. "But I'm hoping I'm nothing. Just me." *With a brain tumor.* She pushed that thought aside to chew on later.

He stared harder and Kylie's courage winced. He shook his head and his brows tightened. "Why are you being so close-minded?"

"I'm not. Believing in all this . . ." It occurred to her that he wasn't talking about her ability to accept all this, but rather, his inability to read her mind.

"She can't help it." Holiday stepped forward. "It's a condition of one of her gifts. She's a ghost whisperer."

Kylie nodded as if to say ditto. Both men's eyes widened.

"Ghost whisperer?" Austin said, and turned to Holiday, but before he shifted, Kylie spotted something that looked like fear cross his expression.

"Like you?" Burnett glanced at the camp leader.

"You've read my file?" Holiday asked.

"It's my job to know who I'm working with."

"Funny, you didn't offer your file to me," she responded. "And you expect me to work—"

"I'll have it sent over. If it really interests you," he countered, his voice dripping with sarcasm.

"On second thought, don't bother," she clipped out. "But to respond to your earlier comment, yes, Kylie's a ghost whisperer just like me." While Holiday's tone lacked the earlier attitude, the brief smile that flashed on her lips contained attitude plus.

"You, too?" Austin shuddered. "I hate ghosts."

"Is she fairy?" Burnett asked, staring and twitching again at Kylie as if attempting to read her once more.

"We're still trying to decipher that," Holiday answered.

"So her parents are not registered as supernaturals?" Burnett questioned.

"No," Holiday replied.

"They could be rogues."

"Be what?" Kylie asked.

"They would have never sent her here if they were," Holiday answered Burnett, leaving Kylie's question hanging.

Kylie's phone buzzed, but she ignored it, not wanting to miss out on any conversation that centered on her.

"Or maybe that's why she's here." Burnett's harsh glare focused on Kylie again. "Were you sent here with a purpose, Miss Galen?"

"No, and my parents didn't do anything wrong," Kylie insisted.

Holiday took a step closer. "If your hearing isn't off, you should be able to tell she spoke the truth."

Burnett nodded. He stood and then focused on Holiday. "You're right. She doesn't seem involved. But I want to be updated on her condition."

Holiday's expression hardened. "I don't see why that is necessary."

"Neither do I," Kylie blurted out, not liking how they discussed her as if she wasn't here.

Burnett ignored Kylie and focused only on Holiday. "You'll comply with my wishes, Miss Brandon, or I'll see to it that my boss finds a camp leader who will."

For the first time, Holiday flinched, telling Kylie the camp leader cared more about her job than she did her pride. "I'm simply curious as to why you're interested in her."

"In addition to watching over this project, I'm in charge of tracking any anomalies in our alliance. Miss Galen qualifies."

"I'm an anomaly?" Kylie blurted out in disbelief.

"Okay, I'll update you," Holiday said, still paying Kylie no heed.

Burnett looked a tad smug, as if he knew he'd won. Then he glanced back at Kylie. "You may go now."

Kylie gazed up at Holiday. "I thought—"

Holiday interrupted. "We have a meeting. I'd appreciate if you two could let yourselves out."

Burnett crossed his arms over his wide chest. "Your meeting will have to be rescheduled. I need you to go through the files with me. Since it appears that Miss Galen is not our suspect, we need to find out who is."

"And you just assume that it's one of my kids," Holiday seethed. "Have you even considered that—"

"Yes, I do assume that. All the evidence points here," Burnett snapped.

Evidence of what? The question lay on the tip of Kylie's tongue, but something warned her not to push it.

Holiday's lips tightened before she turned to Kylie. "We'll meet after lunch. Is that okay?"

Kylie nodded, disappointed all her questions would have to wait, but it didn't mean she couldn't start getting other answers. Standing up, she nodded good-bye, then walked out of the meeting room with purpose. She had things to do. Things to figure out. And first on her list was to find a certain fairy and get her brain scanned for tumors.

. . .

Kylie stepped out of the office, not sure how to go about finding Helen the healer. Her phone buzzed again and she pulled it from her jeans. It was a text from Sara. One word appeared on the screen.

"Negative," Kylie said aloud, and smiled in relief for Sara. She started punching in Sara's number when someone moved beside her. A tall and wide frame cast a tall and wide shadow.

Before Kylie looked up, she somehow knew the owner of that shadow would have jet black hair and light blue eyes. Taking a deep breath, she slowly looked up.

Damn, she hated being right.

Chapter Twenty-two

"Can we talk?"

Lucas Parker's voice sent almost as many chills through her as the slight pressure of his hand against her back. Almost. But not quite.

She fought against the urge to shiver as he nudged her away from the group of kids standing about fifty feet to their left. While his words lent itself to a question, the fact that he was moving, and taking her with him, implied she didn't have a choice.

The warm feel of his hand on the small of her back took her back to last night's dream—the one where they were swimming together. That thought reminded her that she'd interrupted Lucas and his girlfriend earlier today. Kylie blinked, praying she wouldn't break out in a full-blown blush.

"What do you want to talk about?" she managed to ask, but she guessed he meant Derek and her. He'd seemed plenty angry when he'd caught them on the rock—she just didn't know why. She tried to stop walking, but he kept moving her along. Unless she wanted to trip and land on her face, she had no option but to put one foot in front of the other.

Kylie's Reeboks rushed to meet his pace. Then she saw the line of thick trees in front of her and no way was she going in the woods with him. Nope.

"Stop!" She jerked away from his hand and tripped, losing her grip on her phone. It landed with a thud on the grass. And Kylie almost joined it.

He caught her by her forearm and lifted her with complete ease. Catching her breath, she realized the back of his hand rested against her breast.

She stared at his hand, against the swell of tingling flesh, her heart racing—racing from fear and from something else. That something else having everything to do with the dream she'd had last night and where his hand was now. "Let me go," she seethed.

He released her and held his palms out. "I wouldn't hurt you, Kylie."

"How would I know that?" She took a step back and waited to see if he'd say something about knowing her before. Maybe even remind her that he'd saved her from a bunch of bullies. At which time she'd have to remind him that he'd still killed her cat.

But he said nothing. He just stared at her and the expression in his eyes appeared hurt. Like he had that right.

God, did he even remember her? Or Socks?

He passed a hand over his face and asked, "What was that all about?"

What was what all about? Then she thought she knew.

"Derek drew my name. We were just talking." *Unlike what you and your sidekick were doing. And not that it was any of your business, anyway.*

In the bright sunlight, Kylie noticed Lucas's beard stubble, something most seventeen-year-olds didn't have. Then she recalled he was a werewolf and wondered if that explained it. Or was he just one of those guys who matured early, who had a full beard by the time they graduated high school?

"I saw how you two were talking, but that's not what I'm asking about."

"In that case, I'm sorry I interrupted you and that girl." She reached down and picked up her phone.

When she stood back up, he was frowning, but to his credit he didn't try to claim she hadn't interrupted anything.

She couldn't explain why that almost upset her. But damn it. What was wrong with her? An hour ago, she'd wanted Derek to kiss her and now she was having the hots for the guy who killed her cat?

Stress, she decided. Stress obviously brought on the hook-up hormones. Or did a brain tumor do that?

Lucas let out a sigh. "I didn't mean that, either. I meant what did the FRU want with you?"

Kylie pressed a hand to her left temple to assuage the ache and tried to think how to explain it. Then she wasn't even sure she should explain it.

"I don't know." She didn't know enough about what the FRU suspected to make sense of it herself, let alone to explain it to anyone else.

His eyes tightened. "What do you mean, you don't know?"

"I mean, I don't know. Nothing is making sense to me these days."

Skepticism filled his expression and insisted she give him more. But why was he asking? Could he be behind whatever it was the FRU suspected her of doing? Her own suspicion started to build.

"Why do you want to know?" she asked.

"They've been hanging around and I can tell Holiday is upset. I asked her about it, but she said I didn't have to worry. If something's going on, I want to help her."

Kylie remembered Holiday had brought Lucas with her last night when she'd had the dream. Maybe the two of them were friends, but if Holiday chose not to tell him anything, far be it from Kylie to interfere.

"They wanted to talk to me because they think I'm an anomaly. They're trying to figure me out like everyone else is."

The disbelief in his gaze lessened. "Did they do it? Figure you out?"

She shook her head. "Apparently I'm a real puzzler."

"Girls generally are," he said, and smiled. And holy crap, if his smile wasn't one of those that made a girl's heart fall over on itself.

She caught herself from being lured into his smile and mentally slammed on the brakes. Then, because she didn't want to stand there while her heart did somersaults, because she needed to find Helen and see if she could detect a tumor in Kylie's brain, Kylie held up her phone. "I have to make a call."

• • •

It took Kylie twenty minutes to find Helen. During that time, she'd texted Sara a bunch of smiley faces, but had foregone calling her. Now that Sara's trauma was over, Kylie felt justified in concentrating on her own. And the first order of business was to get her brain scanned by a certain half fairy.

Moving across the dining hall, she studied Helen who was sitting at the table, her nose in a book. The girl came across as the quiet but really smart type—the kind who never had to study in school, but wasn't really proud of it.

"Hi," Kylie said when Helen didn't notice her.

Startled, Helen jerked her attention up. A strand of sandy blond hair fell across her face and she brushed it back. "Hi."

Kylie opened her mouth to speak, only to realize she didn't have a clue how to ask if she would check her for a brain tumor. The silence hung heavy and Kylie forced herself to start taking. "I . . . I just . . ."

Noise from the other side of the room erupted and Kylie looked at the other campers. "I'm Kylie Galen. You and I were in the group—"

"I remember," she said in a mellow voice. Kylie didn't know Helen, but she instantly identified with her. She was another cliqueless wonder. A loner. Kylie couldn't help but hope that the girl had someone like Sara who made her life easier.

"Can we talk?" Kylie asked. "Somewhere else?"

Helen glanced over at the other campers, and then picked up her book and backpack.

When they stepped out of the dining hall, Kylie noticed several groups of hungry teens congregating near the building.

She headed away from them, and tried again to find the words to ask Helen. "I was wondering if . . . I sort of—"

"Derek told me," Helen said.

"He did?" Kylie's chest pinched at the thought of Derek trying to help. Behind that pinch came guilt at still not being able to trust him. Was she wrong to be unsure of her feelings for someone who could control them as easily as he could breathe?

"There's a quiet spot behind the office," Helen said.

"Not there." While Kylie didn't think Lucas would already be hooking up again, she didn't want to chance it.

She saw the path back to her cabin was mostly unpopulated, so Kylie headed that way.

They passed a group of kids, laughing at something one of them said. In the midst of the group, she spotted Lucas's girlfriend, and before Kylie could look away, the girl met her gaze and snarled. Why did the she-wolf hate her so much?

Trying not to focus on Lucas or his girlfriend, Kylie glanced at Helen. "Do you think you can help me?"

Helen shrugged and everything from her expression to her posture appeared uncertain. "I've only done it with my sister. I'll try, but . . ."

"But what?" Kylie asked as they continued down the path.

"Aren't you scared?" Helen asked.

Kylie stopped walking. "Should I be?"

Helen did another one of her insecure shrugs. "Maybe. I don't know. All I know is that I'm scared."

Oh, just great. Kylie swallowed the nervous tickle down her

throat. "Is it going to hurt or something?" When Helen didn't immediately answer, Kylie asked, "Did it hurt your sister?"

"No," Helen admitted.

A sigh left Kylie's throat. Second thoughts started building, but then she remembered how badly she wanted to get to the bottom of everything. "I need to know."

Helen motioned Kylie to move behind a row of large oak trees. The girl tossed down her backpack and then looked at Kylie.

"How do we do it?" Kylie asked, her stomach knotting.

"Honestly, I don't know. With my sister I just . . . We were fighting. She had stolen my diary. And then all of the sudden . . ." She let out a breath.

"So we have to start fighting?" Kylie asked, unsure what Helen was getting at.

"No." She shook her head. "It was almost like . . . You know how we can peek into everyone's mind?"

"No, I don't know," Kylie answered, frustration tightening her tone as her headache returned with a new vengeance.

Surprise registered on Helen's face. "You really can't see people's brain patterns? But I thought we all could do that."

"I can't," Kylie answered. "Which is why I don't think I'm one of you guys." She clasped her hands together to keep them from shaking. Her heart lurched at the thought that she honestly might have a tumor. Then her mind went back to the idea of reading brains. "Have you always been able to do it? Always?"

"Sort of. I mean . . . I could do it, but I didn't know *what* I was doing. I just thought it was like closing your eyes real tight and seeing the different splotches of red. But now that I know what it is, it's so much clearer."

Their gazes met and Helen twitched her eyebrows.

"What do you see?" Kylie asked, her heart racing.

"Just your pattern." Helen continued to stare, unfocused like when Kylie looked at one of those posters where if she stared at it long enough, she might see a hidden image. "You aren't like . . . normal people. They have these even waves. Yours is . . . up and down and then you have some weird kind of scribbles. But you aren't letting me read you."

"I don't know how to let you read me." Kylie bit down on her lip and tried to stare at Helen, unfocused to see if she could see anything. Nothing happened, but her eyes crossed.

Blinking, Kylie asked, "Do I have to let you read me before you can see if I have a tumor?"

"No, but . . ." Helen refocused her eyes.

"But what?"

The girl let go of a sigh. "Like I told you, I don't know how it works. With my sister, I had my hands . . ." Helen raised her hands on each side of Kylie's head. "I was . . . holding her head." She hesitated. "Do you want me to try?"

Kylie nodded, even though doing it made her pulse race. Helen placed a hand on each side of Kylie's head. Kylie watched the girl close her eyes. Her smooth forehead wrinkled and her mouth tightened in concentration. Kylie stood there staring and hoped no one stumbled upon them. She could hear the rumors now. Kylie and Helen were making out behind the trees. Right.

Several seconds ticked by, and with each increment of time, Kylie felt more awkward. She was about to call it quits when her head began tingling. The tingles turned to heat. All at once, a comforting warmth radiated from Helen's palms.

"I'm doing it." Excitement rang in Helen's voice. "It's working."

The heat from Helen's hands eased inside Kylie's head. Kylie continued to stare at Helen, trying to read her expression. What was the girl seeing? Should Kylie be calling her mom and having her go out and start shopping for wigs? No way was Kylie walking around bald.

Slowly, the hold Helen had on her head lessened. The fairy dropped her hands to her sides. After two deep breaths, she opened her eyes.

"And?" Kylie blurted out. "Do I have a tumor? Do I?"

Chapter Twenty-three

"Hey, where have you been?" Miranda asked as Kylie dropped down on the bench beside her and Della in the dining hall fifteen minutes later.

"Talking to Helen." Kylie brushed a strand of blond hair behind her ear, her nerves still jumpy.

"Who's Helen?" Della held her glass of "juice"—that's what Kylie had decided to think of it as—to her mouth.

"Helen Jones." Kylie motioned to the quiet girl who had just sat down at another lunch table. While Kylie had invited Helen to join them, she'd declined, saying she'd promised to sit at the fairy table today.

Kylie watched Helen sit next to Derek and lean in to whisper something in his ear. Kylie didn't need super hearing to know Helen had shared the no-tumor verdict. As if to prove Kylie right, Derek met Kylie's gaze and smiled.

Kylie returned the gesture. While she was comforted that Helen hadn't seen any black dots in her brain as she'd spotted in her sister's, the answer moved Kylie closer to accepting that she was . . . well, not all human. And that was not comforting at all.

Della leaned forward and whispered, "How did your interrogation go? Did you find out what they suspected you of?"

"What interrogation?" Miranda's eyes grew round.

Kylie looked around at the crowd. "I'll tell y'all later."

Miranda nodded. "Oh, did you hear we're getting a computer? They're putting one in every cabin."

"Cool," Kylie said, only half listening. Instead her mind chewed on the possibility of insanity explaining her odd brain pattern. For sure, there'd been times she felt crazy—these last few weeks topping the list.

"You'd better get your lunch before they stop serving," Della said.

Kylie noticed that several of the campers were already stacking their trays and leaving. The tumor scan had taken longer than Kylie had thought.

"Yeah." Kylie stood up.

"Oh," Miranda said. "Perry was trying to find you earlier."

Kylie frowned and leaned down. "What did he want?"

"Maybe for you to check his sex again." Della snickered.

Kylie groaned.

Miranda chuckled and then got serious. "I think it was to apologize. He told me that he even tried to get away from you, that you were the one to bring him inside."

Kylie recalled that the kitten, aka Perry in disguise, did try to resist when she brought him in. As he did when she pried his hind legs apart. "He still shouldn't have been peeking in our windows."

"True," Miranda said. "But at least he's willing to apologize. It takes a big person to do that."

"Or a little twerp who's afraid I'll tell Holiday on him," Kylie said.

"She has a point," Della said.

Kylie walked to the lunch pickup window. The elf who had driven the bus stood behind the counter—all three feet of her, the tip of her head barely hitting the countertop. She cocked her head back and looked at Kylie, her brows twitching. "Have we figured out what you are yet?" The elf slid a food tray at Kylie.

"Not yet," Kylie muttered, not liking the fact that everyone at the camp knew about her identity crisis.

"Does your friend need anything to eat?" the little woman asked, frowning.

"What friend?"

The cold brushed down Kylie's right side—his presence as noticeable and as welcome as a paper cut. "You can see him, too?" A wisp of steam left her lips with the words.

"Nah, just feel him. Don't like it, either." The elf backed away from the counter.

Go away. Go away. Closing her eyes, Kylie willed Soldier Dude to leave. When the chill faded as quickly as it had come, she wondered if it was really as easy as just wishing him away. One more thing she needed to talk to Holiday about. Nevertheless, the small victory offered Kylie a tiny sense of control. Real tiny.

Picking up her tray, she went back to join Miranda and Della. Admittedly, she didn't search the room for any guys wearing army garb. Why look for trouble?

"Bad day?" Miranda asked when Kylie dropped her tray rather discontentedly on the table.

"Bad month." Kylie picked up the sandwich and sniffed. "I hate tuna." She felt her throat tighten and swallowed the knot of emotion, swearing she wouldn't cry.

"You like peanut butter and jelly?" Miranda asked.

"Yeah." Kylie looked at Miranda, thinking she was offering to swap. Instead, she was holding out her pinky and waving it at Kylie's sandwich.

The sandwich in Kylie's hand moved. Kylie looked at it, and her mouth fell open. Peanut butter and red jam oozed over the crusty edges of the bread. "Holy crap." Kylie dropped the sandwich back on the tray.

"Wow." Della leaned over. "Can you zap me up a second glass of blood? Oh, make it O negative. I hear that's the best."

Miranda made a face. "I do *not* do blood."

"Why am I not surprised?" Della huffed.

Kylie shut out all talk of blood and shifted her gaze from her transformed sandwich back to the sandwich transformer. "I thought you said you couldn't do magic?"

Miranda made a funny face. "That's hardly enough to call magic. I've been replacing my lunch with peanut butter and jelly sandwiches since I was two. My mom tried force-feeding me liverwurst. Who in God's name eats that stuff?"

"I'd bet I would love it now," Della said.

Kylie's stomach growled and she pulled back the bread to give the sandwich a quick check. "Is it . . . safe to eat?"

"You think I'd poison you?" Miranda asked, clearly offended.

"No, but it could be radioactive or something. I don't know what happens to food when it's . . . zapped here."

"I've eaten my sandwiches all my life," Miranda said.

"Yeah, we see what it did to you, too," Della added, her tone sounding more and more annoyed.

"Go suck a vein," Miranda snapped.

"You got one?" Della countered, and bared her teeth.

"Please." Kylie looked from one roommate to the other. "I beg you, don't start this again." Only when they both seemed resigned to stop bickering did Kylie revisit the idea of eating. Amazingly, she was starved. Getting one's brain scanned must increase one's appetite. Or maybe it was that her headache had finally taken a hike. Either way, she was hungry enough to take a chance and eat a sandwich that had been conjured up by Miranda's pinky finger.

Picking up the sandwich, Kylie sank her teeth into the soft white bread. "It's good," she told Miranda, as she moved the bite around in her mouth, and tried to keep the peanut butter from sticking to the roof of her mouth. "Thank you."

"You're welcome," Miranda said. "And in return, all I'd like is for you to put in a good word for me with Derek—since you don't like him."

Della made a snorting sound. "You are so blind. Kylie's crazy about him."

Miranda's mouth fell open and she looked at Kylie as if waiting for her to rebuke Della's claim. But the peanut butter got caught on the roof of her mouth and Kylie couldn't have spoken even if she wanted to. Not that she was overtly ready to speak up. She didn't know how to answer.

Frustrated at Kylie's silence, Miranda addressed Della. "She said she didn't like him."

"She lied." Della shrugged.

Miranda snapped her head around to Kylie. "Do you like him? If so, just tell me you like him."

"Who does Miss Don't-know-what-I-am like?" Lucas's girlfriend plopped down on the opposite side of the table.

Kylie's gaze shot to the werewolf. Strange. She couldn't ever remember having so much anger or dislike being lopped on her in one cold stare.

She managed to push the lump of sandwich she'd pried off the roof of her mouth to her cheek. "No one," she said, but it came out muffled.

"Really?" The werewolf's lips turned up in something that might have been considered a smile if the smirk accompanying it wasn't so evil. "By the way, my name's Fredericka. I thought you'd like to know the name of the girl who will kick your ass if you even try—"

"Ha. That's funny," Miranda said.

Funny? Kylie shot a look at Miranda and right then the blob of bread, peanut butter, and jam slid halfway down Kylie's throat. She covered her mouth and coughed, which only made the situation worse, because as the golf ball–sized lump of food tried to come up, it lodged between her tonsils. She gasped for air, but got none. Zilch.

"What's funny?" Fredericka's cold stare now focused on Miranda, which might have concerned Kylie if she wasn't slightly preoccupied about not being able to breathe. She started thumping her chest.

Can't breathe.

"You kicking her ass," Miranda shot back.

Hey. I can't breathe here. Kylie reached for her throat, the universal sign of choking.

"I mean, with all the help Kylie would have stopping you and all."

Seriously, I can't breathe. Oh, friggin' great, she was at a camp full of bloodsucking, meat-eating creatures, and she was about to die of asphyxiation from a peanut butter and jelly sandwich.

Fredericka leaned forward, getting closer to Miranda. "You think I'm scared of your scrawny little butt?"

Still can't breathe here, guys.

Finally, Della—you gotta love an attentive vampire— reached around Miranda's shoulders and gave Kylie one extra hard thump between her shoulder blades. The clump of food dislodged from her windpipe. While it hurt going down, at least oxygen started passing.

"Me?" Miranda's voice came out squeaky. "You thought . . . I meant . . . No, no. I didn't mean help from me." Miranda pointed a finger at Della. "She might take you on. She's got this whole vampire combative attitude going, but I didn't mean her, either."

"But she's right," Della said, half her attention on Kylie and the other half on Fredericka. "I'd help Kylie kick your ass in a heartbeat." She curled her lips at the werewolf, showing off her canines.

Fredericka didn't appear concerned. Not that Kylie was certain of anything; she was still working on getting the needed oxygen to her brain, while giving the drama playing out in front of her a wee bit of attention. Hey, if she was about to get ripped apart by a werewolf, she wanted to know the reasons why.

"Then who are you talking about?" Fredericka leaned across the table and a low growl escaped her throat.

"I mean Kylie's ghosts." Miranda said. "She's got like a dozen or so hanging around, or hadn't you heard?"

What? Kylie coughed—good thing the lump of bread had gone down and not up because she would have choked on it again.

"I don't know about you, but I'm not messing with the dead. Don't you remember last year when Holiday talked about the death angels?"

Death angels? Kylie recalled Miranda talking about the legend of dancing death angels at the falls on the bus ride to the camp. She gave up one more cough and then held up her hand. But right before she started talking, she noticed the fear in Fredericka's expression.

Not wanting to come off like a scared rabbit confronting a hungry wolf—even though that pretty much described exactly how Kylie felt—she looked Fredericka directly in the eyes. "Stop." Cough. "I don't want to fight you." Cough. "I don't even know why you'd want to fight me. Or my ghosts."

Hey, Kylie was no fool. She fully intended to take advantage of the fear she spotted in the girl's eyes.

"Just stay away from Lucas," Fredericka warned, but her voice lacked its earlier confidence.

"Me?" All the crappiness of the day, of the last few weeks, zeroed in on this high and mighty B with an itch, and the scared-rabbit feeling faded.

"You know what?" Kylie snapped. "Maybe you should go tighten the leash you have around your so-called boyfriend's neck, because every time I've spoken to him was because he came up to me. Not the other way around."

"You'd better watch your back," Fredericka said.

"She doesn't have to," Della said. "Her ghosts do that for her. Didn't you hear about the little incident that happened at our cabin last night?"

Fredericka shot up and took off.

Kylie pressed a hand to the table and stared after her. "What a bitch."

"Yeah, she was like that last year, too. But we did good," Miranda said, and placed her hand on top of Kylie's.

"We rocked," Della said, and put hers on top of Miranda's.

"Thank you," Kylie said, and looked from one roommate to the other. "Y'all didn't have to stick up for me, and I appreciate it."

"Hey, we're friends," Miranda said. "And that's what friends do."

Smiling at her two new friends, Kylie realized that coming to camp wasn't going to be *all* bad.

Then, letting go of a heartfelt sigh and feeling her bravado kick down a notch, she met Miranda's gaze. "Do death angels really exist?"

Chapter Twenty-four

"And oh, do death angels really exist?"

It was probably the seventh or eighth question Kylie had pitched at Holiday during their meeting thirty minutes later. The moment Kylie's foot had stepped inside the office, the questions just started flowing.

"That's . . . a lot of questions." Holiday smiled and motioned for Kylie to sit down.

Kylie set her phone down on Holiday's desk and took a chair. When she'd left the dining hall, she spent the last five minutes talking to Sara, celebrating the fact that her pregnancy test was negative, but now Kylie was back to focusing on her own mission of finding answers.

"Yeah, and I'm only getting started," she said. "I also want to know what else I could be. The other day you said—"

"Really?" Holiday's brow arched. "So you've accepted that you're one of us?"

The question bounced around Kylie's head. "No. I just want to be prepared if . . . that's what I discover."

The camp leader brushed her long ponytail of red hair behind her shoulder. "I heard you had Helen check you for a tumor."

"Who told you?" Kylie asked, imagining the whole camp teasing her about it. Or even worse, teasing Helen. The girl seemed even shyer than Kylie and the last thing Kylie wanted was for her to get hell because of something Kylie had talked her into doing.

Holiday shook her head. "It wasn't like that. Helen was excited that she discovered how it worked and wanted to share it with me."

Kylie nodded. She understood how Helen felt and didn't begrudge her sharing the news with Holiday.

"But you still aren't a believer, are you?" Holiday asked, meeting Kylie's gaze.

"I could still be . . ."

"Crazy or schizophrenic."

"Right," Kylie said, relieved that Holiday understood.

Holiday sighed as if exasperated and Kylie's relief evaporated.

"It's just I don't think either of my parents are gifted. And you said this is most likely hereditary. Plus, I can't see into people's head and see any patterns. Helen said she could always do it."

"That's Helen. Most of us with ghost whispering powers—it just appears one day." Holiday sighed. "And there could be a hundred reasons why your mom or dad hasn't shared this with you. You . . ." She held up her hands. "What am I doing? My job isn't to convince you. It's to help you find your own answers."

Kylie almost apologized for disappointing Holiday because

she honestly liked her, but how could Kylie just believe this without some proof?

"Let's get back to your questions." Holiday paused as if recalling the list. "Do death angels really exist? I'm assuming you heard about the legend of the name Shadow Falls."

"Yeah," Kylie said. "Is it true?"

"I've never seen the shadows. Of course, it wasn't quite dusk when I was there."

"I mean the death angels?"

"Well, I haven't ever seen a death angel either. But I know several people who claim they have. Some think they exist only in the legends, but since all supernaturals are considered legends, it's hard to say they don't exist."

"Are they known to be evil?" Kylie asked, her curiosity stemming from both Fredericka's fear and Miranda's hesitancy to talk about them later.

"Not necessarily evil. They are thought of as powerful ghosts who are . . . avengers. It's believed that they right the wrongs of the supernaturals. And stand judgment of them."

"Is that why everyone seems so scared of ghosts?"

"Yup, that would be the reason." A smile twitched Holiday's lips. "Frankly, we scare the bejeebies out of most supernaturals. Remember the FRU?"

Kylie nodded and inwardly admitted it scared the bejeebies out of her, too.

Holiday placed her right elbow on the table and then rested her chin in her open palm. "To be honest with you Kylie, death angels per se may not exist, but I see all my ghosts as being a lot like we think death angels are. I mean, I've actually had several protect me in different ways. Sure some of them need something from us, but more times than not they are here to either help us, or to help us help someone else. As scary as this all seems to you, you should know that it's a special calling. Very few supernaturals have this gift. It's said that it is bestowed on only those with worthy spirits, good hearts, and courage."

"But I'm not those things," Kylie said, pleading her case. "On Halloween, I wouldn't even go into the haunted houses."

Holiday chuckled. "I didn't say you were perfect, Kylie. Heaven knows that I have my faults as well. But our hearts want the good to win. We're still afraid, we still make mistakes, but if we listen to what our hearts want, we will find the right way." She rested her left hand on top of Kylie's.

Kylie looked at their hands joined together on the table. "Is being a ghost whisperer a common gift for fairies? And elves?" Kylie remembered the bus driver sensing when Soldier Dude had dropped by for a visit. "At lunch, the elf, the one who drove the bus that brought us here, she knew the ghost was there."

"Yes, there have been studies that say it is more common with fairies and elves. But it's not unheard of for others to have this ability. While certain gifts are bestowed to different species, each being can have less or more, depending on their spirits or their links to the gods and goddesses."

"So what else could I be?"

"This morning when I touched you and you sensed that I was trying to calm you . . . the fact that you could feel that is . . . well, unusual. Generally speaking, another fairy, depending on their level of power, may be able to sense it, but . . . honestly, I've never heard of anyone sensing it through touch."

"So assuming I'm not human, I'm also not fairy?"

"I didn't say that. What I can say is that whatever species your gifts stem from, your lineage to the gods is closer than most. I think you are just coming into your powers and who knows what all awaits you."

Kylie just stared. Holiday acted as though her words were supposed to make her feel better. "But do we know—if I *am* one of you—that I'm not like a vampire or werewolf?" Kylie held her breath as she waited for Holiday to answer.

Holiday shrugged. "I'm guessing if you were of that species, we would have seen some of the normal characteristics that are linked to them. However, there are a few of all species that are what we refer to as atypical. Their heritage is with one species and yet they lack certain characteristics, and are often gifted in other ways. The studies seem to conclude that, perhaps, these individuals are the very few that have combined genetics of two or more species. Not that it has really been proven."

Oh, great. She could be a hybrid. Just like her sociology teacher's car.

"So . . . normally, you really don't have half of one species and half of another? I thought Miranda said they've been mixing forever."

Holiday smiled. "Yes. But generally, the species with the closer lineage to the gods is the one passed on in the DNA. Here again, the gifts of the child may vary, but the basic characteristics seem to remain true for each species, such as the transformation into a wolf, or the need for blood to survive—if the virus is active."

Kylie's mind was trying to wrap around all this information. "Isn't there some blood test that could tell if I'm anything at all?"

"Regrettably, no. Oh, they are still trying, believe me. However, it's legend that the gods made our blood the same as humans, and unidentifiable as a matter of survival. If normals, or even one form of a supernatural, could test for certain species, they might be able to eradicate certain types."

Kylie conceded that point. If she'd found out two weeks ago that vampires and such existed, she'd have been all for trying to eradicate them. But now, after knowing Della, Miranda, Derek, Holiday, Helen, and even Perry—the little twerp—Kylie would never agree to it.

Then she remembered she wasn't the only one who didn't know why she was here. "Is there any kind of supernatural that isn't hereditary?"

"Well, as I mentioned earlier, in rare incidences it has been known to skip generations. Especially in the instances of vampirism. Then there are humans who are simply turned by either vampires or werewolves, but it's suspected that even in those cases, the victims who survive being turned have been touched in some way by the gods. Or demons."

Demons? Okay, Kylie wasn't ready to deal with them just yet. "But you don't think I'm a vampire or a werewolf, right?"

"I think it's unlikely."

Which basically meant, if Kylie wanted to get to the bottom of this, she'd have to go to her parents. And just how in the heck was she going to do that, assuming her parents were as clueless about this as she was? Knowing her mom, if Kylie started asking questions, she'd get herself pulled out of camp and stuck in a loony bin.

During the art hour later that afternoon, Kylie was paired up with Helen and Jonathon. The teen had removed all his piercings except his left earring. Kylie also noticed the way he carried himself, as if somehow becoming a vampire had given him a double shot of confidence. Even Helen seemed quicker to smile and totally comfortable with her new role as fairy/healer.

Kylie remembered Holiday saying how the camp would make most of them feel relieved because they always sensed they were different. Kylie saw that relief in Helen and Jonathon—it was as if they'd finally discovered who they really were. It was just one of a dozen or more things that made her different from everyone else here at camp. She couldn't help but wonder if this failure to identify with her supernatural self wasn't another sign of her not being anything but human.

Their art assignment was to take a walk as a group of three, find a spot, and then sit and sketch the same thing. Kylie, her mind still stuck on seeing the falls, suggested that they take a walk to the waterfalls. She felt pretty sure she could find her way back to where Derek had taken her and then follow the sounds from there. Face it, she was curious, but both Helen and Jonathon refused to go, saying only that they preferred to stay away from that place. Instead, they walked down one of the trails and found an old tree that had been split in two from what she assumed had been lightning.

While Helen and Jonathon got into the whole sketch-a-tree

thing, Kylie spent most her time trying to figure out how to approach her parents. Her mother already thought she was nuts because of Soldier Dude. What would she say when Kylie asked, point-blank, if her mom had any fairy ancestors, saw ghosts, or could transform herself into a unicorn.

Later, when Kylie met up with her hiking crowd, she almost bailed when she found out Lucas was leading the group. Then, afraid ditching would get her into trouble with Holiday, Kylie plastered a cordial look on her face that she didn't really feel, and swore to ignore him. Fifteen minutes into the hike, she realized she didn't have to ignore Lucas because he did a championship-winning job of ignoring her. Half an hour into the hike, and not once had he addressed her personally or even glanced her way. Not that she cared.

It was a downright shame Fredericka wasn't around to see how unimpressed the two of them were with each other. Okay, the truth was, Kylie counted her blessings that she and Fredericka hadn't crossed paths again. Somehow Kylie had to muster up some courage, or at least learn to fake some. Because sooner or later they were bound to come face-to-face again. Kylie's hands began to sweat just from considering it.

And to think Holiday thought she had courage. Ha.

In the beginning of the hike through the woods, Kylie mostly hung with Miranda, when her roommate wasn't chatting it up with the five or six male hikers. Honestly, when it came to the opposite sex, Miranda reminded Kylie a bit of Sara. A little too out there. Then again, it might be Kylie was a tad jealous at how easily both of them could flirt.

Even though Kylie didn't consider herself unattractive,

playing that whole giggly role didn't come easy for her. She was fortunate that Trey hadn't been turned off by her more subdued style.

Thinking about Trey reminded Kylie that he'd called again during art class. He'd left a message, too, but she hadn't listened to it yet. Hey, he'd have to get in line. She had her own issues to deal with. But even as she tried to push thoughts of him away, she remembered him saying in their first conversation, *I just want to see you. I miss you.*

Her chest tightened, because damn it. She missed him, too.

Kylie felt Miranda nudge her with her elbow.

"This is Kylie. We're rooming together," Miranda said.

Waving at the group of guys walking on the other side of Miranda, Kylie quickly went back to checking the trails for water moccasins and pretending she wasn't listening to Lucas's spiel about the camp.

According to him, real dinosaur bones were actually found here back in the 1960s. After a few more minutes, Kylie forgot about feigning disinterest and like the rest of the group—minus a few of the boys and Miranda—hung on Lucas's every word.

Lucas took them up to a creek bed where an archeologist had roped off some prehistoric footprints. Kylie found the whole story fascinating. And it had nothing to do with the fact that Lucas's deep voice sounded hypnotic. She'd always found archaeology intriguing.

"So, are they still excavating the site?" Kylie asked. "Couldn't there be even more dinosaur bones here?"

Lucas turned to her. "Not on camp property, they're not." His tone lost its earlier enthusiasm and his focus shifted back to the others so fast Kylie had no doubt that her being here annoyed the hell out of him. Surely he knew she hadn't chosen to be on his little adventure.

If Kylie had any reservations about his attitude being a figment of her imagination, it died when Miranda whispered, "I don't see why that bitch Fredericka thinks he's into you. From what I can see, he barely tolerates you."

"I know," Kylie muttered, but even as the words left her lips, she recalled how he'd looked at her last night in her PJs.

"I've been thinking about Fredericka and I swear, she's so evil," Miranda whispered. "I'll betcha she wasn't born at midnight. Some supernaturals lie . . ."

Kylie nodded, only half listening, and that's when it hit. "Oh my God, that's how I can do it. Thank you." Kylie gave Miranda's arm a good squeeze, and for the first time she felt as if uncovering the truth was in her reach.

Chapter Twenty-five

That evening, Kylie stayed behind at the cabin when Miranda and Della went to the music get-together at the dining hall. Supposedly, some of the guys were going to sing and had brought guitars, and then, a little later, Holiday and Sky were bringing out some music CDs to play so everyone could dance. Kylie wasn't feeling in the mood to dance. Or even to listen to music. She had far more important things to do. Sitting at the small desk off the kitchen, she reread the e-mail she'd just written, wondering if she should click send or delete the whole thing.

> Hi Mom,
> We got computers in our cabin, so I thought I'd e-mail you instead of call.

Truth was, she figured she could lie better in an e-mail than over the phone.

You know how you are always fussing about me going over
my minutes. Anyway, I'm doing okay.

Another lie. Nothing felt okay. Well, except her friendship
with Miranda and Della.

I have a question. We're doing some crazy horoscope read-
ings and it's partly done by comparing your time of birth to
that of your parents.

And that was the lie that Kylie had been worrying about
saying out loud, but she still felt it was clever.

Can you tell me what time you and Dad were born? And is
there any way I could check and see when Nana and Papa
were born? What about Grandma and Grandpa Galen? Don't
we have like that family tree thing that Grandma filled out?
Did she put the time of their births on it?
Thanks for your help.
Kylie

Kylie's finger hovered over the send button. She almost added,
"please hurry," but decided not to push her luck. If she acted
too anxious about it, her mom would start to ask questions.
Best to play it cool.

Taking a deep breath, she hit send. Excitement shot through
her. If this worked, she'd have her answer. Or at least, she'd be
closer to knowing the truth.

She'd asked Miranda to clarify the whole midnight-born rule, and according to her, there were some humans who were born at midnight. And then there were some supernaturals who were not born at midnight. However, the latter were known as the untouchables—demons, born of the devil.

And while Kylie considered her mom cold, she didn't consider her evil. If one of her parents were part demon, she would have known. Right?

Then there was the whole probability that it had skipped a generation. Which was why Kylie had asked for her grandparents' times of birth. She knew she was dreaming that her mom would have that info at her fingertips, but hey, Kylie wanted answers.

And she wanted them now.

Thirty minutes later, Kylie stood guard over the computer, obsessively clicking NEW MAIL, when her phone buzzed. She ran to the bedroom to find it. As she hurried through the door, she remembered she hadn't listened to Trey's messages yet. He'd called again during dinner, and she hadn't answered then, either.

She told herself it was because she was surrounded by people who could listen in, but she could have walked outside and taken the call.

She could have, but she hadn't.

Deep down she knew that meant something. She just wasn't sure what it meant.

Snatching her phone from the bed, she eyed the screen. Frowning, she took the call.

"Hello, Mom." Kylie fell on top of the mattress. "Didn't you get my—"

"E-mail? Yes, but I don't want to get an e-mail or text. I want to talk to you."

"Okay." Kylie listened as the silence filled the line. See, that was the problem with her and her mom. They really had nothing to talk about.

"Did you have a good day?" her mom asked.

"It was okay." Another awkward moment. "Did you read my e-mail?"

"Yes," her mom said.

"Can you tell me what time you were born?"

"It was late."

Kylie's heart stopped. "How late?"

"I don't know the exact time. Are they feeding you well?"

Kylie closed her eyes. "It's camp food, only slightly better than the school cafeteria. Do you have your birth certificate? That should have the exact time."

"I think it was around eleven. Just say eleven."

"I need the exact time, Mom," Kylie muttered. "I told you. It's for a camp project."

"My birth certificate is in the closet in that box with all those other important papers and old pictures. It would take me forever to find it."

"Please?"

"Why is this important? You don't even believe in horoscopes."

There were a lot of things I used to not to believe in. "Like I said, it's for a camp project. All the kids are doing it." *Can't you do that much for me?* "Do you have Dad's birth certificate?"

"Have you spoken with him?" her mom asked, lowering her voice.

"No," Kylie answered, and the feeling of abandonment swelled in her chest.

"You're not angry at him, are you?" her mom asked.

Hell, yes. He left me to live with you. "Honestly, I don't know what I'm feeling."

"It's not good for you to be angry, Kylie."

Why not? You stay angry at him. Right then, Kylie realized something she should have realized long ago. Her mom was forever angry at her dad. Kylie just didn't understand why.

Her mom sighed. "I need to know if he's coming on Sunday."

"Why are y'all doing this?" It was a question Kylie had never asked. She'd always assumed her mom, being her mom, had one of her temper tantrums and told him to get his stuff and leave. She'd even heard her mom tell him to get out a couple of years ago when she'd walked in on them fighting.

"Doing what?" Her mom asked as if she seriously didn't have a friggin' clue.

"The divorce. That's what."

Silence. "Kylie, that's between your dad and me."

"Like it doesn't affect me? How can you even think this wouldn't affect me?" Tears filled her eyes.

"I'm sorry this is hurting you, Kylie." Her mom's tone came out hoarse. "I never wanted it to hurt you."

Was the Ice Queen crying?

Kylie closed her eyes and felt a few tears slip down her

cheeks. "Will you *please* look for your birth certificates?" she asked, trying to hold back the tears.

"Fine," her mom said. "I'll see if I can find them and I'll e-mail the information to you. If not tonight, tomorrow."

"Tonight would be better." Kylie pulled one of her knees to her chest.

"I'll see," her mom said. Which meant Kylie could expect it to happen tomorrow. "Promise me you'll call your dad about Sunday."

"Bye," Kylie said.

"Kylie. Promise me."

The knot tightened in her throat. "Promise."

Kylie hung up and stared at her phone. What was she going to say to her dad? Oh, hell, why not just do it and get it over with. She started punching in his number, only to realize she'd accidently punched in Nana's old number.

And just like that, it hit. The swell of grief. She missed her grandmother so much. Missed calling her whenever she had some crazy problem with her mom. Missed the way Nana would pat Kylie's cheek and say, "It's all gonna be okay."

A knock sounded at her bedroom door. "Kylie?" Della's voice echoed on the other side.

Kylie closed her phone and wiped her tears from her face. "I'm on the phone," she said. "Can't visit now."

"But, I . . . I have a surprise for you," Della said.

"I don't want a surprise." Couldn't they just leave her alone? For once?

"I'm opening the door. I hope you're dressed."

The bedroom door opened. "I said I . . ." Kylie's words evaporated from the tip of her tongue, or maybe they crawled down the back her throat. That might explain her inability to speak. Then again, it was probably just the shock of seeing who stood beside Della.

Chapter Twenty-six

"I found him sneaking into the camp. Better me, I suppose, than one of the others." Della stared at Kylie. "Do you want to see him?" She gave Trey the up and down look. "He's kind of cute. If you like his type."

Kylie opened her mouth to speak but nothing came out. So she just sat there with her mouth hanging open like an idiot, staring at Trey.

"Hey." He pushed Della aside and moved into her bedroom.

"Not so fast!" Della yanked him back a good three feet and looked at Kylie. "You wanna keep him, or should I toss him to the wolves? I heard they're hungry."

Trey, looking stunned that Della—only an inch or so over five feet—could move him so easily, rubbed his arm where she'd latched on to him and stared down at her.

"It's okay," Kylie managed to say.

"Thanks," Trey said, cutting Della an odd look, and Kylie wasn't sure who he was thanking. Her for agreeing to see him, or Della for bringing him here.

"Okie dokie. Later." Della leaned in. "By the way, no one knows he's here but me. So you're gonna have to sneak him out." Della waved and then stepped out and shut the door.

Trey rubbed his arm one more time and stared at the door before he turned back to her. "That is one weird and strong bitch."

Kylie's shot her gaze to the door, afraid Della would storm back in and defend herself. "She's not a bitch. She's my friend. What are you . . . doing here?"

"What do you think I'm doing? I came to see you."

Kylie shook her head. "You said it would be next week."

"Yeah, but I have a cousin who lives a couple of miles from here. I talked Mom into letting me come up early so I could see you." His gaze shot to the phone in her hands. "I called you at least twice and left messages. Didn't you get them?"

Realizing what he'd done to see her, Kylie felt guilty for not taking his calls or even checking his messages. "I . . . it's been crazy." A few lingering tears slipped from her lashes. She blinked them away and just stared at him. His sandy brown hair hung just a little longer than before and his bangs brushed against his eyebrows. He wore a dark green T-shirt and jeans. Her gaze lowered to his chest. The place she always loved to rest against. Oddly, she remembered him as being buffer. Or was she remembering Derek?

"You're crying." He moved in and concern, honest to goodness concern, filled his green eyes. "Are you okay?"

The compassion in his gaze sent a wave of emotion through her. She stopped caring about what he looked like and just wanted to feel loved. She nodded yes, but the truth slipped from her lips. "No. Everything in my life is falling apart."

Trey moved in and before Kylie could stop him, he was doing what Trey did best, holding her. He'd joined her on the twin bed. Her cheek rested against his chest, and she listened to the steady pounding of his heart. Inhaling his familiar scent, she closed her eyes. She'd give in for a moment. Just a moment. Then she'd push him away.

"Is this about your parents' divorce?" His hands moved tenderly against her back. His touch felt good. Familiar. Normal. Life the way it should be. Like the way it was less than a month ago.

"That and everything else," she said, accepting that she couldn't tell him about the camp and what was happening to her.

"You mean your grandma?" he asked. "I know you two were close."

"Yeah." She pulled back, wiped her eyes, and stared at him stretched out beside her on the tiny twin bed. Silence and sudden physical awareness vibrated in the small room. They were alone. They were in a bed.

It wasn't as if they hadn't been in bed together before. He'd visited her several times when her parents hadn't been home. And they had met at Sara's house a couple of times when her parents hadn't been there. It was just . . . those were the times that things usually went too far. When telling him to stop had made him mad.

"My camp is right next to yours," he said.

She nodded and then blurted out what she needed to say to him before she lost her nerve. "You shouldn't have come here, Trey. I have no idea what kind of trouble I'll get into if we're caught." She did know the number one rule posted: no normals allowed on camp property without permission. And here she was with one stretched out in her bed. It felt wrong. But it still felt right.

"I miss you, Kylie," he said, ignoring what she'd said to him. "Really miss you." He reached up and tucked a strand of her hair behind her ear.

She swallowed. "I miss you, too, but—"

He leaned in and placed a soft kiss beside her lips. Whatever she was about to say got lost in her head. She closed her eyes and even while a little voice inside her told her to stop him, she didn't want to stop this. She wanted him to kiss her, to make her forget.

Oh, yes, she wanted to forget.

His mouth touched hers, slow at first, as if making sure she wanted it, and then he slipped his tongue into her mouth. She loved it when he kissed her like that.

The next thing Kylie knew, Trey had his hand up the back of her shirt and if she didn't stop him, she knew what came next. He would undo her bra. He would touch her breasts, and it always felt so good when he touched her. There was even that one time that she'd let him take her shirt off.

She felt his hands on her bra hook. He deepened the kiss, as if to distract her. She decided to let him do it, too.

But then what? The question bounced around her head. She would stop him, right? She always stopped him. That was the reason he'd dumped her, the reason he'd hooked up with that other girl.

That was when he'd broken her heart.

Opening her eyes, Kylie broke the kiss.

His eyelids fluttered open and she stared at his eyes, searching for a reason *not* to stop him this time. She wanted to lose herself in his eyes . . . to see the gold flecks sparkle.

Oh crap! Trey didn't have gold flecks in his green eyes. Derek had the eyes that pulled her in. Shocked, she put a hand on Trey's chest and recalled how good it had felt to lean against Derek's chest just this morning—how she had felt safe and accepted. "I . . . maybe we shouldn't—"

"Shh. Please don't say it." He put his finger over her lips. "This feels so good, Kylie. And I want to hold you like this, I want to touch you." His hand shifted around to her front and softly passed over her bra, making her breast feel tight. "What's wrong with us being together if we love each other? And you know that's how I feel, don't you? I love you."

I love you. Those three little words played like a slow song in her head. He moved in again for another kiss. She wanted to be loved so badly. And it did feel good, Kylie admitted to herself. It helped her forget.

She let herself become lost in his kisses again. Lost in how his hands moved over her naked skin over her back up to the bra latch. Unlike before, he had her bra unclasped in seconds.

Probably because he'd had practice. Okay, that thought put an end to the warm emotions swirling inside her. Or was it the cold that suddenly invaded the room? Oh, gawd, Soldier Dude was back.

Here.

Now.

Watching her make out with Trey.

"Okay, sorry. I can't do this." She pulled away and stood beside the bed, not looking anywhere but at Trey. *Go away,* she told the coldness, and squeezed her eyes closed.

When she opened her eyes, she felt the chill fade. She focused again on Trey, stretched out on the bed frowning at the ceiling.

"Not again," Trey muttered, and he sounded angry. He always got a little mad when she first stopped him. One time, he even dropped her off at her house without speaking to her.

Without wanting to, she found herself comparing him to Derek. Not just his body, in that Derek won hands down, but his attitude. For some reason, she didn't think Derek would pressure her so hard to give it up.

And then pout like a spoiled brat when she refused.

A tiny ribbon of anger swirled around her other emotions, overpowering passion and hunger and even her fear. "Who do you think you are, Trey? You can't just come into camp and expect me to have sex with you, especially after everything that's happened."

He sat up and brushed a hand over his face. "I didn't come here expecting to have sex." He let go of a deep gush of air. "I came to talk. Fine . . . yeah, I want sex, too. And I don't understand why you keep—"

"You want it enough that you'd break up with me and find someone who would give it to you?" Why she'd asked that she didn't know, because it had already happened.

He frowned.

"Did you sleep with her?" Kylie asked. In her heart she already knew the answer, but for some reason she needed it confirmed.

He didn't say a word. He didn't have to. The confirmation was all over his face.

"Did you tell her you loved her, too?" The thought stung like a paper cut right across the heart.

Even more guilt filled his eyes, and then he shook his head and fell face-first into denial. "No, I didn't sleep with her. And why would I tell her I love her, when I love you?"

Kylie didn't have Della's super lie-detecting skill, but she knew he'd just lied to her. Knew it with certainty and she wanted to throw something at him. "Don't lie, Derek."

"Derek?" He sat up in bed. "Who the hell is Derek?"

"Trey," she snapped.

"Who's Derek?" Trey asked again.

She shook her head. "It doesn't matter. We . . . you and I aren't together anymore."

"So you're together with him?"

She shook her head. Then, realizing what a mistake this had been, she faced the fact that this was partly her fault. "I'm sorry. I should have just told you no when you asked if I would see you. I can't see you now or next week."

He looked so hurt. Just as she'd known he'd been lying about sleeping with that girl, Kylie knew the hurt on his face was real. Trey did care about her. He'd just cared about having sex more.

"Are you seeing someone else? Is that who Derek is?" He

jumped off the bed and stopped right in front of her. "I know I screwed up, Kylie. But . . . please, give me another chance. I really miss you." He reached out to touch her.

She pushed his hand back. "I believe you miss me, Trey. I do. But I can't do this now."

"We don't have to have sex. We can just talk, okay? I'll wait until you're ready, I swear. Let me take you out for a pizza or something. I drove my dad's truck and—"

"I already ate dinner. Where did you park the truck?"

"At the front gate, but please . . ."

"I can't," she said.

"Don't tell me you don't care about me anymore. We dated for almost a year."

"I don't know what I feel." She reached back under her shirt and rehooked her bra. "I'm confused about everything right now . . . except that I know you hurt me, Trey. When school starts up, maybe we can . . . talk. But right now I have to get you out of this camp before something bad happens."

"Like what?" he asked. Something close to disgust crossed his face. "Is it true what they say about this place?"

"What who says?" she asked.

"My cousin and the other campers from last year. They say that all the kids who attend here are juvenile delinquents who were into really weird crap. Real freaks."

Only a few days ago, she would have totally agreed with him, but now . . . "Don't believe everything you hear." She reached down and found her phone on the bed. "Just trust me on this, okay? You've got to go." She gave him a nudge toward the door.

She took him through the woods, staying a few feet from the trail back to the dining hall. Once there, she peered around a tree to make sure the coast was clear. The muscles in her gut relaxed a little when no one was hanging outside. She hurried Trey past the entrance and breathed a sigh of relief when they moved behind the gate to his truck.

He looked down at her. "I do love you," he said.

She only nodded and motioned for him to go.

He reached out and she let him hug her. She even returned the embrace. Her emotions started zipping all over the place again. Deep down, she admitted that while she didn't think she'd ever forgive Trey for dumping her, a small part of her still cared about him. And who knew, maybe by the time school started up again, she'd feel differently. But as for now . . .

As he drove away, Kylie stayed in the parking lot until his taillights faded into the darkness. Standing there, she hated how alone she felt.

When she turned around, she realized she'd been wrong. She wasn't alone. Just friggin' great. Someone stood by the gate, watching her. Kylie couldn't make out who it was, but she prayed it wasn't Holiday or Sky. As she got closer, she recognized her lone watcher.

It wasn't Sky or Holiday.

It was worse.

Fredericka.

Determined not to show any fear, Kylie walked right past her. She got almost to the dining hall when the girl whizzed by and came to a sudden stop in front of Kylie.

She managed to stop right before slamming into the she-wolf.

"So, Ghost Girl had company, huh?" Fredericka said in a condescending voice. "What have you been doing? Screwing in your cabin?"

Kylie wondered if being turned into a werewolf explained the girl being such a bitch, or if she had always been this mean.

"If I was, at least I did it in a bed and not in the woods like some people I could mention."

Fredericka's eyes went from black to a deep burgundy in a nanosecond. Kylie wasn't up on werewolf color trivia, but she could guess that meant anger. That's when she realized that pissing the werewolf off probably hadn't been the best thing to do. Then again, Kylie also knew people like Fredericka preyed on the weak. She couldn't let the girl know how much she really frightened her.

The she-wolf growled. "Do Holiday and Sky know you've been entertaining guests? Maybe I should I fill them in?" Her voice seemed to vibrate from her solar plexus.

Right then, Kylie saw Holiday step outside the dining hall. As badly as she hated the idea of Holiday knowing Trey had been here, Kylie refused to let this B with an itch have something to hang over her head.

Kylie hot-footed it past the she-wolf and stopped in front of Holiday. "Hi. I just had a friend stop by uninvited. I realize it's against camp policy. I wasn't aware he was coming, so I escorted him out and it won't happen again."

Holiday frowned and it looked as if she was about to read

Kylie the riot act. Then her gaze shifted over Kylie's shoulder. When her focus returned to Kylie, the look of anger faded. "Thank you for telling me. Make sure it doesn't happen again. We only allow visitors on parents day. We can't have normals poking their noses around here uninvited."

Kylie nodded. "I understand." And then she took off to her cabin, praying Fredericka didn't follow.

By nine o'clock that night, Kylie had kept her promise to her mom and called her dad. It had been short, to the point, and hurt like a toothache. She didn't mention he hadn't come to see her before she'd been shipped off to the camp. She didn't mention that he hadn't come to get her at the police station, either.

And neither did he.

Basically, he told Kylie he loved her, he missed her, and he would see her Sunday on parents day at ten o'clock sharp. Oh, and he had to go, because he was out with a client.

Hanging up from the sixty-second call, Kylie remembered her mom always accusing her dad of putting his job before family. Kylie thought hell would be announcing a snow day before she agreed with anything her mom said. But right now, Kylie wondered how many inches they were predicting. Going into her bedroom, she dropped on the bed and hugged her musty-smelling pillow, but she didn't cry this time.

Maybe she was cried out, or just too angry at Fredericka. Maybe she was still in some kind of aftershock from her little make-out session with Trey—who she'd accidentally called Derek. Dang it, here she was afraid to like Derek, in case she only liked him because he looked like Trey. Now she was with Trey, and Derek came popping in her head. And don't forget the attraction/fear she held for a certain blue-eyed werewolf. Just how messed up could she possibly get?

Kylie heard the door to the cabin open and slam shut. She had her feet on the floor to go greet Della and Miranda when she heard the tone of the words being slung back and forth between her roommates.

"I called the computer first," Miranda yelled.

"I beat your little witch butt fair and square," Della responded.

"Listen here, you good-for-nothing vamp!"

Kylie stormed into the room. Della sat at the computer, her canines showing and growling. Miranda stood, chin held high, with her pinky finger held out in the air wiggling while her voice spewed something about zits.

"Stop it! I'm sick of this," Kylie yelled. "Can't you two fight like normal people?"

Miranda shot her gaze to Kylie. "Why would we fight like normals?"

"We're not normals," Della retorted. "Neither are you, and the sooner you accept that, the better off you'll be."

"You don't know that," Kylie snapped. "Fine, you two go ahead and kill each other. Just don't leave a mess, because I don't want to get stuck cleaning up any body parts." She swung around to go back to the bedroom when she recalled the reason she'd come out in the first place. She did another about-face. "By the way, if you hear me screaming bloody murder in the middle of the night, don't worry, I'm just having a night terror." She started back to her room.

Della called out. "Stop right there, Miss Smarty Pants! Don't you think for one minute that you're going to go into that bedroom without explaining first?"

Kylie swung back around. "I did explain it. They are just bad dreams."

"Not that. I mean the hot guy sneaking into the camp looking for you. Or did you forget about the little present I delivered earlier?"

Kylie wished she could forget. Seeing the questions in both her roommates' eyes, and knowing that Della could have gotten in a lot of trouble for delivering Trey, Kylie figured they both deserved something. She went to the kitchen table and dropped in a chair. "His name is Trey and he's old news."

"How hot was he?" Miranda asked, and sat beside Kylie.

"On a scale of one to ten, he was an eight," Della answered Miranda, and then looked back at Kylie. "Why is he old news?" She moved away from the computer and dropped in a chair across from them.

"Because he left me for some slut who would put out, that's why."

"Jerk," Miranda said.

"That piece of human shit," Della piped in. "You should have told me, I'd have roughed him up a bit."

Silence fell and the three of them sat there looking at each other. Miranda stretched her hands out on the table. "So if he left you for someone who would . . . put out, does that mean that you've never . . . you know?"

"*You know* what?" Della snapped. "What are you asking her?"

"I want to know if she's done it," Miranda said. "Are you a virgin, Kylie?"

Chapter Twenty-seven

Kylie looked at her new friends and wondered if she should share something so personal. While still a little perturbed at their "normal" remark, she felt a bond with these two. A bond she'd shared only with Sara.

"Yes, I mean, no. I haven't ever done . . . you know. Guess that means I'm not only a freak, but a virgin freak." Kylie stared at her hands a minute and then added, "It just never felt right, okay?"

Miranda leaned forward. "Don't be hard on yourself. I haven't gotten there, either. Hey, don't get me wrong. I came close, but as my uncle would say, this isn't horseshoes, right?"

Both Kylie and Miranda turned to Della, who looked paler than usual.

Miranda slapped her palm on the table. "Spill it, Vamp. We did."

Kylie gave Miranda a light nudge with her elbow. "Della doesn't have to spill anything if she doesn't want to." Kylie leaned back in her chair and decided a change of subject was needed. "Fredericka caught me saying good-bye to Trey."

"Oh, crap," Della said, some of her color returning. "What did she do?"

"She basically threatened to tattle on me, and then Holiday stepped out of the dining hall right then."

"Did she tell her?" Della asked.

"No, I decided to do it myself and not give that bitch the pleasure."

"What?" Miranda asked. "You told Holiday you brought a normal into camp without permission? Did Holiday come unglued?"

"No. She told me not to do it again," Kylie said.

Della cleared her throat. "Did you tell her I was the one who brought him to your cabin?"

Kylie rolled her eyes in grand Sara fashion. "I wouldn't do that, Della." She stood to go check her e-mail on some off chance that her mom had answered her.

"You know what I heard?" Miranda leaned in as if she had a piece of juicy gossip to share. "I heard Fredericka's parents were rogue. Someone had to do some serious arm pulling to get her in here."

"What do you mean by rogue?" Kylie asked, remembering Burnett of the FRU suggesting her parents could be rogue, as well.

"People who refused to adhere to the rules. For werewolves, it mostly means they hunted food that wasn't on the approved list."

"By . . . not on the approved list, do you mean like . . . humans?" Kylie asked, getting a chill.

"Or other supernaturals and livestock. Even pets."

Kylie's mind shot straight to Lucas Parker and his parents. Was that why Lucas and Fredericka were buddies? Because their parents were rogue werewolves?

Della stood and went to the fridge. "Want something to drink?" She glanced back.

"A Diet Coke, please," Kylie said.

"Miranda?" Della asked.

"Diet Coke sounds good."

Kylie stared at the "No new mail" message. "I asked my mom what time she and my dad were born."

"And?" Della set a soda beside the computer.

Kylie picked up her Diet Coke and went back to the table. "Mom couldn't remember, so she said she'd check the birth certificates. She's supposed to e-mail me. When she gets around to it." Kylie dropped back into a chair. "Knowing her, that could be next year sometime."

"Yeah, that's like when they say 'maybe' and they really mean 'no.'" Miranda moved to the desk to check her own e-mail.

Della dropped back in her chair, popped the top of the soda, and took a long sip.

"You can have soda?" Kylie asked.

"Yeah." She frowned. "Why?"

Kylie shrugged. "I don't know. I mean, I saw you eating pepperoni, but I thought vampires could only drink . . . you know."

"Blood?" Della finished, sounding annoyed that Kylie couldn't say it.

"Yeah. Blood." She pushed the word out of her mouth and tried not to turn green.

"No, I can have other stuff. It doesn't supply my body

nourishment and nothing tastes as good as it used to taste. Oh, and some things have really bad effects on me. Like broccoli."

"What happens if you eat broccoli?" Kylie asked.

"Explosive, really bad gas."

Kylie made a face. "I think that happens to everyone."

"Nope." Miranda looked over her shoulder. "She's right. Nothing is worse than a vampire fart. Except . . ." She looked at the screen and started typing. "Except a witch's fart after she eats a bean burrito."

They all laughed. When the moment passed, silence rained down on them again. Della turned her soda can in her hands. "I did it."

"Gross, you farted?" Miranda covered her nose.

"No," Della said. "I had sex."

There was like this reverent pause.

"And?" Miranda finally asked, and turned in the chair.

"It was nice. Really nice. Lee and I had been dating for a year. I loved him. It felt right." Tears filled Della's eyes, but even without them, the pain rang in her voice. "But then I turned into a vampire."

"He couldn't accept you?" Kylie's chest ached for Della, and she remembered how hurt she'd been when Trey dumped her.

Della wiped her eyes. "I didn't actually tell him. I was going to, but . . ." She bit down on her lip. "I went to see him after I was turned, and when he kissed me, he pulled away. He said I was cold and that I must still be sick and he . . . didn't want to kiss me until . . . until I felt warm again."

"What a jerk," Miranda said.

Della inhaled. "How do you tell the guy you love that you'll never be warm again?" Della's chin trembled.

Kylie rested her hand on Della's. "Maybe you should have tried to tell him. Maybe he could have understood if he knew—"

"No." Della shook her head and her sleek black hair moved in a wave around her face. "I don't think so. He's a wonderful guy, but he's so straight-and-narrow second-generation Chinese—like his family and my dad's family. He almost broke up with me when he realized my mom was Euro-American."

"He doesn't sound so wonderful," Kylie said.

Della shook her head again. "It's not all his fault. It's his upbringing. We're raised to believe we're supposed to be perfect. Make the best grades, go to the best schools, get the best jobs. We're not . . ." She bit down on her lip. "We're not supposed to be monsters."

"You're not a monster," Kylie snapped, appalled that Della would say that. And yet deep down, hadn't Kylie considered Della that in the beginning? And even worse, wasn't Kylie afraid she might learn she was a freak of nature herself?

"She's right," Miranda said.

Kylie gave Della's cold hand a gentle squeeze. "If he doesn't love you, then you'll find someone else who will. You're young. You're beautiful. You've got the rest of your life ahead of you." The question formed in Kylie's head and before she could stop it, it spilled out. "Are you immortal? Or are you already . . ."

"Dead?" Della finished for her.

Kylie flushed with embarrassment. "Oh gosh, I'm so sorry. That was so rude. I'm trying to make you feel better and I . . . It just slipped out."

"It's fine," Della assured her. "I'm not dead. Vampires' bodies function differently, that's all. Don't believe everything you read in those teen novels. We're not immortal; we only live to about 150."

"That's a pretty good deal." Kylie looked over at Miranda. "How about witches?"

"Life expectancy is about the same," Miranda said, never looking away from the computer.

"And other supernaturals?" Kylie wondered if she discovered she too was a supernatural, if she'd have an expanded life expectancy.

"Fairies live the longest." Miranda talked while she typed something into the computer. "I think there's one old dude that's like five hundred or so."

"Are you hoping you're fairy, now?" Della asked.

Kylie put her right elbow on the table and dropped her chin in it. "No. Oh, hell, I don't know," she muttered, letting go of a pent-up sigh. "This just sucks. Why can't my mom just answer me for once in her life? I hate not knowing anything."

Kylie looked back at Miranda. "Can't you help me out?"

"How?" Miranda asked, her concentration still on her e-mail.

"You are brave," Della giggled, understanding what Kylie meant. "Don't you remember she screws up her spells?"

"A gift for you." Miranda shot Della a one-finger salute over her shoulder.

Della laughed harder. "At least it's not your pinky."

Kylie ignored Della and their gestures. "Can't you do a spell that makes my mom find the birth certificates and e-mail me the info? Seriously, if you can make a peanut butter and jelly sandwich appear from nowhere, why can't you do this?"

"Well . . ." Miranda continued to stare at the computer. "I tell you what. Touch your nose three times and say Miranda is a goddess."

Kylie stared at the back of Miranda's head. "Are you serious?"

"Serious." Miranda turned around and she didn't appear to be joking. "Come on, touch your nose three times and say Miranda is a goddess."

"And you won't turn my mom into a toad?" Kylie held her left index finger in front of her nose.

"I wouldn't do that if I were you," Della warned.

Miranda scowled at Della. "I pinky promise not to mess up." She held out her pinky.

"And if I do this, I'll get my mom's e-mail?" Kylie couldn't believe she was considering this, but . . .

"Yup." Miranda grinned. "Or you could just come check the computer. Because you just got an e-mail from her."

Kylie jumped up and literally pushed Miranda out of the chair. Holding her breath, Kylie reached for the mouse. She could be one click away from knowing for sure that she was a supernatural.

One click. God, she was so scared.

Chapter Twenty-eight

"Open it already," Della shouted from behind Kylie.

Kylie looked over her shoulder, from Della to her right to Miranda on her left. Taking a deep breath, Kylie looked back at the e-mail and clicked open.

> Hey hon, I was wrong. I wasn't born at eleven o'clock, it was ten p.m. Ten twenty-three to be exact. Your dad was born at nine forty-six a.m. Did you call your . . .

Kylie stopped reading. Neither of her parents was born at midnight. Emotion did cartwheels inside her chest. Heavy emotion. Was this relief? It should be relief.

It meant she wasn't a supernatural.

"See, I told you guys. I'm not one of you." Her chest clutched with a heavy emotion that didn't feel like relief. She didn't want to be one of them, did she? Or maybe what she felt was just disappointment for not fitting in. Again. Wasn't that the story of her life?

Deep down, you've always known you were different. Holiday's words played in Kylie's head. And for the first time, she admitted to herself that Holiday was right. Kylie had always felt different. Always felt like the outsider. But she wasn't . . . different. Well, she might be different.

She just wasn't a supernatural.

This was the proof.

"I don't believe it." Della spoke up first.

Then Miranda piped in. "Holiday mentioned it does skip generations."

"Only in rare situations," Kylie said.

"Maybe your mom's lying," Della added.

Kylie looked back at the vampire. "Why would she lie?"

Della shrugged. "Maybe she's just in a pissy mood because she's getting a divorce. I don't know."

"Your parents are getting a divorce?" Miranda asked.

"Yeah," Kylie said, not even the tiniest bit upset at Della for mentioning it. She may have only known them for a few days but she trusted these two.

"Sucky." Miranda pressed a hand on Kylie's shoulder and squeezed.

"Yeah." Kylie stared back at the e-mail.

"Why are they divorcing?" Miranda asked.

"I don't know. Mom's so . . ."

"Bitchy." Della tossed out the word.

Kylie almost nodded, then stopped. "No. She's not really a bitch, she's just . . . cold, distant. About as warm as a popsicle. I actually heard my dad tell her that a while back."

"So your dad's having an affair," Della said matter-of-factly.

Kylie turned in her chair and stared at Della. "No."

Della made a face. "Believe me, if he accused your mom of being a popsicle, he's found some young 'warm' thing to screw."

"He's not like that," Kylie said with conviction. Right then she realized what she said about her mom being cold.

"And by cold, I meant . . . emotionally, not—"

"I know," Della said. "Don't go thinking you've got to tiptoe around my feelings." But her eyes said differently.

Kylie knew all about pretending to be tough. She'd had a crash course in it these last few weeks.

Kylie looked back at the screen. "Mom, she's just . . . hard to live with sometimes. I don't blame my dad for leaving her."

"So are you going to live with your dad?" Miranda asked.

The question took Kylie back to the day she'd stood in the driveway, begging her dad to take her with him. As much as it hurt to remember, she had to accept the truth—that day, it felt as though when he decided to leave her mom, he'd also decided to leave her.

"It's late and I'm tired." Kylie got up and went to the bedroom and unlike earlier, this time she was able to cry.

The next morning Kylie marched into her meeting with Holiday and placed a copy of her mother's e-mail on the table in front of the camp leader.

"See, I told you so," Kylie said. "Now maybe you can just call my shrink and have her tell my mom to bring me home."

The idea of going back home wasn't nearly as life-altering as it had felt a few days ago. There was even a part of her that didn't want to go—but considering she wasn't supernatural, she really didn't belong here, either.

"What's this?" Holiday glanced back at the note, and her eyes widened when she read it. Looking up, she met Kylie's gaze. "Okay, I admit I'm surprised, but it doesn't really change the facts."

"Why not? You told me that only in very rare circumstances would it skip a generation."

"What about the fact that you see ghosts? That you were born at midnight? Or that your brain doesn't read like a human?"

Kylie dropped into the chair across from Holiday. "I could be crazy. Or like you said the other day, just a freak of human nature and dealing with a super-charged ghost."

Holiday nodded and then leaned forward. "Or . . . maybe the people you think are your parents aren't really your parents."

Kylie's mouth dropped open. "Believe me, with the crap that is going on at home right now, I'd love to believe I was adopted, but I've seen pictures of my mom pregnant."

Holiday opened her mouth as if to argue and then shook her head. "Like I said earlier, this is your quest."

"*Was* my quest. I completed it. I found the answer. I'm just a human."

Holiday propped her right elbow on the table and rested her chin in her open palm. Kylie had begun to think of it as the camp leader's trademark mannerism because she always seemed to do it when she was launching into one of her "Is this how you really feel?" speeches.

It reminded her of her shrink, Ms. Day, who did pretty

much the same except hers was to lean back in her chair and nod.

The worst part was that tactic always worked on Kylie, too.

"Are you really sure of that?" Holiday asked. "Do you really want to leave Shadow Falls Camp?"

"Yes. No. I don't know." Kylie dropped her face into her hands for a second. "I mean . . . right now, everyone is with their own kind. Miranda's with the witches, Della's with the vampires. And I'm . . . well, I'm here with you because I don't belong." Kylie felt like a total outsider—a misfit.

"Is anyone making you feel unwelcome?" Holiday asked.

"It's not that," Kylie said.

Holiday let out a deep breath. "I saw Fredericka last night. If there's a problem—"

"No problem," Kylie said, not wanting the she-wolf to think Kylie had tattled. "This has nothing to do with her." And that much of it was completely true.

Holiday looked back at the paper. "Look, I'll make you a deal. Give me . . . no, give yourself two weeks to think this over, Kylie. If you still want to leave then, I'll personally talk to your mother."

Maybe because deep down Kylie wasn't looking forward to going back home to her mom—or, more likely, because she knew she'd miss Miranda and Della—she decided two weeks wasn't such a big deal.

"You got it," Kylie said.

"Great." Holiday stood up. "And since I may only have two weeks, I think it's time we get serious."

"Serious about what?" Kylie asked as Holiday pulled two yoga mats from the closet.

"Ghosts." Holiday spread out the mats on the floor and then motioned Kylie to sit down. "You have to learn to deal with your ghosts, Kylie."

"I just have one," Kylie said.

Holiday arched a brow. "It starts with one. But believe me when I say others will come. As a matter of fact, they already have come. You just don't remember."

Kylie's stomach began to twist into a knot. "What are you talking about?"

"I read in your files that you've been having night terrors."

Holiday's words sank in. "You're telling me that the night terrors are . . . ghosts?"

Holiday nodded. "Right now, they are coming to you when you're asleep. But eventually, if it happens with you the way it did with me, they'll start appearing when you're standing in line at the movie theater, sitting in a classroom, even out on a date."

Kylie recalled the nights she'd awakened feeling completely terrified, but clueless as to what had caused it. Chills crawled up her spine. "I just want to learn how to turn them off."

A frown appeared on Holiday's face. "That's your choice. But let me put it to you like this. To reach the cut-off switch, you have to pass through a place where spirits like to hang out."

"Is it like a one-time-only switch? Once I cut it off, I won't be bothered again?"

Holiday shrugged. "That depends."

"On what?"

"On how badly a spirit wants to talk to you." Holiday sat down on the mat. "Have you ever done any form of meditation?"

Kylie shook her head.

"Have you heard about out-of-body experiences?"

"No." And she preferred to stay in her body, thank you very much. "So are you saying ghosts can just keep turning my switch back on even if I don't want them to?"

"A powerful one can." Holiday motioned for Kylie to sit on the mat. "Or you can just hear them out and see what they want. The latter works best for me. Now, let's practice some meditation techniques."

The next four days passed in a blur. Kylie tried to talk Della and Miranda into taking a hike to the falls, but neither of them wanted any part of it. It appeared that if Kylie wanted to see the falls, she was going to have to go by herself. There was only one little problem—the thought of facing dancing death angels by herself scared the crap out of her. So she decided to stop fixating over seeing the waterfalls. It wasn't as if she didn't have other things to fixate about. Things like Della and Miranda's persistent bickering. They continued to fight at least once a day. And Kylie continued to break them up before one of them murdered the other.

Kylie spoke with her mom every morning and night, too. When Kylie didn't call her, her mom took it upon herself to call Kylie. The fact that her mom did call made Kylie more aware that her daddy didn't. She told herself it was simply a male thing, that most men didn't call unless they had something to say.

Besides, she'd see him Sunday, which was tomorrow. A fact her mother had been a tad upset about. But please, her mom had been the one who told her to ask if he was coming.

And Kylie was glad she had. She really wanted—needed—to see her dad. And for some reason, probably because she missed him so much, the closer Sunday came, the closer Kylie was to forgiving her dad. Hopefully, by tomorrow her dad would have missed her enough that he would agree to let Kylie live with him when her two weeks were done at camp.

Kylie ate up about sixty minutes talking and texting Sara, who amazingly had completely recovered from her pregnancy scare and was now back in full swing with her new boyfriend—a nineteen-year-old cousin of one of her neighbors.

If Kylie read Sara's innuendos correctly, the two of them would be having sex in the near future. Kylie had come so close to reminding her friend what she'd just gone through, but at the last minute, she lost her nerve. That or she simply decided that saying it would accomplish nothing other than to push her best friend further away.

Sara never excelled at taking advice.

Trey had called twice with the same song and dance. He loved her, he was sorry. If she'd just give him a chance he'd prove how much he loved her.

Kylie suspected his "proof" would include their getting naked. And the more she thought about it, the more inclined she was to keep her clothes on. She'd even asked Trey if he could just be her friend for the summer. But then he'd freaked out when she'd said another boy's name. What would he do if she decided to move on and go out with someone else? Go off the deep end, she suspected.

Why couldn't Trey be more like Derek? She'd asked the half Fae to be her friend, and other than telling her he had wanted her to kiss him, he had stopped coming on to her.

Oh, he was nice. Always spoke to her, even asked about her problems with her parents. They also talked about Holiday's resentment at both of them for wanting to turn off their gifts. Most days, he would even come and sit with her for at least one of their meals. Nevertheless, everything about his behavior spoke only of friendship.

No more hot lingering gazes up close where she could see the flecks of gold in his eyes.

No more special smiles.

No more feeling his breath on her cheek.

No more touching.

Even when he sat beside her, he always seemed to make sure there was a good six inches of space between them.

The fact that she'd see him sitting shoulder to shoulder with other girls stung like a fire ant.

She ignored the sting and told herself it was for the best. She was leaving in a little more than a week. And face it, the best things weren't always fun.

For example, learning how to meditate, trying to get to the off switch to cut off the ghosts, was turning into an all-time dreaded chore. Holiday had her hitting the mat three times a day. They'd tried burning incense, counting, music, and even visualization, but nothing seemed to help. Kylie's mind refused to find an altered state of any kind.

Holiday stayed forever hopeful, Kylie not so much. "It will happen, I promise," Holiday would say after each failed session.

For Kylie, it was just more proof that she wasn't one of them. Not that she really needed more proof, but still . . .

The only thing that left the slightest bit of a question in her mind was that Soldier Dude wouldn't quit showing up. Kylie told Holiday to send him a message to quit wasting her time. Holiday gave Kylie the pat answer of, "It doesn't work like that."

Kylie had learned to hate that saying.

Almost as much as she hated the daily visits with the ghost. Thankfully, he hadn't gone spastic on her with the blood games again, but just seeing him was starting to give her the heebie jeebies. The way he looked at her, the way he stood, it was eerily familiar. Kylie convinced herself that Holiday had been right. Her night terrors had probably been filled with images of him, hence the reason seeing him gave her an odd sense of déjà vu.

Holiday had even suggested Kylie try talking to him, but that idea totally creeped Kylie out. She got this mental image of him opening his mouth only to have worms or blood ooze out. Nope, she'd keep her mouth closed and pray he did the same.

Thankfully, the last few days she'd pretty much managed to stay out of Lucas's and Fredericka's way. But every morning when she waited to see who drew her name in the Meet Your Campmates Hour, Kylie would hyperventilate, worrying one of them would get it.

And today was no different. If they did draw her name, Kylie had already decided to fake a bad headache and beg off.

Sure, Fredericka would probably accuse Kylie of being afraid of her. But best to have her accuse Kylie of it than to have her know it for certain. And if Kylie had to spend an hour alone with the she-wolf, Fredericka would for sure smell Kylie's fear.

Kylie stood between Miranda and Della watching as the campers drew names and announced their companions.

Kylie knew Miranda was praying that Chris, a really cute vampire, would draw her name. Della never seemed to care who got her name, but yesterday Kylie had seen the way the sneaky vampire kept eyeing Steve, one of the shape-shifters.

When Kylie asked Della about it, she denied it, but Kylie noticed Della's cheeks had actually gotten a little color in them. Who knew a vampire could blush?

Derek walked up beside Kylie. "Hey." She smiled. And yeah, maybe her smile was a little wider than normal.

"Hi," he said rather matter-of-factly, and then focused on the campers drawing names. With his attention not on her, Kylie let her gaze move over him. He wore a light green T-shirt that fit tight across his chest. Kylie remembered resting her head against him. She recalled with clarity how good it had felt, and how when she looked up, his lips had been so close to hers.

Blinking, trying not to let her mind go there, she shifted her gaze away from his chest. He wore khaki shorts that hit almost to the knee. His legs were a bit hairy but not at all skinny. She was moving her gaze up when she noticed the Band-Aid on the middle of his elbow joint.

She reached over and pulled his arm closer. "Is this . . . is that . . . You gave the blood?"

"Yeah." His eyes met hers and for the first time in days he

didn't instantly look away. They were having one of those moments that she'd missed.

She gently ran her finger over the Band-Aid. "I'm sorry."

"For what? You didn't do anything."

"Did it hurt?" she asked.

"No." He continued to gaze down at her and it felt like there was no one else in the world but them. She saw the gold flecks sparkle and darn if she didn't want to lean even closer.

"Derek!" a very hyper voice called out. "I got your name!"

Suddenly, Derek was yanked away. Kylie looked up and focused on the yanker—Mandy, a cute brunette fairy.

Kylie watched the girl wrap her arms around Derek's neck and pull him down for a fast kiss. At first, Kylie waited for Derek to look shocked at the girl's show of affection. Instead, he glanced at Kylie for a mere second and then refocused on Mandy, who then stepped up on her tiptoes and kissed the boy again.

And Derek didn't look surprised at all. He looked . . . he looked happy. Then he smiled at Mandy—the same "special" smile he shared with Kylie.

"Great. Are you ready?" Derek asked the too perky brunette.

"Tell me again where this spot is?" Mandy asked.

"How about I just show you instead," Derek answered.

Was he taking her to the creek? Kylie's chest grew heavy. At first, she didn't recognize the emotion and then she remembered feeling it when she saw Trey with his girlfriend at the party. Thankfully, she managed to stomp it down before Derek turned back around.

His soft green eyes met hers. "See you later. Okay?"

"Yeah." She forced a smile on her face that felt about as real as a smiley face. She and Derek were just friends; she had no right to be jealous. And yet . . . why did it hurt so much?

She bit down on her lip. See, this was why she didn't want to start having those feelings for Derek. Because it hurt. Then as if she wanted to punish herself even more, she turned and saw the two of them holding hands and walking away.

"Oh, crappers," Miranda snapped. Kylie turned to look at her, realizing she'd almost forgotten her roommates were even there. Well, Miranda was still there. Della had already left.

"What?" Kylie asked. "Who got your name?"

Miranda made a face. "Not me. *You.*" She gave Kylie an elbow in her ribs. "Or are you telling me you didn't hear who just got your name?"

Chapter Twenty-nine

Kylie swung around and touched her temple, thinking she might as well start faking the headache right now. "Who?"

"Me," came a familiar male voice beside her.

Kylie turned around and faced Perry and then removed her finger. Perry was *not* worth faking it.

"Promise you won't touch my ears," he said, but in his eyes she saw his apology.

"Fine, but don't go turning yourself into anything. It freaks me out."

"You're no fun," he answered, but Kylie noticed he stared mostly at Miranda.

"Yes," muttered Miranda, glancing back at Kylie. "Chris got my name. Wish me luck," she said, and then reached up and let her hair down.

"Good luck," Kylie said, and noticed the frown on Perry's face.

"So where do you want to go to talk?" Perry asked, his gaze

latched on Miranda and Chris as they walked away. Kylie had never seen such a sad-eyed shape-shifter.

"I don't care where we . . ." The idea hit with the subtleness of a dump truck. It was wrong. Oh, so wrong, but she couldn't help herself. "I know just the place by a creek bed."

The next day Kylie stood in the dining room at ten o'clock sharp, waiting on her dad. She had her spiel practiced, knew exactly how she was going to approach the subject of her moving in with him. And it was so much easier that she'd thought it would be.

Last night, her mom had announced that she'd been given a promotion, but it would require some travel. Hence, it simply made sense that Kylie would stay with her dad. Not that she'd told her mom. Nope, that could wait until later.

Derek walked through the dining hall doors. When he spotted her, he came over. Kylie felt her face flush remembering how she'd taken Perry to the rock expecting to find Derek and Mandy there, doing God only knew what. But nope, Derek hadn't been there. So Kylie had simply walked past the big rock and taken Perry into the woods another half mile before they stopped to visit.

Plain and simple, she hadn't wanted to taint the memories of where Derek and she had really gotten to know each other.

And while she'd felt loads better knowing he hadn't taken Mandy to their special place, Kylie wasn't stupid enough to think that it didn't mean he'd taken Mandy somewhere else to do . . . God only knew what. Nor was she stupid enough to blame him for it. How could she when Kylie herself had been the one who'd asked to be just friends? And yet . . .

"You're here early." Derek offered her a friendly smile.

Kylie couldn't help but wonder what kind of a smile he'd offered Mandy when they'd been alone. Had he kissed her? Had he ever taken her to the rock? "Dad said he'd be here ten o'clock sharp."

"So is your mom going to come later?" he asked.

"No," Kylie said. "Mom doesn't want to chance running into him. The world would end if they had to see each other."

"Sorry about that. That has to be tough." He said it with such concern that her heart dipped a bit. All last night she'd watched him and Mandy laughing, sitting shoulder to shoulder. She ached to go back in time and stop herself from telling him she just wanted to be friends. Then again, considering she was probably going home soon, maybe it was best.

"Is your mom coming?" Kylie asked, liking that he'd trusted her enough to tell her his past. *Had he told Mandy anything?*

"Afraid so," he said. "She's a tad overprotective. Has been since . . ."

"Your dad left?" Kylie asked, and lowered her voice.

He nodded and right then, the front doors opened and in came several sets of parents, along with some more campers.

"There she is," Derek said. "I'd better go."

"Good luck," Kylie said, and unable to stop herself she reached over and gave his hand a squeeze. Touching him felt right and . . . wrong. The tingles traveling up her arm were not those that should come from a friend. He stopped moving away and stared at her.

His smile seemed extra warm. "You, too."

Kylie watched him go and admitted that she was going to miss him. Heck, she was going to miss Miranda and Della, too. She wouldn't miss their bickering, but she'd miss them.

Shaking herself out of the melancholy, she tried to find her dad in another group of parents as they flooded in.

Kylie didn't see him, but she did see a set of parents that had to be Della's. A Euro-American woman stood with an Asian American man, scanning the crowd. Knowing that Della hadn't expected them for another hour and had stayed at the cabin, Kylie walked up to the couple.

"Hi, I'm Kylie. Are you Della's mom and dad?"

"Yes, where is she?" the woman asked.

"She wasn't expecting y'all so early. If you like, I can get someone to run to the cabin."

"Is she still in bed?" the dad asked. "My God, I thought this camp was supposed to straighten her out." He looked at his wife. "I'm going to ask for the results of the drug tests. If they don't have them, I'm taking her out of here and placing her in a better facility."

Kylie tried not to react to the harshness of the man's tone. But on the inside, she gave thanks for her dad. So what if he hadn't shown up at the police station, and maybe he should have come to see her before she was packed off to camp, but without a doubt, Kylie felt certain he was loads better than Della's grumpy dad.

"Oh, she's awake," Kylie said, knowing it was probably a lie, but wanting to protect Della from his demeanor.

Giving the room another check for her dad, she said, "I'll tell you what, I'll run and get her."

She walked slowly to the door and took off in a dead run to get Della up and dressed.

An hour later, Kylie sat at the back of the dining hall watching everyone else visit. She'd gotten Della up and to the dining hall in record time. And on the way Kylie had stopped in the office to see Holiday and warn her about Della's father wanting to see drug tests.

Kylie gazed at Della now, sitting and chatting with her sister, while her parents sat stiffly listening in. From the distance, the visit didn't appear to be going well. Della had been tied in knots about seeing them, and after hearing her father's temper, Kylie couldn't say she blamed her.

Miranda's mom and dad showed up about twenty minutes after Della's. Kylie had never seen Miranda appear so insecure as she did around her parents. She sat with her shoulders slumped over and not smiling. Miranda always smiled and her posture wasn't that of the browbeaten child, but that's how she appeared in their presence. Kylie wanted to march over and tell both Miranda's and Della's parents how happy she was to have them as roommates, but for some reason, it seemed hokey.

Derek and his mom had gotten up to go take a walk. He'd actually brought his mom over to meet her. Kylie had to bite back a laugh when his mom brushed a strand of his hair off his brow and Derek blushed. Guys never liked it when their moms made a fuss over them.

"Hey." Holiday came over to where Kylie sat. "Your dad's not here yet?"

"Not yet. He probably misjudged how long it takes to get here. Mom always was the one who figured out the maps and such. And you know men, they'll drive for hours before they stop and ask for directions."

Kylie knew she was close to babbling but she couldn't help it. Babbling was better than thinking about the possibility her dad simply wasn't going to come.

Holiday grinned. "Men. We can't live with them. And it's no fun living without them."

"Do you have . . . someone?" Kylie asked, even though she didn't know if it was too personal of a question to ask her camp leader. "I don't see a ring or anything."

Holiday shrugged. "Well, sometimes no fun is better than putting up with them."

"So you're divorced?" Kylie asked.

"No, we never made it to the altar. I had the ring, had the date, and even the wedding dress. An hour before the wedding, I realized I didn't have my fiancé."

"That must have sucked," Kylie said.

"Yeah, it did."

"Did he ever tell you why?" Kylie asked.

"He said he met someone more compatible. Another vampire."

"Oh goodness, it's not Burnett, is it?"

Holiday's eyes widened. "No. Why would you think . . ."

"He likes you," Kylie blurted out. "Everything time you aren't looking, he's looking at you."

"Please, that man's so arrogant, I'd never . . ."

"He's good-looking," Kylie said.

"I know, damn it." Holiday sighed. "I hate him for it, too."

They both laughed.

Holiday looked over at Della and her family. "Thanks for giving me the heads-up. Her father is a real handful."

"I know," Kylie said. "It made me realize how lucky I am. Wait till you meet my dad. He's not like that."

"I'm looking forward to it," Holiday said.

Kylie knew Holiday was hoping she could take a look at her dad and pronounce him supernatural. Not that Kylie believed it. Her dad wasn't gifted. Well, he was, but not that kind of gifted.

Kylie sighed and looked up at the door and wished he'd hurry up. She needed one of his hugs in the worst way.

Her gaze shifted back to Della and she wondered if her dad ever hugged her. "Do you think Della should go live with other vampires?" Kylie asked Holiday.

Holiday sighed. "It's really hard for a new vampire to coexist with normals. Especially if they live with someone who is controlling. But Della really cares about her family, and leaving them is going to be tough, too. I'm afraid either path she chooses is going to be really hard."

"I hate that," Kylie said, her heart hurting for her friend.

Right then the doors opened. Kylie held her breath waiting to see if it was her dad. Instead, in came Lucas Parker with an older woman. Kylie watched how Lucas caringly held the woman's arm. "Who is that?" Kylie asked.

Holiday looked up. "Lucas's grandmother."

Kylie hadn't considered the probability of running into

Lucas's parents. The last thing she wanted was for them to recognize her—especially since it was obvious that Lucas didn't. "His parents aren't coming, then?"

"Afraid not. His parents were killed right after he was born. His grandmother raised him."

"Not right after he was born," Kylie said, not thinking before she spoke.

"Yeah, it's terrible." Holiday said, misunderstanding Kylie's comment as heartfelt disbelief instead of an announcement of a fact. "I think the files state he was only a week or two old when it happened."

"Oh." Kylie looked away. Then she remembered what Miranda had said about kids born to rogues. Had Lucas lied about his parents because otherwise he'd have been judged? And was the saying true that if one was born rogue, they died rogue?

"Not again," Holiday said.

Kylie looked up and saw Burnett James walking into the room. He wore a huge frown on his face and she didn't have to be supernatural to know something was very wrong.

Holiday pulled out her phone and dialed a number. She frowned and then dropped it in her pocket. "Why is it half the time when he shows up, Sky manages to be unavailable and I have to deal with him by myself?"

Kylie didn't think Holiday was expecting an answer so she just shrugged and didn't say anything.

"Excuse me," Holiday said. "Looks as if I have another battle to win."

Seconds later, Kylie watched Holiday and Burnett walk out

of the room together. Checking her watch, Kylie considered giving her dad a call and making sure he hadn't had a flat tire or something. Of course, she knew her dad was completely capable of changing a tire, because he spent hours teaching Kylie how to do it.

My girl is never going to be stranded. Kylie smiled, remembering how they'd held a timed tire-changing contest. As the good memories played in her head, she decided she had to forgive him for his recent indiscretions. He'd been too good of a dad to hold a few slip-ups against him. She smiled again, knowing her father would totally agree that she should stay with him if her mom was going to be traveling.

Nevertheless, Kylie wasn't smiling an hour later when he still hadn't showed. With crazy thoughts like car accidents running though her head, she pulled out her phone and dialed his number.

He answered on the third ring. "Hello, Pumpkin," he said.

Her chest eased just hearing his voice. "Hi, Dad? How close are you?"

"How close am I to what?"

Kylie's throat tightened. She recalled his words. *I'll be there at ten o'clock sharp.* "Didn't you remember?"

"Remember what?"

The knot in her throat started crowding her tonsils and her sinuses stung. "It's parents day at the camp. You said . . ." She bit down on her lip and prayed he'd laugh and tell her he was right around the corner.

Only he didn't.

"Damn." She heard him inhale. "Honey, I can't come up there today. I'm up to my eyebrows in paperwork from the office. It's been a crazy week."

"But you said . . ." Kylie jumped up and started walking through the dining room before she completely lost it and broke down in the middle of a room filled with parents.

"I said what?" he asked.

"I gotta go." Kylie closed her phone and shot through the doors seeking a place to be alone. Only she wasn't alone. She felt the cold presence following her all the way to the cabin. Anger and hurt filled her chest so full, Kylie could hardly breathe. Hand on the doorknob, she paused. The cold seemed to press against her back, so she peered over her shoulder.

Not only was he there, but like her, he was crying. Only the tears rolling down his face were the color of blood.

Fear tried to find room in her chest, but her anger knocked it out of the way. "Go away!" she yelled at the ghost. "Leave! Me! Alone!"

Chapter Thirty

The next morning Kylie stepped out of her bedroom and was shocked to find Della typing at the computer. Della was never here in the mornings.

"You didn't have an early morning thing to attend?" Kylie asked.

"Not really," Della said. Her mood came off as somber. Actually, all three of them had been pretty somber since yesterday. They hadn't even participated in their usual before-bedtime-chat at the kitchen table. No doubt, after parents day, they all had demons to deal with, and demon-dealing was usually best done solo. Not that Kylie had been alone for a big part of the night.

Soldier Dude had popped in and out all night. She hadn't seen him exactly, but she'd felt his cold presence. She only hoped that she caught on to the whole meditation thing soon so she could put a stop to this.

Della's hands paused on the keyboard and she looked over at Kylie. "I'm sorry if my dad was rude to you. And thanks for coming and getting me like that."

"He wasn't really rude to me." It was you he was rude to, Kylie almost said, but decided Della probably already knew that about him and didn't need to be reminded.

"Yeah, well, he's hard to take sometimes. But believe it or not, he means well."

"At least your dad showed up." Kylie remembered how she'd walked a thin line between lying and changing the subject last night to avoid telling her mom that her dad hadn't come. Her mom would have had a fit if Kylie had told her about his no-show. And her mom's fits weren't pretty. Still, a part of Kylie almost wished she had.

After all, her dad had acted as though he'd never promised to be there.

"Do you want to check your e-mail?" Della asked. "I think you got one from your dad."

Kylie's chest gripped. "No. I'll . . . check it later. *Or not.* Right now she wasn't ready to hear any excuses. Kylie looked around. "Where's Miranda?"

"She's outside. She's hoping to catch a glimpse of Chris but she said she'd wait for us. You ready to go?"

Kylie nodded. "Sure."

Seconds later, she and Della stepped out the door to find Miranda standing at the side of the cabin.

Miranda glanced toward them. "Hey guys, there's a baby bird that looks like it fell from its nest. Oh crappers, I think its wing is broken, too. Poor thing."

Della and Kylie hurried over to join her. Miranda, palms outstretched, had the small bird held up to her face. One of the bird's wings was hanging at an odd angle.

"Can't you just zap it well?" Della asked.

"I wish. But I'm afraid I would . . . screw that up, too," Miranda said, her tone filled with a bit of self-loathing—no doubt a result of her visit with her mom.

Miranda looked at Kylie. "Do you think that girl . . . the one who scanned you for a tumor . . . might be able to heal it?"

"I don't know," Kylie said, and noticed how the bird's eye color had gone from black to blue. Then she noted how the bird stared at Miranda. Call Kylie suspicious if you want, but she'd seen that gaga-look before on a certain shape-shifter's face. She glanced at Della, who met her gaze and then rolled her eyes.

Oh, yeah. It was definitely Perry.

"I think the humane thing to do is break its neck," Kylie said.

"Oh, definitely," Della echoed.

Kylie edged closer. The bird turned his head to peer at her and actually flinched. *That's right, you little twerp, you'd better be afraid of me.*

"You're so cruel." Miranda brought the bird to her breasts, then tucked her chin down to talk to it. "Don't you worry, Miranda's gonna take care of you," she cooed.

"Why don't you check its sex to see if it's a boy or girl?" Kylie couldn't help but snicker.

Miranda's poor-thing expression twisted upside down as she finally caught on to what Kylie was saying.

Miranda glared suspiciously at the bird. "Perry, is that you?"

The sparkles started popping all around Miranda's hands. Miranda jerked her palms from beneath the bird. Landing right on his butt was a red-faced Perry.

"I was just flying by. I didn't . . . I didn't do anything wrong. I wasn't even looking in the windows." His gaze shot to Kylie. "And don't you touch my ears or my neck." He got up and ran off.

"I should turn him into the rat he really is," Miranda said, apparently embarrassed she'd been fooled.

Kylie completely understood Miranda's feelings, then she remembered seeing embarrassment on Perry's face, and she knew why, too. The last person he wanted to look bad in front of was the girl he had a crush on. "You know he likes you, don't you?"

Miranda's mouth dropped open. "No, he doesn't."

Della snorted but didn't say anything.

"Yes, he does," Kylie said. "You should have seen him the other day when you ran off with Chris for the Meet Your Campmates Hour. He looked like a whipped puppy. And the whole time we were together, he kept asking questions about you."

Miranda stood there, her mouth agape. "If he likes me why hasn't he said something? We were even here together last year."

Kylie glanced at Della. "You wanna help me out here?"

"Nah," she said with a grin. "I think you're doing okay on your own."

Kylie turned back to Miranda. "I wasn't here last year, but . . ."

"But what?" Miranda asked.

Kylie shrugged. "I don't think he knows how to tell you he likes you," she said.

"Oh, please. He's not shy."

"He's not shy being a class clown or the class smart-ass. But when you get him alone, he comes off pretty tongue-tied. Honestly, he wasn't half as annoying, either. I personally think the downside of being able to change into anything is the fear that you don't know who you really are."

Kylie stopped and considered her own words. "Gosh, I actually sounded smart right then. Didn't I?"

They all laughed and started walking to breakfast. They were halfway there when Miranda swung around to face Kylie. "You really think Perry likes me?"

Kylie chuckled. "Yes."

Della raised her chin up and sniffed. "I smell loooove in the air."

"I'm not . . ." She paused and then said, "Did you smell it on him?"

"No," Della admitted. "But that's because shape-shifters don't put out the same pheromones. I'm not attuned to what a horny bird smells like."

They all giggled and then started walking again.

"He's cute, though, isn't he?" Miranda asked.

"In a way," Kylie said.

"Maybe a little," Della offered, and then asked, "so, what are you going to do about him?" She placed her hand over her heart to add drama to the question.

Miranda shrugged. "Wait and see if he makes a move."

"Why wait? If you want him, go get him. Don't be a wuss."

"Right." Miranda flipped back her hair and put it up with the band she had on her wrist. "I don't see you putting the moves on any guy."

"That's because I'm not pining over anyone here."

"Liar," Kylie said.

"Please," Della said. "Who do you think I got the hots for?"

"Steve, the tall shape-shifter with sandy-colored hair," Kylie said matter-of-factly. "You couldn't stop looking at his butt the other day."

Della's mouth dropped open and she rolled her eyes. "You are so wrong." She fanned herself with her hand. "But the boy is eye candy to the max."

They all chuckled. "What about you?" Miranda asked Kylie.

"I don't have time to pursue anything."

"You got the same amount of time we do," Miranda said.

"No, I don't." Kylie stopped walking. She hadn't told them about her two-week deal with Holiday, and for good reason. They weren't going to like it. "I . . . Holiday agreed to talk to my mom about my going home after two weeks."

"Why?" both her friends asked at the same time.

"Because I don't belong here. I'm not one of you."

"Bullshit!" Della said. "You just don't want to be one of us. You still think we're freaks. I see it every time the word *blood* is mentioned."

Okay, she might have had a point about the blood.

Kylie still shook her head. "It's not—"

"You can't go," Miranda said, interrupting her. "Who's going to stop Della and me from killing each other?"

"Oh, screw it," Della said, frowning, and looked at Miranda. "Let her go back to her safe little world where the only thing she worries about is if her daddy loves her. If she doesn't want to be friends with us, I certainly don't want to be friends with her. Hell, I didn't like the bitch anyway."

Della shot off so fast Kylie didn't see her go. Miranda stood there staring. "She's just mad. She didn't mean that."

"I know." Kylie bit down on her lip, but Della's words still hurt.

Miranda twirled her ponytail. "I hate to say this, but I don't blame her. I'm mad at you, too." And then Miranda took off.

Just great, Kylie thought. On top of everything else, she'd managed to piss off her two new best friends.

When Kylie got to the dining hall, Miranda and Della were sitting at a different table from where they usually sat. Kylie got the message loud and clear. They didn't want to be near her.

Fine.

Picking up her food tray, Kylie moved to her normal table, feeling a tad self-conscious about being alone. The door opened and Kylie looked up just as Derek walked in. His lips spread into a warm smile, one of his special smiles, that made her heart swell with appreciation. He started walking toward her, and relief filled her chest. She could really use a friend right now.

She continued watching him, suddenly aware that his eyes and smile didn't seem fixed on her. Sure enough, he didn't stop at her table. Kylie counted to ten and tried to wipe the pain from her eyes before she turned to see where he'd gone.

Peeking over her shoulder, she spied Derek cozying up with Mandy, his shoulder fully against hers. Swinging back around, Kylie stared at her eggs and her emotions felt just as scrambled.

She liked him, she didn't like him. What the hell was wrong with her?

Trying to decide whether attempting to eat was a mistake, Kylie heard Della's I'm-pissed voice. Kylie looked up expecting to find Della and Miranda going at it, but she was wrong. Della had her nose in the face of another vampire chick. Then the girl pointed a finger in Della's face and said something in a low voice that Kylie couldn't hear.

Kylie's first instinct was to march over there just in case Della needed reinforcements. Della had stood up for her against the she-wolf, but before Kylie got to her feet, Della took off.

After managing to down at least a half piece of toast, Kylie went out front to find Della. No Della. Instead, some of the other campers were drawing names. She was so not in the mood to chat with someone for an hour, but neither was she in the mood to go back to the cabin where Soldier Dude might appear. Deep down, she sensed that her talking to him yesterday had somehow made him more determined than ever to make contact with her.

She spotted Miranda standing by herself and walked over, hoping she might have gotten over her anger. Unfortunately, Miranda cut her a cold look. Not giving up, Kylie leaned in and asked, "What was the problem between Della and the other vampire?"

Miranda shrugged. "Don't know, she wouldn't tell me. It appears that when she's mad at you, she's also mad at me." Miranda's name echoed from the front and she took off without another word.

Kylie was watching Miranda walk away when she felt someone step beside her.

"You ready?" The deep male voice made her stomach drop. Kylie glanced up into Lucas's blue eyes. "Ready for what?"

"I got your name." He held up a piece of paper.

And I got a headache. Or PMS. Or bad cramps. Just been diagnosed with the flu. She had to come up with something to get out of this. But with his blue eyes focused on her, the words didn't come out. She looked around the crowd to see if the she-wolf was sizing Kylie up for a casket. Fredericka wasn't around.

"I know a place we can go," he said. His hand came around her back to nudge her along.

She took a step, trying to get the words *I can't* to slip out, but they wouldn't come. And just like that she knew why. She wanted to know if he remembered her. Why it mattered, she didn't know. But it did.

"You seemed interested in the dinosaur tracks." He met her gaze. "I know where there are some more. Why don't we go see them?" He guided her down the path that led toward the cabins, and she followed.

It wasn't until he turned to go down one of the wood trails that Kylie sensed something was different. Then she knew what the difference was. She wasn't afraid of him. When had she stopped being afraid of Lucas Parker? Maybe she was just getting immune to fearing supernaturals as a whole.

Questioning the logic behind her lack of fear, she recalled what she knew about him. He'd been raised by rogues. He'd killed her cat. Was it really smart of her to trust him?

She searched her instincts for anything resembling fear, and nope, it wasn't there. What she did find was the memory of how tenderly he'd helped his grandmother into the dining hall. And then Kylie remembered how he'd protected her from the neighborhood bullies.

"You do know that if your girlfriend sees us together she's going to be pissed, right?"

"What girlfriend?" he asked.

She rolled her eyes at him. "The one who is usually attached to your hip."

The muscle in his jaw tightened. "Fredericka is not my girlfriend."

"Oh, so she's just the girl you make out with behind the office, then," Kylie said before she could stop herself.

His frown deepened. "I figured that's what you thought that day."

"So I was wrong?" Kylie purposely allowed the sarcasm to play in her voice. "Do I look stupid to you?"

He stopped walking and swung around so fast that Kylie bumped right into his chest. He caught her shoulders and set her back. The feel of his hands on the shoulder straps of her white tank top sent heat flashing through her chest. But it faded the moment she saw his angry expression.

"No, you don't look stupid," he said in almost a growl. "But you are making assumptions without all the facts, and that's not a sign of intelligence."

Kylie's mouth dropped open at his insult. "So what was she doing, showing you her new bra? Come on. She was buttoning up her blouse when I stumbled on you guys."

He frowned and pushed a hand over his face. "You're right. I'm sorry I said that." He moved his hand and opened his eyes. "I admit you had a right to jump to that conclusion, but you're still wrong."

She offered him another eye roll.

"She wasn't showing me her bra; she was showing me her tattoo. On her shoulder. She got a wolf tattoo and wanted me to see it."

He started walking again and Kylie followed. "Well, she obviously has a serious crush on you."

"I know." He sounded frustrated. "She and I . . . we sort of hooked up last summer at the very end of camp."

"So she *was* your girlfriend." Kylie stopped moving and glanced at him.

He shook his head ever so slightly. "It wasn't even like that. We . . . met up on a full moon, and . . . it shouldn't have happened. But it did."

Kylie had visions in her mind of two wolves playing leap frog, but not quite leaping, and she felt her face flush.

"We haven't even spoken since camp last year. But she shows up here acting as if we're together. I tried discouraging her."

Kylie pretended to be interested in a bird singing in a tree so she wouldn't have to look at Lucas. "She obviously doesn't discourage very easily, or you've done a bad job of discouraging her."

"Probably both. I've even talked to Holiday about it, because she's driving me crazy."

Kylie started walking again. It wasn't her place to ask, but . . . "What did Holiday say?"

"That I'd probably have to be up front with her. But . . . I don't know, I guess I don't want to hurt her."

That or you just like having a girl hanging all over you and unbuttoning her shirt to show off her . . . tattoo. Kylie knew her last thought might be unfair, but it applied to most boys she knew. Heck, even her dad had warned her that teenage boys were generally after one thing.

Not that she was exactly listening to any of his advice right now.

"If you're that worried about hurting her, maybe you do care about her," Kylie said.

"No," he said adamantly, and then added, "okay, I feel sorry for her. She's had a rough time of things at home, and people judge her too harshly for it."

Kylie, knowing Lucas's past, read more into his statement than he knew. Or did he know? Did he realize she remembered him and that she knew he'd lied to Holiday about having lived with his grandmother all his life?

It suddenly occurred to her that when he'd jerked her aside to ask about what the FRU had wanted with her, maybe he'd been afraid she was tattling on him. Was he still afraid she'd tell?

The slightest hesitation about being alone in the woods with him wiggled through her mind, and that's when she realized they were deeper in the woods than she'd ever gone before.

Deep enough that nobody, not even her campmates with super hearing, could hear her scream.

She brushed a strand of hair behind her ear. "Exactly how far away are these dinosaur tracks?"

Chapter Thirty-one

"Not too far," Lucas said. If he was aware of her sudden insecurity, he hid it well.

"They're actually in a creek bed right outside the property line of our camp," he added without looking at her. "But there's this part of the fence that's been cut that we can slip through."

"I didn't think we were supposed to leave the campgrounds."

His focus shifted from the trail to her. "It's only a few feet off the property. Hey, it's up to you." He came to a complete stop. "You seemed interested the other day on the hike. I just thought . . ."

Kylie swallowed hard and glanced from side to side.

His nostrils suddenly flared as if trying to catch a scent. "You're afraid of me again? Damn, I thought you got over that."

"I have," she stammered, and wondered when he noticed her lack of fear. "I just . . . I'm remembering the snake the other day," she lied.

The suspicion in his gaze faded, and he almost looked

relieved. "Don't worry, I can smell those things a mile away, and I'm faster than any water moccasin." He started walking again.

She followed.

They walked without talking for a few minutes. The woods seemed to swallow their footsteps. His pace was fast, but not so fast she couldn't keep up.

"Have you figured out what you are yet?" he asked.

"No. But there's more than a good chance I'm just human."

He stopped abruptly and looked back at her.

Kylie held her hand up in front of her forehead. "Don't do it. And don't say it. I know I don't read like a human. But frankly, I'm tired of everyone checking out my head. It's as bad as guys staring at my boobs."

The moment the last sentence spilled from her mouth, she wished she could suck it back in, especially when she remembered him checking out her boobs the night she'd passed out.

"Sorry. I guess I can understand how that might get to you. Having us . . . stare at your pattern all the time." He grinned.

And damn if it wasn't the kind of smile that made a girl melt. They stood there studying each other and then it became downright awkward. He finally shook his head and started walking again.

They had walked another forth of a mile when she noticed a Band-Aid on his arm. "Did you . . . give blood?" She pointed to his arm.

"Oh, yeah." He looked at the Band-Aid as if he'd forgotten it was there, ripped it off, and tucked it inside his jeans pocket. "I helped Chris with his drive."

"Chris, the vampire?" she asked.

"Yeah," he said as if it was no big deal. And she recalled Derek acting the same way.

"You don't find it . . . strange?"

He arched a brow. "Strange?" He studied her as if he didn't get her question.

Kylie realized the stupidity of her question. Lucas turned into a wolf. Compared to that, drinking blood probably seemed like nothing.

Then he answered, "People donate blood all the time, Kylie."

"That's to save someone's life," she said, just to prevent the awkward silence.

"And vampires die if they don't drink blood."

Kylie wasn't sure if she'd known that, but hearing him say it had her head swimming. "Can't they survive on . . . ?"

"Animal blood?" he finished her question. "They can and do drink animal blood, but to maintain proper nourishment, they need some human blood in their diet. It's the same as donating to the Red Cross."

Without meaning to, she let her next thought slip out of her mouth. "Sick people don't drink it. It's injected into their veins."

"Does it really matter how it gets into their system? Personally, I don't see the difference."

She gave his analogy some thought and felt small and inconsiderate.

"Aren't you rooming with a vampire?" he asked.

"Yeah." But somehow in her mind she'd separated Della the friend from Della the vampire.

"And she hasn't asked you to donate yet?"

"No." And Kylie knew why, too. Della knew how Kylie and even Miranda felt about the whole blood issue. For some reason Della's angry retort from this morning rang in her head. *You still think we're freaks.*

"All the vampires are supposed to get someone to donate. If they fail, they don't participate in the rituals."

Kylie remembered Della hadn't gone to her regular early morning meeting today—then there was the argument Della had with another vampire. The memory of Della standing up to Fredericka flashed in Kylie head, then came the flash of how she'd protected Kylie from her cousin, Chan. Della had been willing to go the limit for Kylie, but Della hadn't even felt comfortable enough to ask Kylie for blood.

You still think we're freaks.

Della's accusation rang again in Kylie's mind.

Kylie didn't consider Della a freak, but in truth, she hadn't accepted her for who she really was, either. Sum it up and it meant Kylie hadn't been much of a friend.

The realization hurt like a punch to her stomach.

"Is it safe?" Kylie asked.

"What?" Lucas asked.

"Donating blood to the vampires. Is it safe?"

"Of course it is. Holiday wouldn't allow it if it wasn't."

Opening herself up to accepting Della took Kylie down other mental paths. "What's it like?"

He shrugged. "It's just like they do it at a doctor's office."

"Not that. I mean, changing into a wolf. I heard some others say it was . . ." She tried to think how to put it.

"Scary?" he asked, and arched a brow.

"And painful," she answered, deciding not to try to sugar-coat it.

"I think it looks worse than it is." He didn't talk for a few minutes and then started again. "It's sort of like a really sore muscle being massaged. It both hurts and feels good at the same time."

"So it's not like Perry when he changes?"

"No, it's not like that. A shape-shifter's body changes on a whole different cellular level and speed. When we change, you can see the process as the body takes on the new form."

"It doesn't sound fun."

"But it is. It's exhilarating." His eyes lit up and Kylie didn't doubt he was telling the truth.

"And what's it like afterward? When you're changed, do you . . . are you still you?"

"Am I still me?" he asked, not understanding.

"Do you think like a human, or do you think like a wolf?"

"I'm not human, Kylie," he answered. "I'm a werewolf."

She felt her face flush. "I just meant—"

"I know," he said, and let go of a deep breath. "When I turn, I have very heightened senses and instincts. To hunt. To mate. To protect what's mine. They could be called very humanlike instincts. However, in werewolf form the instincts are harder to deny."

So maybe his killing her cat hadn't been out of meanness, but more from his instinct to hunt. Until that thought hit, she hadn't realized she'd been trying to find a way to forgive him.

The silence grew awkward.

"And when you're not turned, what are your gifts?" she asked.

"Heightened hearing, smell, strength, and agility."

"So it's the same as a vampire?" She recalled Della pointing out that vampires were the more powerful species, not that Kylie honestly believed her. Della was biased. Then Kylie suddenly remembered one of Della's gifts. "Can you hear my heartbeat?" *Could he also tell if she was lying?*

"Depends. Our strength and senses increase the closer we get to a full moon. But for the most part, our hearing is tuned to listen for intruders moving in and not so much for things such as heartbeats."

She recalled he'd jumped out of the tree the night of the campfire. It struck her as odd that he could do that but a wolf couldn't. Then again, she supposed there were lots of benefits to having fingers and thumbs.

"The fence is right here." He pushed the loose edge of the barbed-wire fence back, and motioned for her to slip between him and the opening of the wire. "Be careful not to get your shoulders cut."

The gap was small. Kylie squeezed by him and her breasts brushed up against his chest. The warm and tingly sensations shot through her so fast that she started to jerk away.

Before she moved, he must have sensed her tension and he pulled her against him. "Careful." His head lowered and his gaze met hers. They were so close that his nose brushed up against hers. "You're going to cut yourself on the wire."

She nodded and slipped through. The fence could have been wired with electricity for the tingles running through her body.

As soon as she was clear, he stepped through and dropped the wire. Their gazes met again. Somehow, she knew he was thinking the same thing she was—about how close they had been to each other. She could still feel the blood flowing to her cheeks.

"It's this way." He motioned her along, but she saw him take in her face—no doubt she was blushing. In just a few minutes, they got to the creek bed. He studied the water. "The water's up a bit," he said. "Usually, it's only trickling down. The tracks are right across the stream. It's only a foot deep, but you might want to take your shoes off if you don't want them to get wet."

Kylie sat down and removed her tennis shoes and socks and rolled up her jeans. He stood over her and watched. She looked up. "You're not going to take yours off?"

"Wet shoes don't bother me."

She stuffed her socks in her shoes and set them away from the water. The splashing sound of water filled her senses. Looking toward the stream, she asked, "Is the waterfall close to here?"

"It's a mile, but on camp property."

"Have you ever been there?" she asked.

"Once," he said.

"Was it as scary as everyone makes it sound?"

"A little," he said. "But I didn't see any shadows." He chuckled.

Was that because he couldn't see ghosts?

"You ready?" he asked, when she sat there thinking.

"You bet." Standing up, she dipped her toes in the creek. "It's cold." She smiled.

"Yeah, but in the afternoon when the sun is at its hottest, it feels great. Up about a half a mile there's a place that's deep enough to swim in. I try to go there at least once a week."

She got a vision of him swimming, and remembered her dream.

He stepped into the water and reached back and took her right hand in his. She looked down at his fingers locked around hers, her mind still trying to push the image of the two of them standing in waist-deep water, her breasts pressed against his chest.

"The rocks are slippery," he said, following her gaze.

"I think I can handle it." She pulled her hand free.

"When you fall on your ass, you'll be sorry."

"I won't." She smirked at him. But on her very next step, her foot and her pride hit a slick spot and without warning her legs slid out and up and she landed on her butt with a big splash.

"Crap." The cold water soaked through her jeans to her butt. Laughter, very deep and very contagious, rang out. He stood over her, his arms crossed over his wide chest, his blue eyes dancing with humor.

"Stop it." Almost laughing herself, she cupped her hand, caught a handful of the water, and tossed it at him.

He laughed harder, but then offered her his hand. She took it this time.

She was on her feet and went to take another step when she slid again, only this time she didn't go down alone. She landed on top of him, her face buried in his shoulder. She raised her head, and watched the cold water rush over his shoulders. Then she saw him looking down at her, still smiling. And looking good doing it, too.

"That's what you get for laughing at me." She grinned.

His chest expanded beneath her as if he took in a deep breath. And suddenly she didn't even feel the chill of the water—all she felt was the warmth of his body against hers.

"And this is what you get for laughing at me." He pulled her up a few inches until his lips touched hers.

She didn't try to stop him. Oh no, she actually climbed up higher on his chest so the kiss wouldn't be awkward. His hand moved up to the back of her neck. He shifted her head slightly so her mouth was more accessible to his. The slightly rough texture of his shaven cheeks felt wonderful. His tongue moved inside. Slowly at first, then without hesitation. Warmth built inside her and she couldn't seem to get close enough to him. Everything felt different from the kisses and caresses she'd experienced with Trey.

More, her instincts seemed to scream. She wanted more.

She ran her fingers through his damp, dark hair, loving how the strands felt. Loving all the emotions swirling through her, over her, making her feel so alive, so new.

Her breasts pressed against his chest felt fuller, and maybe it was the dream driving her, but she wanted to feel him touch her. It wasn't until she heard voices nearby that she came to her senses. She pulled her mouth from his and pushed up a few inches off his chest. His eyes opened and he stared at her with a hooded gaze. She saw the wildness in his eyes, a hunger like she'd never seen before. More than anything, she wanted to be the one to feed his hunger and taste the wildness. Then the voices drew closer. And right then, everything she felt was just too much.

She moved off him, as unsure of these new emotions as she was of her ability to stand up on her own two feet. "We should . . . I heard . . ." She stood.

"They're not coming this way," he said. He sat up and glanced up at her through his dark lashes. Exhaling, he scrubbed his palm over his face. "Damn," he muttered, then looked back up at her. "I probably shouldn't have done that, should I?"

"Probably not," she agreed, even thought she wouldn't give the moment back for anything.

He slung back his wet hair, sending the drops of water reflecting off the sunlight spinning out. "Then forget it happened, okay? Just forget it ever happened."

"I don't think I can forget." She'd be remembering this kiss and this moment years from now. Because as much as she liked kissing Trey, it was as if this was her very first grown-up kiss. Her first real taste of passion. This kiss, the thing she'd felt was somehow more. And God help her, because while she wasn't ready for "more," she still wanted it. And that, she supposed, was the true meaning of passion.

Aware of the awkward silence building between them, she looked around. "Where are the tracks?"

"There." He pointed her to the edge of the creek.

She moved over there, slowly. Staring down at the prints, she pretended an interest in them. He suddenly stood beside her, casting a long shadow. When she looked up, she caught him staring at her chest.

She glanced down and saw that the water had made both her satin bra and white tank top practically invisible. Her nipples, still tight and tingling, pushed against the fabric.

She crossed her arms.

"You should wear my shirt." He tugged his wet blue T-shirt up. Kylie watched as his shirttail shifted upward, exposing a very hard abdomen. The hem of his shirt inched higher, and she took in the cutest inny belly button she'd ever seen. And then his chest. Solid. Hard. A few drops of water glistened against his skin. Her heart beat to the sound of passion again.

Realizing she stared, she turned away. "Maybe you should just promise not to look and keep your shirt on."

"I *might* be able to do that. But the six guys that are about to arrive in less than thirty seconds might not be so cooperative. Then I'll have to teach each of them a lesson."

"I thought they weren't coming this way?"

"They turned around." He started putting the shirt over her head. She raised her hands and helped him. With the shirt in place, he offered her half a smile. His gaze lowered to her chest.

"Much better." He reached out and brushed a wet strand of hair off her cheek. "You have no idea how beautiful you are, do you?"

The voices were at the bank of the creek now. Not that Kylie cared. Every instinct she had was zeroed in on the man standing in front of her and the compliment he'd just given her.

He made her feel beautiful. He made her feel sexy.

"You ready to head back?" Lucas asked.

She nodded, but right before she turned, she heard her name. "Kylie?"

Damn if she didn't recognize the voice, too.

She looked back to the bank and found herself staring at a very puzzled-looking Trey.

Chapter Thirty-two

"Do you know him?" Lucas asked, his bare arm brushing against hers in a protective manner.

Too stunned to speak, Kylie managed to nod. And then Trey started over, splashing through the water.

"Everything okay?" Trey asked.

He didn't look at her. Instead, he kept his gaze riveted on Lucas. Or rather, on Lucas's bare chest.

"Yes," she said, finally finding her voice. "We . . . we were just looking at the dinosaur fossils."

"Is this Derek?" Trey's tone was full of accusation. Not that he had a right to accuse her of anything, considering everything that had happened between them. But the hurt in his eyes was genuine and it tugged at her heart.

"Trey, this is my friend, Lucas. Lucas, this is Trey."

Both boys stared at each other. Instead of exchanging handshakes, they offered each other cold, unfriendly nods.

"We should go," Kylie said to Lucas, and nodded a good-bye to Trey.

She started walking across the stream. Lucas fell in step beside her. She almost slipped again, but Lucas caught her, bringing her fully against his chest as Trey watched from the other side of the stream.

"Boyfriend?" he asked, releasing his clasp on her waist.

"Ex." She got to the other side and sat down to put on her shoes, but she could still feel Trey watching her. She knew all too well how he felt. The same way she'd felt seeing him and that girl at the party. Poetic justice, just dues, turnabout was fair play—a bunch of emotional qualifiers skipped around her head, but truth was, she felt none of them.

"Why did he ask if I was Derek?" Lucas asked.

"It's a long story." And one she didn't want to share right now. As she tied her shoes, guilt tied knots in her chest. She shouldn't feel guilty.

But she did.

Shoes on, she stood up and started walking, never looking back. Her emotions ran like wild horses in her mind.

Lucas held out the fence again and she slipped through—without brushing up against him this time.

As soon as she knew Trey couldn't see her anymore, she stopping thinking about him and started thinking about the kiss. Needing to feel grounded, she started putting it into perspective. Yes, it had been a good kiss, but it hadn't been more than a kiss.

Right?

They hardly spoke on the walk back. And she hardly looked at him, because seeing him without his shirt was . . . making it hard to think. When they had almost gotten to the camp trail,

Kylie realized she hadn't gotten the one answer she wanted from him. Did Lucas remember her?

She tried to find a way to ask without it sounding as if she wanted him to remember her. As if she thought what they'd shared as children had connected them. It didn't.

How could it, when he'd even suggested she forget the kiss? Her chest began to tighten just a little. God, why did his saying that have to hurt so much?

She took a deep breath. Just add that question to the growing list she'd started since coming to Shadow Falls.

While the rest could probably wait, this one couldn't.

She wanted to know—needed to know—if he remembered her.

Just blurt it out. Just blurt it out. She saw the clearing in the woods ahead and knew her time with him was short. She might not talk to him again before she left.

"You know, you kind of remind me of someone," she said.

"Do I?" He didn't look at her.

"Yeah." She waited for him to ask who.

He didn't ask. Instead he said, "I get that a lot."

They came to the clearing and stepped out on the trail. His gaze met hers. "I have to go. I'm leading another hike." He turned to leave.

"Lucas?" she called after him, and he swung around. She pulled off his shirt and handed it to him. He took it.

She pulled her damp shirt away from her bra. It wasn't completely dry, but no longer as transparent.

She saw his gaze lower to her chest briefly, then he met her eyes.

Do you remember me? "Thanks for . . . showing me the dinosaur tracks."

He nodded. "You're welcome." He hesitated, and then said, "I'm sorry, Kylie."

She knew he was apologizing for the kiss. First, he tells her to forget it ever happened and now he apologizes for it. Her chest clutched.

Then he took off again and Kylie stood there with one thought running through her head. *She wasn't sorry. She wasn't thrilled Trey had stumbled upon them. But neither was she sorry.*

Kylie had just put on some dry clothes when she heard someone come into the cabin. Stepping out of her room, she spotted Della standing by the open fridge drinking . . . something.

Blood. Kylie forced herself to accept it. Her friend was a vampire and vampires drank blood, had to have it to live. It was time for Kylie to face things. "Hey."

"I'm not talking to you." Della screwed the top on the bottle and placed it in the vegetable bin as if to hide it.

"I don't blame you. I haven't been a very good friend."

Della turned around. "Is this your way of saying you're not going to leave?"

Kylie tried to think how to answer that. "I don't know yet. I told Holiday I'd give it two weeks. So I guess I shouldn't say one way or another until then."

Then, before she lost her nerve, Kylie moved in and stretched out her arm, rubbing a finger over her vein in the crease of her elbow. "Do you have the stuff to do it?"

Della's brow wrinkled. "To do what?"

"To draw blood. Derek said that you guys were trained."

"I didn't . . ." Her eyes widened. "I never asked . . ."

"I know, but you didn't ask because you knew I'd say no. Right?"

"That's part of it." Della continued to study her.

"And the other part?" Kylie asked.

"Because you just stopped being afraid of me. I didn't want you to look at me like a monster."

"You're not a monster," Kylie said. "You're just a vampire."

"And you don't see that as a monster?" Della asked.

"Not when I realize it's you."

Della hesitated. "My parents would think I was a monster. Lee would think I'm a monster."

"Screw what they would think," Kylie said. "You're not a monster." She held out her arm. "You need blood to live."

"I can survive just drinking animal blood for the summer," Della said.

"Why should you when I've got extra?"

"You'd really do it?" There was a catch in Della's voice.

"Well, I heard that once you agree to it, you can't take it back," she teased.

"I wouldn't hold you to it."

"I was joking. I want to do it."

"Do what?" Miranda asked, stepping into the cabin.

Kylie looked back. "I'm giving her some blood."

Miranda's eyes widened. "Seriously?"

Kylie nodded. "She offered to fight Fredericka for me. I owe her that much."

Miranda made a face. "Oh, hell, if you're gonna do it, then I've got to do it."

"No, you don't," Della said.

"Yes I do. Because we're a team. All of us."

Della's eyes grew moist. "I don't allow witches on my team."

"Tough titty, vamp," Miranda said. "Because you got one." Miranda held out her arm. "Let's do it. But it better not hurt. I hate needles."

"I can't do it until we get it cleared with Holiday or Sky."

"Then let's go get it cleared," Miranda and Kylie said at the same time.

Right then, a toad, aka Miranda's piano teacher, plopped down at her feet. "Not again," she seethed, and eyed the toad. "Won't you ever learn?" Miranda pointed her finger at the amphibian. "Keep this up and I swear, I'm reporting your butt to the police."

"Maybe you should," Kylie said.

Miranda looked at Kylie. "Yeah, but he never . . . All his offenses could be explained by accidents—trying to show me the right keys on the piano, that kind of thing. The only way I know he was really doing it was because of the spell."

"I'm telling you," Della said, "we should cook his horny ass. Or give him to the werewolves. I heard they love toads."

The toad jumped across the room and then faded into thin air. Kylie got curious. "When he pops in here, is he disappearing from wherever he is?"

"Yup," Miranda said. "But except for the first time, it's happened when he's alone. Or at least that's what I think when I peek into where he ends up when he goes back. I think he gave up teaching piano lessons."

"Well, at least that's good," Kylie said.

Miranda's eyes grew round as if she just remembered something. "Is it true that Lucas got your name this morning?"

"Yeah," Kylie admitted.

"Oh, shit." Della pushed Kylie into a kitchen chair. "Start talking. What happened?"

Miranda dropped into a chair. "Yeah, spill it."

Kylie did spill it. It all rolled off her tongue so fast she couldn't stop it. And not just about the kiss. She told them about Lucas living next to her, about her cat. She told them about the amazing kiss and about the whole mess with Derek and Trey—including her mixed-up feelings for Derek after he'd moved on without giving her so much as a second glance. When Kylie finally shut up, Della and Miranda sat there, their eyes wide and their mouths hung open in disbelief.

"Damn," Della said.

Miranda leaned back in her chair and sighed. "I wanna be kissed like that. I'm so ready to be swept off my feet."

"That's easy," Della said. "Why don't you go find Perry and lay one on him?"

Miranda shook her head. "Please, if the guy doesn't have the balls to even tell me he likes me, he's not going to have the balls to kiss me."

"Then put a spell on him to make him grow a pair," Della said.

They all laughed. And then Kylie's phone began to ring. She glanced at the caller ID and saw her dad's number on the screen. Her laughter faded into a frown. And then, just because she didn't want to let anything ruin the mood, she reached down and turned off the ringer and then slipped the phone back in her pocket.

The next day and a half flew by. It helped that there were no more bouts of drama—no surprise visits from Trey, no confrontations with Fredericka, not even any arguments between Miranda and Della. They had donated blood and it felt right.

And then night fell.

Kylie woke up in a cold sweat. She sat up in her bed, knowing the ghost was here. Then Kylie realized she wasn't in her bed. She wasn't even at camp.

Her heart raced as she tried to make sense of her surroundings. She knew she wasn't in Texas anymore. Not even in the United States, for that matter. It felt . . . foreign and yet somehow familiar, like images she'd seen in the Gulf War movies her mom loved.

Kylie stood outside of a small house on a plot of land devoid of trees and grass. It was hot. Not Texas hot, more dry desert heat. The sun had set and the time seemed caught between light and dark. The smell of burning rubber and wood, of devastation, filled her nose. Plus there was noise. So much noise. It was as if someone suddenly turned up the volume because the noise around her was deafening—there were screams and loud pops—bombs echoing off in the distance. Gunshots. Someone was yelling for her to follow them. "It's not our problem," the male voice screamed.

What's not my . . . She heard the wailing—a woman, Kylie realized. A woman screaming for help, screaming in pain.

Fear climbed up Kylie's spine and she knew whatever was happening to the woman was terrible. And unjust. Kylie didn't want to be a part of it. Didn't want to see it, didn't want to know about it. Too ugly. *Not my problem.*

What was not her problem? Confusion filled her mind.

It's a dream. Just a dream. Wake up. Wake up. She tried to remember how Dr. Day had taught her to stop the dreams, but she couldn't. She closed her eyes really tight and opened them, hoping she'd be back at her cabin.

She wasn't. Somehow she'd moved closer to the house and to the screams. The woman was in the house. Someone hurt her. Who? Why? What did it all mean? Why was Kylie here? Why was she stuck in a war movie? Or was it a movie? No, a dream.

Her mind tried to compute the questions. *No time,* a voice deep inside her demanded, *only time to feel, to understand.*

Why did she need to understand?

Her questions faded and she felt completely present in the dream again, in the havoc, in the ugliness of war. She felt an enormous guilt for not wanting to be involved with the woman. If she ran, if she ran right now, she knew she could catch up with the others and get away.

Choices ran through her head. She could live if she left now. But could she live knowing she'd allowed this to happen to the woman?

No. She couldn't. She glanced down at an assault rifle in her hand. Just like the ones from the war movies. She had to stop whoever was hurting that poor woman.

Kylie kicked in the door and aimed her gun at the man hunched over the woman. "Stop it!" Kylie screamed, but it wasn't her voice making the demand. It was a man's voice.

Kylie froze for a second, then she saw that the man had a knife. She saw the woman, her clothes ripped, and blood covering her face and hands, as she scrambled away from her assailant.

The man swung around to face Kylie. He rushed forward, his bloody knife held high. Her finger on the trigger tightened. She saw him fall and felt no remorse for shooting him. He was evil, she knew it.

A young boy came running in the front door. His dark hair and eyes seemed haunted and older than his years. "No!" he screamed when he saw the bleeding woman huddled against the wall. He fixed his eyes on Kylie.

He started yelling something in a language Kylie didn't understand. He pulled a gun from his pants pocket and aimed it. Aimed it right at Kylie.

Pop. Pop. Pop. She heard the shots. She didn't feel them, but she knew she'd been shot—she also knew when she fell to the floor she was dying.

Suddenly, she stood in the corner of the room looking at the boy and the woman. Her gaze shot to the body lying in a heap, the body she'd just left—the person she had been. Soldier Dude. Blood streamed down his face. He reached inside his uniform and pulled out a letter. He brought it to his lips and with his last breath, he kissed the envelope.

Kylie's heart ached for the loss. She didn't know him, but she cared. Cared that he had died. Cared that he had died trying to save someone.

The woman sat up, looked at the dead soldier, and started screaming again, and so did Kylie.

When she woke up, she was still screaming, standing with her back against the kitchen wall in her cabin. Miranda and Della, dressed in their pajamas, stood in front of her, staring.

Kylie let go of her tension and felt herself slide down the wall. Her throat felt raw, her heart raced.

"She's having a night terror," Miranda said from far away.

Kylie wanted to believe it, but no. She'd never remembered the others. This time she remembered. Somehow she knew that this had been more than just a dream. This was how Soldier Dude had died.

Kylie sat there for a good ten minutes, assuring Della and Miranda she was fine. When they finally went back to bed, Kylie returned to her bedroom. Realizing she couldn't sleep, she got dressed and went to see Holiday. The camp leader had told Kylie if she ever needed her, night or day, she could come to her cabin. Kylie was about to find out if Holiday really meant it.

Moving down the path toward Holiday's cabin, Kylie couldn't help but notice how the night seemed void of noise. Not a bird, not even the shuffle of a raccoon. In her mind, she heard the woman's screams again and saw the soldier take his last breath. Tears dampened Kylie's face. She brushed them away, not wanting to be crying when she got to Holiday's cabin.

Suddenly, the dark silence shattered. Kylie heard arguing in the woods. The voices were gone just as quick as they'd begun, though. The hairs rose on the back of her neck. She ignored the fear of the unknown and focused on what she knew. The soldier was dead. He'd died trying to save someone. She kept walking. Holiday's cabin was only another five minutes away.

She took another step, and that's when she felt someone move into place behind her.

That's when she felt the hand grab her arm and jerk her back.

"You shouldn't be out now," the eerily familiar voice snarled.

Chapter Thirty-three

Kylie swung around. It felt as if her heart jumped up and slammed against her tonsils. As soon as she saw it was Sky, Kylie breathed a sigh of relief.

"You scared me," she said.

When Sky's hold tightened, Kylie's relief started to vanish. "I . . . I need to speak to Holiday. She said if I needed her, I could come. It didn't matter what time."

Sky continued to stare, but her grip finally lightened. "What do you need to see her about?"

"I had another bad dream. Only I remembered this one. The ghost was there."

Sky dropped her hold and then stepped back as if she wanted no part of Kylie's ghost. "Do you know which cabin is hers?"

Kylie nodded. Sky motioned for Kylie to continue, and she did. Even so, Kylie felt Sky watching her as she took each step. Kylie wasn't sure why and then it finally hit her that Sky probably thought Kylie was going to or coming from a hookup with a boy.

Kylie stopped in front of Holiday's cabin door and knocked. A few seconds later, the camp leader, wearing a big night shirt, opened the door.

"Kylie?" Layers of concern filled Holiday's voice. "Is everything okay?"

The distress in Holiday's voice opened up Kylie's floodgates again. Tears formed in her eyes and her throat grew tighter. "No." Kylie shook her head side to side. "It's not okay."

Holiday pulled Kylie inside and wrapped her in a solid hug. Kylie allowed herself to be held by someone who seemed to understand. When the hug ended, Kylie told her, "I think I know what the ghost wants from me."

When the sun rose, Kylie still sat on Holiday's sofa, going over and over the dream. The camp leader confirmed what Kylie had suspected. It hadn't been a normal night terror, but an out-of-body experience. The ghost had brought Kylie into his last memories. Holiday agreed that Kylie could be right, that the ghost might have been accused of committing the crime he'd died trying to stop, and now he wanted someone to let the world know he wasn't the villain. Nevertheless, Holiday also said that it was seldom that easy.

"Do you think he's going to try to do this again?" Kylie asked, hugging her knees. While she wouldn't deny that she had a newfound respect for the man, even found her heart grieving for him, she didn't want to do this again. Every time she remembered that woman's screams, remembered pulling the trigger to kill the woman's attacker, she felt sick.

Holiday squeezed Kylie's hand. "I don't think ghosts realize it's as hard as it is on us. They can be relentless at times."

Kylie shook her head. "I can't do this, Holiday. I'm not brave enough." Her insides started shaking again.

Holiday sighed. "You're doing fine. And I'm here whenever you need me, Kylie. Why don't you go to your cabin and get some sleep? Take the day off and just rest."

"What if it happens again?"

Holiday reached for a pad of paper. "I'm giving you my cell number and if you need me, I'm just a phone call away."

Isn't that what her father had said? But another hug from Holiday and Kylie almost believed her.

Around noon, Miranda and Della brought Kylie some lunch. "You didn't have to do this," Kylie insisted, and picked at the pizza.

"You donated blood. I'm obligated to you for life," Della teased.

"What about me?" Miranda asked. "I gave blood, too." She held up her arm to show off the Band-Aid.

"Yours wasn't that good," Della teased, and then she looked at Kylie again. "Derek asked about you at breakfast this morning. He said he needed to talk to you about something."

Kylie sighed. With everything else, did she even have it in her to start thinking about Derek? "Did he say what it was about?"

"No, but he looked serious."

"Oh," Miranda added, "you missed the excitement, too. You know Chris, the vampire? He and that blond werewolf—I think his name is Nathan—they got in a fight. Sky had to break it up."

"There was blood all over the place," Della said. "And it smelled so good."

"Why were they fighting?" Kylie popped a piece of pepperoni into her mouth.

"A reason?" Miranda asked. "Everyone knows vamps and wolves don't get along. Especially the males." Miranda shot a glance at Della, who was already frowning.

"Not true," Kylie said. "Lucas even gave blood to Chris. They're roommates."

"And some of the vampires didn't want him to take it," Miranda said.

"Why not?" Kylie asked.

Miranda shrugged. "Stupid prejudices. One of them said they didn't want to be indebted to a dirty dog."

"That's just a stupid rumor," Della said. "I don't know if anybody really said that."

"Yeah, but that's what everybody's saying happened. Oh, and guess what else you missed?" Miranda started twisting in her chair. "Guess who sat at our table?"

Kylie saw the twinkle in Miranda's eyes. "A bird with a broken wing."

Miranda grinned. "How did you know?"

"Because you've got that goofy grin and started dancing, stupid." Della laughed.

"I don't have a goofy grin," Miranda snapped.

"No fighting. I'm trying to digest my food." A minute later Kylie asked, "Anything else happen?"

"The FRU showed up again," Della said, her voice more serious this time, and then she rose and walked to the computer. "I didn't hear anything, but that tall dark guy was all over Holiday, reading her the riot act about something."

Kylie took a drink of her diet soda and told Della and Miranda what she knew. "So, something is going on, guys. And whatever it is, it's serious. On the second day at camp, Burnett told Holiday that if 'something' didn't *stop* happening, they would close the camp down."

"Close it down?" Della swung around from the computer. "They can't do that. This is what keeps us sane and keeps us from killing each other."

The computer let out an e-mail-alert beep. Della glanced at the computer and then back at Kylie. "You got another e-mail from your dad."

Kylie dropped her pizza, suddenly not hungry anymore. She still hadn't spoken to him. Kylie knew she was wrong to keep dodging him, but so was he. He'd told her he would come to the parents day. Add the fact that Kylie felt he'd also stopped loving her, and the whole daddy subject was just another demon she needed to tame. And she intended to do it. Sometime later. When it didn't hurt so darn much to think about.

"Holiday didn't look happy," Della added. "Especially when they brought Lucas into the office."

Kylie's gut clenched. "They talked to Lucas? What did they say?"

"I don't know," Della said. "But he looked mad enough to kill."

When Miranda and Della left a short while later, Kylie lay back down. But sleep evaded her. And not just because she was afraid a certain ghost would snatch her up for another trip down memory lane. She thought about Holiday and wondered about the mess with the FRU. She wondered about Lucas. Did they find out his parents had been rogue? Did Lucas think she was the one who said something?

Her mind raced and she didn't know which problem to give herself over to, or how to stop thinking about it all.

She'd already logged in about forty minutes talking to Sara this morning, listening to her go on and on about Phillip, the new guy she was seeing. Then Kylie had spoken to her mom and lied like a big dog. *Everything at camp was just peachy.* When Kylie heard a knock on the cabin door, she was thrilled over the distraction.

But not so thrilled when she opened the door and found Lucas standing there. Okay, she was thrilled he was there, but why couldn't she have looked better? She looked like she'd just crawled out of bed, which she had, while he looked . . . great. He stood in her doorway, with one hand behind his back.

She opened her mouth to say something but couldn't even get out a normal greeting. It wasn't just lack of sleep, either. No, it was remembering their kiss.

And how he'd told her it had been a mistake.

"Hi." He grinned as if he knew she was tongue-tied. "Your roommate, the one with the tri-colored hair, said you weren't feeling good."

"Yeah, but I'm feeling better now," she managed to eke out, and then said, "I heard the FRU talked to you?"

He nodded. "It was nothing."

She sensed that was a lie.

"I got you something." He shot her his killer smile.

And darn it if she didn't just melt into a puddle. Holding on to the doorknob, she asked, "What did you get me?"

"I went to town to pick up some stuff for Holiday and . . . I found it." He suddenly looked guilty.

He pulled out his arm, and Kylie expected to see a bouquet of some inexpensive flowers. Not a wiggling, mewing black and white kitten.

Her breath caught.

"I think you should take it. It doesn't like me too much."

Kylie took the kitten and cuddled it against her chest. The thing was so small it almost fit in the palm of her hand. She stroked the feline's forehead and heard the tiny thing purr. Was she dreaming? She had to be, because the kitten had the exact markings of her cat, Socks. The cat he'd . . .

Her gaze shot up to his. "You remember?"

He nodded. "Of course I do." There was a minute of silence. "I should . . . go." He started to walk away and then turned back around and came back to the door. He leaned his arm against the frame and met her eyes. Something about his posture told Kylie whatever he was about to say was serious. "Kylie, I swear, I tried to stop him. It was the first and last time we fought."

"Stop who?" she asked.

"My dad. He was bigger and a heck of lot faster than I was then. But I tried." He took another step back and then pointed to the side of the porch. "The litter box supplies and cat chow are there."

Kylie just nodded. His admission about his dad having been the one who killed Socks had sent a shock through Kylie's system. All these years she'd assumed . . . "Do you want to come in? Help me set it up?"

For a second, she thought he was going to say yes. Then he looked deeper into her eyes and she saw some of the wildness of desire she remembered from the kiss. "I'd better not."

"Why?" she asked, knowing his refusal wasn't just about coming inside. He was saying no. No to the possibilities running through her mind each time she thought about him. No to the possibilities of more kisses, and their getting to know each other for real.

"It wouldn't work." he said. "There's some things going on in my life right now. It's not a good time, believe me."

She couldn't accept his dismissal, not without trying. "You know what they say about waiting for the perfect time, don't you?"

He closed his eyes. "I can't drag you into this, Kylie."

"Drag me into what?"

Opening his eyes, he reached out and passed a finger over her lips. "You are so innocent. And I am so tempted." He dropped his hand. "But I can't. Take care of yourself, Kylie Galen."

His final words sank in and they sounded a lot like good-bye. She reached out and grabbed his arm. "Are you leaving?"

His gaze met hers. He didn't answer her, he didn't have to. She saw it in his eyes.

"Is this about the FRU?" she asked.

He let go of a deep breath. "I can't . . ."

She dropped her hand. "I never said anything about you to them or Holiday. I swear it."

He smiled but it was the saddest smile she'd ever seen. "I know." Tucking both his hands into the tips of his jean pockets, he looked at her. "You know, I didn't think you could get any cuter than you were when you were six. But I was wrong." He leaned down and his lips lightly touched hers. It happened so fast, she barely felt it.

She wanted so much more than that quick compliment and chaste kiss. "Are you leaving?" she asked him again.

He didn't answer. He'd moved off the porch. Kylie stood by the door and watched him walk away. And although he never told her for sure, she knew. She knew Lucas Parker was going to disappear from her life again.

Less than an hour later, Kylie heard someone knock again, or make that pound, on the cabin door. She'd just made it into the living room when the cabin door swung opened with such force it slapped against the cabin wall.

Kylie saw Burnett first, followed by a very unhappy Holiday.

"You don't walk in uninvited," the camp leader seethed.

"He was here. I can smell him." Burnett glared down at Holiday.

"I don't care. You respect my wishes, or I'll take it up with your boss."

"You already have." The vampire's eyes tightened with anger.

"Well, I'll do it again," she said.

"I have to find that kid," Burnett growled. "I don't have time to play nice." The vampire focused his gaze on Kylie.

"Sorry we barged in," Holiday said.

"What's wrong?" Kylie asked. She didn't have to ask who they were looking for.

Burnett took a step toward her. Holiday grabbed him by the arm to yank him back, but he didn't budge.

"Where is he?" Burnett demanded.

"Kylie, have you seen Lucas Parker?" Holiday countered in a calmer voice.

Kylie swallowed. "He came to check on me about an hour ago. But he left."

Burnett leaned his head to the right as if listening to her heartbeat. "Did he tell you where he was going?"

"No," she said. And she was so glad he hadn't. "Why? Why are you looking for him?"

Burnett just stood there staring.

"He's not a bad guy," Kylie said.

Burnett swung around and walked out. Holiday took one step after him and then glanced back at her.

"He's not a bad guy," Kylie repeated to Holiday.

"I have to go," Holiday said. "I'll come by in a little bit."

Holiday shot out, trying to catch up with Burnett. Kylie stood there in the living room and remembered again the day Lucas had popped his head over the fence and told her to make sure she didn't leave her new kitten outside. All this time, she'd considered his words to be an admission of guilt. She'd blamed him unjustly, painted him as some evil individual.

And Kylie wasn't doing that again. In her heart, she knew whatever they were accusing Lucas Parker of, he hadn't done it. And if he had, there had been a damn good reason.

Chapter Thirty-four

"Change back or I'll neuter your ass right now!"

Miranda's warning jarred Kylie awake shortly before three that afternoon.

Not that Kylie wanted to wake up now. For all she cared, Miranda and Della could duke it out this time. Kylie pulled a pillow over her face when Miranda's threat repeated itself in her head.

Neuter? Della didn't have a pair of balls to remove. So who was Miranda threatening?

Oh, no. Socks, Jr.?

"Fine," Miranda's voice rose again. "You asked for it."

"Stop!" Kylie screamed, and shot out of bed just in time to see Miranda holding the kitten and wiggling her pinky at it.

"You were so wrong," Miranda snapped. "It's not me he likes. He was in bed with you."

"No, no." Kylie pushed her hair back and tried not to laugh. "That's not Perry."

"Then who is it?" she asked.

"It's not anyone. It's a real kitten."

"He fooled you again."

"No. He's not fooling me. That's a real kitten. Lucas gave it to me."

"Lucas?" Miranda's eyes widened. "That's what I came to tell you. He's missing. The FRU have been looking everywhere for him."

"I know," Kylie said.

"How do you know?" Della asked, popping into the bedroom.

The kitten let out a pathetic meow. Kylie took the scared feline from Miranda. "Holiday and Burnett came here looking for Lucas earlier today."

"Was he here?" Miranda asked.

"No, he'd already left." Kylie hesitated. "What do they think he did?"

"Beats me," Miranda answered.

Kylie hugged the kitten closer.

"Whatever it is, it must be pretty bad," Della said. "They even brought human cops out to talk to Holiday. He's up to his eyeballs in trouble."

After Della and Miranda left, Kylie sat in the living room floor playing with Socks, when Helen knocked on her door.

"Hey," Kylie said, and asked her to come inside.

"I heard you weren't feeling well."

"It's nothing," Kylie said, wondering if Helen had come to

offer her healing powers. And then she noticed something amiss in the girl's posture, as if the girl wanted to say something but couldn't spit it out. At first Kylie almost worried she'd had second thoughts about Kylie having a brain tumor.

"What's wrong?" Kylie asked.

"It's stupid, really." Helen said. "But . . . I needed some advice."

"From me?" Kylie asked.

Helen nodded. "You see, I kind of like Jonathon, but I don't think he knows I like him. And I've never been good at things with guys. I was hoping maybe you could . . . you know, tell me how to do it."

"Me?" Kylie said, and almost laughed. "Seriously, I'm not the person to come to with this."

Helen looked disappointed. "But I've never even had a boyfriend. And I don't know anyone else I could ask."

Kylie stared at Helen and remembered the girl had gone the extra mile to help her. "I've only had one real boyfriend. And because I'm not . . . flirty, I just went for honesty."

"Like what kind of honesty?" Helen asked. "Because I don't see myself as flirty either."

Kylie shrugged. "It sounds dorky, but I just asked him if he had a girlfriend. When he said no and asked why, I just said that I was sort of thinking that I liked him. I mean, I know so many girls who do the whole flipping hair, giggly thing, and maybe that works best. Then again, honesty worked for me once. Maybe it will work with Jonathon."

And maybe Kylie thought, if she could just figure out what she felt, maybe she would give honesty a try again.

• • •

The next few days were something of a blur. And not a good blur, either. Kylie and Holiday weren't getting anywhere with the meditation. Della and Miranda's bickering was at an all-time high. Trey was calling and leaving long messages on Kylie's phone. Kylie couldn't stop thinking about Lucas. Oh, and her dad had called her mom and told her that he hadn't visited Kylie the last week and that Kylie wasn't answering any of his e-mails or phone calls.

Her mom gave her hell for it, too.

"You lied to me," her mom had accused.

"No, I just let you believe he came."

"Same thing. And . . . and . . . you can't get mad at your dad," she insisted.

"Why?" Kylie asked. "You're always mad at him."

Then her mom got her panties in a wad because Kylie's dad insisted on coming out this weekend. At first, Mom had said she wouldn't come. Now she was back to being furious, and saying she was coming and that they were just going to take shifts visiting.

Guess who she expected to take care of all the scheduling?

Right. Mom expected Kylie to do it.

The only positive thing happening was that Soldier Dude hadn't returned. Kylie wanted to believe he was gone for good. Holiday wasn't convinced, though. Then again, Holiday wasn't in the best of moods lately. When Kylie asked what was going on, Holiday just shook her head and said it would work itself out.

Kylie had also asked Holiday about Lucas. The camp leader

let out a big sigh of frustration and said she couldn't talk about that. Kylie had to bite her tongue to keep from telling Holiday that trust was a two-way street. It would be nice if Holiday wouldn't be so secretive.

The tension Kylie saw in Holiday seemed even more pronounced in Sky, which struck Kylie as odd. Because so far, the werewolf leader seemed immune to the frustration brought on by the FRU's constant visits. Kylie got the impression that Holiday and Sky were having problems.

If that wasn't bad enough, the tension from the two leaders seemed to be having a bad influence on everyone else. There had been another fight, this one between a witch and a fairy.

"Told you witches and fairies don't get along," Miranda had said the day she, Kylie, and Della stumbled upon the fight being broken up by Holiday.

"What are you going to do if I discover I'm part fairy?" Kylie asked Miranda.

"Damn," Della said. "Did you just say what I think you said?"

"What?" Kylie asked, clueless.

"Are you finally admitting that you're not all human?"

With everything else going on, Kylie hadn't given the whole human or not human issue a lot of thought. And strangely enough, it didn't even seem to matter anymore. Okay, that wasn't true. She still wanted to know, but if she did find out she was supernatural it wasn't the end of the world. As a matter of fact, it was the idea that she might not be "special" that seemed to bother her more.

"So?" Miranda asked her.

"I am whatever I am," Kylie said.

Miranda started to say something and Della held up her hand. "Shh."

Kylie and Miranda paused and listened. All Kylie could hear was the background noise from the wildlife park.

"What do you hear?" Kylie asked, almost worried Chan had returned.

"The animals," Della said. "They are seriously pissed."

"At what?" Miranda asked.

"Like I would know," Della said. "But I've never heard them so . . . angry."

Right then, Helen came up beside Kylie and leaned in to whisper, "It worked. I asked if he had a girlfriend and it was just like you said happened to you. He asked me why and I told him I was thinking I might like him. And now, we're going to go on a picnic tomorrow, just to get to know each other better. Thanks."

Kylie gave Helen's arm a squeeze. "That's great. Come by before the date and Miranda can fix your makeup. Won't you, Miranda?" Kylie looked over at her friend.

"I'd love to," Miranda said.

"Thanks," Helen said, and ran off.

Saturday morning, Kylie stood back from the crowd waiting to hear who they'd be paired with for an hour and finished her conversation with her dad. She'd finally given in and called him on Friday. He'd acted like nothing was wrong, never even said anything about not coming last week, or about her not answering his calls or e-mails. He told her he was looking forward to seeing her on Sunday and then he started talking about a trip he was taking to Canada in a few weeks.

Kylie explained that her mom was also coming tomorrow and that they would have to take shifts. Kylie was positive that her dad would tell her that whole shift thing was stupid, that they could both just visit her.

Maybe deep down, a tiny part of her hoped they would both come at the same time, and then, miracles of miracles, maybe they would take one look at each other and decide they'd missed being together.

That's the thing about miracles. They didn't happen that often. Her dad didn't call the shift thing stupid. As a matter of fact, he seemed just as adamant not to see her mom as her mom was not to see him.

"How about I show up after lunch?" he asked. "And I'll call first to make sure she's not there."

Kylie bit her lip to keep from asking him where her real dad was. Every since a divorce had been mentioned, her father had changed. Completely, wholeheartedly. Parents weren't supposed to do that to their kids. She was certain it was written in the parents' rulebook.

"Fine," Kylie said. *And if you don't show up, don't worry. I don't think it will hurt as much the second time.* "Later, then," she said, and closed her phone.

"You ready?" a male voice said from behind her, leaning in close to her ear. "I got your name."

Kylie recognized Derek's voice. She'd managed to evade him all week. Not to be mean, but out of a basic need for sanity.

Her life was already a friggin' mess. She didn't need to add anything else to it. Besides, he had a girlfriend who was probably more than happy to spend time with him.

She turned around. "You already had my name," she said.

"I got lucky a second time." There was something about his voice, as if he worried she wouldn't believe him.

She didn't. "You did it again, didn't you?"

"Did what?" he asked, but she knew darn well that he understood exactly what she meant.

"You traded some more blood for my name, admit it."

He shrugged. "I wouldn't have to if you'd quit avoiding me."

"I haven't been—" She didn't want to lie to him, so she just shut up.

A couple of people walked past and he leaned in. "If you really don't want to go, you know I won't make you."

She looked up and saw the total honesty in his gaze. He hadn't touched her, so she didn't think he'd altered her emotions, and yet . . . everything inside her shifted. How could she have such strong feelings for Lucas and still be angry with Derek because he'd hooked up with another girl? It didn't add up.

Then again, why should it? Nothing in her life made a lick of sense lately.

"I've been worried about you," he said, and his voice sounded so concerned . . . and so warm.

"You mean when you weren't with Mandy?" she asked. And then she wanted to kick herself for acting as if she had a reason to be jealous.

He looked a little uncomfortable. "That's sort of what I wanted to talk to you about."

"I don't do relationship advice," Kylie said.

"I heard you do. Helen said she talked to you about her crush on Jonathon. Miranda mentioned talking to you about Perry. And what's that other vampire's name . . . ?"

Kylie let out a breath. "Fine, for some unknown reason people think I'm Cupid." But she didn't want to play Cupid for him and Mandy.

"Maybe you're related to him," he said, sounding serious for a moment.

Kylie's heart did a tight squeeze. "Could I be?"

"Some supernaturals are descendents of the gods," he said.

"Would my parents have to have been born at midnight? Or is that one of the instances that it could skip a generation?"

He shrugged. "I wouldn't know. But I bet Holiday would. You want us to go find her?" he asked, apparently willing to give up part of his hour to help her get an answer.

"That's okay. I'm meeting with her after lunch."

"So, my possible goddess." He did one of those old-timey bows. "Can I have the pleasure of your company for an hour?"

She grinned at his antics. "If you promise to behave." Or did she want him to?

"That takes all the fun out of it, but I promise." He shot her a sly look and she saw that his eyes were twinkling.

They started walking and he hesitated. "Same place? Or does the thought of the snake scare you?"

"Same place is fine." A nervous tickle did a slow dance down her spine. It wasn't about the snake, but about the memory of how close she'd come to kissing Derek that day.

They walked down the trail in silence. The sun did its

magical thing again of casting sprays of light through the trees. Kylie couldn't help but wonder what it was about being with Derek that made everything feel . . . enchanted.

"Is it you?" she asked as they got to their spot.

"Is what me?" he asked.

She eyed him with skepticism. "Are you the reason that everything feels . . . magical and so vivid? The colors, the smells, the way sun streams in."

"Oh, that's just my charm." His tone came off teasing.

"Seriously?" she asked. "Are you doing this?"

He laughed.

"Stop laughing," she insisted.

He stopped, but he didn't stop smiling. "Okay, seriously, I don't know what you mean. I'm not doing anything. It's just pretty back here."

He jumped up on the rock and held his hand down.

She hesitated and looked at his hand.

"I promised to behave," he said.

She took his hand and he lifted her up. She sat beside him, but not too close.

He pulled a knee up to his chest. His jeans looked well-worn but comfortable, and his T-shirt was a dusty green. It wasn't tight, but snug enough that it showed off the width of his shoulders. It might have been the shirt he'd been wearing when she met him. He looked really good then, and still did. Right then, Kylie wondered how she could have ever compared him to Trey. Derek was so much hotter than her ex-boyfriend.

"So you and your girl are having problems?" Kylie blurted out, trying to change the course of her thoughts.

"You could say that," he answered in a sly voice, and she watched him run a finger across his chin. Her gaze studied his lips and she wanted to taste him.

"What's wrong?" She blinked, ignored the slyness in his tone, and hoped hearing him talk about Mandy would chase off her thoughts of kissing him.

"Well, she thinks I have a thing for another girl."

Kylie felt her stomach tighten. "Do you?"

"No."

Okay, that hurt, but she tried to deny it. Oddly enough, the advice she'd been giving to everyone else, to be honest, seemed almost impossible for herself. Maybe in part because she wasn't even sure what she felt.

"But," he continued, "I think I sort of led her to think that."

"Why?" Kylie asked.

"I hoped she'd be jealous. Maybe appreciate me a little more."

"And how did that work for you?" Kylie asked, believing those kinds of games didn't end well.

"I don't know. Did you get jealous?"

Kylie looked up at him. "I . . . you mean, me?" She shook head. "But you and Mandy are—"

"Friends," he said.

It still wasn't fitting together. "But you . . . she kissed you."

"You obviously haven't ever noticed her in a crowd. She's a serial kisser. I think her parents are French."

Kylie tried to digest what he was saying. Harder yet was digesting what she felt. She liked Derek. Really liked him. And she was attracted to him. Maybe it wasn't the same intensity that she'd felt for Lucas at the creek, but it was real. And in some

ways even more real than the explosive attraction she felt for
Lucas.

And Derek hadn't left, the little voice in her head said.

"You okay?" he asked.

"Yes. No." She shook her head. "I'm just befuddled." Okay,
there. She'd given honesty a shot.

"I know," he said.

She remembered he could read her emotions and really
wished he wouldn't. The fact that he figured things out before
her didn't feel right. A breeze stirred her hair and a strand got
caught in her lips.

He gently brushed the stand back. "I'm just relieved you're
not mad at me."

"Give me a few minutes," Kylie said. "It could change. My
emotions are all over the place lately."

He grinned.

She felt herself being lured again by his smile. She shook her
head. "Derek, I just—"

"Kylie, I didn't tell you this to pressure you. I'm telling you
this because I realized how stupid it was trying to make you jealous. It occurred to me that it could totally backfire. What am I
saying? It did backfire, because you wouldn't even get within ten
feet of me."

She bit down on her lip. "I'm sorry. It's been a crazy week."

"You're going through a lot. That's another reason I wanted
to see you. I sensed you're stressed."

What all could he sense? Kylie wondered. Did he sense her
stress involved Lucas? Had he sensed she was jealous? Kylie remembered the day she'd seen Mandy kiss Derek.

"You're right. I was jealous of you and Mandy. But I still don't know if . . . I don't think—"

He held up his hand. "I'm fine with being your friend. But I'm not going to lie to you this time. I'm hoping it becomes more. But until it does, I'll respect your wishes."

She looked at him and found herself falling for him a little more. "You can do that?"

"You bet." He leaned back on the rock and put one hand behind his head. The position did wonders for his arms and chest. "Especially now that Lucas is gone," he said, and from his tone, Kylie somehow knew that Derek suspected a lot more than she wished he did.

Chapter Thirty-five

Oh, God. Did Derek somehow guess that she'd kissed Lucas? Could her emotions give that much away? Kylie didn't know. But neither did she want to ask.

So she lay back on the rock and looked up at the trees. The sound of the nearby waterfalls seemed to stir in the trees. Her mind went to the legend for a second, but then Derek's nearness was a much more intriguing thing to think about.

They didn't talk. Derek shifted his arm closer until the back of his hand brushed up against hers. That little touch sent tingles coursing through her body.

"Your mom coming tomorrow?" she asked.

"Of course. She never turns down an opportunity to embarrass me."

Kylie giggled, remembering how Derek had blushed when his mom had straightened his hair. "She loves you."

"She treats me like I'm three." He paused. "Your mom or dad coming?"

"Both," Kylie said. "Or so they say." Her dad had lied once.

"Did you know the world might end if they accidentally have to be in the same room together?"

"Is that what's got you so stressed?"

"Some of it."

He turned his arm over, slipped his hand into hers, and offered her a gentle squeeze. "I care about you. I don't like seeing you upset." His warm hold on her hand tightened again. He'd promised to behave, but she supposed he didn't see holding hands as misbehaving.

She wasn't sure she could call it that, either. She did know it felt good—sort of like a hug. His palm felt warm, not unnaturally warm, but just one person reaching out to another. "I care about you, too."

"Good," he said, and she could almost hear the smile in his voice. They didn't talk for the next few minutes, and then he asked, "Is the ghost another part of what's stressing you out?"

"Yup." Feeling safe with him, she told him about the dream she'd had of the ghost, and how she thought the ghost wanted her to help exonerate him of a war crime he didn't commit.

Derek listened as she rambled. Realizing she'd done most of the talking, she asked, "Do you still want to turn your back on your gift of communicating with the animals?"

"Yes. I'm getting really good at tuning them out. Holiday says if I keep this up, soon I won't even notice them. Of course, she says that as if it's a bad thing." He paused. "What about you? You still want to kick your gift back?"

The fact that Kylie had to stop and think about her answer left her a little surprised. "It scares me," Kylie said. "I don't think I'm brave enough to do it. But since the dream, I just keep thinking about the soldier. How brave he was. He knew when he went back to save the woman that he wouldn't live through it. I wish I knew his name so I could find out if he was accused of doing something he didn't do. And if he was, then I want to find a way to make it right." She closed her eyes for a second. "But you know what's weird?"

"What?" Derek's fingers wiggled in her hers.

"Every time I see him, he looks familiar. Like I know him from somewhere."

"Maybe you do."

"Maybe," Kylie said. "But I've even asked my mom if we had anyone in our family who ever served in the military and she said no."

Derek shifted beside her. "Did Holiday say how a ghost picks the person they attach themselves to?"

"She said it could be all kinds of ways. I could have passed by somewhere his spirit was, or it could be personal."

Derek raised his arm to check his watch. "I hate to be the bearer of bad news, but our hour was up thirty minutes ago."

"That is bad news." She closed her eyes. "Derek?"

"Yes."

"Thank you."

"For what?" he asked.

"For everything." She rolled over and looked at him. And heaven help her, but she wanted to kiss him so bad she could scream. And if the look in his eyes was any indication, she wasn't the only one wanting.

He moved in just an inch. She could feel his breath on the

corner of her mouth. He was so close, she could count his lashes, but it was his lips that tempted her.

"Kylie." The way he said her name made her melt a little more.

"Yes," she managed.

"You're making it hard for me to keep my promise."

"I'm sorry." She almost kissed him then. Almost. But knowing it wouldn't be fair to him, or herself, she didn't do it. Not yet.

The next morning Kylie sat with her mom and watched her check her watch for the tenth time. Kylie couldn't help but wonder if her mom hated being with Kylie so much, or if it was the thought of her dad showing up that made her mom so eager to leave. Probably both.

"I'm so glad it's working out here," her mom said, straightening her tan suit jacket. The color did nothing for her olive complexion and dark hair. It only enhanced what looked to be dark circles under her eyes.

"Your friends seem nice, too." Her mom glanced over to Della and her parents at the table in front of them.

Kylie had introduced her to both Miranda and Della when she arrived. Her mom leaned in. "The hair is a bit much on that one girl. But if you tell me she's not too wild, or doing drugs or anything, I guess I have to believe you."

"She's not wild, Mom," Kylie muttered. Silence followed, and Kylie knew what it would be like living with her mom, dealing with her mom's prejudices and awkward silences. Kylie could feel the chill from across the table. Not a ghostly chill, either.

Or was it?

Kylie shifted her gaze across the room and saw him standing in the corner, staring, crying more tears of blood. Her heart gripped and Kylie really wished she knew his name so she could help him.

"Are you sure we don't have any family in the military?" Kylie asked her mom again.

"Positive, dear." She looked at her watch again. "Your camp leader—what's her name? Holiday? She seems nice, too."

"Holiday is nice," Kylie said, remembering how she'd exchanged glances with Holiday after she'd met her mom and seeing the camp leader shake her head no, as if to say, her mom wasn't supernatural.

"Okay, I guess I should go," her mom said. "Do you want to walk me to my car?"

Kylie spied the clock on the wall. Her mom was leaving thirty minutes early. *So much for mother/daughter quality time.*

"Of course." Kylie got up. As they passed Della and Miranda with their parents, Kylie realized neither of them seemed particularly happy. Tonight's table chat, a nightly ritual, was going to be more like a whine session.

Kylie and her mom walked to the parking lot without talking. Thankfully, the ghost didn't join them. When her mom turned around to say her final good-byes, she reached out and gave Kylie's arm a squeeze.

Kylie's chest tightened as the memory of needing a hug at Nana's funeral came barreling back at her.

"You know, some moms hug their kids."

Shock crossed her mom's face. "Do you need me to hug you?"

"No," Kylie said. *Who wanted a hug you had to ask for?* It was like having to ask for an apology.

"Bye, Mom." Kylie turned around and went back to the dining hall to wait for her dad. She didn't look back and watch her mom drive away, even though she knew her mom would be waving and expecting Kylie to do the same. From now on, no hugs equaled no farewell waves.

Kylie almost didn't recognize him. First, where was the touch of gray lining his temples? Second, his hair was not naturally two-toned. And for sure, he didn't wear it in a spike cut. She wasn't even going to talk about the clothes he wore. Old men should never, ever wear tight jeans.

"Is that him?" Holiday asked.

Kylie wished she could lie and run out the back door, but her dad spotted her across the room and started over to her.

"Is he a supernatural?" Kylie asked, fighting the embarrassment and looking back at Holiday's twitching brows.

"No." She let out a big sigh. "But that doesn't mean—"

"I know," Kylie interrupted.

"How's my pumpkin?" Her dad pulled her into a tight hug. Kylie closed her eyes and tried to forget how he looked and just let herself soak up the comfort of having his loving arms around her. Tears filled her eyes and she swallowed hard, praying she could contain them.

"I'm okay," she muttered, and pulled back. Her sinuses stung, but the tears didn't fall.

"Is this one of your friends?" her father asked, motioning to Holiday.

Kylie looked at Holiday's camp-leader badge and wondered if her dad's dye job had fried his eyesight.

"I wish." Holiday held out her hand. "I'm Holiday Brandon, one of the camp leaders."

"You're kidding me," her dad said. "You can't be a day over twenty. And you don't look like any camp leader I've ever seen." His smile widened and his gaze shifted down Holiday's shapely form.

"No kidding." Holiday eased her hand from her dad's.

Kylie gawked at the man who had been her rock, who had been there through skinned knees, mom arguments, and even boy problems. The reality rolled over her like a dump truck. Her father was flirting. With Holiday. Holiday who was . . . well, at least fifteen years younger than her dad.

"What happened to the gray in your hair, Dad?" Kylie blurted out.

Her dad looked back at her. "I . . . I don't know."

"Well, excuse me," Holiday said, and Kylie could swear she saw a smile appear in the woman's eyes. "I'll let you two visit."

Or not, Kylie thought. She didn't know this man, and she wasn't all that sure she wanted to get to know him, either.

• • •

"He wasn't like that before," Kylie said a little over an hour later, still fighting the urge to cry.

Kylie's dad had stayed less than an hour. Holiday, as if sensing Kylie was upset, asked her to go with her on a run into town to buy some supplies.

"Divorce is hard on people," Holiday said. "Trust me, when my parents divorced, they went totally bonkers, too. Mom even got breast implants and started borrowing my clothes."

"How did you survive?" Kylie asked.

"You just do. Of course, large ice cream consumption helps." Holiday smiled as she pulled into the ice cream shop parking lot. "What do you say? Wanna feed our worries with creamy, sweet, cold stuff?"

Kylie nodded.

Holiday reached for the door. "Follow my lead. First we have to sample at least five flavors each, then we order a triple scoop."

Kylie laughed. "What worries are you feeding?"

"Are you kidding? Do you know how many hours I've been stuck with Mr. Big, Bad Vampire?"

"Burnett," Kylie said, understanding. "Why don't you just say yes?"

"Yes? Oh, no. Over my dead fairy body. He's as irritating, rude, and obnoxious as he is . . . hot."

"So you're in love, huh?" Kylie teased.

Holiday pointed a finger at her. "Keep this up, and you won't get any ice cream."

As Kylie and Holiday fed their faces with everything from

chocolate mint to banana chocolate fudge, Kylie, hyped up on sugar, let a question slip that she normally wouldn't ask. "How do you know you're in love?"

Holiday licked her spoon clean of her cotton candy–flavored ice cream. "You don't ask easy questions, do you?"

Kylie spooned up a bite of butter pecan. "Nope."

Holiday studied her ice cream. "I've thought I've been in love several times. A few times with my heart and even more times with my hormones."

Holiday's answer described Kylie's situation with Lucas and Derek perfectly. Kylie spooned up a bite of ice cream. "And none of those worked out?"

"Nope. That's the tricky thing about love. It walks like a duck, quacks like a duck, and smells like a duck. But after you sleep with it a month or so, or get dumped at the altar by it, it starts smelling more like a skunk."

Kylie leaned forward to ask. "Is this your fancy-dancy way of telling me I shouldn't sleep around?"

Holiday pointed her spoon at Kylie. "Nope, it's my fancy-dancy way of saying you gotta be careful." She leaned in. "Just because a guy rings your bell, doesn't mean you have to toot his horn."

Kylie laughed and so did Holiday.

Holiday stirred her ice cream. "If I could go back, I wouldn't have slept with three of the guys I did. But you can't go back. And the memories. Bad, bad memories are tattooed on my brain." She tapped her spoon against her forehead. "You can't even get them lasered off."

Kylie nodded. She had a few bad memories of her own that she couldn't shake, so she totally related.

When they finished their ice cream, they walked next door to the used bookstore. Kylie happened to catch the title of a book that had been left on a shelf. *Overcoming Dyslexia.* Picking up the book, she flipped through it and wondered if Miranda had ever read it.

She walked over to the counter and asked if they had any other books on this subject. The lady took her to a whole section of books about different disabilities. Kylie selected three more on coping with dyslexia and paid for them.

Holiday was still browsing, so Kylie stepped outside and took in the small town's main street. It was quaint. Antique stores, specialty shops, and even a candy store—the kind of place her parents used to drag her to when she was a kid.

A couple walked past holding hands and Kylie tried to remember if, on any of those trips, her mom and dad had ever acted like they were in love. She couldn't recall ever seeing them holding hands. They always did their own things when they were out. Her dad played golf. Her mom shopped.

Kylie had just moved over to Holiday's van when she spotted another couple step out of the bed-and-breakfast. They were kissing. Not the quick, touch of lips kind of kissing, but tongues moving in and out of each other's mouth like they were in heat or something. The kissing quickly progressed to the butt-grabbing stage. *Find a room,* Kylie thought, wondering if they knew they had an audience or if they even cared. Ahh, but wrong or right, Kylie couldn't look away.

Mostly because alarm bells were sounding in her brain.

There was something familiar about them.

She watched the woman's hands slip into the front of the man's jeans. Kylie's mouth dropped open. Gross. That was so lewd, yet Kylie, now hiding behind the van, still couldn't turn away. When the couple finally parted mouths and the guy turned forward, recognition hit.

Kylie gripped the side of the van, her knees suddenly feeling like jelly.

"Oh, my God."

Chapter Thirty-six

Dad?

Kylie grabbed the door handle to keep herself from falling face-first onto the street. What was her dad doing . . . doing with . . . Kylie's gaze shot to the woman, or she should say, shot to the "girl." Kylie recognized her dad's new assistant whom she'd met last month at a company picnic. The girl was in her third year of college.

Still leaning against the van, Kylie did the math. While math wasn't her best subject, she figured the girl to be about four years older than Kylie herself.

And just like that, Kylie figured out a bunch of things. Like how her father's six pairs of underwear ended up being grilled—how her mom's countless cold-shoulder moments toward her dad suddenly added up to be fair justice.

Realizing the couple had walked to where they might spot her, Kylie moved to the other side of the van. And the cold that followed her around the van told Kylie she wasn't alone. Yet, too emotionally distraught to think about the ghost, Kylie concentrated on not barfing up the triple scoop of ice cream she'd just consumed.

Holiday arrived shortly. "You okay?"

"Great," Kylie lied, too embarrassed, too horrified to give details. Bad enough her father had flirted with Holiday, but to see him with someone who probably still treated her skin for acne, well, it was just too much.

On the way back to the camp, Kylie looked at Holiday. "Do you know what qualifies as justifiable homicide?"

"No." The camp leader laughed. "But if I have to put up with Burnett much longer, I might become an expert. Who are you thinking of offing?"

"My parents." The vision of Kylie's dad groping his assistant filled her head and her chest ached. "Or maybe just my dad."

Kylie waited a few more minutes before she dropped the bomb. "Do you think . . . you could hold off a few more weeks before you talk to my mom about my going home?"

Holiday didn't look at her, but Kylie saw the smile of victory in her profile as she continued to watch the road. "You betcha."

Monday night, almost everyone hung out at the dining hall to watch movies. Kylie, Miranda, and Della had stayed up way too late Sunday night nursing the wounds inflicted by their respective parents. Then Kylie and Miranda went over the books Kylie had bought on dyslexia.

"This won't work," Miranda said, frustrated at just trying to read the first chapter.

"What if I read it to you?" Kylie said.

Miranda looked up at Kylie and her eyes went misty. "You'd do that?"

"You'd do it for me, wouldn't you?" Kylie asked.

"In a snap," Miranda said.

Hence, the two of them had stayed up way too late. So instead of hanging out to watch a movie, Kylie headed back to her cabin.

When she opened her cabin door, the smell hit her and she wrinkled her nose. She obviously needed to clean the litter box. Then Socks, the little ball of fur Lucas had given her as a farewell gift, stuck its head out from under the sofa and hissed.

"Come here, sweetie," she cooed, but dang it if the kitten didn't go deeper under the sofa. Her phone buzzed. Kylie pulled it out of her pocket, saw that it was her mom, and placed the phone on the coffee table and tried to coax the kitten out.

After several failed attempts, Kylie gave up. "Fine, sleep under the sofa." Frustrated and tired, Kylie started pulling her shirt off over her head and went to get her PJs on.

When she reached her dresser, she heel-kicked off her tennis shoes and pulled out her favorite nightshirt. Slipping off her bra, she dropped it on a chair. Then and only then did she raise her eyes to the mirror.

Her breath hitched. It took her mind a second to compute what she was looking at in the reflection. And another second to get friggin' mad.

"Get out of here, you twerp!" She hurried and slipped on her night shirt before turning her full fury on Perry, who had transformed himself into a lion and was stretched out and taking up her whole bed.

"Out!" Kylie seethed.

The lion roared.

Kylie grabbed her boobs beneath the nightshirt and raged, "You finally got a peek at your first set of boobs, didn't you? You are so . . . so pathetic. And don't you think for one minute that I won't tell Miranda about this, either."

She reached down and picked up her shoe and threw it at the beast. "Out!" The animal roared again. "I swear to God, Perry, if you don't sparkle your ass out of here, I'll pin both your ears behind your head and break your neck."

The room's temperature suddenly dropped a good fifty degrees.

"Don't scream," a male voice said. "And don't make any sudden moves."

Kylie's heart slammed against her ribs when she saw the soldier standing beside her night table. It wasn't so much that he was there that had her mentally stammering, it was that he'd spoken to her.

She took in a deep breath. A wisp of steam escaped her lips as she exhaled.

Goose bumps rose on her flesh. She crossed her arms to fight the chill. "The lion isn't real," she managed to say. "It's Perry. He's a shape-shifter."

The soldier wasn't bleeding this time. But the memory of the dream, of seeing him dying on that dirty floor came hurtling back. Her heart ached for him. Now that he was finally talking to her, would he tell her his name? Oddly enough, even mentally referring him as Soldier Dude didn't feel right. He deserved more respect.

"It is real, Kylie," he said as the lion roared again.

She reached for her other shoe and hurled it at Perry.

"Kylie, listen to me." The ghost's voice grew louder, firmer. "That isn't Perry. It's real. And it's dangerous. Don't provoke it. Move to the door. Get out, now."

His words sank in and she stared harder at the lion.

The lion who was not sparkling back into human form.

The lion who stood up and leapt from the bed.

The lion who moved in front of the door and prevented her from escaping.

The lion, who paced back and forth while sizing her up as if trying to decide what kind of sauce he wanted her served with.

Kylie didn't, couldn't, look away from the lion, but she spoke to the ghost. "Okay, the door thing didn't work. Got any other ideas?"

"Stay calm." His words rang the same time the animal roared, sounding angry. Hungry.

"That's kind of hard to do." She shivered, both from the cold and the thought of the lion's teeth ripping open her rib cage.

"He's waiting for you to run. If you stay calm, it will give us some time."

"Time to do what?" she asked. The lion dropped down on the floor and started cleaning his paws. Was he washing up before dinner?

"Time to think of something else," he answered.

Hearing her own teeth chatter, she glanced over at the ghost. "Can't you . . . make him leave?"

"If I could, he would already be gone." Sincerity added deepness to his voice. In spite of her panic, something about the ghost struck that chord of familiarity again. As if she knew him, or maybe as if she should know him.

"What's your name?" She tried to stop shaking, but couldn't.

"Daniel Brighten," he said.

She let the name bounce around her head, trying to find a connection. Nothing clicked. Blinking, she met his blue eyes again, watching as a strand of his blond hair fell across his brow. "Why?" she asked. "Why are you following me around? Is it about how you died?"

"No," he said. "I needed you to know that I didn't have a choice."

Why did he need me to know that? Kylie flipped her gaze from him to the lion every other second. "Do I need to tell someone? Did you get accused of hurting that woman?"

"No."

The lion stood back up and Kylie's breath caught. She looked around for something to defend herself with.

"Don't do that," the ghost said.

"Don't do what?"

"Don't grab the chair."

She gazed back to him. "Can you read my mind?"

"No, you were looking at it."

"I'm scared," she admitted.

"I know, but if you grab it, the lion might feel threatened."

"Yeah, well, I'm kind of feeling threatened, too. The beast is supposed to be next door at the refuge, not in my bedroom." Kylie suddenly remembered Della telling her that the animals sounded angry. Was the lion angry at her now? "How did it even get here?"

"I don't know, but let's worry about that later."

A deep rumble sounded from the lion's chest. Kylie wasn't sure if that was his angry noise, but from where she stood it sure as hell was his scary noise.

"Don't panic, Kylie. He can smell it."

Daniel was right, Kylie decided. Animals, like supernaturals, could smell things like fear. She inhaled slowly. *Think about something else. Think about something else.* Her mind found a topic and she looked at Daniel again.

"Is Nana, my grandmother, in heaven?"

"Of course she is."

"If you can visit me, why hasn't she?" The steam from her lips snaked up to the ceiling.

"I was here first."

"Where were you first?" Her teeth chattered again.

"Waiting until you were old enough to understand. They only allow one spirit to come to you at a time, until you are able to cope."

"Well, they were wrong." She looked back at the lion.

"Wrong about what?"

"I'm not ready to cope yet."

He smiled.

Kylie hadn't meant it to be funny. "So you've actually seen Nana?" New goose bumps started forming on top of the old goose bumps. Kylie knew she would feel warmer if the ghost left, but the idea of being alone with the lion didn't thrill her.

"She is not a woman who can be missed," he said. "Not even in spirit form."

Curiosity struck. "Did you meet her before . . . before she died?"

"A long time ago." His light blue eyes, combined with his blond hair, pulled her in for a second. She studied him. And then it happened.

She saw inside his head. She was doing what all the other supernaturals could do. Seeing his pattern. A tiny thrill ran through her.

Blinking, she continued to look at his pattern. He had vertical lines and then some odd kind of writing, like Chinese, or prehistoric symbols. "You are . . . were supernatural, weren't you?"

The lion let go of another roar. Kylie flinched as the beast stood. "I think he's hungry," she said. "I think I should get the chair now, don't you?"

The ghost didn't answer. Kylie noticed the temperature rising. Oh, shit. Even the ghost feared being eaten alive. Only he couldn't be since he was already dead.

Just as she might be soon if she didn't think of something quick.

Tears filled her eyes. She was alone. All alone. And then the lion tossed his head back and forth and lunged at her.

Chapter Thirty-seven

Kylie shot behind the chair, thinking about using it as a weapon, but when she looked up, the lion had backed up. He poked his face out the bedroom door as if something out there had caught his attention.

Then Kylie heard it, the kitten. The lion took a step out of the bedroom. She could go slam the door, push the bed against the wall.

And listen as the animal ate her kitten alive.

"No!" She rocked the chair back and forth to get the lion's attention. "Come here, you ugly foul-smelling monster."

The lion backed up, growled, exposing his teeth, and shook his mane at her.

For some reason, she thought about the soldier and his choice to die as he went back to save the woman.

I'm not going to die. I'm not going to die.

"Daniel, please come back," she called out, not wanting to be alone.

The cold brushed over her skin again. "Holiday is getting help."

The lion came closer to the chair. New tears filled her eyes. "Don't leave me again, okay?" she begged.

"I won't," he said. "I never wanted to."

"Kylie?" Holiday yelled out from the living room.

The lion charged at the door. "Don't come in," Kylie screamed, and shook the chair to keep the beast's attention in case Holiday didn't hear her.

Kylie heard retreating footsteps. "Burnett is on his way to get a sedative gun," Holiday called. "He's just a few minutes away. Are you safe?"

Safe? She had a lion in her bedroom. But if Burnett was on the way, maybe . . . Kylie started to answer when she heard more voices.

"No," Holiday said.

"No what?" Kylie asked.

"It's too dangerous," Holiday said as if talking to someone else.

Footsteps sounded from the cabin's living room. The lion growled. Derek appeared in the doorway. His soft green eyes met hers, and then shifted to the lion. Fear flickered in his eyes, and she felt the same fear as he did.

The thought she might have to watch the lion attack Derek sent her heart bouncing against her ribcage. "Leave, Derek," Kylie said, trying to sound calm even though she was a breath from screaming. "Listen to Holiday."

"I can do this," he said in a confident voice. "I have the gift, remember?"

Derek took a step into the room. The lion shook his mane and growled.

Derek didn't move. He stared at the beast. Then he started unbuttoning his shirt.

"What are you doing?" she asked, and while the idea of seeing him without his shirt tempted her, this was so not the time.

"He doesn't like how I smell."

"Then for God's sake keep it on so he doesn't eat you."

"It's okay." Derek tossed his shirt back into the living room. He looked even better than she imagined. Then, holding his palms out, he took another step forward. The lion roared, but didn't charge.

Derek took another step. This time, the lion lunged for him, almost taking Derek's arm in his mouth.

"No." Kylie started rocking the chair to get the animal's attention.

"Stop that," Derek ordered.

"It stops him from getting you."

"Kylie, you're making him mad. Trust me, okay? Stop!"

The firmness in his voice got her attention. Soldier Dude stood silent in the corner, so she couldn't stop shivering.

"I'm going to come over to you," Derek said. "I want you stand behind me. Then we're moving out the door. You go through first and I'll shut it. You understand?"

Almost as if the lion knew Derek's plan, he growled and faced Derek, but backed up closer to Kylie. Each step Derek took, the lion took another closer to Kylie.

A urine smell filled Kylie's nose. The big cat's backside hit the chair and knocked Kylie against the wall.

When she refocused, she saw Derek now stood inches from the lion. So close that the beast's mane brushed up against his bare abdomen. Derek's muscles tightened and his upper body appeared hard, almost chiseled.

"Now ease out from behind the chair, Kylie," Derek said.

"Do as he says," Daniel said, speaking up.

Kylie moved her foot and the lion slammed his head into Derek, and almost knocked him down.

Derek rebounded. "Slowly, Kylie," he said, as if he didn't realize the lion could open his mouth and use him for a chew toy. "Slow and easy."

She inched out, afraid to even breathe, and then Derek caught her arm and eased her behind him. She placed her hands on his bare sides. The palms of her hands pressed against his warm skin.

"That's good. Now we're going to do baby steps back until we're out the door. You're doing good. Keep going."

Kylie felt the door's threshold against her heel. Derek reached around to the left for the doorknob, and the lion lunged and swatted his claws at Derek.

Derek's hiss filled Kylie's ears, and she knew the beast's claws had ripped into his skin. "You okay?" she asked.

He didn't answer, just reached again for the knob. The lion roared, but didn't charge this time. Kylie continued to move backward into the living room as Derek slowly followed. As he closed the door, Kylie saw Daniel smile.

"You did it." Holiday rushed inside the cabin. Kylie stood there, hugging herself, her insides trembling, and feeling sick to her stomach.

"Help me move the sofa to the door in case he decides to charge it," Derek said.

As Derek and Holiday moved the sofa against the door, Kylie noticed blood dripping down his hard abdomen.

"You're . . . hurt." Her teeth chattered so hard she could barely talk. She pointed at him and felt a cold sweat drip from her forehead.

"Just scratched," he assured her.

She took the steps separating them and fell against him. She didn't care that she was getting blood all over her favorite nightshirt, either. She dropped her face against the warm wall of skin and muscle and continued to shake.

He wrapped his arms around her. Holiday moved in and placed a hand on her back.

Kylie didn't know which one of the fairies were doing it, or if it was both—she honestly didn't care—but the thousands of tiny pinpricks of panic started to fade. She felt safe and that was all that mattered.

She buried her face deeper into Derek's naked shoulder, loving how he smelled, how it felt to be this close to him.

"Put Kylie down in one of the other bedrooms," Holiday said.

"No. I'm fine." Kylie raised her head, but didn't want to leave the comfort of Derek's arms. She needed this for just a little longer. He was so warm and she was so . . . cold.

Kylie saw Daniel standing behind Holiday. He smiled at her and then faded. "Thank you," Kylie said, hoping he heard her.

"You're welcome," Derek answered.

Kylie looked back to offer Derek his own verbal gratitude, but a loud *whack* stopped her. The cabin door slammed open so hard it sounded like it had cracked. Burnett came barging into the cabin, his eyes glowed red, and he held a big rifle in his hands.

"You promised me that you wouldn't come up here," he seethed at Holiday.

"I changed my mind," she said, not sounding at all remorseful.

The lion roared on the other side of the door and Burnett roared with him. "I'll take care of that first, and then I'll deal with you."

"Yeah, well, good luck with that." Holiday smirked.

Burnett started toward the door. "Wait." Derek set Kylie back. "Let me calm him down so he won't think you are killing him."

At first Burnett appeared doubtful, but then Holiday nodded. "Fine," Burnett said.

Kylie couldn't say she'd offer the beast that much courtesy, but deep down, she admired Derek for doing it.

The two men eased the sofa away from the door. Burnett pressed his ear to the door and then said, "He's on the other side of the room." Then he reached for the knob.

"Be careful," Kylie said.

Derek looked back at her and smiled. "Piece of cake."

"You don't have to stay here," Kylie told Holiday, who pulled a chair beside Kylie's bed about an hour later. The camp leader had personally cleaned Kylie's room to remove the stench of the animal.

Holiday leaned in and whispered, "It's this or I'll get my ass chewed out by Mr. Big Bad and Handsome. So just pretend like you need me until he leaves. Now that they've taken the lion, I don't think he'll hang around longer than a few more minutes." Sitting back in her chair, she bit down on her lip. "Boy, am I glad Derek was around."

Something occurred to Kylie. "Couldn't one of the witches have stopped this?"

"If I could have found them," she said. "They were all out on a hike with Sky. I knew Burnett had just left here to go back to the wildlife park, so I called him."

"What was he doing at the wildlife park?" Kylie asked. Then she said, "What's going on, Holiday? How did the lion get here? Who put it in my room? And don't tell me that it's your job to worry, either."

It didn't appear as if Holiday was going to answer. Her expression turned grim, and she dropped her hands into her lap. "You're going to find out tomorrow, anyway."

"Find what out?"

"Someone is raiding the wildlife park. Killing the very animals the park is trying to save. Most of the animals killed have been on the endangered species list. Of course, the government didn't waste any time blaming us, either. Any strange crime happens anywhere and someone is pointing to the supernaturals."

"They think one of us is doing it?" Kylie asked.

Holiday bit down on her lip. "Not only do they believe it, but as of this afternoon they have proof. At least they think they do."

"So someone here is doing this?" Kylie asked.

"They found a blood trail leading back to our camp."

"But the lion wasn't killed," Kylie said.

"No, but the fact that it was here just makes things worse. Someone had to help that animal escape."

"And someone put it in my room," Kylie said.

"That or it could just be a coincidence," Holiday said. "He could have wandered into any cabin."

"But the cabin door was closed," Kylie said.

"Maybe one of you left it opened. Then he might have hit it and shut himself in."

"Or someone put him here," Kylie said.

Holiday reached out to touch her again, to calm her, and Kylie held up her hand. "I'm okay."

Falling deeper into her pillow, Kylie stared up at the ceiling. "Do they blame Lucas for this?"

Holiday was quiet for a moment. "He's being looked at as a possible suspect."

"I don't believe it," Kylie said. "He's not like that."

"I know, but . . . I can't convince them of that. Especially since Fredericka took off this afternoon."

"She did?" Kylie watched Holiday nod, and she felt the tiniest bit of jealousy. "Do you think she's with Lucas?"

"Knowing her, yes."

Kylie clutched her hands together, accepting she had to get past Lucas, but still refusing to believe he was guilty. "Are they going to try to shut down the camp?"

Holiday's frown deepened. "If they can't get to the bottom of this, they'll try. I'll fight it with every ounce of fairy dust I have in me, but . . . it may take more than me."

Silence filled the room and then Holiday said, "Burnett's going to hold a meeting tomorrow and probably interrogate everyone. I wish I could stop him, but damn it, with all the evidence, I can't even argue with him that it's not one of us. But throwing accusations around in a group of adolescent supernaturals is sure to backfire."

"Do you really believe someone here is doing it?"

"Yeah. Either that or someone is trying awfully hard to make it look like we're doing it."

The door to Kylie's bedroom opened and Burnett stuck his head in. "Are you going back up to the office?"

Holiday's expression changed to fake concern. She rested a hand on Kylie's shoulder. "I'm afraid she needs me. We'll talk tomorrow."

Burnett wasn't fooled, that was apparent by his expression, but he didn't argue, either. Well, as long as one didn't call slamming the door an argument.

"Jerk," Holiday muttered.

"I can hear you," he retorted from the other side of the wall.

Holiday frowned. "I swear, he's this close to me siccing a death angel on his ass." And she didn't try to say that quietly, either.

"I thought you didn't know if they really existed," Kylie whispered after a few minutes. If she'd thought they existed, she would have asked Daniel Brighten, the soldier, to go find one. Then she recalled what Holiday had said about all ghosts being angels. For sure, Daniel had been a big part of what saved Kylie.

She leaned close. "All I have to do is threaten and even big bad vampires usually piss in their pants."

They both laughed and then Kylie said, "He saved me, didn't he?"

"Derek?" Holiday asked. "Yeah, I would say he did."

"No. I mean, Derek did save me, but it was the ghost who told you, right?"

"Sort of," she said. "Because he's attached to you, he can't really communicate with me. But he found someone who could." Holiday reached down and squeezed Kylie's hand. "Nana said to tell you she loves you. But she wished you wouldn't have let them bury her wearing that purple lipstick."

Kylie got tears in her eyes and laughed at the same time. After a few minutes, she said, "I finally did it."

"Did what?"

"I saw into someone's mind." Kylie almost told her it was the ghost's mind that she'd been able to see, but for some reason she wasn't ready to talk about that. It was as if she needed to digest it all first. There were a lot of things she needed to digest.

Holiday grinned. "Welcome to our world, girl."

Kylie's smile was weak, but it was real. "Does that definitely mean . . . that I'm one of you guys?"

"Yup." Holiday brushed a strand of hair from Kylie's cheek.

"When you saw Nana, did you check if she had been a supernatural?"

"I did. She was human." Holiday gave Kylie's hand a squeeze. "How do you feel about this new development?"

Kylie let out a deep breath. "A little scared. A little relieved. Now I just want to figure out what I am."

"You will, Kylie. The answer is here. It always is."

Chapter Thirty-eight

Holiday was right.

Not about Kylie discovering what she was. It had been five days since Kylie had almost been a lion's dinner, and her identity crisis was still alive and thriving.

The thing Holiday had pegged right was Burnett's method of solving the wildlife crimes backfiring. As soon as he announced that someone at the camp was guilty everyone started pointing fingers. The vampires accused the werewolves because most of the animals killed had been from the feline family and everyone knew werewolves hated cats.

The werewolves accused the vampires of doing it because their blood supply was low. The fairies accused the witches because they sometimes used tiger blood in some of their spells. The witches accused the fairies because everyone knew fairies were sneaky little bastards. Someone pointed out that the shape-shifters were known to use wild animals as sport to hunt and conquer them.

Then, the finger-pointing stopped being species-directed and certain unlucky individuals got suspicion slapped on them. Lucas and Fredericka got voted to be the most likely guilty parties. Then Derek's name got thrown in the hat because he could communicate with animals, and everyone knew he didn't want the gift. Then because Kylie was still considered "the weird one" with a strange pattern and a closed mind, her name got tossed into the guilty hat as well.

Kylie had even forgotten herself and went to Della and accused her cousin Chan of being the culprit. Maybe he really was one of the Blood Brothers gang. Della did what Della always did. She got furious.

Tension at the camp was at an all-time high. People had stopped participating in the Meet Your Campmates Hour, and Holiday and Sky were having a hard time just keeping everyone from killing each other.

Then there was the tension between the two camp leaders.

Kylie had walked into the office and overheard them tossing verbal punches. Sky insisted it was time to throw in the towel and close down the camp. Holiday insisted right back that it would be over her cold fairy body before she let them close it down. Sky accused Holiday of being a martyr and unrealistic, and Holiday accused Sky of having lost her faith in the school and of half-assing her job this year.

Kylie didn't know Sky very well, but she knew enough to agree with Holiday. For some reason, Kylie had never warmed up to the werewolf camp leader. In some ways, the woman even reminded Kylie a bit of her mom. Cold, uncaring, and closed-off.

Not that Sky might not have reasons for joining the ranks of the Ice Queen Sorority. It appeared that Kylie's mom sure as hell did.

It was funny how all of a sudden Kylie saw the relationship between her mom and dad differently now. Yeah, her mom was cold, but her dad was a cheater. It sort of became a "what came first, the chicken or the egg" kind of question. A question Kylie didn't have the answer to.

While it still hurt something fierce to think about the divorce, Kylie had decided to try not to make it her problem. Face it, she had enough fires to put out in her own life. Heck, she'd almost become kitty chow. In the back of Kylie's mind, she still wondered who wanted her harmed badly enough to put the lion in her room. The only name that came to mind was Fredericka. But if she believed Fredericka guilty, did that not put more suspicion on to Lucas?

Thoughts of Lucas snuck into Kylie's mind more than she wanted. Now at least when they showed up, they had to compete with thoughts of Derek. He and Kylie hadn't been alone since the whole lion scene, but he sat with her and Miranda and Della sometimes during meals. Every now and then, she'd catch him looking at her with more than friendship, but good to his word, he never put any pressure on her.

Nope, the pressure she felt came from herself. One minute she'd make up her mind to just walk up to him and kiss him. The next she'd find herself thinking about her dad, about Trey, and she'd wonder if giving herself to a relationship was worth the heartbreak that seemed to follow.

And then there was the whole issue of trying to figure out

what she was. For some reason, she felt that once she got that solved, she'd be free to make other life choices.

Kylie walked back into her cabin, stopping to sniff the air for beast smells. Nose still up, she felt her foot being attacked by Socks. Scooping the little fellow up in her hands, she brought him to her face.

Whenever Socks was running amok, Kylie figured the cabin was free of beasts and ghosts. Daniel had only dropped by a few times—each of which would send Socks scrambling under the sofa. Not that Socks had to stay hidden long; Daniel was back to short visits and he'd stopped talking.

"So the coast is clear, huh?" Kylie asked Socks.

"Except for a very happy witch," Miranda said, barreling out of her bedroom to give Kylie and Socks a hug.

"Let me guess," Kylie said. "Perry finally grew a pair and kissed you."

"No," Miranda said. "I'm beginning to wonder if he ever will. But forget about him right now, because I finally did it. Well, with your help, of course."

"You did what?" Kylie asked.

"I got rid of Mr. Pepper."

"Of who?"

"My piano teacher."

"Oh gawd, tell me you didn't let Della cook him."

"No. I figured out what I messed up with the curse, and reversed it. I used those books to help me figure out what I could have gotten backwards—words, letters. It was like a puzzle, but I finally figured it out." She held her arms up in the air in victory. "I'm toad free."

Kylie laughed.

"And . . ." Miranda continued, "the best part is that Mr. Pepper checked himself into a mental hospital."

"Because he has a thing for young girls?"

"No, because he's been dreaming he's a toad, but . . . he confessed to the doctor that he was worried about his attraction to little girls." Miranda laughed. "I sort of dropped in on his first session. But what's important is maybe he'll get some help."

"You did good," Kylie said.

"No. We did good. I wouldn't have done it if not for you. And while I'm not sure I'll ever make High Priestess, I still might be in the running. You're my hero, Kylie Galen."

"And I'm not?" Della asked, walking out of her bedroom.

"Sorry," Miranda said. "You'll have to try harder next week."

Kylie put Socks down so he could attack Della. For some reason, the kitten loved her Donald Duck slippers.

Kylie watched the kitten take swats at Donald's bill and then reality wormed its way into her good mood. "We may not have next week. They really may shut the camp down if they don't find out who is terrorizing the wildlife park. We've got to stop pointing fingers and do something. I don't know about you guys, but I don't want to go home."

"Did something else happen?" Della asked.

. Kylie told them what she'd learned when she'd stopped by Holiday's cabin. "They almost snagged the white tiger."

"How?" Della asked. "I thought that vamp from the FRU was guarding the place."

"He is, but someone broke into the lion's fences again, and

while Burnett was investigating that, someone cut the fence to the tiger's cage."

"Poor animals," Miranda said.

"Yeah," Kylie answered, remembering Derek saying the lion that had shown up in her cabin had been confused and scared. "Wait," Kylie said. "Why didn't I think of this before?"

"What?" Della and Miranda asked at the same time.

"I think I know how to get to the bottom of this."

Chapter Thirty-nine

"It doesn't work like that," Derek said ten minutes later, wearing his shirt completely unbuttoned. No doubt Kylie had banged on his cabin door after he was already undressed.

Kylie glanced at his chest and noticed that his scratches were healing. "What do you mean, it doesn't work like that? I thought you could communicate with animals."

Derek closed the cabin door and moved her off the porch as if he was afraid one of his roommates might be listening.

"It's not like I can ask them questions. I hear or, should say, sense their emotions. And not even all of them."

"You said the lion told you he didn't like how you smelled."

"He didn't tell me. He thought it." Derek shook his head. "It won't work, Kylie."

"But it has to." Her throat tightened. "They're going to close down the camp, Derek. I'm just getting a grip on the whole non-human stuff, I can't leave now."

He studied her face for a moment. "I know, but—"

"It's not just about me, either. You've seen what's been

happening at the camp. Everyone is turning on each other. Everyone says the camp is what helps keep peace among all of us. If they think the various supernatural gangs are bad now, think of—"

He put a finger to her lips and she fought the desire to slip her hands inside the opened shirt and hug him. "I'm not disagreeing with you. But I just don't think it will work."

Right then she remembered. For Derek to be able to turn off his gift, he had to continue to shut them out. Yet he'd saved her from the lion. She hadn't even considered his sacrifice until now. How could she have forgotten that?

"I'm sorry." She closed her eyes a second. "It's because of your gift, because you have to stop using it. I forgot—"

"No," he said. "Okay, yeah, maybe a little."

"It's okay, Derek," she said, seeing guilt in his eyes. She remembered that only a few weeks ago she would have eaten worms to send her gift packing. "It's not fair of me to ask you to do this." She turned to leave.

He grabbed her by her arm. "Wait." His gaze met hers. "I was serious when I said it was only a little part of why I'm hesitating. To be honest, I'm this close to saying the hell with it and playing the Tarzan role."

She saw from his expression that he told the truth. "Hey," she said. "That Tarzan role saved my life. Don't belittle it."

"I know, and that's why I'm thinking about accepting it. But this is . . . over the top. It's not like I can sit down and have a chat with the animals. It doesn't work that way."

"How do you know?" Kylie asked. "Have you tried?"

"No, but . . . others have this gift. And if I could actually do that, Holiday would have said something."

"Holiday has said a thousand times that everyone's gift is different. Look, I know you said that so far all you hear are their thoughts, but somehow you communicated with that lion not to make hamburger meat out of us."

"Okay, if by some miracle I can actually communicate with them, it still won't happen. That FRU James guy wouldn't let me near the animals. He had me in the office again today. He thinks I'm involved. He even accused me of doing it to impress you."

Kylie considered going to Holiday right then, but she knew Holiday would worry someone might get hurt and would say no. She tilted her chin back in defiance. "Then we don't ask him to let us in. We sneak in."

"Sneak by a vampire? That's like trying to fool Superman."

"Yeah, but I happen to know what his kryptonite is."

"He has a kryptonite?" Derek asked.

"Yup. And her name is Holiday."

Kylie admitted this might be a long shot, but when it was your only shot, you made the most of it. And that's what she and Derek had done. They had to acquire a little help to pull it off, but she was dang proud of her plan.

Kylie and Derek waited a few hundred yards away from the wildlife park gates, hidden behind some trees. According to Della, that distance would be far enough that Burnett couldn't smell them. Kylie clutched the maps of the park she'd printed off the Internet from the computer in Holiday's office.

Once Burnett was out of the way, getting into the camp was going to be a piece of cake. Well, it was when you had a certain eye-color-changing shape-shifter helping you out. And to make sure they didn't run into any unexpected surprises, Della would make a sweep of the park, and then stand as lookout.

Their biggest concern was if Derek's ability would allow him to learn anything from the animals. He was skeptical.

Kylie wanted to believe in miracles.

Her phone rang. "Done," Miranda said.

Which meant Miranda had managed to get Holiday's cell phone and send Burnett the 911 message, a ruse Kylie knew he would not be able to resist. Helen, gracious enough to help, was right now having a meltdown by the creek that required Holiday's help. The longer Burnett searched for Holiday, the more time Derek would have with the animals.

However, first they needed Burnett to leave. And he did a few minutes later, when he slammed the door to the office and disappeared into the night.

"Looks like he's in a hurry," Derek whispered.

"I think he really cares about Holiday." Kylie's heart pinched with guilt for scaring Burnett. To make up for it, if things calmed down, Kylie might help get the two of them together.

"Ready?" Derek asked.

She nodded. They ran toward the park, knowing the clock was ticking.

Perry had the gate open for them when they arrived. "See

ya." Because his presence might upset the animals, he took off, sparkles falling around him as he transformed into an eagle and disappeared into the dark sky.

"It still freaks me out to see that," Della said, stopping at Kylie's shoulder.

"What did you find?" Kylie asked, knowing their time was short.

"One guard, human—sleeping on the job—in the back office." Della paused. "Are you sure you don't want me to come, too?"

Kylie shook her head. "I think the less people involved, the more likely the animals will communicate with Derek. Go back to the camp and let us know when Burnett heads back. Hopefully in time for us to get out."

Having already studied the maps, Kylie and Derek took off to the section called the "lion's den" first. Lion's den? That so didn't have a good ring to it.

While there were some stars out, the moon, as if stingy with its light, only peered out from behind a cloud every now and then. Even the animal sounds seemed more ominous than usual, or maybe Kylie's perception was warped because she knew they were trespassing—basically breaking the law. Either way, she found herself moving closer to Derek.

"The lions are right around the bend here," he said.

She wasn't sure if it was cat urine or something else, but the stench hit her nose. "I can smell them." The odor took her back to being trapped in the room with the beast. Her emotions started jamming to the tune of panic.

"Relax," Derek said.

The fact that he could read her emotions still unnerved her. "I'm trying."

"There's something I need to know," he said at the same time as a lion's roar rang out.

"What?"

"What are you going to do if we learn that Lucas is behind this?"

"I'll do the same thing I'll do if we discover someone else is behind it. Tell Holiday." She paused. "But that's not what we're going to find."

"You seem really sure he's innocent."

She could feel Derek studying her. "And you seem really sure he's guilty."

"That's because the evidence says he is."

"It's all circumstantial."

"For someone who was scared shitless of the guy, you sure have changed your tune."

Kylie realized where this conversation could lead and she wanted to call it over. "I just want to find out who's doing this and pray it stops them from closing down the camp."

"Me, too," he said.

Feeling a blast of icy wind brush against her, she wrapped her arms around herself.

Derek studied her. "Is the ghost here?"

"Maybe." She looked around and didn't see him. "He's only come back a few times since the lion incident and he never stays but a few seconds."

"Maybe he'll help us out the way he did then."

"Maybe, but I'm hoping we don't need any help," she said, and the coldness left as quickly as it had appeared.

They stopped at the fence. "This is it." Derek peered through the chain-link fence.

"Are they here?" She couldn't see them.

"Yeah. Behind the tree and beside the pond over there."

"Do they know we're here?" Kylie asked.

"Hell, yeah."

She took a small step back from the fence. "How are you going to do this?"

He chuckled. "I was waiting for you to tell me."

"You're serious?" she asked.

"Partly," he said, sounding a tad insecure.

"Okay." She bit down on her lip. "Can you read them?"

"Right now, all I'm getting is that they see us as a threat."

"Why?" Kylie asked at the same time as another wild animal noise—maybe an elephant?—filled the night. "Surely that's not all they're feeling."

"They're males." He snickered. "We don't elaborate on feelings."

"Real cute," she muttered.

"I thought so." He grinned.

"This is serious." She nudged him with her elbow.

"I know." His smiled faded. "I told you I didn't know if this would work."

"Just concentrate," Kylie said. "Ask them what they're afraid of in your mind."

He leaned his head on the fence and closed his eyes. She

watched him. Time crept by, one minute, two. She had to bite her lip to keep from asking him if it was working.

Then thinking if she concentrated, too, maybe it would be better, she moved against his back and placed her hands on his sides. *Why do we scare you? Why do we scare you?* She repeated the question in her mind.

"Kylie?" Derek whispered.

"You getting something?" she asked, hoping.

"I was until . . ."

"Until what?" she asked.

"Until you pressed your breasts against me. And thinking about them beats lion chatter hands down." He chuckled. "You're going to have move back."

She stepped back and gave him a swat on his back.

He laughed, but then went back to concentrating.

She heard a rustle behind the fence. "I think one of them is coming."

"Shh," he said.

She hushed, but when the lion pounced on the fence, she let go of a scream as loud as his roar. Jumping back, heart pounding, she landed on her butt.

"That's the same lion, isn't it?" she asked, staring at the creature who stared at her. She would never forget his eyes, golden and hungry.

Derek didn't answer. He didn't even turn around to offer her a hand up. Then she noticed how he stood frozen, eyes open, staring at the beast as if . . . as if they were having a mental chat.

Staying where she was on the ground, so as not to disturb them, she lifted her hands to dust off the gravel. She hadn't given her hands one dusting when she felt herself being lifted off the ground.

She screamed, and another hand slapped over her mouth.

Derek swung around but before he could even take a step forward, a blond guy had him by the throat, pressing him into the fence. The lion roared behind him.

"Not so loud." The voice didn't sound even slightly familiar. From the coldness of the touch, Kylie knew the person who had her was a vampire, or something equally cold-blooded.

Derek struggled to free himself. The lion's roar grew more threatening.

"What do we have here?" her attacker asked.

Kylie managed to look at him. Auburn colored hair. Red glowing eyes matched his hair. Definitely vampire, she decided, noting his fangs that hung slightly over his bottom lip.

"Looks as if someone is hungry," said Red, the vamp holding her against him. "Bet the kitty would like to eat a young tender thing like you. Problem is, so would I."

"What the hell?" The blond guy who had Derek by the neck yelled out, and then he dropped in a dead faint to the ground.

Kylie noticed the intense look on Derek's face, and she knew he'd done something to the blond. Then Derek's gaze shot to her and Red.

"Get your hands off her," Derek said, his voice hoarse.

Kylie saw him lunge forward, but out of the sky two more guys dropped, each grabbing one of Derek's arms. He struggled.

"Excuse me," Kylie's attacker said. "I think I'll go have a snack." He jumped back at least twenty-five feet, taking her with him. They landed with a thud. Kylie's whole body jarred and she bit the edge of her tongue.

Hard.

She tasted blood as it pooled onto her tongue.

She tried to pull away but the vampire's strength made her feel as capable as a bug against a fast-approaching windshield.

"Oh man, you smell good." The vampire raised her off the ground and turned Kylie's head toward his. "Pretty, too." He studied her for a second as if reading her pattern and then his mouth came down on hers.

She knew he drank her blood and wasn't kissing her, but she wanted no part of it. No part of him.

Fight. Fight dirty. She remembered dating lesson number one that her father had taught her. Pulling back her leg, she let go with everything she had and kneed that bastard in the balls.

She hadn't even considered if vampires had the same weak spot. But the vamp's scream proved they did. However, she could have foregone being tossed through the air like a rag doll. Her back slammed against the fence and she slid down to land with a clunk on the ground.

Everything in her said she needed to stand up, get ready to fight. But unable to breathe, it took everything she had just to open her eyes.

She saw the two vampires who had been holding Derek had fallen to the ground like the one earlier.

"Kylie, you okay?" Derek suddenly appeared standing over her.

"She's mine," said a gravelly voice.

Helpless, Kylie watched the vampire who kissed her snatch

Derek up by the neck, and throw him across the fence and in with the lions.

Kylie heard the lions roaring and envisioned them ripping Derek apart. "No!" she screamed.

The vamp looked at her as if she were the prize in the box of cereal. "What are you?" he asked, and reached down to pick her up.

An enormous cold showered her. Colder than anything she'd ever felt. Icy needles touched her skin, cut through her human tissue, and found its way to her bones. For a second, her arms and legs felt paralyzed.

Then suddenly Kylie was standing. The vamp held someone in his arms. Then Kylie realized he had *her* in his arms. His eyes now glowed an even hotter red.

Oddly enough, she wasn't afraid. She waited for him to get closer, sensing she could deal with him. But not knowing how.

From the corner of her eye, she saw Derek pull himself over the top of the fence.

"I said don't touch her." Derek jumped off the fence at Red.

Red dropped her body and knocked Derek back against the fence. "You don't know when to die, do you?" he growled.

Another dark figure dropped out of the sky and hit Red so hard he fell to the ground. Kylie recognized Della instantly.

Derek turned back to check on Kylie's body, but another dark figure slammed him against the fence again.

Without thinking, Kylie moved forward. She grabbed the vamp holding Derek and slung him away. She watched in a kind of daze as the vamp's body flew thirty or forty feet in the air to land in a patch of woods.

When she looked back, Derek stared right through her.

"Wow, did you see that?" she asked Derek, but he didn't answer.

He joined Della in sparring with the vamp she'd kneed in the balls. The taste of the guy's mouth still lingered on her tongue and she wanted to spit. But first she moved in, found an open spot, tightened her fist, and swung. The vamp flew backwards and landed in a crumbled heap.

Both Derek and Della swung around and stared at each other as if confused.

"Kylie?" Derek screamed.

"Yeah," Kylie answered, but then she watched Derek run over to her body on the ground. He turned her over and for the first time she felt the shock run through her system. If she wasn't in her body, where was she?

Derek screamed her name and then said, "Breathe, damn it. For God's sake, Kylie, breathe." He shook her.

Oh, crap. Was she dead?

Chapter Forty

Looking down at her clothes, Kylie realized she wore army fatigues. She was . . . she was in Daniel Brighten's spirit body again—just like in the dream. *Did that mean she wasn't dead?*

She looked back at her own body and saw that Derek was fighting off two more vamps to keep them away from her. Della swooped in to help.

Remembering she could help them as Daniel's ghost, Kylie took a step toward them. But just like that, she realized she was back in her own body. She pushed herself off the ground, determined not to just lie there. Moving, however, caused her a ton of pain.

Someone else suddenly appeared and fought beside Derek and Della. Kylie squinted at their newest ally.

Sky?

Floodlights flared to life. The night's darkness, along with several of their attackers, scurried away like rats.

Burnett, along with a few other FRU-looking people, seemed to come at them from all sides. They grabbed a couple of the vamps and locked them in handcuffs at both their wrists and ankles.

Derek rushed over to Kylie. "Are you okay?"

She nodded, although her body was hurting in places she didn't know could hurt.

"What the hell happened?" Burnett demanded of Derek. He reached for Derek as if prepared to slap a pair of cuffs on him.

"It's my fault," Kylie insisted. "I made him do this."

"She did not," Derek insisted.

"No, it was my idea." Della surged forward.

"No, they're all lying. It's not their fault." Sky moved in.

Everything seemed to go silent for a long moment, and then Derek spoke up. "Sky planted the blood that you guys found that led back to the camp. She helped those rogues take the animals. But she came to our defense in the end."

Kylie knew Derek had learned this from his mind meld with the lions. The lions had talked to him, just as she'd hoped they would. A tiny bit of happiness about being right swiveled through the chaos of the moment, and she let herself savor it.

"He's telling the truth." Sky held out her arms to be cuffed.

Burnett put the cuffs on her. "Why?" he asked, staring at her as if disgusted.

"They . . ." she said looking at the captives, "have my sister. Threatened to kill her if I didn't help them get the camp shut down." Sky glanced at Kylie. "I could do it when that was all they wanted, but this . . . They promised no one would be hurt. I don't know how the lion got in your cabin, Kylie, I swear. I was told to take the witches out for a hike. I knew they were planning something, but hadn't thought . . . They said no one would be hurt." She shook her head and looked back at Burnett. "I was only trying to save my sister."

"They? Who are 'they'?" Burnett growled, and looked at the two vamps cuffed on the ground. One of them growled at Burnett and fought against the handcuffs. Two of the other FRU men subdued him.

Kylie suddenly realized the red-haired vampire, the one who'd first grabbed her, had gotten away. And for some reason that thought sent chills down her back.

"The Blood Brothers," Sky answered. "The vampire gang."

"And why did they want the camp shut down?" Burnett asked.

"They feel as if the camp is corrupting potential members," Sky answered. "And from what they said, they aren't the only ones thinking it. Most of all the rogue gangs are starting to rebel against the camp."

"Do you know where they're keeping your sister?" Burnett asked, and Kylie heard the slightest hint of sympathy in his voice for Sky's dilemma.

"No. But my father's hired someone to find her."

Holiday came rushing forward. Her gaze shot to Sky wearing cuffs. "What are you doing?" she asked Burnett.

"My job," he answered, and started walking Sky away.

Holiday shot forward. "You let her go—"

"He can't, Holiday," Sky said. "He's right. I screwed up. I'm sorry."

"What are you sorry for?" Holiday asked.

Sky looked back at Derek. "Tell her," she said.

Burnett looked at Holiday almost as if to say something, and then he nudged Sky to start walking.

Holiday looked back at Kylie, Della, and Derek. "Someone better start talking. And fast."

Holiday had a doctor rush to the camp and go over everyone inch by inch. Other than a few scrapes and deep bruises, they were pronounced fine. It was after two in the morning at that point and Kylie's muscles ached like a bad devil and she wanted nothing more than to go to bed. But apparently Burnett had other plans.

Kylie and her partners in crime—for some reason, Helen, Perry, and Miranda had all confessed to being part of Kylie's plan—were told to wait in the dining hall. Holiday and Burnett walked in. Kylie saw the shadows of pain in the camp leader's eyes; no doubt Sky's betrayal had cut deep.

Burnett started the dialogue, or you could call it the chewing down. He referred to what they'd done as stupid and foolish. He told them they were lucky that none of them had been killed. Yada yada yada.

And he was right.

But Kylie would have done it again in a heartbeat.

She sat there and took her punishment like the rest of them. Yes, she knew sneaking into the park hadn't been without some risk, but she hadn't planned on going to war with a vampire gang. All she'd wanted to do was get Derek to the animals so he could possibly get some answers.

Which, by the way, had worked. Not that Burnett mentioned that in his ass-chewing.

"Did you even realize that they had outnumbered you by five? I can't believe . . ." He continued his rant, reminding them they were supernaturals and they were supposed to be smarter than that.

A question popped into Kylie's mind and before she could stop herself, it slipped out of her mouth. "Are you still going to close down the camp?"

Burnett, not happy about being interrupted, frowned. "If this is the kind of behavior we can expect, we have no choice."

Enough. Enough. Enough.

When the word scraped across Kylie's mind the third time, she stood up. "We did the only thing we knew to help."

She hadn't a clue where her assertiveness came from, perhaps exhaustion, but she couldn't seem to stop herself.

"You seem to have forgotten that we didn't plan to get into an out-and-out brawl with a vampire gang. All we wanted was to get Derek close enough to communicate with the animals and find out what the hell had been going on."

"You should have come to us," Holiday said.

While her heart went out to the camp leader, Kylie had a point to make. Since she'd already pissed Burnett off, she might as well keep going.

"Why should we come to you?" Kylie asked. "You didn't trust us enough to tell us what was going on. Yes, we know you're the camp leader, but we're not in kindergarten here. You say we're here to learn how to cope in the outside world but then you try to shield us from anything that might be the least bit unpleasant. And let's say if we did come to you with this, I don't think you'd let us do it because you'd be worried it could be dangerous. And then there's you." Kylie pointed to Burnett.

"That'll be enough," Burnett snapped.

Not hardly. "Even if Holiday had agreed to let us do it, there's no way you would have let Derek in the park because you thought we were all suspects."

"Ditto," Derek said.

"Amen," Della said.

"You go, Kylie," Miranda snapped.

Everyone else in the room nodded their heads in agreement.

"That's not important," Burnett charged.

"Yes, it is." Holiday held up a hand to silence the tall, dark, and menacing vampire. "Kylie's right. I don't like it, but she's right."

Holiday took a deep breath. "I have the tendency to be a tad overprotective." She looked at Burnett. "And you have a tendency to be . . . well, a jerk."

Burnett's expression was a cross between shock and anger.

"I'm just being honest." Holiday glanced back at Kylie and the rest of them. "And to answer your question, Kylie, Burnett has already informed me that thankfully the camp will not be closed down."

Everyone in the room let out a yelp of victory.

"As a matter of fact . . ." Holiday glanced at Burnett as if almost asking permission to continue. He frowned but nodded. "As a matter of fact, Burnett has also just informed me that my request to turn Shadow Falls Camp into Shadow Falls Camp Academy has been granted."

"Like a full-time school?" Kylie asked.

Holiday nodded and Kylie saw her gaze seek out Della. "We're hoping this will help alleviate some of the strain of the newly turned supernaturals who find living with normal parents impossible. It will allow them to maintain contact and hopefully prevent these families from completely severing relationships."

Kylie grinned and glanced back at Della, who appeared as if she might start crying.

"And," Holiday continued, "while it's true, I did just call Mr. James here a jerk, and true, he is one, I'd also like to point out that tonight his boss informed me that . . . contrary to what I thought, he's been a supporter of the school. His boss said he's been our advocate all along. So like it or not—and for the record, I don't like it—he is deserving of our respect."

Burnett had his arms crossed over his chest, staring holes at Holiday. Kylie suspected the camp leader didn't glance at him just to piss him off.

"That said," Holiday motioned for the door, "it's very late and since tomorrow is parents day, we have to be up and at our best in the morning, even if we have to fake it."

Miranda, Della, and Kylie walked out together. "Chan wasn't there," Della said. "I would have smelled him."

"I know," Kylie said.

"Who's Chan?" Miranda asked.

"I'll explain it later," Della said, and then she looked back at Kylie. "When Sky said that she didn't put the lion in your room, she was telling the truth."

"I thought she was," Kylie said. But something about that whole incident still didn't read true. Not that she'd ever really find out.

They started toward their cabin when Kylie saw Derek. "You two go," Kylie said. "I want to say good night to Derek."

"Do you smell those hormones?" Della asked Miranda.

Kylie frowned at Della as they walked away and then she turned to find Derek.

"Hey, wait up," Kylie called to Derek.

He turned around and started moving toward her. When they met in the middle, he was smiling. "I liked how you stood up to Burnett and Holiday," he said.

Kylie shrugged, unsure where she'd gotten the courage to do it, but lately she found herself speaking her mind. She didn't think it was altogether a bad thing, either.

"And I liked how you stood up to the vampires earlier. What did you do? They kept dropping."

He grinned. "Apparently, I have the ability to shock their systems with emotional overload. It was pretty cool, wasn't it?"

"Yeah, it was," she said.

He studied her. "Your ghost was there, too. Wasn't he?"

"Yeah," Kylie said, not really ready to share the whole out-of-body experience thing.

Their gazes met, held. "It worked didn't it?" Kylie said. "You communicated with the animals. That's how you knew about Sky, right?"

He nodded. "Yeah. You were right."

She thought she heard something in his voice—like regret. "Are you upset that it happened?" Like flies on a bad banana, guilt buzzed around her chest. He'd done it for her. "If you are . . . I mean, I'm sorry that—"

He reached out to put a finger over her lips. "You don't need to apologize. I'm glad I did it. To be honest, it felt right. Tonight felt right." He pushed a strand of her hair behind her ear and left his hand there. "We did good. We make a good team."

"You've saved my life twice now. Three if you count the snake." She looked up at him, at his soft smile. His hand touching her neck felt so good. So right. Without thinking, she moved up on her tiptoes and pressed her lips to his.

He wasn't the one who started the kiss.

Nope. She did that.

He wasn't the one who deepened the kiss.

Nope. She did that, too.

He wasn't even the one who moved in closer.

Nope. That would be her.

Not that he seemed to mind.

But he was the one who moved his tongue inside her mouth. Deep inside her, she heard a little voice say, "Oops."

She pulled back. They were both breathing hard. She wasn't sure either of them had breathed this hard when they'd been fighting rogue vampires.

He opened his eyes and looked at her. "Wow."

Kylie inhaled, still trying to catch her breath, trying to clear her head. She stared down at her shoes, because looking him in the eyes right now seemed too much. She hadn't meant that to happen. Or had she?

He ran his finger under her chin and tilted her head up. Damn. He was going to make her look at him. Then he'd probably ask the question she couldn't answer.

"What was that, Kylie? Just a thank-you for saving your life . . . or was it more?"

Yup, that was the question she was afraid he'd ask. "I don't know," she answered honestly. "Maybe just a weak moment."

He laughed. "Do me a favor." He leaned closer.

"What?"

"Whenever you're feeling weak, come see me."

She went to give him a thump in the chest, but he stopped her. He brought her hand up to his lips, his green gaze never shifting from her eyes, and he gently kissed the top of her hand. The moisture of his lips sent a shiver, a wonderful kind of shiver, all the way down her spine.

For some unknown reason, that second kiss wreaked more emotional havoc than the first had. And that's when she noticed how beautiful the sky was. It appeared . . . enchanted. The stars twinkled like something out of a Disney movie. Was Derek doing this? Was he using his gifts and making her see things differently? And did it matter if he was? She didn't have the answer. "I should . . . should probably go. Tomorrow is parents day."

"I'll walk you to your cabin." He arched a brow.

"I'm not kissing you again," she blurted out, before she thought about it.

He laughed. "I bet you will."

She knew he was right, but . . . "Not tonight."

"I figured that. Good thing I'm patient."

Derek's kiss and maybe everything that came before it had helped Kylie not think about seeing her mom—about what she would or wouldn't say about seeing her dad making out in the middle of town. Then there was the other question she had to ask. The question that made Kylie's entire insides twitch.

The question Kylie hadn't let herself think about.

But now, standing in the dining hall, waiting for her mom to arrive, Kylie wondered if she shouldn't have been thinking about it. Face it, some things just weren't meant to be blurted out.

Her mom walked in and Kylie saw her scanning the room for her. Kylie took the second to just notice her mom. Like her brown hair, her brown eyes. Like how Kylie didn't look anything like her. Except for the nose. She'd for certain gotten her mom's little ski-lift nose.

"I almost didn't find you," her mom said as they sat down at one of the least crowded tables. Her mom's butt wasn't on the seat when she said, "You haven't been getting enough sleep, have you, Kylie?"

Was it some kind of mother radar or something that made a mom know these things? "Just restless," Kylie lied.

Her mom leaned over the table and whispered, "You aren't having those dreams again, are you?"

"No," Kylie said.

Her mom cut her eyes in that don't-lie-to-me stare.

"I swear."

"Okay," she said.

"Hello, everyone," Holiday said at the front of the hall. "I know I don't normally address you on these visits but I've got some news I'd love to share. First, I'm sorry to have to tell you that due to family issues, Sky Peacemaker, my co-leader of the camp, has to take an unplanned leave of absence."

Kylie had to admit, Holiday managed to explain it without really lying.

"However," Holiday continued, "we are in the process of looking for a replacement. Until then, we have a temporary— just temporary—replacement. And I'd like you to meet Mr. Burnett James. He comes highly recommended."

Kylie wondered if Holiday knew how telling the second "just temporary" was? The fact that she was going to have to work with Burnett was no doubt eating her alive.

"My second news . . ." Holiday then went into her spiel about the camp becoming a boarding school.

Kylie watched her mom as Holiday did her dog and pony show. She half expected her mom to stand up and applaud and scream out, *Freedom at last, freedom at last.*

Oddly enough, her mom was able to hide her excitement. Kylie felt a shot of guilt scratch across her conscience. How unfair was it that Kylie wanted to sign on full-time to the school, and yet she was going to be pissed at her mom for wanting the same.

After Holiday finished, Kylie looked back at her mom and said, "You want to take a walk? There are some paths through the woods that are nice."

Her mom looked down at her feet. "Sure. Luckily I wore tennis shoes."

Kylie decided to take her mom to a less woodsy trail that ended by the creek. It wasn't as nice as her and Derek's spot, but still pretty. She went by the cabin to get a blanket for them to sit on.

Her mom meandered around the cabin. "This is sparse, but nice."

Socks came running out of her bedroom and attacked her mom's shoelaces. "Oh, it's sooo cute."

Her mom picked up Socks, Jr., and held it up to her face. "Whose kitten is it?"

"Uh, mine."

Her mom looked surprised. "Okay, but don't you think you should have cleared that with me first?"

"I . . . yeah, I guess I should have," Kylie said.

Her mom continued to stare at the feline. "Do you know what cat this reminds me of?"

"Socks?" Kylie said.

"Yeah. Do you remember her? We had that cat when you were born. Your dad got it for me the day we had our first sonogram. He was so excited, he . . ." Her mom stopped talking and blinked as if to chase the memory from her mind. "Yeah, cute kitten." She put the feline down as if she half blamed the kitten for bringing on a painful memory.

Kylie saw the emotion in her mom's eyes, and she wished she could punch her dad. She swallowed the knot forming in her throat and went to grab a blanket.

They walked in silence, and then her mom asked, "You are calling your dad now, aren't you?"

Kylie almost lied, but then said, "The phone works both ways, Mom. If he wants to talk to me, he can call."

"Honey, men aren't always good at—"

"It's not men we're talking about. It's Dad."

"I'm sure he didn't intentionally forget about coming to see you. His work sometimes can be challenging."

"Really?" Kylie asked. "Is that why you barbecued his shorts on the grill?"

Chapter Forty-one

Her mom continued alongside Kylie, walking through the path in the woods. "I'm not very proud of doing that."

"You should be," Kylie said. "I think it was very fitting."

Her mom looked at her before speaking. "He's just going through something right now, Kylie. That's all."

The fact that her mom would defend him pushed Kylie over the edge. "Yeah, he's going through his super-young assistant."

Her mom stopped and grabbed Kylie's arm. Tears filled her mom's eyes. "Oh, baby. I'm so sorry."

Kylie shook her head. "Why are you apologizing? Are you having an affair, too? I swear, if you're seeing someone my age, I'm divorcing both of you."

"No. I would never . . . I didn't want . . . you to find out. You were always so close." Her mom held a hand over her trembling lips for a second. "How did you find out?"

Kylie sensed it would hurt her mom to know that her dad brought the bimbo with him last weekend, so she lied. "I caught him in a lie."

She shook her head. "He never was good at lying."

Right then, Kylie wondered how good her mother was at lying. Did her dad even know the truth? She stopped moving and closed her eyes and considered the question she needed to ask.

"My, this is pretty," her mom said.

Kylie opened her eyes and found her mom looking over at the stream. "Yeah." Kylie moved closer to the stream and stretched out the blanket for them to sit.

Her mom sat down and stared at the water. "Is there really a waterfall here?"

"I'm told there is," Kylie said, hoping to keep the frustration about never having seen the falls from her voice. And right then, she decided even if she had to go alone, she was going to see that falls—for some crazy reason, it seemed important that she went. "I've never seen it, though."

"Why not?"

Kylie shrugged. "Supposedly, there's a legend about there being ghosts there. Most everyone is afraid to go there." Me included, Kylie thought, but didn't say it—not that it would stop her next time.

"Really?" Her mom looked intrigued. "I love ghost stories, don't you?"

"Sometimes," Kylie answered honestly, and glanced away so her mom couldn't read anything in her expression.

"Well, it's peaceful here," her mom said. "I like it." She leaned over and patted Kylie's hand. "Thanks for bringing me here."

Call Kylie a coward, but she shelved the question she didn't want to ask, and went for the less explosive topic. One her mom should be happy about. "What do you think about the camp turning into a boarding school?"

"Your camp leader sounded happy about it," her mom said, still staring at the water.

"What do you think about me signing up?"

Her mom's head snapped around. "What? Hon, that's a boarding school. That means you live here."

"I know," Kylie said, honestly surprised at her mom's reaction. "Just think, you wouldn't have to put up with me." Kylie tried to go for a teasing tone. But if her mom's expression was any indication, Kylie missed by a long shot.

"No," her mom said. "Let me make this clear. Hell, no. You have a home and it's with me."

Two things, two huge emotional realizations hit Kylie at once. One, she really wanted—no, make that needed—to stay at Shadow Falls Camp. Somehow, some way, she had to convince her mom to let her do this. And the second realization was that her mom didn't want to get rid of her. Kylie had been so sure, so certain that given the choice her mom would have packed Kylie a little knapsack and had her out the door in no time.

With her emotions playing bumper cars in her heart, Kylie didn't know what to say. "I . . . I really like it here, Mom."

"You like it at home, too," she said.

Not anymore, was her true answer, but that suddenly seemed cruel. "But . . ."

"If this is retaliation for the divorce—"

"It's not," Kylie said. "I promise. I just . . . It feels right here. I'm getting to know who I really am. Remember how you used to tell me that I had 'belonging issues' because I didn't want to

join any of the clubs or teams at school? Well, here, I belong . . .
I belong here, Mom."

"You have Sara. You two are as close as sisters."

"I love Sara. I always will, but we're not . . . as alike as we
used to be. We don't even talk every day now. She's found some
other girls to hang with and honestly, I don't fit in with them."

Her mom's eyes grew worried. "But—"

"Mom, please . . ." Kylie saw she'd made headway because her
mom wasn't arguing nearly as adamantly as she normally did.
Then Kylie remembered another trump card. "You said your new
job would require lots of travel. What do you think you're going
to do with me when you're gone?"

"Well, your dad will take over."

Kylie cocked her head. "Do you think I want to go over to
his place while his girlfriend, who is practically my age, flaunts
herself all over him?"

"Then I'll turn down the promotion," her mom said. "You
are more important to me than . . . than any job." Tears filled
her mother's eyes.

Tears filled Kylie's eyes at the same time. She couldn't help
herself. Then because it just felt right, she reached over and
wrapped her arms around her mother.

"I love you," Kylie said, and held on. She held on tighter
than she had ever held on before.

Her mom didn't pull away. She patted Kylie's shoulder. It
wasn't the warmest embrace, but it had potential. Then, not
wanting to push her luck, Kylie pulled back.

"I'm sorry," Kylie said.

"For what?" her mom asked, and Kylie noticed her mom's

face was a splotchy mess. Another thing they had in common that Kylie hadn't realized.

"I'm sorry," Kylie said. "I really don't want to hurt you. And it's not as if you have to make a decision today. I'm here all summer, but I really do like it here. And Holiday said the students could come home on the weekends. There would be all kinds of vacation days. And I'm only three hours away. Heck, you work out of your home so you could even move closer."

Her mom sighed. "But you're my daughter, baby." She ran her hand over Kylie's cheek. "I don't want other people raising you."

"Mom, would you get real? I'll be seventeen in a few months. You've already raised me." Kylie hesitated and then added, "Besides, you should be dating and stuff."

Her mom's eyes widened. "I don't think I'm that brave."

"Why not? You're beautiful and with a new wardrobe, you could be . . . hot." Her mom was much prettier than the tramp her father was involved with right now.

Her mom sighed. "When did my little girl grow up?"

"I don't know." Kylie grinned and lay back on the blanket. Her mom followed her lead and lay back. They listened to the creek water flow and stared up at the blue sky peeking out through the white cotton-ball clouds. Maybe it was Kylie's imagination, but she could almost hear the falls even from here.

Finally, Kylie sat up. Her mom did the same. "Mom, can I ask you something?"

"Sure, hon."

Kylie looked at her mom and just blurted out the question. "Who is my real dad?"

Chapter Forty-two

Kylie saw her mom flinch. She didn't look at Kylie, almost as if trying to decide what lie to tell.

"The truth, Mom," Kylie said. "I need to know the truth."

Her mom finally looked at her. Both tears and panic filled her big brown eyes. "Who? Did your dad . . . tell you?"

Which dad, Kylie thought, but didn't say it. She knew the one her mom meant.

Relief flowed through her. Her dad knew. Kylie hadn't wanted to believe her mom could have lied to him all these years. Then Kylie's relief vanished and she wondered if this was what the divorce was really about. Had her dad just discovered he wasn't Kylie's biological father? Her heart tightened at the thought that the divorce was her fault.

"No, Mom, I promise. He didn't tell me. It was just . . . a feeling." That much was true. She didn't have proof, she hadn't even asked Daniel. But the odd feeling that Daniel looked like someone she knew had finally made sense.

He looked like the girl she saw in the mirror every morning when she brushed her teeth—the same blue eyes, the same blond hair, the same bone structure. They even walked like each other.

And then there was his brain pattern. She kept seeing it in her head and then she remembered how Helen had described Kylie's pattern.

But she couldn't tell her mom any of this.

"Plus, I don't look like Dad at all," Kylie said instead.

Tears dampened her mom's cheeks. "Oh, baby. I'm so sorry, baby. I'm so sorry."

"What happened?" Kylie asked. "Please tell me the divorce isn't about this."

"No, baby." Her mom wiped her tears, and started talking. "I met him, Daniel Brighten, at the gym. He worked there. He was . . . I don't even know how to explain it, but to say he was charming. Almost magical. I fell in love with him the moment I laid eyes on him."

Her mom stared off at nothing as if remembering. "He asked me out. On the first date, he told me that in three weeks he was set to ship out for the Gulf War. Three weeks was all we had. I know it sounds so wrong, and I'll lock you in your room if you ever do this, but . . . after that first date I knew he was the one. By the third, I was . . . There was nothing I wouldn't do for him. We were inseparable.

"When he left, he told me that when he came back, he was going to marry me. That he'd introduce me to his family. They lived in Dallas, so I'd never even met them."

Her mom's breath hitched. "Two weeks after he was deployed, I realized I was pregnant. In my next letter, I told him." She bit down on her lips, and more tears flowed. "He stopped writing. I thought . . ." Tears rolled down her cheeks. "At first I thought it was because he didn't want the baby." Drawing in a deep breath, her mom wiped her face. "About two weeks later, I saw his obituary in the paper. Now I don't even know if he got the letter."

Kylie's heart clutched and she remembered seeing Daniel pull the letter from his pocket to his lips. Tears filled her own eyes and she fought the need to tell her mom about her dreams, about Daniel coming to see her.

Her mom wrapped her arms around her knees as if she was cold. Kylie knew he was here. He stood beside her mom, looking at her with so much love in his eyes that Kylie's own tears came faster.

"I was . . . only eighteen years old," her mom went on. "My mom might have understood, but my dad, he was . . . it would have killed him. Your dad—I mean your stepdad—we had dated off and on through high school. He . . . always claimed he loved me."

She held her head up. "He called me right after all this happened. I told him it wasn't a good time. He didn't take no very easily. He showed up at work and I went out and had coffee. I told him. I don't know why I did. But I needed a friend."

Her mom turned and looked right at Kylie. "He did what most men wouldn't do. He got down on his knees and asked me to marry him, right then."

Kylie thought about her dad, how much he must have loved

her mom to have done that. But what happened to that man now? How could he be the same man who . . .

Her mom continued. "He asked for one thing, one promise. He never wanted anyone to know that you weren't his." She pressed her hands against her lips again. "Your real father was gone. I was desperate. I never . . . never realized how hard that promise would be to keep."

Kylie reached for her mom's hand.

"The day you were born, it was like seeing your dad all over again. You are so much like him."

I know, Kylie thought, and gave her mom's hand a squeeze. Then she looked up at Daniel Brighten.

"I know, if he'd lived, he would have loved you so much."

Kylie closed her eyes and then the words popped out. "I think he does love me. I think he loves you, too."

Her mom did it then. She wrapped her arms around Kylie and hugged her. It wasn't quick, and not even awkward. It was just right.

They stayed there by the creek for another couple of hours. Talking about everything. She told Kylie about the whirlwind love affair she'd had with Daniel. They even talked about Nana.

"You know," her mom said. "The day of the funeral. It took everything I had not to find me a tissue and remove that God-awful purple lipstick they put on her."

Kylie laughed. "I'll bet Nana would have appreciated it." And right then Kylie felt another breeze whisk by. It was cold, but it wasn't the same cold as Daniel's. Kylie smiled and knew Nana's spirit was close.

"Nana was special," Kylie said.

A while later, they started back through the woods. Their shoulders brushed up against each other as they walked. Her mom reached over and squeezed Kylie's hand. "Your dad," her mom said. "The man who raised you . . . he loves you. I know you're mad at him."

"I have a right to be mad," Kylie said.

"I know," her mom answered. "I'm mad at him, too." She hesitated. "No, I'm furious. But I don't think he could have loved you more if you were his own. This is just . . . a midlife crisis." She stopped walking. "Or maybe the truth is something I don't even want to admit."

"What?" Kylie asked.

"He loved me, Kylie. In the beginning, he loved me so much. And I . . . never loved him like I loved Daniel. I never told him, but he knew it. And in time, I . . . God help me, but I resented the promise he asked me to make. Every time I looked at you, I saw your real father and I felt as if I was lying to you. Lying to myself. The marriage suffered. Our relationship suffered." Her mom waved a hand between them. "It was easy to blame him, but honestly, I'm just as much at fault. I didn't have to make that promise."

Her mom reached over and brushed Kylie's hair back. "He was a good father. For years, most of those sixteen years, he was a good husband. He deserved a woman who loved him as much as he loved her. He never had that. How unfair was that to him? Maybe after all that time, he just couldn't handle it anymore."

Kylie knew her mom had made valid points. Things she

should consider when she reevaluated her relationship with her dad. "He could have just asked for a divorce. He didn't have to start cheating with someone practically my age."

"I'm not saying he's right. Or that he's perfect. But he loves you, baby. He loved you even when he didn't have to."

Before her mom left, she made Kylie promise to call her dad again soon. It was a promise Kylie intended to keep, but not today. Probably not even tomorrow.

"Why does romance have to be so complicated?" Kylie blurted out as she barged into Holiday's office later that night.

Kylie had been in her room since her mom left, thinking about her dad and mom and Daniel and comparing all that to what she felt for Lucas and Derek. It wasn't the same thing, but in some small way, it almost felt like it was.

Holiday looked up from the paper on her desk. If the woman's expression was any indication, she was in about the same mood as Kylie. Confused and hurting. No doubt, Holiday and Burnett had butted heads again.

"Good question," Holiday answered. "I personally think the gods did it just to piss us off."

Kylie dropped down in the chair across from her desk.

Leaning back in her chair, Holiday studied her. "You've been quiet all day. Did the visit with your mom go okay?"

Kylie decided to spill the beans. "Daniel Brighten, the ghost, is my real father."

Holiday nodded. Not the reaction Kylie expected.

Kylie felt her gut tighten. "If you tell me you knew this all along, I'm gonna be so pissed."

"I didn't know." Holiday held up her hand. "I suspected. There's a difference."

"You should have told me."

"It doesn't work like that."

"Well, I don't like how it works," Kylie barked.

Holiday let go of a sigh. "Sometimes I don't, either."

They got quiet. Music from the dining hall wafted into the room. A party was going on. A celebration of sorts for not having to close down the camp and for the decision to make the camp a boarding school. For many of the campers, it would be a lifesaver.

"Everything else okay?" Holiday asked.

"Yes." Then Kylie felt that if she didn't get it all out she would burst. "No, it's not okay. I like two guys. One left so that should make it easy, right? Especially since the one who left is probably off having kinky sex with his she-wolf. But no, I've got my mom, my dad, and Daniel's story in my head telling me how it's not fair to care for someone if you care for someone else." She stopped talking just so she could breathe.

"I'm sure that not's easy," Holiday said.

"Oh, I'm not finished yet. It gets better, because this guy, the one I like, has the power to toy with my emotions. And when I'm with him, I feel as if it's too good to be true. That makes me wonder if maybe what I'm feeling is real. Maybe he's just using his power to make me think I really like him."

Holiday frowned. "I don't think Derek would do that."

Okay, Kylie knew Holiday would figure out who the boys were, but hearing his name made Kylie's chest clutch.

"Then again," Holiday said. "Derek is male. Their logic isn't the same as ours."

"So you agree; he could be doing this, couldn't he?" Kylie asked.

Holiday looked as if she'd been put on the spot. "He could, but again I don't think Derek is that type."

"I don't think he is either, but . . ." She closed her eyes. "I'm just feeling so confused."

Holiday sighed again. "I wish I could tell you it gets easier when you're older. But where men are involved, there always seems to be some bafflement."

"And then there's Daniel," Kylie seethed. "Now that I need for him to show back up so I can ask him what the hell I am, he's not cooperating. He's off playing golf or poker with St. Peter or whatever men do in heaven. Or heck, maybe he's found himself some hot too-young girlfriend like my dad has and decided to drop me in the grease, too."

Holiday laughed. "Have you considered that maybe Daniel wants you to find this out for yourself?"

"Oh, that's so not fair," Kylie said. "Your parents didn't die or anything and leave you to go scrambling around to find out what you were. You were born knowing it."

Holiday shook her head. "Everyone's journey is different. Why don't you make that your next quest?"

Kylie slammed back in the chair. "I don't want another quest. Why can't it just be easy?"

Holiday grinned. "Easy is no fun." She sighed. "As much as I hate admitting it, if men were easy to figure out, they probably wouldn't be as much fun as they are."

"Yeah, but feeling as if your life is raining chaos isn't fun. And that's what I've felt for the last two months."

Holiday frowned and reached over and patted Kylie's hand. "And I'm about to make some things even more difficult for you."

"What?" Kylie pulled her hand away from Holiday.

The camp leader frowned and pulled a letter from her desk drawer. "I wasn't going to give you this, but then . . . I remembered what you said about me being too protective."

A wiggle of concern shot through Kylie. "You know, being protective is good sometimes."

"No. You were right," Holiday said.

"Is it from Daniel?" Kylie stared at the envelope.

"No. It's from Lucas."

"Just shoot me now." Kylie banged her head on the desk.

Holiday giggled. "It can't be that bad." She reached over and gave Kylie's hand another squeeze. "You are a special girl, Kylie. If I had to guess, I'd say these two aren't going to be the only ones who will jump through fire to get your attention." She stood up. "I think I'm going to go sit in on the party for a while. Stay in here as long as you want."

"Holiday?" Kylie said her name without turning around.

"What?"

Kylie looked back. "Did Lucas write to you, too?"

Holiday nodded.

"Do you know if . . . if Fredericka is with him?"

Holiday's eyes shifted. "Yes."

"Thanks." Kylie turned around. Holiday's footsteps faded into the sound of the music from next door. Kylie pulled the letter closer. She remembered how it had felt to kiss Derek—hot, safe, except for the little doubt that her emotions were being manipulated.

Her kiss with Lucas had been . . . hotter, but nothing about it had felt safe. Maybe that was even why it had been hotter. Risk and passion seemed to go hand in hand.

Kylie stared at the letter. Was there anything that Lucas could say in that letter that would change the fact that he'd left, that he was with Fredericka—a girl he admitted to having sex with? A girl he'd even admitted caring about.

No, Kylie thought. There was nothing Lucas could say to change that. Any more than her dad could change what he did to her mom. Or what Trey had done to her.

The music seemed to call out to her. There was a party going on and she should be there. She folded the letter and put it in her pocket. She deserved to just enjoy tonight. Later, she'd find out what Lucas had to say.

She stood up, turned to leave. The cold hit her so fast, her breath caught, then, the room filled with a thick fog.

Okay, this was different.

The thought no more went through her head when Kylie knew how different. This wasn't Daniel.

She tried to relax. But face it, this ghost business was going to take some getting used to. "Daniel?" She said his name almost hoping she was wrong.

A section of fog slowly lifted. A woman, no more than thirty, with long dark hair, stood there. She wore a beautiful white gown, or it had been beautiful at one time.

Kylie's heart thudded against her chest bone as she took in the bloodstains. The woman looked at Kylie with dead eyes, eyes filled with so much hopelessness that Kylie wanted to cry.

"Stop him," the woman said. "Stop him, or he'll do it again."

"Who?" Kylie asked. "Who did this?" Kylie gripped her hands together and wished Holiday hadn't left. "Are you looking for Holiday?"

The woman didn't answer. Instead, she faded into the fog. Kylie stood there, hugging herself against the cold, as the fog rose and disappeared into the ceiling. Slowly, the temperature crept back up.

"That is so unfair," Kylie muttered.

"What's unfair?"

Kylie swung around. Derek stood in the doorway. Dressed in faded jeans and a light blue shirt, he looked . . . good. Safe. She met his eyes and she saw the affection he held for her.

Right then, she decided that for tonight she was going to forget.

Forget about the letter in her pocket.

Forget about not knowing what she was.

Forget a certain woman wearing a blood-soaked gown.

Forget that she still hadn't made the trip up to the falls.

Even forget that her mom still hadn't agreed to let Kylie stay at the school.

Tonight, she just wanted to listen to some music, and sit next to Derek—shoulders touching.

"You going to the party?" she asked.

"I've been there. Waiting on you."

"Then let's go."

Kylie started moving toward the dining hall, and Derek followed her. She paused at the threshold, and he bumped into her. Hit with déjà vu, she remembered almost the same thing happening the first time she'd walked through these doors.

She'd been so scared, so certain that she would hate it here. Then again, she'd also sensed that her life was going to change. And yeah, she had been right about that.

"Are we going inside?" Derek asked, brushing up against her. His breath felt warm against her neck.

She nodded, but she just stood there wanting to take it all in. She saw Miranda chatting with Perry. The shape-shifter had yet to admit he liked Miranda, but Miranda was patient. Helen sat with Jonathon who played a game of chess with another vampire.

Della, sipping a glass of blood, stood watching the game. Since learning about the Shadow Falls Camp turning into a boarding school, Della had seemed to lose some of her pent-up anger. Not all of it, but some.

"You okay?" Derek asked, leaning even closer to her ear. He felt solid and so warm standing behind her and right now that was what she needed.

"Yeah." Kylie spotted Holiday sitting with Chris, listening to him play his guitar.

Looking across the room, Kylie found Burnett leaning against a wall, his attention so locked on Holiday that the world could end and he wouldn't notice. Yup, Holiday was his kryptonite, all right.

A sense of belonging filled Kylie's chest. She looked back at Derek and smiled. "Yeah," she repeated. "I'm okay."

Kylie's story continues!

Read on for a preview of the next book
in C. C. Hunter's Shadow Falls series

Awake at Dawn

Available from St. Martin's Griffin in October 2011

"You have to stop it, Kylie. You have to. Or this will happen to someone you love."

The spirit's ominous words flowed from behind Kylie Galen and mingled with the crackle and pop of the huge bonfire about fifty feet to her right. The frigid pocket of air announced the spirit's presence loud and clear, even if the words were only for Kylie's ears and not for the thirty other Shadow Falls campers standing in the ceremonial circle.

Miranda stood by Kylie in the human chain, completely unaware of the ghost, and gripped Kylie's hand tighter. "This is so cool," Miranda muttered and looked across the circle at Della.

Miranda and Della were not only Kylie's closest friends, but her cabinmates.

"We give thanks for this offering." Chris, or Christopher as he referred to himself tonight, stood in the middle of the circle and raised the sacred goblet up to the dark sky as he blessed its contents.

"You have to stop it," the spirit whispered over Kylie's shoulder again, hindering her concentration on the ritual.

Closing her eyes, Kylie envisioned the spirit the way she had appeared to her several times now: mid-thirties, long dark hair, and wearing a white gown—a gown covered in blood.

Frustration bounced around Kylie's already tightened gut. How many times had she pleaded with this spirit to explain, to tell her who, what, when, where, and why? Only to have the dead woman repeat the same warning.

Long story short, ghosts just coming out of the closet sucked at communication. Probably as bad as beginner ghost whisperers sucked at getting them to communicate. Kylie's only option was to wait until the ghost could somehow explain her warning. Now, however, wasn't the optimum time.

I'm kind of busy right now. So unless you can explain in detail, can we chat later? Kylie kept the words in her mind, hoping the ghost could read her thoughts. Thankfully, the chill running down Kylie's spine evaporated and the night's heat returned— Texas heat, muggy, thick, and hot, even without the bonfire.

Thank you. Kylie tried to relax, but the tension in her shoulders remained knotted. And for a good reason. Tonight's ceremonial event, sort of a show-and-tell, was another first in her life.

A life that was so much simpler before she knew she wasn't all human. Of course, it would help if she could identify her non-human side. Unfortunately the only person who knew the answer was Daniel Brighten, her real dad. She hadn't known he existed until he'd paid her a visit a little over a month ago. And he'd obviously decided to let Kylie deal with her identity crisis all on her own.

He seldom visited anymore, bringing a whole new meaning to deadbeat dads. Yup, Daniel was dead—died before she was born. Kylie wasn't sure if they offered parenting classes in the hereafter, but she was tempted to suggest he find out. Because now, when he did drop by, she would catch him watching her and just when she started to ask him a question, he'd fade away, leaving only a cold chill and her unanswered questions.

"Okay," Chris said, "release your hands, clear your mind, but whatever you do, do not break the circle."

Kylie, along with the crowd, followed his directions. Yet as she released her hands, Kylie's mind refused to clear.

Was her deadbeat dad afraid she was going to ask for sex advice or something? That always had her mom disappearing from a room—running around in search of another give-this-to-your-teen pamphlet. Not that Kylie had actually asked her mom for sex advice. Honestly, she was the last person Kylie would go to for *that* kind of advice. The mere mention of her being interested in a boy sent her mom into a panic as the letters S-E-X practically flashed in her mom's eyes. Thankfully, since Kylie had been shipped off to Shadow Falls Camp, the supply of sex-related pamphlets had declined.

Who knew what she'd missed this last month? There might have been a few STDs discovered that she didn't know about. No doubt her mom was stockpiling them for when Kylie went home for a visit in three weeks. A visit she wasn't looking forward to, either. Sure, she and her mom had sort of mended their not-so-good relationship since her mom had confessed about Daniel being her real dad. But the new mother/daughter bond felt so fragile.

Kylie couldn't help but wonder if their relationship wasn't too delicate to actually spend more than a few hours together. What if she went home and found things really hadn't changed? What if the indifference with her mom still existed? And what about things with Tom Galen, the man Kylie had believed to be her real dad all her life, the man who had walked out on her mom and her for a girl only a few years older than Kylie? Kylie was mortified at seeing him sucking face with his way-too-young assistant. So much so, she hadn't even told him.

A late-night breeze brought the smoke from the roaring bonfire into her face. She blinked the sting from her eyes, but didn't dare step out of the circle. As Della had explained, to do that would have shown a lack of respect to the vampire culture.

"Clear your mind," Chris repeated and handed the goblet to a camper on the other side of the circle.

Closing her eyes, Kylie tried again to follow Chris's directions, but then heard the sound of falling water. Jerking her eyes open, she looked toward the woods. Was the waterfall that close? Ever since Kylie had learned about the legend of the death angels at the falls, she had felt driven to go there. Not that she longed to come face-to-face with any death angels. She had her hands full dealing with ghosts. But she couldn't kick the feeling that the falls called her.

"Are you ready?" Miranda leaned in and whispered, "It's getting closer."

Ready for what? was Kylie's first thought. Then she remembered.

Was Miranda freaking kidding?

Kylie stared at the communal goblet being passed around

the circle. Her breath caught when she realized it lacked only ten people from being placed in her hand. Drawing in a deep, smoke-scented gulp of air, she tried not to look disgusted.

Tried. The thought of taking a sip from a container after everyone had smacked their lips on the rim landed somewhere between gross and nauseating in her mind. But, for sure, the biggest yuck factor was the blood.

Watching Della consume her daily nutrition had gotten easier this last month. Heck, Kylie had even donated a pint to the cause—supernaturals did that sort of thing for their vampire friends. But having to taste the life-sustaining substance was a different matter all together.

"I know it's sickening. Just pretend it's tomato juice," Miranda whispered to their friend Helen, standing on the other side of her. Not that whispering helped in this crowd.

Kylie looked across the circle of supernatural campers, their faces cast in firelit shadows from the bonfire. She spotted Della, frowning in their direction, her eyes glowing a pissed-off gold color. Her acute hearing was only one of her gifts. No doubt, Della would call Miranda on her "sickening" remark later. Which basically meant Kylie would have to convince the two of them not to murder each other. How two people could be friends and fight so much was beyond her. Playing peacemaker between the two was a full-time job.

She watched another camper raise the goblet to her lips. Knowing how much this meant to Della, Kylie mentally prepared herself to accept the glass and take a sip of blood without barfing. Not that it stopped Kylie's stomach from wanting to rebel.

Gotta do this. Gotta do this. For Della's sake.

Maybe you'll even like how blood tastes, Della had said earlier. *Wouldn't it be cool if you turned out to be a vampire?*

Not, Kylie had thought, but wouldn't dare say it. She supposed being vampire wouldn't be any worse than being werewolf or shape-shifter. Then again, she remembered Della practically crying when she talked about her ex-boyfriend's repulsion to her cold body temperature. Kylie preferred to stay at her own temperature, thank you very much. And the thought of existing on a diet that mainly consisted of blood . . . ? Well, Kylie seldom even ate red meat, and when she did . . . cook that cow, please.

While Holiday, the camp leader and Kylie's mentor, had said it was unlikely for Kylie to start exhibiting any huge metaphysical changes, Holiday had also said anything was possible. Truth was, Holiday—who was full fairy—couldn't tell Kylie what her future held, because Kylie was an anomaly.